AMANDA HAZARD MYSTERIES
BY CONNIE FEDDERSEN

CHARACTER WITNESS

R.A. Forster

Pinnacle Books
Kensington Publishing Corp.

http://www.pinnaclebooks.com

PINNACLE BOOKS are published by

Kensington Publishing Corp.
850 Third Avenue
New York, NY 10022

Pinnacle and the P logo Reg. U.S. Pat. & TM Off.

First Printing: April, 1997
10 9 8 7 6 5 4 3 2 1

Printed in the United States of America

Prologue

"Got your basic cleaner in forty-gallon drums." Arthur grunted as he grabbed one and rolled it toward the stainless steel cart. "Bad stuff. Bad." He shook his head and gave the drum another twirl, held it against his substantial thigh and looked at the kid. "This is going to clean up any of the gunk you're gonna find, and you're gonna find some real gunk, kid, 'specially over there in that building that looks like a sausage. That's where you're headed, 'kay?"

"Absolutely. No problem. I can handle anything. You want me to do the windows, too?"

Arthur rolled his eyes. This kid was green as green could be. "You see any windows in that building?"

Arthur grunted again and twirled the drum hand over hand. The drum toppled when he let it go and rumbled as it settled down. Arthur glanced over his shoulder and saw the kid's anxious face. This kid was okay. A real go-getter. Arthur liked to help that kind along 'cause he didn't see many of 'em.

"You know this place gives you help on tuition for school if you want to do more than push a broom." Arthur lifted the top and sniffed the green crystals like a gourmet, dumped some into a small, plastic-lidded jar, and attached it to the side of the kid's metal cart. He opened a smaller can and sniffed again. He jerked his head. "This one's strong. You wear gloves when you get to them sinks, okay?"

"Okay. Sure. Whatever you say. I want to do it right." The black-haired kid took his place behind the cart. It was almost as big as he was. "I know about the tuition. The benefits are real good, too. My sister works here. She started at the bottom, too. Now she's an analyst over in the space division. Tysco's been real good to her. Me, I'm going to do better than that. You just wait and see."

Arthur slapped the kid on the back. "I wouldn't doubt I'll be seeing you in a suit one of these days. Just remember to treat the bottom folk like me good when you get up there on top."

"You bet. You bet, Arthur. I'm going to be the best, but I'll never forget all this."

Arthur gave him one of those old, evil-eye warning looks that was filled with admiration. "You ain't there yet, kid. Till you're some big manager, you don't forget all what you gotta do here."

"No problem. I got it straight. Dust the desks and the chairs, empty the wastepaper baskets, don't take anything from the desks or open the drawers. Dust the sills on the windows dividing the manager's offices from the main room. I get a break after two hours. I do the bathrooms next. Then breakfast after the next two hours. Then you're going to take me over to the cafeteria and we're going to dress that down before the office workers get here."

"You got it, my man." Arthur put his hand up. The kid high-fived him and beamed. "See you in four, back here. First breakfast's on me."

They went their separate ways, the kid humming. He dusted with a flourish and waved at someone vacuuming way down a hall; but, for the most part, he was alone and happy to be that way.

Tysco was a wonderful place. While he worked, the kid checked out the drawings on the walls that showed the stuff Tysco manufactured. Stuff that helped feed people, stuff that helped educate people. The stuff that helped kill people he didn't think about. That was in a whole other section, and special people cleaned over there. Besides, it was depressing to think a company this big, a company that would pay him to go to school, a company that had a credit union, could do anything that wasn't good and helpful and excellent. There was the space division, too, and that was exciting. Maybe when he'd paid his dues and learned enough, he'd work in the space division like Verna. He'd make things that reached up to the stars. That would suit him. His ma always said he reached for the stars.

Invigorated by the vision of his future, undaunted by the tasks that lay before him, the kid didn't even stop for his first break. Someday he'd run the whole place and someone would give a speech about how he'd been one hell of a janitor.

Gently he swiped at a wedding picture on the last desk in the row and adjusted it just so. More pictures were stuck to bulletin boards. A big pink bow had been left on a table. The calendars with funny sayings on them were all turned to the next day. The kid smiled at these testaments to the human face of this big, now dark place. People were happy and busy here, and he wanted to be a part of it all.

Stuffing his rag in the back pocket of his bright-orange jumpsuit, the kid whistled and headed across the hall to the bathrooms. He couldn't remember which container held the floor cleaner and which was for the toilets and sinks. Making his first executive decision, he poured the crystals from the smaller pail into the sink and turned his face away just in case the stuff blew up or something. It sure smelled like it should. When nothing happened, the kid smiled, replaced the canister and pulled on the huge gloves that were meant for larger hands than his.

Ten minutes later he looked back on a gleaming row of porcelain sentinels.

"Good job." He patted himself on the back, then pushed open the stall door of the first john.

One, two, three. Only six more to go. The kid was sure no one had ever done such a fine job.

Grinning, he whacked open the fourth door, and that was when his jaw dropped. He stepped back, embarrassed beyond belief. There was a guy on the john. A guy in a suit on the john. Oh Lord, a manager doing his business! The kid stumbled back until his butt was up against one of the newly cleaned sinks.

"I'm sorry. It's my first day. I didn't think anybody would be here. . . ." The kid was sweating; his mind was going a mile a minute. ". . . I'll get out of here till you're done. I can't tell you how sorry I am. I really, really am. . . ." He leaned forward as he started to walk out. But when he passed that stall, the one where the guy was doing his business, it dawned on him that it was awful quiet in there. Not like embarrassed quiet. Not like rude quiet. Quiet like scary quiet. "Sir? Hey, sir? Are you all right?"

He touched the door. It swung open again. The kid blinked, then froze. The stall door swung gently back with a mild little clunk and bounced against the locking mechanism. The kid swallowed. The place was way too hot. He was sweating bad. He called once more.

"Sir?"

Mechanically, the kid pushed open the door once more. He didn't bother to push it again.

The man in the suit—the man sitting up so weird on the toilet—was dead.

"What kind of craziness is this, to try to fix something that isn't broken? You're not broken, and I'm not going to let anyone—not anyone in Los Angeles or Washington—try to fix you."

The thunderous applause made Carl Walsh feel like a god, but no one would ever have known it by his expression. Humble, a tad surprised, a bit delighted was how he looked. It was the expression of a man who was just saying what everyone else knew. He was one of the gang. He was just hanging out with the rank and file. He was a politician.

Today, the street corner where he planted himself was the

Beverly Wilshire and the folks who'd stopped by for a chat were the three-hundred members of the court reporters' union. Carl had been briefed on their concerns, tweaked the speech someone else had written for him, then convinced this group that he had what it took to fight Washington now that he'd conquered City Hall. Not that Washington had a damn thing to do with their problems, but it made them feel important to think that.

He called to them through the last spattering of applause.

"I know you feel like you're alone and you don't like being told you're expendable. I understand that, because I'm there every day. I'm responsible for sorting out the many voices in the city the way you are responsible for sorting out the voices in the courtroom. No machine can do what I do, and no machine can do what you do!"

This time he let passion come into his voice and was rewarded with whoops and hollers of ecstasy. He'd pushed all the right buttons without breaking a sweat. The courts were pushing for electronic recording. If that happened, the reporters would be out of a job forever. Court reporters made a lot of money. The judges didn't. There were more reporters than judges. Reporters could give more to his campaign coffers, and there were more of them to cast a vote. So, Carl Walsh talked to the court reporters' union, not the judges association.

"I'm asking for your support now, at the beginning of my campaign, not the end. You're not an afterthought. You, above all, know how important it is to keep the human touch in the business of lawmaking. Make me your senator from California and I'll keep the humanity in politics. Thank you for having me. Thank you for your support."

The woman at the head table was up and shaking his hand. He was looking her in the eye when he pulled her close and turned to face a camera that was suddenly pointed their way. She was in seventh heaven. He couldn't remember her name. Only the most important names, dates, and details were kept in his head; and at this moment, he was scanning the crowd to confirm that no one on the A-list was present. Buoyed by the good words, the pats on the back, Carl was grinning when he was pulled forward.

"Mr. Walsh." Another woman was tugging on his arm. "This is Mr. Pullet. He heads the division."

"Happy to meet you. What a great turnout." Walsh shook the man's hand heartily. "I can't thank you enough."

Carl led the man away, escaping the dais and his hostess in one swift move. With a few well-chosen words, a guy-to-guy slap on the back, Carl lost Mr. Pullet and fell into step with his two bodyguards. Carl could barely remember their names either, even though his life rested in their hands. They would follow him to the ends of the earth. Right now he just wanted them to walk him to the facilities.

On his way, he gave the high sign to two men who were headed his way and picked up his pace. Life was glorious. The spring in his step was meant to propel him into fast-forward; instead, he collided with a man coming out of the rest room. The bodyguards reached for the mayor; the mayor grabbed the man, and everyone righted everyone else.

"Sorry. I wasn't looking where I was going. Stupid of me, really."

"Sure, tisn't a problem. No problem at all," the other man assured him, and then they looked at each other.

"Gerry O'Doul!" The mayor laughed; and even he, seasoned politician that he was, couldn't keep the surprise out of his voice. "How are you?"

I thought you were dead.

"Well, well. Look who I've run in to. Mr. Mayor, is it?" Gerry chuckled.

I'm glad you're so predictable.

His gentle voice, the last whisper of an Irish brogue that Carl Walsh's father swore—with grudging admiration—was put on for the jury, hadn't changed. It was the only thing about Gerry O'Doul that hadn't. "What's this I hear about your leaving us for Washington? We'll be calling you *senator* then, I suppose."

"I sure hope so." Carl smiled broadly. Gerry, still kicking, took Carl back to a time when he'd proudly watched his father and dreamed of the wondrous things he would do when he grew up. Carl sighed. Never in a million years had he dreamed he would do some of the things he had. The business of the city had had class in Gerry's time; Gerry still had it. Carl knew he did not.

"Wouldn't your father be proud of you! Why I remember when we used to stand against one another in court—me at the defense table, he the prosecutor. We made fine enemies, we did."

"You think I could ever forget? I was weaned on those stories. We had many a dinner where the name Gerry O'Doul was taken in vain." Carl chuckled. "My dad used to talk about you often before he died."

Gerry leaned closer to Carl. Memories were such a lovely connection, so useful. Gerry was happy to see that he could still connect with the handsome, more practically connected Carl Walsh.

"Did he, now? So long ago, 'twas. So many are gone now. Things change so quickly, don't they, Carl? One minute you're surrounded by great friends and great enemies; the next, you're alone."

Gerry's eyes misted. Carl Walsh reached out and put his hand on the old man's shoulder. Something flashed. A photo op. Carl thought there was something sad about that. Gerry turned into the flash even though the intent was to capture Carl doing his thing. It went off again, and Gerry didn't miss a beat. He brought back the misties for an encore. "So he talked about me? That's lovely, sure 'tis."

"Absolutely."

The crowd around Carl had diminished, but people still hung on the periphery of his space in an ill-defined circle, waiting for his ear. There was a ringing. A portable phone was handed to Carl. He took it, simultaneously nudging Gerry along with him to the semi-privacy of the anteroom. "'Scuse me a second." He listened. Gerry waited patiently, reading the signs of a happy man and noticing that Carl was trying very hard not to appear too happy. He couldn't have chosen a better time to bump into his old friend's son.

"Good news?" Gerry asked the minute the phone was folded.

"The best." Carl nodded, no longer beaming. "First term, city budget was down by three percent." Strangely, Carl didn't look Gerry in the eye. How surprisingly modest he was.

"If that isn't wonderful! That's what it's all about, making a difference."

"I'm going all the way no matter what, Gerry." Carl seemed to be talking to himself, but Gerry wasn't quite ready to be discarded. He put his hand on the younger man's arm.

"Success is powerful, Carl. Just remember, it doesn't always bring what you expect," Gerry warned.

"Then again, sometimes it does," Carl bantered back. He rejuvenated himself with that thought. "Listen, I've got to . . ." He held his hands toward the men's room.

"Of course. So ungracious of me." Gerry laughed and took a step back.

"Don't rush off. I've got a half hour or so before my next appointment; we'll have some coffee."

"No, no, no. I'm running, too, I'll have you know." Gerry was as proud as punch but kept a tight rein on his excitement. "I'm taking on a new associate. O'Doul & Associates is going to be back in business, Carl."

"That's great. Got the old fire lit again, huh?" Carl shook Gerry's hand heartily. "Well, you just let me know what's happening. Maybe I can ride your coattails, get some good press standing next to Gerry O'Doul."

"Be happy to oblige, Mr. Mayor. Happy, indeed. I'd be especially proud if we could be seen shaking hands on a bit of the city business before you're off to conquer Washington."

"Gerry, you never change. My dad always said once you set your sights on something you were dangerously tenacious. He also said you were so smooth when you saw an opening that nobody saw the bite coming."

"Your father was a smart man. I'll ask for only a moment, Mr. Mayor, to try to convince you O'Doul & Associates is as fit as a fiddle and ready to perform. You've got the business.

Last I read, it was almost thirty-six police officers alone who were being sued by the citizens of your fiscally well-run city."

Carl Walsh cocked a wry grin, knowing it was useless to try to deflect Gerry's advances. Sidestepping had never worked with his father either.

"Call my office for an appointment. But I'm not promising. Shay, Sylvester & Harrington is still the city's firm of record. I'd hate to get on Richard's wrong side even for you, Gerry."

"I wouldn't either." Gerry's voice lost some of its twinkle; his eyes darkened just a shade. He recovered nicely. "Besides, I'm a little long in the tooth to cause Richard any trouble. He might even find it amusing that I'm mentioning this at all. Crumbs is what I'm looking for, Carl. If you don't ask, you'll never know what you might have had." He raised his hand, the signet ring he'd worn since the day he graduated from law school flashing as they parted company. Gerry shot back a last reminder, "Crumbs is all, Carl."

Gerry walked sprightly out of the Beverly Wilshire alone, a small, content smile on his face. There was change in the wind. A second chance had come his way, and Carl Walsh had a big 2 emblazoned on his forehead. Poor boy didn't have a clue what was about to hit him.

Behind him, Carl was watching. Gerry O'Doul had a spring in his step that a man half his age would envy. Carl allowed himself one small sound that he thought underscored the surprising pleasure he felt at seeing Gerry and being reminded of his father. Actually, it sounded more like a noise to ward off an evil spirit. Carl Walsh felt as if someone had just walked over his grave. The phone rang again. He flipped it open and turned away from Gerry O'Doul's retreating figure.

"Yes?" He listened. "Of course. Of course, I'm thrilled." He listened a bit longer and responded as he knew his caller wanted him to. "I can't thank you enough. We're a great team. Nothing can stop us now. The election is in the bag."

Carl flipped the phone closed, thought of the man on the other end, and wished he were more like Gerry O'Doul.

Then Carl Walsh changed his mind and thanked his lucky stars he wasn't.

* * *

"Your three o'clock is here, Mr. Jacobsen."

"Show him in."

Richard Jacobsen laid his fine hands on the desk, his eyes darting over his office. Everything was in order: There was good news to tell; the future looked bright; the billing statements were on target, and, of course, the relationship with this particular client could not be paralleled.

The door opened.

Richard rose to greet the handsome young man with dark hair and the look of someone on the way up. Richard had always admired that look. He only wished he had had it as a young man. He could have gone so much further, so much quicker. But what was a little time? Richard, a firm believer in fate, knew that it was better this way. The look of success might have made him stand out sooner, but his history, and those he had fatefully encountered in the last few years, put him light-years ahead of his more comely peers. Money, power, prestige. Richard Jacobsen had all this city had to offer; and soon, he would make the country his business. She had always wanted this for him, and he appreciated her sacrifices that had brought him to this point. Luckily, the young man coming through the door wanted quite a bit, too. He was willing to do just about anything to get what he wanted, and that benefited Richard quite nicely. Unfortunately, neither this man, nor the woman who gave her life to him, understood what drove Richard Jacobsen. His lips tipped up just a tad. Even he, humorless as he was, thought that was quite amusing. They would be so amazed—or would it be appalled?—to know what passion drove him.

"So nice to see you. And right on time."

"I'm glad to be here. Have you spoken to our friend?"

"Yes. Everything is on schedule. He's elated."

"Fine. Fine."

The younger man walked straight up to Richard Jacobsen. They met beside his desk, looking at each other the way men will who understand their power over one another. They were both very clear on that.

"I haven't been able to find anything in the office regarding the problem we had this morning. I searched everywhere."

"Not to worry. Everything's been taken care of." The younger man didn't look convinced. Richard put his hand on his shoulders and said sincerely, "I promise. You needn't worry. I needn't worry. There's nothing that can change what's already been done, but you'll never have to ever think about it again."

"Didn't anyone ever tell you never to say *never?*" the young man asked peevishly.

"No," Richard answered quietly. In his business he saw lots of people upset over lots of things. He knew what to do. The hand on the man's shoulder was surprisingly tight. Richard slipped it down toward the elbow. He held on a moment, then, with the gentlest of pressure, led the man across the huge office. "You'll want to freshen up."

"Yes, that would be good," the young man said. He didn't look well at all. Richard felt terrible that he hadn't noticed the moment he came in. That had been terribly inconsiderate.

"Do you need anything?"

"No, I have it all. Right here." He patted his breast pocket, and Richard thought it was dangerous to carry something so important so casually.

"All right. I'll wait. I've blocked off the afternoon for you."

The young man looked over his shoulder. He smiled for the first time. It was shaky, but a smile nonetheless.

"It won't take that long. It never does."

"There's always a first time," Richard answered quietly as the other man walked toward Richard's private bathroom.

It was only after the door had shut that Richard remembered her picture was still there. He wished he'd remembered to put it away.

Richard was, after all, a very, very private person.

"Dorty & Breyer, how may I help you? Miss Cotter? Yes, I believe she's here. Just a moment, and I'll connect you."

She pushed the hold button and zoomed around the reception desk.

"You didn't fool anyone," Cherie called, but Kathleen barely gave her a glance. By the time Kathleen was in her chair, Cherie was kneeling on her credenza, her arms dangling over the top of the carpeted wall that partitioned their cubicles. She tapped Kathleen's head with a pen. "You can't disguise that voice of yours. No way."

Kathleen brushed at her hair. Cherie tapped again when Kathleen pushed the line that was lighted.

"Kathleen Cotter, may I help you?" Her voice was back to normal. Sweet and girlish in pitch, professional in tone. The caller didn't seem to sense her duplicity. Kathleen listened intently, then hung up without another word. Cherie waved a hand, hoping to catch Kathleen's peripheral vision.

"Earth to Kathleen. Who was it? I hope it was a murderer. We need something to perk this place up. I don't have anything fun to do."

"No, it wasn't a new client. It wasn't anyone. I mean, it was someone. He wanted to know if I was going to be busy Saturday night."

Cherie tapped Kathleen's head again and laughed, but it didn't sound as if she were happy. "You've been holding out on me. I didn't know you'd started dating again."

"I haven't, and what that caller had in mind wouldn't be called dating anyway. He just saw me on the commercial that's all. Will you stop it!" Kathleen brushed away Cherie's pen and stood up so fast the other woman almost lost her balance. By the time Kathleen was standing in the opening of Cherie's cubicle, the other woman was settled on the credenza, her legs dangling, her arms crossed. "You know, you've been getting very strange over the last few months. We're attorneys, Cherie, not children. I really think you should start acting like you take your profession seriously."

"Oh, you mean like pretending you're the secretary then running to your chair and pretending to be a lawyer."

"I am a lawyer." Kathleen raised her chin proudly. "Dorty & Breyer may not be a fancy firm—"

"It's the McDonald's of the law, Kathleen. We're legal bimbos." Cherie grabbed her cigarettes without taking her eyes off Kathleen.

"It's a general law practice and the people who come here need us. They haven't anywhere else to go. You should be proud of that. I know I am."

"Oh, yeah, so proud you're going to leave. You're going to go to Beverly Hills, la-de-da." Cherie lit her cigarette and inhaled deeply, letting her statement slap Kathleen in the face. They'd never been best of friends outside the office, but inside they clung to one another. There was no one else except Jay Dorty, and neither of them would want to cling to him.

"You've been going through my desk." Kathleen's red lips pulled tight. It wasn't anger that flared, but disappointment. She never indulged in the former without the latter, and the former usually crept up on her late at night when there was no one to yell at.

"I wasn't snooping. I was in your desk looking for something and I just happened to see that letter. I mean, wow, what can I say? Beverly Hills and everything. Geez, you start fixing yourself up a little bit here and there, and suddenly you're not good enough for this place. You're even too good for Riverside. You went all the way to the top."

Cherie sniffed. She took another drag, tossed back her head, raised her chin, and exhaled loudly. Kathleen had seen the tough girls in high school act like this. She hated women who acted like they were better than everyone else when everyone else could see they weren't. Funny thing, though, all those everyones were usually intimidated by those girls. That was the funny thing.

Cherie, tired of looking at the cloud of gray smoke above her, swung her head back and let her lids lie low over her eyes. "Are you going? 'Cause if you expect a going-away party, I can't afford it."

It sounded like an accusation, as if Kathleen were contemplating murder.

Kathleen sighed and plopped herself in Cherie's chair, crossed her legs, and considered the other woman. One arm was crooked to hold her cigarette up; the other was crossed over an androgynous chest. Her color-stripped hair was pulled back in a short ponytail. Cherie wouldn't look Kathleen in the eye. She probably thought Kathleen wasn't worth the effort.

"I was going to tell you about it when I decided what to do. Really I was." In truth, Kathleen had thought of sneaking out in the middle of the night just to spare Cherie's feelings. After all, news like this would be like announcing she'd won the lottery just when Cherie showed her the dollar she'd found in the gutter. "I was just waiting for the right time."

"Well, when was the right time going to be? I mean, when were you going to drop this on me? When we had a couple of new clients and this office needed both of us? When my car broke down and I didn't have enough money to repair it and needed a ride in? When my ex called to let me know that he'd found another perfect woman? Get real, Kathleen. This isn't the kind of news I would want to hear, now is it?" Another drag. The chin went higher. "I thought you were my friend."

"I *am* your friend, Cherie." That wasn't exactly true, but Kathleen didn't want to disappoint her. She tried again. "I mean, I'm your friend but that kind of thing goes both ways, you know. I could just as easily ask why you're not happy for me? I think a real friend would be excited for the other one, don't you?"

Kathleen uncrossed her legs and considered her black patent pumps, on sale because there wasn't much call for Italian square-toed, high-heeled pumps in Banning, California. Kathleen had bought them just because they were beautiful and different. There was nothing Kathleen loved more than something that looked beautiful, something with color and form, something other than the desert and a sickroom and a mother who could only speak about disappointment and despair. Listening to Cherie, Kathleen remembered so well the words that had made her long for a change of scenery. They were words that had changed things around until Kathleen felt everything not quite right was her fault. Her mother had the knack. Cherie had the knack. Kathleen had had enough.

"I'm thirty. I've never been out of Banning except to go

shopping at the outlets near Palm Springs and to go with my parents for a weekend in Las Vegas when I was eleven. I went to law school just down the road in Riverside. I've never been challenged except to see how patient I could be waiting for my time to live. I've tried very hard to be kind to everyone; in fact, I've bent over backward to be kind to everyone.

"Now, given all that, you can see why I didn't rush to you with this incredible news. I'm very patient; I was trying to be kind so I wouldn't hurt your feelings by leaving you here, and I was trying to be cautious because I know I'm ripe for disappointment. I know what this place is and, until this moment, I wasn't sure I could leave it behind. Dorty & Breyer is predictable and safe. I could probably work here until I retired or died. There's a lot to be said for that."

Finally, Kathleen paused for breath. That was more than she'd ever said about herself at one time in all her years. She felt better already.

"On the other hand, I could go to Beverly Hills to work with an uncle I haven't seen in fifteen years, a man whom I admired greatly and who disappeared without a word to me . . . a man neither of my parents would talk about in all those years. I don't know what I feel about him because I've never been the kind of person to hate. I'm not even sure I carry a grudge. But I do know what I think about his offer to have me work for him. It's an opportunity no one else is going to give me because I come from Banning and I'm thirty and I didn't have enough guts to grab for the brass ring before this. And all you've done by trying to make me feel guilty for wanting to go, and for having the chance to go, is to make my decision for me. I think it's the best thing that happened to me, thank you very much. I'm going to leave here and not look back."

"Well, then, I guess that shows what your home counts for," Cherie said. "Guess that shows what it means to live your whole life in a place that you can just leave it in a snap. Guess that shows what your commitments count for, doesn't it? I mean what are you going to do with your caseload?"

Kathleen was already halfway down the hall. "I wouldn't walk out on the firm."

"You think you're going on an adventure?" Cherie called and Kathleen stopped for a moment. "You're not. Just remember I'm the one that said that. They'll chew you up and spit you out, Kathleen Cotter. I don't care how much you think you've learned from those dumb magazines. They'll see right through you. They will. I don't care if you graduated top of your class. It was still a second-rate school. You won't be able to handle anything bigger than a thirty-dollar divorce. They'll know that the minute you open your mouth."

Cherie laughed until Kathleen turned her head. She didn't bother to look at Cherie; she just stood there, her face in profile. Cherie stopped laughing just in time to hear Kathleen's voice, hurt and suddenly hard.

"At least I'll have tried. And another thing, I won't hate you for trying to make me feel bad about it . . . so that puts me two steps ahead right there."

There didn't seem to be anything more to say. Much as Kathleen wanted to apologize, to beg forgiveness for putting herself before others the way her mother had always insisted she do, this time she wasn't going to. This was the beginning of a new life—her life—finally. She was going to take a chance and grab this opportunity, unless, of course, she got there and her uncle came to his senses.

By the time she'd reached the only office with a real door, Kathleen considered the notion that Beverly Hills would roll up its sidewalks the minute she appeared, the way Cherie said. Then again, they might love her. Kathleen threw back her shoulders and put her hand on her hip. She was as good as anyone in her situation could be and she worked hard. There was always that. Holding the good thoughts, Kathleen raised her fist and knocked on Jay Dorty's door.

"Come."

She went in.

Jay was hunched over his desk, a bad imitation of an imitation heirloom that served its purpose beautifully. It was as big and intimidating as the balding man seated behind it. But now Jay and Breyer and Dorty were over. She was Kathleen Cotter, soon to be associated with the firm of O'Doul & Associates.

She wouldn't be intimidated by anyone. Still, she faltered a bit when Jay slid his eyes up briefly. He never made eye contact.

"Mr. Dorty?"

"Yes?"

He had been laboring over a letter. He did that a lot, yet she never saw a stack of mail waiting for the postman. Once she had offered to take his correspondence to the post office. He hadn't spoken to her for a week. That's when Cherie had become her friend, ushering her out of the office and explaining what was what. Dorty's name was on the door; they labored for Dorty; it was useless to try to be friends with a man who had invented an imaginary partner. Kathleen had taken her words to heart, yet secretly longed for some sort of connection, professional-to-professional. Now, before she made it, she was going to sever it. Kathleen hated leaving something so important undone.

"Jay." Kathleen cleared her throat and changed her tact. She was headed west, to Beverly Hills, she might as well start acting like someone who would do that. "Jay, I have something to tell you. I'm leaving Dorty & Breyer."

She waited. The pen wasn't scratching anymore. Slowly, Jay Dorty sat back. His eyes slid from the top of her blond head to the middle of her knees. Her ankles were hidden by the desk or he would have traveled the whole route. He looked downright surprised; and when he looked her in the eye again, he actually looked sad. Kathleen answered him with an equally sympathetic look, then remembered what she was about.

"I want you to know how much I've enjoyed working here. Not only did I learn a lot handling all those personal injury cases and divorces, but I was honored when you asked me to be your spokesperson on your cable commercial." She smiled, closed-mouthed. It made her eyes crinkle mischievously. When he didn't smile back, she recomposed herself. "But, Jay, I've got an offer and it's big. I'm going to work in Beverly Hills."

Jay Dorty put his hands over his eyes and bowed his head. Kathleen felt horrible. It had been wrong to come on so strong; her voice softened, but the message was clear. "I'd like to leave as soon as possible, but I'll stay as long as you need me. As long as my clients need me.''

Jay dropped his hand. His eyes were red rimmed, but there were no tears. He took a great deep breath through his great broad nose.

''No problem. Take off whenever. Cherie can pick up the slack.''

He was scribbling again.

Kathleen smiled wanly.

That hurt.

When she left his office, she had no idea that Jay Dorty was regretting her departure. There was no one, after all, who left a room the way Kathleen Cotter did.

Chapter One

"Excuse me. I'm sorry to bother you."

The woman stopped and looked Kathleen's way. Her eyes were shaded by the brim of a beautiful straw hat. Beneath the shadows and the sunglasses were fabulous cheekbones. Beneath the woman's throat were equally defined and impressive collarbones that stuck out further than her nearly concave chest. She hitched an impossibly large straw bag over her shoulder and shifted what little weight there was from one expensively sandaled, beautifully manicured foot to the other.

A huge diamond on her ring finger sent a blinding prism Kathleen's way, but Kathleen still managed to see that the woman looked her up and down, seemingly with great interest. Kathleen would have blushed under such scrutiny if she hadn't already been flushed with the heat. Obviously, she didn't quite measure up to Beverly Hills' emaciated chic. Kathleen smiled her apology. The woman did not smile back. Kathleen moved a bit closer, ready to beg if she had to. She was already half an hour late, and that was not a great way to impress your new employer.

"I wonder if you could direct me to the office of Gerry

O'Doul—1820 Beverly.'' The woman started at the sound of Kathleen's voice.

"What's he do?'' she drawled, covering her odd curiosity beautifully. Now Kathleen was surprised. She had thought Beverly Hills was an intimate town where everyone knew the rich, powerful, and famous.

"Attorney,'' Kathleen answered patiently.

"Divorce?'' The woman tipped her small, round sunglasses to eye Kathleen closely over the rims. Kathleen shook her head, truly uncomfortable now.

"Criminal,'' she answered helpfully. The glasses were back on the woman's nose.

"I've been married to a few of those, but they never went to jail.'' She licked her lips and almost smiled. It had been a joke, after all. The woman was peeved and bored. "I don't know. Sorry. Can't help you. Maybe you want to check your information. Look in the phone book.''

She turned away. Kathleen thanked the woman's back and went the opposite way only to be stopped a moment later.

"Are you looking for South or North Beverly?''

"South,'' Kathleen called back, and the woman pointed toward Wilshire Boulevard.

"You've got to cross over.''

Kathleen nodded. She hurried on, and as she passed, the woman lowered her glasses and put out her hand without touching Kathleen.

"You're not . . .'' she said.

Kathleen hesitated, turned full face so the lady could get a good look at her. She knew she was nobody, but for some reason this woman wasn't sure. "No, you're not.''

Now she was sure. The lady ducked into a shop where the windows were stuffed with linens the likes of which Kathleen had never seen. But there wasn't time to linger over beautiful things she couldn't afford. He was waiting for her, ready to settle her into a new and exciting job, a new apartment, a new life. She crossed Wilshire Boulevard, resisting the urge to stand in the middle of it and throw her arms heavenward in thanks.

Her steps slowed halfway down the block. The restaurants

were charming, smaller and not as elegant on this side of Wilshire, and there were no big office buildings. Kathleen looked at the numbers and ignored the strange feeling that something had changed the minute she crossed from North Beverly to South. On she went, hesitating when she crossed Olympic. Kathleen looked longingly behind her. She could still see the grand boulevard, Wilshire, legendary as the real estate on which sat the finest shops and hotels in Los Angeles. It was far away. In this block there was a change again. Office buildings still lined both sides of the street, but now they were yellow brick and beige stucco, not marble.

Kathleen stopped.

She looked up. She looked back, then up again.

She'd arrived.

Number 1820 South Beverly was right in front of her.

This was where she would make her mark. 1820 South Beverly didn't look quite as impressive as she'd imagined . . . until she looked at the door. Now *that* was impressive.

Touching the shining brass plate on the heavy glass door as if it were the portal to Oz, Kathleen gripped the handle, opened it, and slipped through. The door shut with a whoosh, and she was sealed inside. It took a moment for her eyes to adjust to the dim lights and for her to realize she was actually in a small lobby instead of the hushed reception area of the fantastic suite of offices she had expected.

A green EXIT sign hung over a door at the far end of the narrow room like a personal invitation. At a ninety-degree angle, another sign indicated stairs were available if she wanted to take some time ascending to great heights. To her left, the brass-doored elevator dominated the mole-colored wall. On her right, a brass-encased information board was mounted like a fine painting, complete with display light. The floor was real marble, nature's pink veins pumping tasteful life into the creamy white. How lovely! How appropriate. How like the man himself.

Kathleen checked the board. O'Doul & Associates was on the second floor, a chiropractor on the third. Kathleen focused on the fact that each commanded a full floor. That was a very,

very good sign. She called for the elevator and punched the
button for the second floor. Banning and life as it had been
were left behind in the marble lobby while the bevel-mirrored
elevator took her one floor up to her destiny.

This was it.

The doors opened.

She deserved a break.

She walked up to the door with the tasteful legend O'Doul &
Associates.

She would work hard.

She turned the knob, ready to take her place right next to
her uncle.

She was going to be a star.

Kathleen wanted to cry.

Her cubicle at Dorty & Breyer was better turned out than
the offices of O'Doul & Associates. Kathleen looked behind
her to make sure this door wasn't the gateway to a time warp.

The rug, brown flecked with beige, was shag and worn near
the door. She turned twice, eyes down as her navy-and-white
spectators did a little dance on the offending carpet. The floors
should have been hardwood and gleaming . . . at the very least
carpeted in a tight-weave, New England gray, bright and well
cared for. The walls were covered with grass cloth, yellowed
in places where the light came through the old-fashioned blinds.

Kathleen's knees wobbled, but she refrained from sitting
down for fear the chairs in the corner were what they seemed—
naugahyde rather than real leather. There was a desk but no
receptionist, a less-than-streamlined console but no calls. There
was an ashtray the size of Texas, rough and fired in chocolate
brown, like the pots sold at the Banning street fair. A basket
with a dusty silk plant nestled tight in the corner as if it knew
that this was a fake foliage graveyard; Gerry O'Doul's office
was a nightmare of seventies chic. She hated the seventies but,
above all, Kathleen hated the silence.

"Hi!"

Kathleen almost jumped out of her skin. She was on the last quarter turn of her little shuffle, stopping cold as she came full circle.

"I'm sorry. Didn't mean to scare you."

The girl smiled. Her hair was long, dark, and straight. Big, round, thick glasses magnified her eyes. A skirt that had the look of Bette's Banning Boutique swirled about her ankles. Kathleen closed her eyes briefly and realized that the thought made her homesick. If she left now, she could make it back in time to beg Jay for her old job. She could apologize to Cherie for her arrogance. She could. . . . Her lashes fluttered. Her eyes opened. She couldn't do a thing until she got out of this place.

"It's okay. I'm sorry, too. I'm not usually so jumpy."

"Are you here to see Mr. O'Doul?"

An imaginary tail tickled between Kathleen's legs as a big neon *NO* flashed so brightly in her brain she was sure it seared right through to her forehead. Then conscience kicked in and shame came with it. Gerry O'Doul hadn't promised her a pot of gold; she'd just assumed he was sitting on it. On the other hand, looks could be deceiving. People were always telling her that, weren't they? Maybe he just didn't like to spend money on furniture. Maybe all the associates were out to lunch. She clutched her bag. Who was she kidding? The law offices of Gerry O'Doul had stopped functioning. There was nothing deceiving about that.

"Yes, I am." *She would just say hello.*

"Is he expecting you?"

"Yes." She felt sick. He would see how wrong this was, too.

"I'm sorry, I don't remember an appointment, miss." The girl's eyes narrowed, elongating behind the amazing glasses. "You're not. No . . . you couldn't be. You're not Mr. O'Doul's niece are you?"

"Kathleen Cotter." Kathleen's hand went out. She was on automatic pilot. The girl looked at it, then back up at Kathleen.

"He said you were—well, he just said—I mean he didn't say you looked like . . ." Kathleen's brow beetled. The girl seemed so horribly uncomfortable. Kathleen's outstretched hand was getting heavy. "I'm sorry. Hey, sure, Miss Cotter. He's really been looking forward to your coming. So've I. It can get really lonesome around here sometimes." The girl shifted the bag she was carrying into the crook of her arm and took Kathleen's hand and shook it vigorously. The scent of eggs, bacon, and salsa floated between them. "I'm Becky. I do the books. I do other stuff, too."

"Kathleen," she said stupidly.

"Yeah, you said. I just didn't want to seem too familiar. Mr. O'Doul is so proud of you. I know all about you. His niece the lawyer. He was tickled pink when he got your letter about your mother." Becky's mouth rounded to an O of self-recrimination. "Oh, I didn't mean he was tickled to hear your mom died. He was tickled to hear from you because he always wondered how you were doing. He used to tell me all about when you were a kid. I've heard it for ages, how much he adored you."

Kathleen lowered her eyes to check for shackles around her ankles. Becky had just slapped them on and thrown away the key. Kathleen couldn't have felt more disloyal.

"How long have you worked here?" Kathleen moved with her toward the desk. Becky sat herself down along with her brown bag and Styrofoam cup.

"Want some?" she asked, ripping open the bag and holding out something that looked as if it might be alive. It was a breakfast burrito that could have fed half of Banning. Kathleen shook her head.

"How long have you been here?" she asked again. "Working with Mr. O'Doul, I mean?"

"It seems like forever," Becky took a bite of her burrito. Kathleen's stomach lurched. She wasn't feeling well at all. To be forever in brown-shag heaven with the real Beverly Hills only steps away was as overwhelming a thought as was the scent of Becky's breakfast. Kathleen moved a step away. Then she realized that wasn't all that made her stomach churn. There was something else in the air. It was the smell of failure. Failure and breakfast burritos. She could get both in Banning.

"A long time," Kathleen muttered. Becky was just too happy to be specific.

"Let's see, I've been coming in three days a week for about two years. Then last year he cut me down to two days a week. I do the books, you know, just whatever he needs done." She leaned forward as if she and Kathleen were old friends. "To tell you the truth, I think he has me come in 'cause he's lonely."

Kathleen's heart stopped beating. Lonely was a word she'd heard once too often from old people. Hearing it now, Kathleen knew what was really bothering her. The offices of Gerry O'Doul reminded her of a sickroom.

Slowly she willed her heart to beat again even as her mother's voice niggled at the back of her mind. Kathleen could hear her discourse: Shame on you for being so shallow, so self-centered, so mean-spirited. Stay where you're needed. That's what the young do.

Fine, Mother. Fine.

She was all those miserable things. Selfish, shallow, and self-centered. She'd do penance. But if she didn't get one really good reason to stay, she'd walk out the door because she wasn't that young anymore and she had already paid a peck of dues.

"What about his clients? He must need you more often than that to deal with his clients?"

"Oh, sure. We see clients now and again. But mostly he just leaves me paper stuff to do. He just leaves it for me in this box." She touched something to the side of her desk. Indeed, it was a box, one that was covered with shelf-paper. There was nothing in it, and Becky didn't seem to mind at all. "He goes to court, too."

Becky brightened as she tried to paint a glowing picture of O'Doul; unfortunately it was obviously faded after its years in the spotlight. Lord, what had happened? Gerry O'Doul. Defender of the Road Warrior. Gerry O'Doul, a man she had studied about in law school. Gerry O'Doul, beloved and dapper uncle, rake who had deserted her and whom she had still loved through the years. She was in the wrong office. This was the wrong Gerry O'Doul.

"I feel really bad eating in front of you." Kathleen blinked at Becky. She'd been dreaming. Not just for a moment but for years. Becky grinned. "Are you sure you don't want to share? You know, Mr. O'Doul will be here any minute. He called before I ran out and said he'd be up in a few minutes." Becky put her feet up on an open drawer. "Between you and me, I think he's gone off to the barber. He wanted to look real special for you. I kind of got the feeling it's been awhile since you two have seen each other. I mean, maybe there was some kind of, well, you know . . . kind of maybe a falling ou—" Suddenly Becky shook her head. "Boy, you sure don't look like I imagined you would."

It was time to go. Kathleen didn't want to be a twenty-year-old, part-time receptionist's best friend. She didn't want to be a thirty-year-old, out-of-work attorney. She didn't want to be in a place where she'd be surrounded by opportunity and not have the tools to take advantage of it. Gerry O'Doul was not powerful, rich, or successful anymore, and she wasn't fifteen and gangly. She knew exactly how she looked, tall and big and noticeable. Blond and full-chested and full-hipped if she were to put a fashionable spin on things. The last thing Kathleen wanted was to have this girl constantly reminding her that she wasn't what was expected either. In another minute, her heart would break.

Without another word, only a mumble of apology—as much to the absent Gerry O'Doul as the curious receptionist Becky— Kathleen Cotter fled. Reaching for the door, sidestepping toward it, head turning so she wouldn't have to look at Becky's surprised and unsatisfied expression, Kathleen took her leave.

But the powers that be weren't ready to make it easy on her. As if on cue, the door opened, but not for her to run through. The man of the hour had arrived.

"Kathleen Cotter." Gerry O'Doul smiled and the heavens opened up. "Look what a beautiful woman you have become."

Kathleen's shoulders dropped. She almost swooned. Not because she was disappointed her escape had been foiled, but because she had no idea how much she'd missed him. Damned if she weren't happy to see him. How wonderful, after all her lonely years with her parents, to have arms held out to her in welcome. There wasn't much to do but walk right into them. She stayed put instead.

"Uncle Gerry?"

"Sure, do you have to ask?" he chided with a gentle chuckle.

Dropping his arms, he took no offense that she hadn't come to him. He understood how time worked. It stretched so far that one couldn't see the happy beginning with so great a distance behind them. And time could be cruel when it snapped back, jumbling the joys and disappointments into a great confusing bubble. They would discover one another again in another length of time or an explosive moment. He didn't have as much time as she, but there would be enough. Of that he was sure.

"No." She tripped over the word and tried again. "No." She shook her head. "I'd have known you anywhere." She smiled truly as the shock wore off. He smiled back, broadly, to her demure expression. A Hallmark moment. Kathleen hadn't believed in them until now. She would have preferred they remained a thing of the imagination.

"Then let's get reacquainted, for sure I'd not have known you anywhere."

With that, he came to her and took her elbow, gentleman that he was. Graciously, he steered her across the horrid brown shag and past Becky's desk as if they were gliding across a dance floor. He was leading, and the dance would be a spirited tango. He tilted his head to confide in her but spoke to her shoulder. Kathleen was so much taller.

"Vile food she eats, but you'll find her just the ticket when you need work done. You two girls will get along just fine." He patted Kathleen's hand and sent a smile Becky's way.

Kathleen looked over her shoulder to see the last bit of egg-stuffed tortilla disappear into Becky's mouth as she looked fondly at Gerry O'Doul. Kathleen could swear there was a teardrop in the corner of the secretary's eye. Thankfully, Kathleen wasn't as given to high emotion.

All she had was a lump in her throat.

*   *   *

Kathleen inched across the room, deftly stepping over the small tear in the carpet as she looked at the wall of pictures. Hanging there, caught in his prime, was the Gerry O'Doul she remembered. Her uncle Gerry was dapper with his well-styled silver hair and perpetual tan. He'd looked ageless then—just as he did in these pictures. There he was with Sam Yorty, the diminutive mayor who ran Los Angeles before the San Diego Freeway ran through it. Gerry with Cardinal McIntyre. Gerry with Chief Davis. Gerry with Ronald Reagan. Gerry with . . .

"Here you are, my girl."

. . . hair.

Kathleen blinked and looked away from the pictures. The wavy silver hair was gone, leaving only a meticulously slicked-down fringe of white and a few long strands that lay across his otherwise bald dome. Gerry smiled, underscoring the fact that his narrow face was no longer cut and clipped but gently cradled by his fine bone structure. His translucent skin was barely wrinkled, but it was lightly spotted with age. His ears were bigger than she remembered.

"Kathleen?"

She shook her head and focused on his eyes. They still sparkled but the deep blue had faded like well-washed denim. He held a crystal champagne flute toward her, a bottle of champagne sat sweating in an equally impressive silver bucket on his exquisitely carved desk. Here, in his inner sanctum, were the last trappings of his heyday. She looked away. She couldn't bear to be surrounded by reminders of what had been if she were Gerry O'Doul. She couldn't bear to look at these reminders that she was too late. This wasn't the opportunity she had imagined, not the chance she had counted on.

"Thank you, Uncle Gerry," she said quietly.

Gerry lay the edge of his flute against hers. The ting made Kathleen think of the final drink on New Year's Eve. Kathleen never cared for New Year's Eve. It always meant the end of another uneventful year rather than the beginning of an exciting new one. Kathleen sipped. The glass stem was heavy between her fingers, the lip fragile beneath her own; as heavy as her heart, as frail as her emotions.

"I can't believe how you've grown," Gerry said.

"Tall," Kathleen muttered, both hands now grasping the flute.

"And beautiful. How you ever became so glamorous is beyond me. Your mother never was one for fashion."

"Mom was sick for a long time. She watched television. I looked at magazines."

Kathleen stiffened, embarrassed that she had shared even that much with him. Magazines had been her inspiration, her training ground for the real world when she would finally be free to step into it. She'd learned her lesson well, but the world was disappointing her now. She wanted Gerry to understand it had been hard and lonely in those rooms; she wanted him to know how much she'd longed for the life he had. She wanted him to see her disappointment.

Gerry didn't seem to notice, his joy was so great, and she couldn't bring herself to tell him exactly how she felt.

"Look at you, Kathleen. Sure, didn't I think Jean Harlow was waiting for me when I came in. A tall Jean Harlow to be sure. I usually don't like a woman's hair short like that, but on you it's wonderful. So tall and shapely, and dressing like a woman should. Feminine. That's what women have forgotten. A brain, too. Ah, but aren't you a class act, Kathleen Cotter. You'll be the darlin' of the press. The judges won't be able to resist you." He raised his glass again and drank to the glory that was his niece.

"Uncle Gerry, please—" Kathleen twisted her shoulders. Big. That's how her mother had described her. Her father had never managed more than a glance after puberty and hardly more than that before. She put herself together well, and Gerry was kind. But Gerry was also blind in his old age.

"Now, now," Gerry laughed, "we can't have any of that, now, can we? No uncle in here. These are the offices of Gerry O'Doul & Associates, and I am here toasting the best associate a man could have. I'm so proud of you, Kathleen. Passing the bar and all. I wish I had known sooner. I wish . . ."

The light in his eyes dimmed. Kathleen turned away, embarrassingly aware of the years of silence that stood between them. Gerry moved past her, full of vim and vigor. He'd had enough of the moment.

"So, you like my pictures?"

"I always loved your pictures. Mom used to show me every one." She reached out and touched one she remembered best. When she had first seen it, her hands had been dirty from playing her child games; now, her nails were filed ovals and painted to match her lips. She had changed. "You're the reason I became a lawyer. I wanted to be just like you."

"And so you are like me. You inherited my genes. Style and brains." He gave her a wink and chuckled. His collar bobbed about his neck like a starched life preserver. He grinned. Could it be that he really didn't sense her despair, her absolute shock to find him in such a state?

"I can't exactly say I followed in your footsteps." She moved away, suddenly tired and needing to rest. No, not rest. She needed distance. She needed to try this all over again with a completely different result. "You know, I haven't really been doing the kind of work I'm sure you need help with. Dorty & Breyer is just a small office in a strip mall, Uncle Gerry."

He held up a finger and waggled it at her. Kathleen smiled weakly.

"Gerry, I mean." She tried again. "What I'm trying to say is, I don't really think I have the skills you need in an associate. It was wrong of me to lead you on. I should have sent a resume after you asked me to come here. This is Beverly Hills, after all." She looked around and out the window, as if trying to reassure herself that was a true statement. "I don't think I'm—"

"Now, don't you sell yourself short, Kathleen," Gerry O'Doul clucked. "I wouldn't have asked you here if I thought you couldn't do the job. I know in my bones you're a fine lawyer. It's not all knowing the law. It's the image that counts. Image is half of everything, don't I know? Just look at you. Dressed so smartly. A knockout. A voice that will sing like the angels to a jury as soon as we get something to take to court. That's important, Kathleen, the voice I mean.'' Kathleen opened her mouth to use the voice he so admired, but he was like a verbal dervish. ''And smart, Kathleen. I can see you're smart. It's behind your eyes. But more than that, you're a woman of substance.''

''Uncle Gerry, please.'' Her hands were clammy. Someone had turned up the heat.

''Don't deny it. Most young lawyers aren't like you.'' Gerry set aside his champagne flute and sat back in his high-back chair. It almost engulfed him. He looked right at her and, for a brief and unnerving instant, she saw the man who had so courageously wielded his persuasive powers in court for decades. His gaze was steadfast, his eyes deep with thought, his decision-making powers sure in a world that often waffled. ''You are a decent person, Kathleen, and that's why the law needs you. That's why I need you. I believe your letter was a sign. I was almost ready to quit.''

Kathleen was stunned, then she grabbed the straw.

''You're at an age when you should retire, Gerry,'' she insisted, slipping onto a chair, leaning over his desk, and giving him a sincerely concerned look.

''I said *quit*, Kathleen. There's a difference. I know what you saw when you walked in here. This isn't the poshest address I've ever had. Times changed. Fashions changed. It wasn't that I lacked the skill, Kathleen; I lacked the style people wanted in their lawyers. I would never deal from the bottom of any deck. I won cases based on the law of the land and my wits, not the entertainment value of a defense. When people stopped wanting that, I couldn't change. But now I see the pendulum swinging again. I've watched, I've listened. It's time for me to move again. I'm just not as spry as I used to be. I simply can't do it on my own. Who else could I trust to see the vision but you, Kathleen? Even as a child you recognized that one must never give up on a dream.''

Kathleen half started out of her chair, frustrated and set in motion by her own guilt. She didn't want Gerry O'Doul to need her. She'd fulfilled her familial obligations long ago. She had been nurse to her mother, scapegoat for her father. She

had done everything that was expected of her. Half her life had
been given to the discharge of those responsibilities, and she
wouldn't take them up again.

"You don't even know me, Uncle Gerry. I was a girl in
high school when you last saw me. A lot has happened since
then, and some of it I'm not too happy about."

"You're right. High school was a long while ago. But now
I see the woman who sits here, and I can see your life behind
your eyes. I know that you sacrificed a career to care for your
mother. I know your father was difficult to live with."

"No, that's not how it was. I just didn't do anything to
change my life or my job," she insisted, uncomfortable with
the heroic role in which he tried to cast her. He was supposed
to be the hero.

"And you lived in a small town where opportunities were
limited." Another excuse became forgiving fact.

"I didn't have the ambition, Gerry; that's why I haven't
done more and gone further." She scooted farther up in her
chair and laid her arms across his desk, her hands folded as if
pleading with him to stop recasting her so she could stop
putting herself down. He was giving her credit for high-minded
decisions when, in reality, her life had been comfortable and
had slipped away from her and part of it was his fault. He'd
left just when she'd dared to dream.

Unaware of her pain, Gerry twisted the knife with a loving
flourish. "And you took the opportunity when it came along.
Smart girl! Beautiful girl. My niece for sure."

That stopped her. Kathleen looked away. That, at least, was
true. She had taken the opportunity he'd held out to her. This
time she couldn't blame him when she was the one who had
done the taking.

"Uncle Gerry . . ."

"Gerry."

"I appreciate all this, but I can't stay. I can't work with
you."

Her hands slid off the desk and into her lap. The blue dress, the white piping, the red nails. She should be waving the flag instead of burning her bridges. The thought of going back to Banning, a hot and barren place with small-town problems, was so hard to imagine. But she wouldn't be an old maid holding the arm of a legal legend as he limped toward one last hurrah. Better a small fish in a small pond than a bit of muck in the Koi pool.

"Kathleen."

Gerry O'Doul's voice lost its vitality, and Kathleen couldn't look at him. She could be mediocre without his help, but she couldn't face being a shadow on the wrong side of the bright streets of Beverly Hills.

"Uncle Gerry, I just didn't think it would be so overwhelming." She offered a small and useless shrug, knowing now she would never tell him the whole truth, but this miserable reunion had to come to an end.

"So, it's not disappointment. Well, 'tisn't that nice to know? You had me worried." Gerry nodded sagely and Kathleen knew, whatever he was thinking, he was off base. "Beverly Hills is a world away from Banning, isn't it, Kathleen? My goodness, of course you didn't think it would be so overwhelming, did you? Don't you worry; you'll get used to it. We'll be such a team. We'll be having the old office in no time. Did I tell you I had a view of Chanel? They used to know me in there. For Christmas, all my lady clients received a bag from Chanel. Those days will come again." Gerry O'Doul leaned across his desk, his face alight, his narrow shoulders ready for some weight. "It's all about style, Kathleen. Style and character and brains. You have all three. I will make the rain; together, we'll make the strategy and I'll send you off to adventures in the law that you have only dreamed of. It can happen, Kathleen. I know it can. You must believe, too. You must."

"But, Uncle Gerry . . ."

At that feeble attempt at objection, the door flew open with such force that it sent the pictures on the wall ashivering. Kathleen twirled in her chair, spilling some of her champagne on her new dress. Gerry hardly moved, though it sounded like

the earthly plates were on the skids. Her last thought of Gerry
O'Doul was that, on top of everything else, he must be hard-
of-hearing. Then Kathleen Cotter sat still and allowed her senses
to be assaulted by the images and colors and sounds that made
up the formidable presence of Louise Brooker.

Chapter Two

"You've got to do something, Gerry. Whatever it is you have to do, I want it done now. Got it? Go to court. Sue those bastards at the insurance company. I want you to grind 'em to a pulp. I want you to chew 'em up and spit 'em out."

Kathleen snorted a laugh. The image of Gerry O'Doul chewing anything other than three-minute-eggs was funny. But Louise Brooker gave Kathleen a look that would curdle milk, so Kathleen stopped laughing. She rearranged herself to get a better view, but Louise was moving behind her chair, breathing fire. Kathleen twirled herself the other way just in time to see Louise plant herself to the right of Gerry's desk. Not only was Gerry cool under fire, he seemed to sit a little taller in his chair, energized by the woman's fury. He looked at the banshee with the seriousness of a judge. It was clear that every word falling from those rather generous lips was of the utmost import. The lady—and Kathleen used the term lightly—put her large hands on the desk, fingers splayed.

Her nails were painted the palest pink. Small diamonds, implanted on each talonlike tip, twinkled from all except the middle one. On that was etched the most marvelous miniature of Elvis Presley, resplendent in his white jumpsuit. Those nails seemed strange on a woman who reminded Kathleen of a bull terrier. Her chest came into the room well before she did. Big, broad shoulders were thrown back to hold up the whole shebang. That half of her body seemed precariously perched atop nonexistent hips and the skinniest legs Kathleen had ever seen. The woman was an inverted triangle curiously posted on big feet crushed into a pair of high-heeled, platformed, patent-leather slides. Barbie-doll feet came to mind. On her back was a white-leather jacket studded with a rainbow of faux jewels that matched the ones on each finger of her hand. Her skirt was leather, too—the kind that goes from cow's carcass to yours for $29.95. Her hair was big; her mouth was big; her eyes were small, and Gerry O'Doul's attention was all hers.

"Louise, my dear girl. What brings you here in such a state? Sit down. Sit down properly in a chair." Two lovely roses of color bloomed on the apples of his cheeks.

Standing, Gerry came round the desk. Graciously, he held the chair next to Kathleen. Louise looked at it, then gave Kathleen the once-over as if she expected Kathleen to move. Kathleen couldn't have moved if she'd wanted to, and she didn't want to. The woman sat in the chair Gerry held, albeit reluctantly.

"I thought you were Melanie Griffith, for a minute. You're not." Kathleen was of no more interest. The lady opened her mouth and Kathleen could swear she saw words forming deep in that cavern. "Gerry, they turned me down. They won't give me my money! Look at this."

She unzipped her large bag with intertwined G's printed all over it. Kathleen was hit broadside by a scent of questionable taste. Louise fumbled inside and pulled out an envelope that had a streak of waxy color on one end. It matched her lips. Kathleen had leaned close to watch her progress until Louise gave her the evil eye and pulled her bag close. When Kathleen was safely away, Louise tossed the envelope Gerry's way. Clandestinely, she searched in her bag again and came up with the top and bottom of the wayward lipstick. She put them back together, talking the whole time.

"Those stupid idiots at that insurance company denied my

claim. They told me I couldn't have Lionel's benefits. I don't understand it. It was part of the deal. We went to court. You got me that money. Not that we ever, ever expected . . . well, you know . . . but damn, I want my money."

"Louise was Lionel Brooker's wife," Gerry explained. Kathleen nodded and raised a hand, hoping to get a word in edgewise and escape. She wasn't quick enough.

"Ex-wife, thanks to you," she cooed, lobbing the ball gently back Gerry's way.

"It wasn't a terribly difficult divorce," he admitted humbly.

"Only because you handled it so well." Louise pursed her lips and threw Gerry a kiss. Gerry blushed, pleasing his client. A tingle of distaste ran up Kathleen's spine.

"But Lionel died. Tragic." Gerry shook his head sadly. Kathleen swung toward Louise and waited for the explanation she knew would come. It wasn't the one she expected.

"Jerk. Idiot. Asshole," Louise cried. She gave Kathleen a curt look, " 'Scuse me. But the man did it on purpose."

"He died on purpose?" Kathleen crossed her legs; her skirt slid up an inch. Louise watched, assessed the competition, and then checked out her own gams. Satisfied of her superiority, she then satisfied Kathleen's curiosity.

"I suppose a lady would put it that way, but I've never been accused of being a lady." This didn't seem to bother her. "The fool killed himself. He killed himself on purpose. Get it? Suicide," she explained to Kathleen, the idiot child. "Look, look." She reached over the desk and took the paper from Gerry, handing it to Kathleen. A pink, diamonded nail poked at the third paragraph of the letter. "Lady, if you're divorcing your husband, you take this lesson to heart. I was supposed to get his life insurance if he died. I was supposed to still be paid for the years—the best years!—I gave him when he was alive. I never thought he'd die; but just in case, you know, we got a little something extra. Fate is funny. I read my horoscope every day, and I know how fickle things can be. So Gerry," she batted her lashes Gerry's way. From her profile Kathleen could see those lashes were no more real than her formidable breasts. "Gerry went to court. He convinced the judge that I needed

to be cared for in the event of my ex-husband's death. You're
a man among men, Gerry. You saw how hard it was for me
to cope after the divorce. I have no skills. . . .''

Back to Kathleen.

"So then the fool dies. In the john where he works, no less.
Ugh." She shivered and the light from her faux jewels danced
across her rigid jaw. "I don't know that I'd expect anything
less. He was a wimp. Worked in an anthill, lived in the forest,
died in the john in a stall. He hid from the world. No backbone."

"Louise, please. You said yourself Lionel was a good man,"
Gerry reminded her, but her memory was more selective.

"I *thought* he was a good man with a future," Louise shot
back, forgetting her Sunday manners. This was a woman-thing
anyway. She put one hand on the arm of Kathleen's chair,
conspiratorially. With the other, she reached for Kathleen's
champagne and downed it in one gulp. "You know what I
mean. The disappointment in finding out the man you love isn't
the man you think he is can be devastating. It's all about
character and ambition. Well, old Lionel had plenty of character, but he had the balls of a flea. A woman can't live with a
man like that. Not a woman like me, with needs. You understand? Now it seems he didn't even have any character either.
I was duped." She lowered her lashes and patted Kathleen's
forearm. "That means *taken advantage of,* honey." She didn't
wait for Kathleen to indicate she understood. "He was wily.
All that sweetness and accommodating crap. The man planned
and schemed and did it on purpose just to spite me. He did it
on purpose, and I want justice."

"Kathleen, please?" Gerry motioned for the letter. It passed
between them. Gerry pulled out his glasses and looked again
as Kathleen looked at him. Concentrating on business, Gerry
dropped the solicitous attitude and checked out the document.
When he looked up, that sweet, sweet smile was in place.

"Louise, I would be doing you a disservice if I told you the
insurance company wasn't within their rights. Have you read
the policy?"

"Don't be ridiculous."

"Well, the insurance company knows what's in their documents. There was a twenty-four-month exclusion, Louise. If Lionel did himself in within twenty-four months of the issuance of the policy, the policy became null and void. They owe you nothing.'' He shook his head and passed the letter back. Louise ignored it.

''What do they know? This isn't a situation like in the policy. I mean, that's talking about a crazy person, and, believe me, I know Lionel wasn't crazy. What I didn't know was how mad he was at me. He planned this, Gerry, down to the last minute of his life. I know that as well as I know my own name. If he was nothing else, Lionel was the smartest man I know. He read everything. He knew everything. He understood this policy, and he waited until he knew it was the right time. This was like a big joke. I tell you, Gerry, he knew about this thing— this exclusion deal—and he killed himself just before we made it over the hump. One lousy day to go. And I admired that twerp long enough to marry him. I thought if nothing else he was on the up-and-up. Now I see he was just like every other man. Selfish. Selfish. Selfish.''

Kathleen opened her mouth, raised a finger. Who was she to point out that Louise was the one who had married the man in the first place? Who was she in any of this except someone who wanted to leave in the worst way?

''I think I should just come back some other time,'' Kathleen said quietly, hoping to escape under cover of Louise's barrage.

''Louise.'' Gerry chuckled.

''Gerry.'' She talked over him, then glared at Kathleen, who sat back down rather than disturb her further. ''I don't want to hear about it. I don't want any double-talk, and I sure as heck don't want to sit here and chat. I just want to go to court.''

''I have no double-talk for you, Louise, but I would be remiss if I didn't tell you that you don't have a leg to stand on, dear. The agreement is very clear. I tell you that in front of a witness. I would be hard-pressed to take your money fighting a cause like this.'' He gave Kathleen a look filled to bursting with such embarrassing affection she thought she'd die.

''Money, schmoney,'' Louise scoffed. ''It's the principle of the thing. I want what's mine. I want it if it takes forever.

Honey—'' She poked Kathleen with the pads of her fingers for fear of breaking a nail. ''—you watch. I'll get what's mine. You take note. Now—'' back to Gerry ''—let's get the ball rolling.''

"Well, if you insist.'' Gerry stood up and gave Louise a bow, walked around the desk, and was at the door with his hand on the knob when she shrieked at his back.

"Gerry! I want to get started now.''

"Of course, Louise,'' Gerry said sweetly as he slipped through the door. ''I'm leaving you in the best of hands. Kathleen Cotter, this is Louise Brooker, your client. Louise, this is Kathleen Cotter, one of the best attorneys on the face of God's green earth and the newest associate of O'Doul & Associates.''

There were five Styrofoam cups on the desk in front of Kathleen. Four sported perfect, pink lip-prints. The hue had an underlying neon glow that undulated against the white spongy stuff. The fifth was still untouched, filled with cold coffee the color of bark. Even a more-than-healthy serving of cream couldn't make the coffee palatable. Fortunately, the client's taste was broader. She seemed to love the stuff.

The coffee suited Louise just fine, as did the chair in which she sat. Louise Brooker had made herself right at home while Kathleen was still trying to shake herself out of the shock that she had somehow become a functioning employee of O'Doul & Associates. During the last few hours Kathleen had stepped into the outer office to chat with Gerry about this odd turn of events only to find that he'd flown the coop. Louise had squawked that time was awastin', so Kathleen had returned, vowing only to take notes so Gerry could pick up where she left off. After the third hour, Kathleen stopped taking notes and started wondering how she was ever going to stop Louise from talking.

"Did I tell you how we met?'' She popped another breath mint.

Kathleen shook her head, trying to regroup and keep her eyes from crossing. Her eyes itched. She wanted to rub them but resisted the urge, knowing she would only succeed in annihilating the eyeliner on one eye while leaving the other intact. Unfortunately, Louise took that negative little shake and the quick blink of Kathleen's eyes as a sign that she had somehow missed a really important part of her story. She launched, once again, into the saga of Lionel and Louise.

"We met in college. Well, I wasn't really in college. I was waitressing at What a Dish Pizza just around the corner from where Lionel was living. He used to come in all the time. A cheese man. Simple, you know. I swear, I think of it now, the place where he lived, and I think it really wasn't more than a flophouse. But he was a college man. He seemed so romantic. Suffering before conquering the world, you know." She waved her hand in the air and Elvis went flying. Mesmerized, Kathleen watched—the pink lips, the pink nails, the blue-shaded eyes that never left hers. She had to give Louise credit. She looked you in the eye when she talked.

"Anyway, I thought it was just damn romantic. This guy with long hair—my, he was pretty!—kind of slim, with those hip-huggers they used to wear in the sixties. He was like, from another time. I wasn't that old when I met him, so that's probably what marred my judgment about Lionel." This time the painted Elvis found its way beneath the beehive hairdo and gave her head a little scratch. Kathleen decided this was Louise Brooker's equivalent to Pinocchio's nose-growing.

"Mrs. Brooker, I think . . ."

Kathleen's voice seemed to strike a chord. Louise leaned forward. She wasn't about to lose her audience. The nails danced on the wood. Kathleen sat up straighter, her posture even more perfect in defiance of Louise's proposed domination. It didn't help. Louise could talk faster than Kathleen could become indignant.

"Well, it doesn't matter how old I was, does it? I married him. We did it in a field—I don't mean *did it.*" She guffawed at this seemingly hilarious double entendre, and Kathleen saw that beneath the flamingo-pink lips, Louise Brooker had a charming overbite. She smiled. A mistake. Louise, egged on by Kathleen's obvious distaste for her humor, charged ahead.

"And don't call me *Mrs. Brooker*. Where was I? Yeah. Okay. I meant, we *got married* in a field. I had this great dress. Spent every last dime I had on it. Figured, what'd I need money for? Lionel was about ready to graduate with a degree in business management. He was going to graduate school while he worked. It was going to be wonderful!" Storm clouds darkened the horizon of her memory. "The jerk. The idiot. He promised me the world—right there in our wedding vows—the world!"

Louise flopped back against the chair, her lips pulled tight. Her overbite now seemed predatory. She was mad. Kathleen was fascinated. Riding Louise's emotional roller coaster was an eye-opening experience. Kathleen ran her fingers through the spiky, long, almost-platinum bangs, then let her head rest on her hand.

"Well, Lionel had a pretty funny view of the world. I thought he meant we'd be on easy street, you know? Stuff. Clothes and traveling. Maybe go to Graceland. Maybe get me a diamond. Maybe even a house. I didn't really want kids, but what the heck. If he held up his part of the bargain and wanted a few little yard-monkeys, I'd oblige. But noooooo. Lionel wanted to be part of the world. I mean really part of it! Geez, can you imagine? He wanted to commune with it. Every hour he wasn't working, he was out listening to the sound of the wind, reading poetry, walking in the damn fields. It was one thing to be married in one; I didn't want to live in one."

Louise closed her eyes, thinking back and back, her edges softening with each memory that presented itself. "I don't know, I think I really did love him at first. I mean, there were so many things. He was gentle. He was kind. He thought of others before himself. I liked that. Always others before himself." She smiled sweetly, her eyes still closed. Then they opened, narrow little slits through which sparkled eyes that had been opthamologically altered to match her shadow. "And then that all got so damn annoying, if you know what I mean. Ever had anyone do everything you wanted?"

"No, I haven't." Thrown off guard, Kathleen's intent to dominate deflated. Her mind's eye flitted over three-dimensional memories of an overbearing and didactic father, a mother who was so cautious and needy that Kathleen had caught her fear of everything for a while. Finally there was Jim Farley, her fiancé, a man who, like a boy, was easily satisfied. Kathleen had mistaken that quality for maturity and contentment. She had been an idiot. She had waited and waited for the kind of passion Louise talked about. This woman scoffed at it; Kathleen just now understood that she would kill for it.

"No, I've never had anyone want to give me the world," Kathleen said quietly. She was half out of her chair when Louise waved her down. Kathleen stood up.

"Figures." Louise wasn't ready to let her go. "It was a war of the wills. You don't know how awful it can be. Lionel would be listening to his whale-noise recording and I'd say, 'How can you listen to that stuff?' Next thing, there'd be country-western on the stereo. He knew I liked country-western. He'd put the whale-noise tape away in its own little place till I'd go out shopping or something. He'd fix dinner. I'd say, 'Aren't we ever going to have anything except vegetables?' Next night, there'd be a big steak. That sort of thing just bugged me, you know, 'cause I don't think he got any pleasure out of that kind of stuff. I think he just did it 'cause he was a worm."

"Maybe he loved you," Kathleen suggested impatiently.

Louise snorted and eyed Kathleen. There was a challenge there, but Kathleen didn't know what game they were playing. She tried again.

"Maybe he was afraid of you." Kathleen understood that.

"Me?" Louise chortled as if that alone were enough to debunk such a theory. "There'd be no reason. I never hit him. I yelled a lot, but Lionel just told me he loved my spirit. Hey, I gave him spirit. I gave it to him for ten years. The best years of my life. Now look at me. Used goods. That's why Gerry could get me that insurance policy. He knew what was what. He's a good attorney. I hope you're going to be just as good. I don't know. You sure you've been practicing long enough? You look kind of young to me."

"I'm old enough." Kathleen sighed. "But I don't think I'll be handling this matter. I'm helping Mr. O'Doul out today. . . ."

"I meant you just looked young for a lawyer. That's all,"

Louise ignored the last part of Kathleen's statement. Elvis and her four other fingers were back in her hair. This time she was patting it around, fidgeting with all the nooks and crannies. Louise was ready to explode. She was a too-sexy-for-the-world-and-not-ready-to-go-over-the-hill babe and she seemed to find Kathleen Cotter less than acceptable.

"Hey, look, Kathleen, I know it's tough for someone like you to understand, but I spent a long time trying to make Lionel happy. The judge knew that. Everybody knew I didn't have anything to fall back on after we divorced. I wasn't any college-educated person who could go out and call up a good-paying job just like that." She snapped her fingers and made a lovely little pop. "I just wanted a little insurance for my old age in case I didn't find the right guy for me, in case something happened to Lionel and he couldn't pay the alimony. I just want a little bit for myself. I deserve it, know what I mean?"

"I do, Louise. I truly do," Kathleen said, never taking her eyes off the other woman. Kathleen had lived her whole life with people who deserved one thing or another.

To look at them, they were as different as night and day, but that one word, *deserve,* made them sisters in an odd sort of way. Louise Brooker was greedy and lazy. Kathleen pulled her own weight, but both of them thought they deserved something from the men in their lives who had made the future look bright.

"Fine." Louise picked up her purse. "Long as we understand one another."

"Good." Kathleen looked toward the door. No one appeared to bail her out, and Louise was hanging out expectantly.

"So what now? I deserve that money, and they're saying Lionel killed himself too early. How can someone kill themselves too early, I ask you? The judge said I deserved something if Lionel died. I have a court order."

"I'll discuss this with Gerry. In fact, I'll discuss it with him right now," she said tightly.

"Okay." Louise hitched her bag and gave Kathleen an appraising look. "If you're going to be in court, you may want to spruce up a bit. Nobody's going to notice you dressed down like that.''

Louise gave Kathleen the once-over, not quite sneering when she reached the two-toned, high-heeled, career-girl sling-backs on Kathleen's feet. She shivered. There was nothing more to say, so Louise Brooker left, throwing a *bye* at Becky as she sashayed past the girl's desk.

Kathleen followed on her heels, barely waiting until the door was closed.

"Where's Gerry?"

"In his office?"

Becky blinked. Becky nodded. Ms. Cotter didn't seem quite as nice as when she'd walked in, but then she'd spent a few hours with Mrs. Brooker. That was enough to make anyone testy. Kathleen headed into Gerry's office; Becky got up to rifle through the file drawers that happened to be right next to the door Kathleen left open.

"Here's the notes on Louise Brooker, Uncle Gerry." Kathleen laid the legal pad in front of him and stepped back. She was not uncivil.

"Thank you, Kathleen. Interesting woman, that." He studied the papers through his bifocals and beamed. "Ah, I see she told you all about Lionel. A thorough job, Kathleen. All the high points."

"She told me everything, including the best place to get inexpensive underwear in Santa Monica. Uncle Gerry, this woman can't go to court with this and you knew it two hours ago. I think now you'd better make it very clear to her that this is a lost cause."

"Nothing is ever quite a lost cause, Kathleen, if the client is intent."

"Then I'm sure you'll find some wonderful twist to make this all come out right."

"But, Kathleen, I thought we decided you would lead on this one." Gerry sat back, his face a play of astonishment and disappointment.

"*We* didn't decide anything, Uncle Gerry." Kathleen's voice shook, more out of frustration and disappointment than anger.

"Louise Brooker was very interesting. I'm sure you have many very interesting clients, but I can't stay here. This would be so wrong. I was expecting something—" She actually shivered. "—different. And it's not your fault I didn't find it," she added quickly. "I'm so happy we're going to be talking again, but I just don't see that this is really going to work—you know, as far as work goes. I want one thing, you another. Our perceptions are different. We'll become bitter, miserable people if we try to do this. I know because I've already gone through this with my parents. I don't want to be bitter, Uncle Gerry. I just wanted something really different than what I had. I've got to kind of rearrange my thinking, Uncle Gerry. You can see that, can't you?"

Gerry O'Doul sat back and eyed his niece. He tented his fingers. On his hand was a signet ring. It looked too large on his finger. He put those fingers against his forehead, and Kathleen hoped he wasn't going to make a scene. When he raised his eyes, Gerry O'Doul looked straight at her without judgment.

"Yes, I understand. Crossroads are a serious matter and you must be very careful now. A young woman like you has so many options. To stay here and help me might not be the most advantageous move for you. I should have made my situation clearer. I should have told you that I was counting on your help, rather than misleading you into thinking this was an opportunity. I only wanted to make up for all those years between us. I wanted to leave you a legacy. I simply couldn't do it without help." Gerry O'Doul sighed. He seemed to shrink inside his clothes. He touched his maroon silk tie. "Who else would have understood what it was I wanted to accomplish? 'Tis my fault, Kathleen. My fault, indeed, that you've traveled so far and been so put upon. I can't apologize enough."

He was shaky when he stood up. Kathleen almost reached out for him. Gerry let his fingers trail across the desk as he shuffled toward her. He stopped a pace away, a full head shorter, and put his hand on Kathleen's shoulder.

"I appreciate your coming for me, Kathleen Cotter. You've made this old man proud and given me a moment of hope again. I'll always be grateful for that. Thank you, dear girl. Now—'' He bucked himself up, but it seemed to take all his energy. ''—will you be driving back tonight?''

Kathleen stared at him, stunned at the turn of events. She couldn't shake the feeling that she was supposed to do something now, but she couldn't figure out what it was. Gerry started again.

''Do you have enough gas? Would you like to stay for dinner? Sure wouldn't I be honored by that? Ah, but how selfish of me; you probably want to get a head start on traffic. And I'll have work to do looking at Louise's problem. Poor thing needs money, I'm sure. I only hope I can manage this for her. Long days can be so tiring. But, there, that's none of your concern, now, 'tis it?''

Sometime between Gerry's inquiry about traffic and his self-censure, he had gone over to the door of his office and was standing next to it. Kathleen looked at him, then back at the notes on his desk. Slowly, she followed him to the door, unable to part the waters of confusion that were bubbling in her brain.

''I—well—I guess I'll just drive back now.''

''Fine. Fine then.'' He nodded and spoke quietly, like a priest. Another touch on her arm was light, as if she were just a memory and already gone. ''We'll at least stay in touch, Kathleen. I don't want to lose the only family I have. Losing a business partner is hard, but losing you again—'' He shook his head sadly. ''—my only living relative. Ah, that would be such a terrible thing.''

Kathleen nodded. ''No. I mean, yes. Of course we'll stay in touch.''

''Fine, then. Fine.'' Gerry kissed her cheek. ''So lovely, Kathleen. What a pleasure it would have been.''

Before she knew what had happened, she was being ushered through the outer door; and before it closed, she heard her uncle ask Becky for the address of ''that old-folks home'' that had sent him some information. Then the door shut, and Kathleen faced the elevator. If she went in, would she drop off the face of the earth?

* * *

"Wow," Becky breathed, looking at the closed door. "That was really sad."

"Yes, 'twas," Gerry agreed. "Sad, indeed."

"I know how much you wanted her to stay, Mr. O'Doul. I'm sorry she didn't. She seemed like a nice lady." Becky crumpled her midmorning snack trash in deference to the solemn mood.

"Oh, indeed. The best," Gerry agreed cheerily.

He walked back into his office and retrieved the champagne bottle and the silver bucket. "Would you be kind enough, Becky, to do something with this?"

"Sure, Mr. O'Doul." She scurried toward the bathroom and, when she returned, Gerry handed her Kathleen's notes.

"And, Becky, two copies, if you don't mind."

"Two?"

The door opened and Kathleen stood there, resplendent in her simple sheath with the white piping and the champagne stain, her well-cared-for spectators, her purse, and her miserable expression.

"Yes," Gerry said to Becky as he smiled at Kathleen. "Two will do nicely."

Chapter Three

The sun came through the trees like God's fingers nudging the earth awake. It was a precious moment, one he had always loved. She had watched him through this same window as he lost himself in the morning moments before getting into their little car and heading off to work.

He drove through the trees, up and down the winding road that led away from their house. He drove to the intersection that red-flagged civilization and finally to the freeways that took him to his good job thirty miles away. That job paid for the small, neat house off the beaten path in a canyon in the Santa Monica Mountains. It paid for the gardening tools that helped them raise their organic food, the bunnies who were their children, the short trips to Yosemite to commune with a different kind of nature.

That job paid for his past mistakes, too, and he never complained about that. She adored his sense of responsibility, his ability to look behind and see what had gone wrong then look ahead to make things right. He was a man of exceptional sensitivity. He was such a good man. Gone now, he left behind an empty place in the little house and her heart. But he'd also left behind some unfinished business she didn't understand in the place she never went. She would have to take care of that business to keep his memory pure and to save herself. Though she was afraid to go below, she was more afraid not to. Today, she would break the last corporeal tie with him and hang on to the spiritual ones.

Turning from the big window, she went to the smaller one by the fireplace and lifted the lace curtain. She looked beyond the clearing even though she couldn't see the rabbit hutch. Perhaps a moment with them would give her courage, a moment cuddled on the cool earth with a warm little body nuzzled against her face. She bowed her head and decided not to walk in the forest and visit with her friends. To do so would mean defeat. Her courage was ephemeral; and if she didn't try it out now, this instant, she would lose it. Turning on her heel, she went back toward the big window and the door beside it.

Carefully, she snuffed out the incense burning in the holder he'd made from a pine cone that sat on the table he'd hewn out of a tree trunk. Taking another moment, she closed her eyes, laid her hands across her chest, and breathed in the woody scent. Tears came to her eyes, though she wasn't standing close to the spiral of smoke. Perhaps it was the flash of his face— the gentle, loving expression she remembered—that brought the tears. It would be wonderful to see him once more, to have him here to hold, now that she was afraid.

Shrugging into her sweater, she opened the door a crack. She peeked out, scanning the land she knew so well, the land that now seemed so alien. It seemed quiet enough, but then it had seemed quiet the day her husband died, too. Death could come stalking in the dark, the light, when you least expected it. Death came from strangers, and it came for reasons she didn't understand.

Knowing this, she slid out onto the porch, lay against the rough wood of the house, and waited. When nothing happened, she hurried, head down, to her car, a vintage Beetle, and started the engine with a prayer on her lips.

That's when she began to shake.

She was actually going below. To the city where people moved too fast and made decisions about her life when they didn't even know her. The thought of driving the freeways, negotiating the downtown streets, finding the room she wanted and standing up to the people she didn't want to see made her feel sick. But the sounds in the night, the voices she heard through the darkness, were more frightening still. And, most terrifying of all, was the sense that somehow, if she didn't do something fast, someone might make sure she joined her husband sooner than the Goddess wanted. Much as she cared for him, much as she would love to lie next to him again, she didn't want her new bed to be cold and dark and six feet under.

So, she drove away without knowing that company was coming to her house in the woods. This time it wasn't coming through the front door; it was moving through the trees and brush behind her cottage.

"She's gone," the first visitor called to his companion. The second man stood up, his knees cracking under his great weight. He took a deep breath of fresh, forest air.

"About time. I got bit sitting here. I hate bugs. I hate nature. Can't believe it. Something bit me. Look." He pulled down his dress sock to show that, indeed, he had been bitten.

"Looks like a spider." The other man peered closely at the wound. "It's real round. Probably a spider."

The first one shuddered. "That's disgusting. Think it's gone up my pants?"

"I don't know."

His friend moved forward, branches crackling and breaking as he pushed through the trees instead of seeking out a path. He didn't like the outdoors any more than his cohort did, but he wasn't going to be a sissy about it. Behind him, he heard the huge man hurrying to catch up. They were almost at the clearing when he was called. Turning, a reprimand on the tip of his tongue, the man looked at his partner, who was grinning from ear-to-ear.

"Hey, look what I found. Bunnies!"

The big man opened the wire door on the hutch and grabbed one by the neck. His expression softened as he held it up so that they were nose-to-nose. The rabbit's little pink nose twitched; the man's long, hooked one did the same. Suddenly, he gripped the bunny hard, whacking at the side of his neck as he did so. What happened next wasn't quite clear to the man who watched; he couldn't really understand the words that bellowed from the man's belly, but the end result of his outburst sent an amazingly clear message. The man didn't like nature.

The big man stood in a semi-circle of white, fluffy, dead rabbits, not a one giving a twitch about anything anymore. The big guy held a hand to his neck. There were tears in his eyes.

"I got stung. Some goddamn thing stung me. Check for the stinger. I'm not going any farther till you check to see if I'm swelling. I could die from a bee sting. They say you can die from a bee sting. Come on, take a look."

The other man, just as big, just as mean, checked out the dead rabbits, realized that six necks had been broken in a blink of an eye, and decided he would not be the seventh to get on the big guy's bad side. Dutifully, he checked the size eighteen neck, confirmed there was no stinger, then asked politely:

"Can we go on now? Please?"

"Yeah. Let's do it this time. Let's get the hell out of here."

His friend nodded and led the way to the front door of the cottage where he jimmied the flimsy lock. They went inside, and he thanked his lucky stars that the little rabbit lady had gone before they walked in.

"Tony, good to see you."

"You, too, Bob."

They met with a clasp of hands, centurions holding one another's metal-clad forearms in a fleeting bond of brotherhood before the bloodshed. Bob let go first. Tony's grin faltered. It was just another day, after all. Bob opened the door to Judge Kelley's courtroom; Tony pushed open the bar. They both turned left to the defense table and settled their briefcases before they settled themselves.

"What do you figure? Ten minutes on this thing?" Bob snapped gold hasps on a burgundy-colored portfolio and withdrew a manila folder of insignificant proportions.

"For you, maybe. I'm guessing I'll have a go at it with a

trial. You're probably in and out.'' Tony pulled at the tasteful brass-buckled belts that kept his huge case intact. It yawned wide, but he had no more paperwork than his colleague.

They both sat, checked their watches, and completed the ritual with smiles—no teeth.

"Two minutes and the other team forfeits. Kelley runs this courtroom to the wire.'' Tony passed the time.

"No cameras around to play to so he might as well get on with things,'' Bob noted dryly. Tony snickered.

"Judge just can't think of anything to say without a script, right?'' Tony poked his pal.

"I hear he went to the Springs for a tan because it's tough for him to get dressed in the morning without makeup,'' Bob chortled. Both of them were just bored enough to revert to nine-year-old humor as they waited for the day to start.

Tony twirled in his chair, just to be sure there wasn't anyone interested in their conversation. He gave a nod to his client, who sat quietly behind him, and noted a group of schoolchildren farther back. One could never be too careful. An out-of-favor judge might somehow make a comeback. Then their asses would be grasses if he got word they'd been disrespectful. He chuckled, thinking that mighty creative. Asses. Grasses. Whoever said lawyers had no sense of humor was dead wrong.

His eyes flicked over the spectator pews one last time. Only the bag lady from Sixth Street had come in recently. Nothing to worry about. He checked his watch again. The opposition was late. The day was theirs.

Judge Kelley's bailiff was out and singing, "Everyone please rise. Department 33 of the Los Angeles Superior Court is again in session, the Honorable Donald Kelley, judge, presiding.''

Tony and Bob stood, this time their hands clasped in front of their most private parts, their legs spread apart ready for the games to begin. They were fearless in the arena, and the emperor was taking his seat.

Kelley looked up from under well-formed brows, touched the edges of his carefully tended mustache, spied the two, and checked out the empty counsel table. He looked good. Palm Springs always helped. His blue eyes sparkled behind the tasteful, gold-rimmed glasses. The tie that peeked out from the top of the robe was knit and taupe, a color he favored, one that set off his excellently groomed, silver-gray hair. When he spoke, it was with a casualness that belied the sharp mind that had been called into question of late.

"In the matter of Brooker v. the Estate of Lionel Brooker, et al., counsel please make your appearance for the record." He looked up from his papers and smiled pleasingly at the attorneys.

"Tony Maglio for the estate of Lionel Brooker, Your Honor."

"Bob Morton representing All Life Insurance, Your Honor."

"Gentlemen." The judge nodded. "I see that the offended party has seen fit not to make an appear—"

Kelley sat up straighter. In the rear, the courtroom door banged open. The bailiff's hand was on the butt of her gun, her attention arrested by the commotion caused by the two women who hurried in.

The one in the brown suit figured it out first—they had not exactly been subtle and court was in session. She stopped and checked out everyone who was checking her out. Her eyes rested on the judge and she blushed. He raised a brow. The nip and tuck of her suit conjured up visions of *The Thin Man*, long cigarette-holders and longer legs, black-and-white nights where the curtains were drawn and everything was left to the imagination. Kelley should have held himself in contempt, because he could see the lady in brown was only concerned with the lateness of the hour.

She stumbled, then righted herself. She mouthed *sorry* before resuming her step and giving the woman behind her an opening. When he got an eyeful of her, Kelley had a few other thoughts about contempt. This one was resplendent in turquoise. Her dress ended just south of the flattest rear end he'd ever seen and stretched across the most amazing breasts to cross his threshold. Her hair was teased into a shape that reminded him of a mushroom cloud. Her lips shimmered deathly white, lined with a color he could only describe as clay. She seemed to be pushing the other woman forward, but the blonde in brown wasn't going anywhere without some sense of decorum. She pushed back slightly, glanced over her shoulder with barely hidden disdain, and came up the aisle as if she were headed to a wedding—with a shotgun at her back.

"Ladies. You have arrived." Kelley retrieved his smile. After all those months in front of the cameras, little could phase him. He turned to the lady with the briefcase.

"Kathleen Cotter? Counsel for—" He consulted his notes. "—Louise Brooker, ex-wife of the deceased?"

Louise moved as if she would speak, but it was Kathleen who got the words out first. After all these weeks, she'd learned to talk fast.

"Yes, Your Honor." The judge smiled at the sound of her voice. She would never have made it in talkies; but in a place like this where strident was the norm, her inflection was a welcome change. "I apologize to the court for our lateness. I'm new to the area and . . ."

"And I assume, madam, that you are Louise Brooker?" Kelley pinned Louise with a graceful turn of his head. This wasn't grammar school; he didn't want an excuse. Kathleen caught Louise out of the corner of her eye. Louise was radiating toward the bench. Kathleen prayed she wouldn't wink.

"You got it, Judge." They pushed through the bar as one unit, Louise scooting tightly after Kathleen.

"We apologize, Your Honor. Kathleen Cotter for Louise Brooker, for the record."

Kelley referred to his papers. He let his eyes slide toward Louise once more, as if to make sure she did, indeed, exist.

"She didn't want to pay five dollars an hour for parking, Judge," Louise piped in, taking his eye contact to mean he'd like her input. "She's new in town, so cut her some slack."

Kelley raised a brow and digested that incredible piece of information. "Let the record so reflect that Ms. Cotter is, indeed, the attorney of record. You may strike the editorial on our parking fees."

The day had begun.

The lawyers took their seats, Kathleen after her two opponents. From the corner of her eye, she checked them out. Expensive clothes and briefcases—even the estate's attorney, and this was not a wealthy estate. The two looked right back at her, fully composed.

Kathleen took a deep breath, focused on the judge, and prayed she could dispose of this matter quickly, erase whatever feeling of duty she felt toward Gerry, and run for the hills before he found some other oddball client to throw at her. At this rate, she'd make a name for herself in Los Angeles law and it wouldn't be the one she'd hoped for.

"Mr. Morton, we'll start with you, if you please."

Morton obliged. His suit was gray, his shirt white, his tie striped in shades of blue. He seemed rather handsome until you looked closely. His carefully coifed hair was receding, his chin multiplying, his eyes creased from long hours spent over paperwork and short intense hours in the sun pretending he was relaxed. She bet he didn't look so great naked. She held onto that thought and opened her briefcase, wincing as the latches opened with a resounding snap.

"Your Honor," Morton began apologetically. "I hesitate to even take the court's time pointing out the obvious. In the last month since we were served with papers regarding this matter, we have done nothing. We have not offered to settle, nor have we spent our time preparing for a court battle. Quite simply, there can be no battle when there is no basis for confrontation. Quite simply, Ms. Brooker will not be paid benefits to which she is not entitled."

He cleared his throat as a matter of course and continued.

"There has been no discovery, no witnesses to depose. Why? Because the facts are not contested. I cite section 4801, subdivision B of the Civil Code for the proposition that support obligations terminate with the death of the obliger spouse. I would also like to point out that our policy stands in its own defense. It is a basic policy that in no way veers from industry standards in language or intent. Regulations, rules, and policies are clear for all to see and understand. This, in our estimation, is a frivolous lawsuit brought by Ms. Cotter on Ms. Brooker's behalf, and we would request a Summary Judgment in this matter and a dismissal of this suit against All Life." It was a poignant moment. He looked Kathleen's way as if she were the one who hadn't read the fine print before signing on the dotted line. "If there are any questions regarding the language of the policy, I would be happy to go into it chapter and verse. I would even be happy to draw a diagram should Ms. Cotter be inclined to spend her time trying to figure it out visually."

"I doubt that will be necessary," Kelley muttered cheerfully, oblivious to the insult. He'd heard them all, and this was rather mild as affronts went. Kathleen, on the other hand, shot Bob Morton a look. It wasn't as good as the one her mother had used to put her in her place, though, and Morton remained cocky and confident.

"Ms. Cotter?" Kelley turned his judicial klieg light on her.

"Your Honor." She stood up slowly, her knees weak now that the moment had come for her to speak. She was in Los Angeles, not Riverside. She was far from home and alone, tackling this appearance under emotional duress.

"Your Honor." She cleared her throat, too, but it didn't seem to have the same calming effect on her as it did on Bob Morton. "It's not fair."

Kathleen had Kelley's attention. She had everyone's attention, including the pod of schoolchildren in for an afternoon outing. This was an argument they could understand. They were disappointed when there was more.

"Excuse me, Your Honor." Kathleen swallowed. Her mouth was dry. "I meant it isn't fair, in this instance, to decide upon settlement based strictly upon the letter of the agreement between Lionel Brooker and All Life Insurance. As in many instances with this great law of ours, there is often the spirit to consider. And if ever there were a case where spirit counted, it's this one. In the case of Mr. Brooker, the spirit was definitely willing but the flesh was weak. Please note the decision for the plaintiff in Tintocalis v. Tintocalis where the defendant had neglected to pay the premiums in a similar situation. The court ruled that the death benefit was to be paid because no one should suffer by the act of another."

"And we agree, Your Honor," Bob Morton crowed. "All Life should not suffer because of Mr. Brooker's intentional demise. I point to Tintocalis, also, and say that the obligation to sustain support falls directly on the estate. And, I can cite Lucas v. Elliot.''

Tony moved in his chair and whipped out a pen. Furiously, he made notes. The first was to kill Bob Morton.

''We must consider Mr. Brooker's intent to care for his ex-wife, Louise Brooker, when we discuss this matter. It is the spirit of that intent that I ask Your Honor to rule upon. Tintocalis specifically states that intent could be taken into consideration. . . .'' Kathleen went on.

''Your Honor.'' Bob Morton stood up slowly, raising a finger though the gesture was unnecessary to gain attention. ''While I can think of no one seemingly more capable of weaving an intriguing fairy tale than Ms. Cotter, we are not here to wax poetic about intent and love and the spirit of anything. Tintocalis never ruled on intent and *could be* is not a legal concept. We are here to determine whether, under the law, the agreement made between Lionel Brooker and All Life Insurance is binding.''

''Thank you so much for reminding me of that, Mr. Morton,'' Kathleen responded, hoping that sounded appropriately cool. Damn Gerry. She'd told him she'd never made an argument of any length. In her previous life, before Gerry's idea of professional heaven, she had been arbitrator, not aggressor. The man facing her had never arbitrated or acquiesced.

Taking a deep breath, Kathleen put on the face she and Gerry had practiced over the last week—a mask of surety drawn with cosmetics and practice. She hoped someone would be impressed. ''The spirit of Lionel Brooker was as strong in its belief that there are rights and wrongs in this world that supersede the mandates of committees that attempt to regulate life with rules. His life proved that everyone had to live by the rules, but not be ruled by them. Lionel Brooker wanted his ex-wife to be cared for in the eventuality of his death. To that end, and in very good faith, he paid the premiums on an insurance policy for one year, three-hundred-and-sixty-three days. On day three hundred and sixty-four, one day before the suicide clause would have been null and void, Lionel Brooker did something that was an aberration. It was an act that contradicted his generous spirit. Believe me, Your Honor, when Lionel Brooker took his life, he wasn't thinking about a clause buried deep in insurance paperwork.''

Kathleen moved forward. It was so hard to stand behind that table, far away from the judge, with no jury to speak to. If she were going to connect, it had to be now. Kathleen wanted them to know she could attest personally to the fact that the best of intentions sometimes didn't mean a happy ending and nobody should suffer because good intentions went awry.

"Judge, we don't know what drove Mr. Brooker to such a terrible step. To take your own life is not as much a decision for death as it is a belief that life can't go on. I grieve for Mr. Brooker, Your Honor, I really do.''

Kathleen let her eyes roam the courtroom. There wasn't anyone who didn't believe that last statement of hers. No one except Louise, who sat with her chin buried in her hand, her eyes rolled to the ceiling.

"I do,'' she said again. Louise deflected the reassurance by shifting noisily in her seat. Kathleen turned away from her, disgusted. What did this woman care about anyone's feelings? "But whatever drove Mr. Brooker to take such drastic action, it was beyond his control. I'm sure of that, Judge. So, since his action was beyond his control and the intent to financially care for Louise Brooker was so well-documented, I tell you that All Life cannot hold us to the letter of their agreement with Mr. Brooker. A previous court ruling established Mr. Brooker's generous intent; he proved that his spirit was willing to follow through on his promise. The fact that he killed himself a mere day before the agreement was to be nullified in terms of the suicide clause does not point to a meanness of spirit. If Lionel Brooker wished to somehow teach Louise a lesson about greed—'' Kathleen resisted the urge to look at her client.''— he could have taken his life at anytime and his action would still have had the same effect. Mr. Brooker didn't count the days to his death; he acted without thought except to end whatever pain he was in. When he deliberately pursued the means to provide for Louise, he was acting in good faith. He was acting according to a court order, and All Life should reciprocate with equally good intentions."

Kathleen moved back to the table and picked up the papers that waited there.

"Your Honor, I have research that will show how precarious a suicidal—"

Beside her, Louise drummed her fingernails on the table. Today, they were blue. Elvis was gone, replaced by a white-bearded man. Kathleen thought it was a summertime Santa. Louise coldly held up her middle finger for Kathleen to see that it was Kenny Rogers.

"Your Honor." Morton interrupted, his middle-aged face set in an expression of remorse as if he were terribly sorry he had to push his big, long, sharp pin into Kathleen's balloon. "We have no need of a psychological profile. The insurance policy fulfills the court's directives. All Life is not responsible for the deceased's actions after the policy was put in force. And while we are not as unfeeling as Ms. Cotter would like to lead you to believe, we have our rules. What is the law if not rules written down so that everyone can understand what their responsibilities and liabilities are. The spirit of the law is a thing of Hollywood. Scriptwriters trot out the concept when they can find no other means to bring drama to a matter that is exceptionally well-defined. Mr. Brooker indicated he had read the policy. His signature is acknowledgment of that. He accepted the parameters."

"But my client didn't have the opportunity for input, Your Honor," Kathleen said without thought, "Your Honor, if I could simply submit these reports from leading psychiatric journals, I'm sure—"

Bob Morton pushed his pin in farther.

"Mrs. Brooker's presence or agreement was not stipulated, Your Honor. Had it been, All Life would have been happy to comply. Please—" He opened his hands to show there was nothing up his sleeve. "—these are ridiculous objections. Ms. Cotter wastes our time."

"Yes, Your Honor, I understand that it wasn't stipulated, but if I may cite—"

"What she's trying to say is, it wasn't fair 'cause I didn't know about this clause-thing and I was the one who was going to get screwed by it. If I had known, I would have had it taken out."

Horrified, Kathleen swung her head toward Louise. The woman glanced disdainfully back, then grinned at the judge, thrilled with her own input.

"Your Honor, I apologize—" Kathleen began, but Don Kelley ignored her and Bob Morton derided her.

"It seems Mrs. Brooker believes she is God, Your Honor. No one can change an exclusion clause except All Life, and I assure you we would not have been so inclined."

"I wouldn't have let him sign it! We would have done something else. We would have made other arrangements," Louise shot back.

"Your Honor, a moment with my client, please." Kathleen held out her hand as if she could stop this nonsense like a crossing guard, but Kelley was having a darn good time. He had no intention of calling a truce. He pointed at Louise with his pen, like a spider nudging the unsuspecting fly into the web.

"Mrs. Brooker, are you telling this court that you had prior knowledge of your ex-husband's desire to take his own life? Are you telling this court that you wished to defraud the insurance industry by insisting on a substantial policy minus the exclusion clause so that you could cash it in, knowing your ex-husband would meet his death by his own hand? If you are telling this court that you would have refused the policy because of said clause, then you must have suspected your husband was so inclined and that, madam, would constitute fraud."

"Fraud! No way, José." Louise shot out of her chair. Test her by fire and she'd willingly have the flame lit. "Lionel was the last person I'd expect to check out that way. I've lived long enough to know that anything is possible and, sure, I would have made sure there weren't any strings attached to that policy."

"Your Honor, this is ridiculous. My client does not speak for—" Kathleen cried, appalled at the turn of events.

"Kathleen!" Louise howled in frustration.

"There you have it." Bob from All Life was jubilant. "This

suit must be dismissed, and charges brought against this woman!''

"All right, enough.'' Kelley sat back in his big, black chair and drew a finger along his mustache trying to hide his smile. It had been fun, and now it was time for business. "Mrs. Brooker, sit down. Mr. Morton.'' Kelley raised a brow, and the attorney took his seat. Kathleen was the object of Kelley's interest. "Ms. Cotter. You're new to our district, but you are not new to the law.'' Don Kelley spoke conversationally, as if they were just having a bite of lunch instead of his handing her head to her on a plate. "Can you honestly stand there and tell me that you contest the fact that All Life is within their rights to set boundaries on the policies they sell?''

"No, Your Honor,'' Kathleen admitted miserably.

"Are you going to contest the fact that Mr. Brooker did not know what he was signing?'' Don Kelley shifted his chin to his other hand.

Kathleen's head hung figuratively lower. She whispered in her angelic voice. "No, Your Honor.''

"Is there any reason that I shouldn't grant the All Life motion for Summary Judgment since we all agree that the company is well within their rights to set the rules for their policyholders and to deny benefits should those requirements not be met?''

"No, Your Honor.''

"Then, Ms. Cotter, the only thing you can possibly contest is that Mr. Brooker is not dead.''

"Of course, he's dead.'' Kathleen chuckled pleasantly, grateful the judge had resorted to levity. Yet when she looked up, he wasn't laughing.

"Then will you argue that he didn't kill himself?''

"He killed himself.'' Louise again. "He resented paying me money because I was taking his farm!''

"Louise, stop.'' Kathleen pushed hard and Louise fell off the left heel of her shoe, crumpling just enough for Kathleen to get her down in her chair.

"Your Honor. My client is distraught. She doesn't know what she's saying.''

"I can see that, Ms. Cotter.'' He sighed, accepting a note

from his clerk, muttering while he read it. "So, if you don't agree with your client, then you must believe that Mr. Brooker did not kill himself."

"Perhaps not." Kathleen's mind whirled as she tried to figure out how she could extrapolate an argument to defend that statement from the psychiatric reports.

"And what evidence do you have that there was foul play?" Kelley jotted a note back to the clerk, then cradled his chin in one hand and toyed with his mug with the other.

"I didn't suggest foul play was involved." Kathleen raised her chin, peeved that he should get his jollies at her expense.

"Your Honor," Bob Morton called. Kathleen looked over. The schoolchildren were filing out of the courtroom, uninterested in Morton's objection. "I really must object. I assume Ms. Cotter has read the police report, at least. And if she hasn't, then she is insulting the integrity of this court by playing these little games without doing her homework. Is it her intent to wear us down? To confuse us? Well, I, for one, say this court cannot be confused any more than it already has been by her nonsense."

"Mr. Morton?" Kelley raised a brow and pushed at his gold-rimmed glasses. "Are you speaking for this court?"

Morton, to his credit, back-pedaled with grace. "I only meant that this court's calendar has been confused by this frivolous suit, Your Honor. Certainly it was not directed at—"

Kathleen's eyes narrowed with satisfaction. Morton's whole foot might not have made it into his mouth, but a goodly portion had. Unfortunately, Kelley had tired of both of them.

"Never mind. Never mind." The judge waved them away. He was ready to take the ball and go home. "I've heard enough. I will grant the motion for Summary Judgment and dismiss the case against All Life."

"Thank you, Your Honor."

"Oh, damn," Louise muttered, throwing her hands up to her face. Kathleen glanced at her client only to see the identical nail portraits of Kenny Rogers winking at her.

"Your Honor." Tony Maglio moved in for the kill now that Bob had mortally wounded the opposition, no expressions of professional offense on his face. His style was that of the good guy. He grinned openly. The court was his locker room. He snapped his towel Kelley's way.

"We move that the estate of Lionel Brooker be held not liable in this action also, for the same reasons that All Life has expressed. We also believe there are no contested issues here. The estate should have no liability because Lionel Brooker did, indeed, provide for Louise Brooker as stipulated in the previous ruling. He secured the insurance policy as directed. Louise Brooker, by accepting the policy when it was forwarded and signing the receipt for said delivery, agreed that stipulation had been fulfilled. Lucas v. Elliot is again cited. Had Mr. Brooker not purchased life insurance, the estate could be charged. However, he did. Therefore, I see no reason why we should be in front of Your Honor arguing the matter."

"Three minutes, Ms. Cotter," Kelley muttered.

"Lionel Brooker did not contest Louise Brooker's request for a life insurance policy to protect her in the case of his death. He sought out All Life; he paid the premiums. That goes to intent, Your Honor. Lionel Brooker proved that he intended to provide for my client no matter what. If the insurance company is not liable, then the estate must be. This is based on the previous court's ruling. Louise Brooker is entitled to support."

"Ms. Cotter." Judge Kelley clipped her name off like the end of a good cigar. He smiled. He was ready for another chat. "How long have you been practicing law?"

"Eight years, Judge."

"Still close enough to graduation that you must remember your classes in law school. There was probably one professor who conducted a discussion of state of mind?"

"Yes."

"Do you remember hearing that it is impossible for a third party to attest to state of mind?" Kelley was grinning. Sitting high above the proceedings, his comely looks made the sharpness of his lesson something akin to a smiling executioner.

"Yes."

"Then, Ms. Cotter, unless you are going to produce a note from the deceased—" His fingers twisted like a magician. "—

call a mystery witness who happened to be in the stall next to Mr. Brooker before he did the deed, or call a psychic who will attest to what Mr. Brooker had in mind regarding his estate on the day, and dare I say, at the moment of his death, I would suggest you think twice before going down this road.''

"But—'' Kathleen began.

Judge Kelley raised one finger and waggled it. His clerk passed him another note. This one seemed to amuse him. Kathleen raised her chin. It felt like the Rock of Gibraltar, but she managed to keep it up while he did some housekeeping. Louise wiggled in her seat and recrossed her legs. If movements were words, Louise's would all be spelled with four letters.

"You blew it,'' Louise whispered. Kathleen's shoulders went back, ready for any slings and arrows. "Gerry should have been here.'' Under her breath once again. "That old man's got more on the ball than you'll ever have.''

"Be quiet, Louise.'' Kathleen never moved, not her head and barely her lips. Judge Kelley rolled his baby blues, then glared as best he could at the bad girls in school.

"I think we're going to have to continue this discussion with the estate of Lionel Brooker. I believe that there is some merit to the case against the estate—though, without the life insurance policy, I imagine the ex-Mrs. Brooker will find it less lucrative than she imagined. Legally, though, I don't see—''

"Excuse me?''

Those two little words wafted forward from as far back in the courtroom as it was possible to come. The huge seal behind the judge seemed to tip forward as the sweetest voice—sweeter than that of Kathleen Cotter—floated across the expanse of pews and over the shining wood of the bar and into the well to lay itself in front of the man in black.

Judge Kelley squinted though there was nothing to obstruct his view. Tony turned—not exactly turned—but moved his very straight body as if he were taking a ride on a lazy Susan. Louise flung herself over the back of her chair. Kathleen took two tiny steps and twisted her head. Bob Morton stopped packing his briefcase, and the woman who had spoken, a woman so very small and delicate that visions of Thumbelina came to mind, seemed to shrink under their scrutiny.

"I beg your pardon?" Don Kelley's voice softened as if he were talking to a child. From their perspective, it appeared as if the woman might indeed be younger than anyone imagined. Her long hair was parted in the middle; her clothes were just a bit too big. Her long cardigan sweater hung over her narrow shoulders as if it weighed on her mightily without giving any warmth. She wore no makeup; her eyes seemed nothing more than circles of dark, for the lashes were too light to define the shape of them. Her mouth remained a tight and fretful line that was too narrow to make a statement or be considered attractive.

"Miss, do you have business before this court?" Kelley called out.

"I do, sir," she said in a voice only a fraction stronger than before. Although they all looked at the woman, one man acted. A man Kathleen hadn't really noticed before. He said something to Tony as he sidestepped out of the pew where he had been sitting. Kathleen wasn't sure if it were a muttered curse or an expression of sorrow. She couldn't hear anything more. He was hurrying toward the woman. But she was quicker still.

Instead of waiting for him to reach her, she seemed to anticipate his moves and sidestepped, ducking around him so that he had to turn and follow her with hoarse, quick whispers of objections. Questions were thrown her way, but she ignored them all. Kathleen knew this must have taken a great deal of courage, the same kind of courage it had taken to object when her own father had told her she'd never be a lawyer.

"I don't want anything," she called to the judge, waving a childlike hand as if that would make him understand how sincere she was. The man caught up with her. She turned back to him as he put his hand on her arm. "I don't want anything," she snapped, instantly embarrassed by such a display. Her attention was back on the court, her bovine eyes darting Louise's way. Kathleen could have sworn she saw a flicker of fear behind those eyes. "She can have it all. I mean it, Judge. Louise—" She looked directly at the ex-Mrs. Brooker. "I don't want any of it. No money or whatever Lionel had. I'd like to keep the house; but if you want that, too, it's okay." She looked at the judge with big, big, frightened eyes. "Please, Judge, just give it all to her."

"Mr. Maglio?" Kelley wanted an explanation but was so fascinated by the woman he never took his eyes off her.

"Yes, Your Honor. I apologize for this interruption. This is highly irregular. I'll take care of it." Tony headed toward the man and the woman, circled both with his long, well-clothed arms, and tried to step them backward to the door.

"Mr. Maglio! What are you doing? This court is not in recess."

"Please, Your Honor," he called back, unwilling to release the quietly feuding couple. "I need only a moment to straighten this out, Your Honor. This is Edward Brooker, Lionel Brooker's brother and executor of the estate. I beg Your Honor for a short recess." He was still hurrying them to the door, but Kelley was as curious as any of them.

"And the lady?"

Tony Maglio stopped. His shoulders sagged. He would have preferred not to have added another iron to the fire, but now there was no choice. Facing Judge Kelley, he was about to speak, but it was Louise who spilled the beans. Losing interest in the whole affair, she muttered *Lionel's wife* just before the little woman started to cry and Judge Kelley called a recess.

Chapter Four

"She just wasn't worth talking about, sweetie."

A new twist. Louise was throwing endearments at Kathleen like stones.

"Why didn't you tell me about her! Lionel had remarried and you didn't think that's important? That is information that actually might have been helpful, Louise. You've told me every stupid little thing I didn't need to know a hundred times. In all that time, don't you think mentioning a new wife might have been something I might have found interesting?" Kathleen controlled herself admirably considering the fine line Louise was walking.

"My problem was with Lionel and my part of his money." She jerked her head in the general direction of the hall where the little lady had been shooed by Lionel's brother and the attorney. "She's a nothing, sweetheart. I don't deal with nothings. I learned my lesson with Lionel. He turned out to be a big, fat, sensitive zero. Looking at her makes me sick. It only goes to show how right I was about him. He could have had me. He could have made me happy, and I would have given him everything. But we get divorced and he goes to that wimpy little dishrag. It's insulting."

Kathleen paced behind Louise, who was taking her own sweet time touching up an already perfect makeup job. Kathleen glared at the other woman and wished she had the guts to tell her that perfect paint-by-numbers does not make a masterpiece just as slight-of-build and soft-of-voice does not a dishrag make.

Then she caught sight of herself in the mirror, looking away just as quickly. She couldn't lie to herself. No matter how well-drawn the mask, it was still painted on to hide what was underneath. Louise hadn't offered the information, but then again Kathleen hadn't asked.

"Look, Louise, you hired me to—"

"I hired Gerry, honey." She flicked at her eyelash, and a perfect sphere of mascara flew toward the mirror. Kathleen's face burned as red as the lace bra that peeked from under Louise's turquoise top. Louise had met her mark; she'd hit below the belt.

"You hired O'Doul & Associates. For the time being, I am the associate, and Gerry assigned me to your case because he knew I could handle it." Kathleen stopped pacing and took her share of the blame. "I should have stuck with my original gut feeling and stuck by my advice, as an attorney, not to pursue this matter." Louise raised a well-plucked eyebrow and Kathleen's guilt trip was over. "As a woman I should have told you I thought you were greedy and ungrateful."

"But you didn't, did you?"

Louise was done. She turned around slowly and planted her flat behind on the square sink. An incredible amount of cleavage heaved toward Kathleen as Louise Brooker crossed her arms. The red lace was now well-hidden. "Okay, Sister Kathleen, let's talk."

"We've talked enough. If you don't want to give me information that can help you, then I don't know what you want to talk about."

"Sure you do, honey. We need to lay our cards on the table, clear the air—" She smiled wickedly. "—bare our breasts." Louise chuckled, but her amusement didn't last as long as Kathleen's embarrassment. "I gave you plenty of chances to do that these last few weeks. From the minute Gerry joined us at the hip, I was ready to give you the benefit of the doubt. I figured, if the old man thought you had it, then you did. But what I saw that first day, and what I saw in that courtroom, just proved what I figured out the first time I laid eyes on you. You're an okay package and Gerry O'Doul may be your uncle, but you haven't got half the balls or the brains he has.''

"If that's meant to shock me, you're wasting your breath."

"I don't want to shock you. I just want to do what's right. I wanted to clue you in so you don't go on thinking you're cut out for the big leagues." The door opened. Both of them looked toward the young black woman who gave them a glance, took a second look at Louise, then hurried into a stall. Kathleen moved closer, but Louise didn't care who heard her. "I know what I want. I figured, if nothing else, you'd do your best to please Gerry and get it for me. Or maybe you'd try your hardest because you had some pride. But now you're trying to weasel out of your responsibility by telling me it's my fault you're not going to win. Hey, where were you when I was talking? I gave you what I had, and you didn't even do me the courtesy of asking me questions. We lost because of you.''

They heard the toilet flush, and the stall door opened just as Louise wrapped up.

"Baby, all was lost long before that little broad showed up. You look good in your own way, but get you out there in the ring and they KO you without lifting a finger. You don't have style. You don't have a mouth on you. You're not even quick on your feet. Your arguments sounded like a grocery list. You got all quiet when you should have stood up for me, so I had to try to do it myself. So, I'll just go on back to Gerry and tell him he takes this thing on or I take my business somewhere else. I believe in this. I need an attorney who does, too."

"It has nothing to do with faith. What I needed was a case with merit,'' Kathleen muttered, never taking her eyes from Louise's.

"A good lawyer doesn't need merit. They need brains, and you had enough time before this hearing to use yours. Gerry didn't need to know about that woman to get me the insurance policy; you shouldn't have needed to know to get me the benefits. Admit it, that mouse doesn't mean anything."

Louise was wrong, Kathleen was sure, but she wasn't exactly sure why. Kathleen turned on her heel and walked into a stall. She locked the door and sat down to think.

When the answer came to her, Kathleen flung open the door triumphantly, forgetting to pretend she had gone into the stall for any other reason than to hide.

"Of course it's important. She wants to give . . ." Kathleen looked right. ". . . you . . ." She looked left. ". . . everything." Triumph turned to defeat. Louise Brooker was nowhere to be found. Resigned, she hitched her briefcase and followed her client. "The woman wants to hand over the estate. We probably wouldn't even be here if we'd known that."

As she opened the door and stepped out into the hall, Kathleen looked for Louise. She looked right and spied the second Mrs. Brooker halfway down the very, very long hall. Kathleen started toward Lionel's lady, who stood arguing—or at least trying to argue—with Lionel's brother. Her tiny hands moved quickly; his expression was earnest and frustrated. No matter how benevolent her opponent, the woman was obviously losing the battle.

Kathleen's steps quickened when the argument suddenly intensified. The man was angry and Alice in Wonderland was hanging her head, poking at the elevator button. Even from the quickly closing distance, Kathleen could see the lady was crying and desperate. Kathleen's pace quickened as something clicked in the back of her mind. Here was a woman agitated to the point of physical distress, a woman exhibiting all the signs of fear. Yes, fear, and that meant there was more here than met the eye. High emotion had no place in a simple disposition of an insignificant estate.

Kathleen almost ran. The elevator door was opening. The blond-haired woman turned. The man took her arm, only to release it when she shrank from him in horror. The man backed away, putting one hand to his brow, the other on his hip, arm akimbo. The regular Joe was back, not as intimidating as she had imagined a moment ago, and the doors were closing on a sad woman, not a character out of central casting. Mrs. Brooker's body was now framed by the closing steel. With the thrill of optical illusion, it seemed as if those doors were pushing her tiny body together, compressing her until soon there would be nothing left. Kathleen would never know what there was in this estate that was worth a threat, a fight, and a great deal of fear.

"Wait!"

Kathleen's arm was in the air; her breath was tight in her chest. She sprinted the last few steps, but she was too late. The doors closed. The woman was gone. She turned to the man who was simultaneously turning away from her.

"I needed to talk to her," Kathleen said to his back. He walked with a slouch, whether of defeat or nature she didn't know. She spoke to him again, scooting around to come parallel with him. "Is she all right?"

The man stopped, hands in his pockets. His jacket didn't fit well. It wasn't expensive. His face was long, his nose a bit too short to balance the eyes and lips. He looked at Kathleen with little interest. He'd been around lawyers too long now to really believe she was worried.

"She's fine, I'm sure. She's a nut. Pure and simple. A nut. Like everyone in California. Lionel was weird, but a real good guy. How strange could it be here?" He shook his head. "Well, I'll tell you. I'm from Michigan. Lionel and I didn't know each other very well, but I thought he was a neat guy."

"Was he?"

The man seemed startled by the question. His eyes swam with tears. Kathleen had hit a nerve no one else had bothered to seek out.

"Yes, he was. My brother was the most giving man I've ever known. He was a lot younger than I was, but even when he was little he would just as soon give you the last of whatever he had rather than keep it for himself."

"Then he was a kind of a martyr?" Kathleen almost lost the man on that one.

"No, he was a true and generous spirit. Hard to believe somebody could change that much, isn't it? Hard to believe that he suddenly became a drug-user selfish enough to take his own life." The tall man sighed again and ran a hand over his eyes. "I'm sad he's gone. I'm sad he went the way he did. I was happy to take care of his estate, though. You know, do something to show that I still felt a connection. Besides, I didn't think it was a big thing. I mean, what could a guy like him acquire that would take so much time to take care of? Lionel didn't care about a whole bunch of material things."

He began to walk. Kathleen fell into step and listened.

"Besides, I'm ten years older than Lionel. Who would have thought he would kick off before I did? Stupid idiot." The man sighed. "He and Sarah lived in a canyon, raised animals, had a vegetable garden. They worshipped all this natural-world nonsense." The man shook his head at their stupidity. Kathleen assumed in Michigan there wasn't time to worry about worshipping anything. "And then there are the nuts. Lionel sure knew where to find them."

Kathleen looked up to see that he had spied Louise. Lost in their own thoughts, the two of them stood and watched her. Kathleen was aware that those thoughts were probably identical.

"Mr. Brooker, I'd like to depose you," Kathleen said politely.

"Because Sarah showed up? Because of her, you're going to make this more than it is? It should be over by now. I need to go home. There's nothing I could tell you that I haven't told you in the last few seconds. Lionel was a super guy. He loved Sarah. Weird as they were, they were perfectly suited to each other. Then he killed himself. Who's to say what went on in his mind? There, that's it. I just want to go home."

His tired eyes were still trained on Louise, who lounged against the wall folding a piece of gum before she popped it in her mouth.

"I've got to do my job, Mr. Brooker. I've got to try to get as much as I can for my client. But if Lionel loved his new wife as much as you say, you may want to try to set the record straight so she won't give everything away. Lionel would have wanted that, wouldn't he?"

"Why bother? You want everything. I can't fight that."

"I want what's fair," Kathleen assured him.

He glanced from Louise to Kathleen. His tired eyes looked her up and down, then he laughed and walked away, his last comment trailing behind him and meeting its mark.

"Fruits, nuts, and liars."

Kathleen pulled her old plaid robe around her and scratched the back of her leg with her sock-clad foot. She was watching her landlord fix the sink and thinking about her miserable day. Sarah Brooker's face haunted her. Louise's words riled her. Gerry's assertions that she had done her best rang less than true. And there was something else that niggled, something that she'd been trying to tell herself ever since she got home. She just couldn't quite grasp what it was and her new landlord's chatter wasn't helping.

"You'll love it. Come on. You haven't been out since you've been here. You haven't even unpacked your stuff." He gave the wrench one more twist. He was a joy to watch.

"No, thanks anyway." She was moping. There was no challenge Paul loved better than destroying a good mope.

"Come on. It's a producer's house."

Paul stood up and wiped his hands on the towel on the sink. He dangled that last tantalizing bit of information as if it were a carrot. He was the most gorgeous man Kathleen had ever seen. Tall. Dark. Gay. When Paul had been fired from his job as an exotic dancer, Gerry had successfully argued that, being gay, Paul could not be a threat to any of the ladies he entertained and, therefore, he had been discriminated against. The settlement was substantial and Paul's gratitude unbounding. He could never repay Gerry for his brilliance, but he kept trying. Kathleen's rent in his West Hollywood apartment complex was next to nothing.

"No, thanks. It was a lousy day. I think I'll just sit here and lick my wounds."

"Oh, sure, I've had days like that, too. You're right. A party isn't what you need. Maybe you should go see Gerry?"

Kathleen shook her head.

"Right again. If you're feeling *that* bad, only someone who

loves you will do, and I don't mean love like relative love."
He winked. "I don't know what I'd do without William. When
I was so low those days during the lawsuit, he was the only
one who kept me sane." Paul pocketed his wrench and smiled.

"How do you do that?"

"What?"

"How do you fix my sink and still look so clean?"

"William may adore me, but he also does the laundry. He'd
have my head if I made more work for him." Paul chuckled
and patted her shoulder as he left. "If you change your mind,
call us before eight."

He left Kathleen to wallow in her misery. At least she did
that well. She watched two hours of news, managed a microwave pizza bread, and balanced her checkbook by the time
Paul and William checked with her at eight to see if she'd
changed her mind. She was in bed by nine-thirty, staring at the
ceiling while images of Louise and Sarah Brooker, Lionel's
brother, and Judge Kelley floated through her head. They
seemed to make a comfortable party of four, but no matter how
hard Kathleen tried to join them at their table, there was never
one more chair. Gerry popped in for a command performance,
a maitre d' in the muddled cafe of her mind. Tony Maglio and
Bob Morton floated by on their way to another table, smiling
at her as she drifted into a less-than-restful sleep. When her
nightmare dinner was served and the great silver dome was
taken off the platter, the waiter announced the special of the
evening was Lionel Brooker. But Kathleen was too far away
from the table to see him. Too far away . . . and in the small
part of Kathleen's brain that still fought sleep, she realized this
wasn't so odd. In reality, she had no idea what Lionel looked
like. Strangely, though, Kathleen Cotter's last thoughts were
of Paul and William, William and Paul, and how very, very
happy they were—together.

That did it!

She was awake and excited at one in the morning, inspiration
coming to her in that never-ending dream. She had the answer
and no one to tell at that hour. So Kathleen Cotter showered,
put her face on, and sat in her robe at the small kitchen table

to make notes. By six, she'd been to the bakery, purchased the largest coffee cake she could find, and left it at Paul's door with a note of thanks. At eight-thirty, she was at the office, waiting for Gerry O'Doul. He came in six minutes later, and Kathleen began to talk. Gerry listened, trying very hard not to let the tears in his eyes show. He had never been happier in his life, and he had a funny feeling Kathleen hadn't either.

They filed a motion for reconsideration in the matter of Louise Brooker v. All Life Insurance by ten and, thanks to Gerry's intervention with Judge Kelley's clerk, had an appearance scheduled for eleven the next day.

That evening, Kathleen brought Paul and William a bottle of champagne. Love, she said, was always an inspiration and they had given her a ton of it—inspiration, that was.

Chapter Five

This time Gerry sat with Louise behind the bar. Kathleen wore burgundy and the look of a kid on Christmas morning. Louise wore a mini-skirt that matched her orange fingernails. Kathleen had no interest in the rocker of the day. Judge Kelley's shirt was white, his tie gray, his black robes fresh. Bob Morton was dressed in a suit the color of summer sand. They were all assembled to find out if Kathleen had brought them to this courtroom once again to waste their time or pique their interest.

"Kathleen Cotter for Louise Brooker," she said following the court courtesies.

"Bob Morton, Your Honor, for All Life. And, for the record, not happy to be here, Your Honor."

"All in a day's work, Mr. Morton," Kelley quipped. Obviously a morning person, his smile was radiant as he turned it on Kathleen. "Good morning, Miss Cotter. Didn't really expect to see you again on this matter."

Kathleen took his benevolence as a sign of good fortune. She kept her mouth shut and let Kelley lead.

"You've been granted this hearing based on your motion for reconsideration in the matter of Louise Brooker v. All Life Insurance." He pushed aside his notes and crossed his arms

atop the high desk. I must say, I granted this motion out of
curiosity, and a bit of coercion on the part of my clerk. I cannot
imagine what you have to bring before this court that was not
brought to light day before yesterday. However, I'm hoping it
will be something that will start my morning out right. So, you
will proceed."

Kathleen cleared her throat, fully aware that Bob Morton
was pouting.

"Thank you," she said sweetly. "I was devastated after my
last appearance in your court. Not because I believe I had been
treated unfairly, not because you hadn't given our argument—
slim as it was—due consideration . . ."

"Your Honor, could Ms. Cotter just get on with it?"

"Cool your heels, Mr. Morton. She'll get to it soon enough,
won't you, Ms. Cotter?" Kathleen made a mental note to always
jockey for the morning calendar.

"Absolutely. I do appreciate the time you're giving me."

Kathleen chanced a glance behind her. The deep glint in
Gerry's eyes offered encouragement, but his expression was
that of only mild interest. Louise squirmed beside him. Kathleen
faced the bench without giving her a second glance. Kathleen
reached for inspiration. For a minute it wasn't there. No visions
of mother and father rooting for her, no sense of friends cheering
her along. When it finally came, she was surprised to see that
it came from inside her. Tenuous though this courage was, she
grabbed it, held it, and spoke.

"When last we met, Your Honor, you asked whether or not
I understood that a third party cannot attest to state of mind. I
assured you that I did, indeed, understand that. I would not
waste the court's time attempting to argue that point. I will,
however, ask the court to reinstate the action against All Life
on the basis that there is, if not life, a certain amount of commu-
nication after death that allows the deceased to speak for himself."

"Your Honor, please." Bob Morton was on his feet. His
please, pulled out like taffy, was left like a sticky lump on
Kelley's bench as a warning not to step in the mess. Kelley,
being a curious sort, ignored Morton's less-than-subtle advice.

"Go on, Ms. Cotter."

Base hit. Now she'd steal home.

"As I was saying, I believe that there is a certain life energy left behind by the deceased that speaks for itself. I believe that there are other ways to address proof of intent, Your Honor. I believe that I can prove that, while Lionel Brooker did, indeed, die from a self-administered lethal dose of drugs, he did not intend to take his life that day. I say *intend*, Your Honor. This is the crux of my argument for reconsideration."

Kathleen could stay still no longer. She wandered from behind the counsel table, considering the floor, raising one hand ever so slightly. She was thinking hard, having a conversation with her best friend and, today, that best friend was the Honorable Donald Kelley.

"If there were no intent to die at the moment Lionel Brooker inserted the needle beneath his skin, then there can be no question of suicide. A suicide is, by definition, the act of killing oneself on purpose. On *purpose*." She verbally underlined the word, then paused, like a preacher allowing for a moment of reflection. "What I do believe is that Lionel Brooker's intent— his purpose—was to get high. He may have wanted to enjoy himself or relieve himself of some pressures he had been experiencing. I believe he intended to suspend time for a few moments, but certainly not an eternity, and I believe I can prove that."

"Based on what, Your Honor! The man is dead. We've already established that no third party can speak to the deceased's intent." Morton raised his voice. He didn't even bother to get up. Kathleen didn't waste her energy on him. She was hot. He knew it and he was scared. Instead, she kept her eyes on Don Kelley and waited for divine intervention from the bench. When it didn't come, she had no choice but to forge ahead.

"Lionel Brooker's behavior speaks for itself. I will show that Lionel Brooker did not fit the profile of a suicide, persons who have specific consistencies as documented in journals of medicine and psychology. I propose to show that in his work and, especially, his personal life there were no pressures so great that suicide was desirable or an option."

Kathleen dropped her voice a note, came close to placing her clasped hands on the high bench in an attitude of supplication the way she and Gerry had determined she should, but that wasn't her style—yet.

"I promise, Your Honor, if you give me this chance, I will prove to you by the deceased's own actions that the *intent* to kill himself was never there. I will prove that the clause which has excluded benefits to my client based on the purposeful taking of one's own life is null and void."

That was enough. Slowly she walked back to the counsel table, looking at Morton as she continued speaking.

"Yes, Lionel Brooker is dead. No, he didn't commit suicide." She was behind the table locking eyes with Judge Kelley when she said. "Yes, Louise Brooker is entitled to collect the death benefits from All Life. I can prove all this is true. That, not the time spent in this courtroom, is what upsets Mr. Morton but because All Life is going to have to live up to its obligation and pay Louise Brooker a quarter of a million dollars."

Kathleen sat down. She sat straight in her chair and hoped Gerry O'Doul, along with everyone else, was duly impressed. Louise had even stopped fidgeting.

"Mr. Morton?" Judge Kelley lowered the checkered flag for All Life.

"Your Honor." He stood up and buttoned his jacket. "I find this a great deal of nonsense and beneath my dignity to even argue this position."

"I see. Then I suppose I can do nothing less than grant Ms. Cotter's request."

"Your Honor," Bob Morton sputtered, "I didn't mean I wouldn't argue. I only meant that it was beneath me to try and make sense of what Ms. Cotter proposes." He was talking fast now, knowing he had lost some footing. Kathleen liked Judge Kelley more with each passing minute. "There is the coroner's report on Mr. Brooker that rules, in unequivocal terms, suicide."

"It reads overdose," Kathleen muttered. Morton talked fast, but it was clear Don Kelley had heard her.

"That is the only proof needed in this matter, and if Your

Honor considers such a request and agrees to this motion, you will be setting a dangerous precedent. You will be setting this court up for reversal on appeal. I can promise you, All Life will appeal.''

Kelley's sunny disposition clouded, and his eyes turned icy.

"The day this court rules on the basis of political expediency, counsel, is the day these robes will be discarded," Kelley said. "And anyone who suggests otherwise is on shaky ground."

"I only meant that All Life cannot allow a ruling in favor of Ms. Cotter to pass. It would wreak havoc with our system, void such a clause immediately, and take away our privilege to make our own rules. Your Honor, I cite Cramer v. Biddison where it is clear if the obligor spouse violates an order to maintain life insurance, a constructive trust may be imposed against his estate. That is where the road to justice lies. I never meant to imply—"

Kelley waved Morton away.

"I know what you meant, Mr. Morton. Your argument has as much clarity as Ms. Cotter's. I choose to rule in favor of Ms. Cotter, for her argument has not only clarity but conscience and creativity. It is a powerful combination. I charge you to remember that when you are before this court." Lacking a gavel, Don Kelley stood up and finished the proceedings with an authoritative touch to his fine mustache. "You have the option of a pretrial conference. If either of you believes there will be a chance to settle this matter out of court, I suggest you do so."

"I doubt that will be possible, Your Honor," Morton said, his pride clearly wounded.

"Fine." Kelley opened his calendar, motioned for his clerk, and addressed counsel. "Trial is set two months from this date. Both parties will be present and ready with their arguments. I heartily recommend you attempt to make nice with one another. In the event that you are not able to, I look to Ms. Cotter to bring a resoundingly convincing argument before this court—" He gave another one of those looks to Bob. "—so that it will not feel its time has been wasted or its judgment flawed."

"Yes, Your Honor. Thank you, Your Honor. Thank you."

Kathleen rose in deference and gratitude to the man on the bench. She didn't move an inch until he was away. The minute he was behind closed doors and the clerk was on to other matters and the bailiff had lost interest and Bob Morton was packing his things, she whirled to Gerry.

"We did it," she whispered.

"Well done, Kathleen," Gerry whispered back. "*You* did it." There was a catch in the back of his throat. "I always knew you could."

But Kathleen wasn't listening any longer. She beat back the sudden feeling of invincibility, hiding behind the comportment of a woman who wasn't sure of her own worth. But she did know her stock had suddenly gone up. When she smiled at Bob Morton, he pushed through the bar without so much as a word to her. She snapped up her briefcase, as if for the first time it really belonged to her and she really belonged in this place. She felt wonderful as she, too, took her leave. Gerry was waiting and they walked out of the courtroom together.

"Sure, wasn't it lucky you decided to stay with me to see this through," he said as he took her arm. It didn't escape her notice that his grip was firm.

"I'm glad I could help."

The pesky little revelation that Gerry could have done as well, if not better, than she danced around them both as they headed for the door. He hadn't needed her. He had taught her. She had learned and she resented that now, in this moment that should have been her triumph.

"Help! Why Kathleen, you're a veritable good-luck charm. I stopped into the office to find a new client has already come our way. Personal injury. An old, but lovely, lady. I thought perhaps you might handle it." He pushed open the door, following the way Louise had gone.

Kathleen slowed, holding the door open a bit longer than necessary to buy time. But no one came behind them. She had no choice but to walk with Gerry, so she said what was on her mind.

"I don't think I should take on anything else, Gerry. I thought we'd agreed I'd help you out with Louise. We should probably leave it at that."

"Oh, Kathleen, I wouldn't be asking if it were something terribly time-consuming. Sure, don't I know that you could handle this with one hand tied behind your back, and the lady is old. She'd most likely feel more comfortable with another woman when it comes to discussing her injury. Hip, you know." Gerry took Kathleen's arm and leaned a bit more heavily. It was a subtle rearrangement of his weight that whispered need. She looked away, resisting the urge to tsk. Gerry smiled.

"But, of course, you're right. I'm sorry. Silly of me to forget. I just thought it would be all right since Judge Kelley isn't going to hear Louise's case for two months. I thought it might be interesting for you to have something to break up the investigation. No problem. I'll handle it. Though I do have Mr. Craig's incorporations to deal with. That man has more schemes going than a barker at a carnival. And, of course, I have the small problem with Mr. Sargeant's will. The man says he's terminal, but he said that the last time we looked at his will . . ."

"Gerry. It's not a problem. I can do it. Really. But then I'll start looking around. I think it's best." Kathleen's jaw was as tight as a guitar string.

"That's so kind, Kathleen. Thank you. And, of course, our arrangement still stands. Of course." Gerry let go of Kathleen's arm, leaving her behind to wonder if he'd heard her at all. Amazing how his gait had suddenly improved and his voice become almost boisterous the moment she acquiesced. Kathleen smiled ruefully and wondered if she'd ever catch on. She followed Gerry, whose arms were held out to the formidable Louise.

"There you are. You left so quickly. Sure, aren't you proud of our Kathleen?"

"Yeah, she did just what you told her to do." Louise hefted her white-leather saddlebag higher and slipped her thumb through the gold ring that held strap and bag together. Louise didn't even have an inch to give, so Gerry took it from her.

"Ah, but the strategy, that was hers. All hers. She's brilliant, my Kathleen," Gerry grinned, unaware or unwilling to acknowledge the voltage that crackled between the two women, Louise's generator by far the more productive. "What now, Gerry?"

"Well, Louise, my dear, that's for Kathleen to say." Kathleen stood at Gerry's back and he graced her with a loving look.

"Right. But you're still checking everything. Now that the mess has been cleared up, I don't want any more snafus, okay?"

"There haven't been any snafus, Louise," Kathleen said. Louise pegged her with a shimmering, golden gaze. Today the eyes were hazel, the eyelids Inca-like. "I'll report once a week. Unless there's something significant to talk to you about. Then Gerry and I—" Kathleen turned for his corroboration but Gerry wasn't listening. His eyes were locked on a target not too far away, just over Kathleen's shoulder.

Kathleen followed his gaze and let hers rest on the small, unattractive man who walked down the hall of the courthouse as if he owned it. Kathleen was about to ask who he was when she realized Gerry no longer knew she existed. His face was a play of caution and curiosity.

Gerry moved quickly around Kathleen, walking toward his quarry, hailing the man convivially. He hurried, as if he would regret the action if he stopped to think about it. The other man saw him. He stopped. He waited. They came together, subtly wary.

The stranger smiled like a warrior with his foot on the neck of a fallen enemy. But that passed, leaving only a pleasant expression of recognition by the time the two men shook hands. It was a curious meeting to observe.

"Gerry," the man said quietly with a baritone that was exceptionally pleasing. He looked directly at her uncle, yet Kathleen knew he was well aware that she and Louise straggled behind. She was also quite certain the man had assessed them both and reached conclusions that would never be altered.

"Richard." The two men shook hands. The contact didn't seem pleasing to the small man. Gerry pretended not to notice. "I thought you'd given up litigation and left that to those impressive underlings of yours."

"I like to keep my hand in. Sweating over budgets can be so boring. I learned that from the best before he turned me out. I see the master is still following his own advice."

"That was a long time ago, between you and me." Gerry chuckled, and the other man smiled as if to say how silly old differences could be. "Now I've got another young lawyer to worry about." He motioned for Kathleen to come closer. "Kathleen Cotter, my niece. Newly associated with O'Doul & Associates and only moments ago triumphing over All Life Insurance, thank you very much."

"That *is* impressive." The man with the thin, brown hair and the softly colored eyes gave her a moment's attention. Kathleen shook his hand. It was soft, too. She had the distinct impression that those eyes held secrets of immense proportions. But they didn't linger on her. She had no secrets. She obviously was no challenge, and his gaze drifted back to the man who was.

"Kathleen, Richard Jacobsen is the man who has wrapped up all the city business. General partner at Shay, Sylvester & Harrington, don't you know? He'll have to watch us, won't he, Kathleen? I've already talked to Carl about snatching away some of the city problems."

Richard Jacobsen smiled pleasantly. "You'll be stepping on my toes then, Gerry."

"Ah, it would be hard to even make you wince, Richard. We'll settle for the crumbs and be licking them up with style."

Kathleen shifted from one foot to the other, unsure of what was passing between them, only sure that an undercurrent pulled them into some pool where they, and no one else, had treaded water before.

"Yo, Gerry, I gotta go." All three turned toward the sound of Louise Brooker's voice, surprised to find her still hovering on the outskirts of their odd triangle.

"Louise, Louise, my dear girl, I'm so sorry. Come here and meet Richard. Richard, the client on whose behalf Kathleen spoke so passionately. Louise Brooker, the brave woman who is going up against All Life with O'Doul & Associates by her side."

Richard Jacobsen's expression shifted, or so it seemed to Kathleen. It may have been a trick of the light or a genuine look of concern that flitted lightly behind those eyes or it could have been a subtle look of surprise. But who didn't look surprised upon meeting Louise?

"I hope your business with the court is finished now," he said politely.

"Not likely," Louise shot back. She nodded. "Nice to meet-cha." She then left, seemingly satisfied with the day's proceedings. For a moment, Kathleen wondered where Louise was going. For a second, Kathleen wondered if she'd be lonely. Then, she realized that opportunity stood at her elbow and she paid attention to it.

"Louise can be a little abrupt," Kathleen apologized. Richard Jacobsen turned his head toward her, but not until he had apparently satisfied his curiosity about Louise Brooker. He smiled at Kathleen as if to say they alone understood how things could be with difficult clients.

"I trust the problem is as colorful as the lady herself?"

"All the adjectives one could use for Mrs. Brooker, you could use for her problem."

Richard looked back to Gerry. Kathleen was thrown back in deference to the bigger fish in the pond.

"Did I read about it in the papers, Gerry? The name sounds familiar."

"No, no you didn't. An odd sort of thing. Louise's ex-husband committed suicide at the Tysco headquarters. Now she wants the insurance premiums that are being denied because of an exclusion. If the poor man had only waited another day or two, I'm afraid O'Doul would be out of a fee. One of those unusual things that keeps us in business, rest poor Lionel Brooker's soul." Gerry chuckled. It was too small a thing to bore Richard with, and Richard had never had much of a sense of humor anyway. "Kathleen will take care of it. Lovely way she's managed on the strategy. Chip off the old block, Richard. I wouldn't be surprised if her performance were written up in the journals."

"I'll look forward to reading about it." Richard stood up

straighter and bowed toward Kathleen. "Best of luck to you, Ms. Cotter. I wish we had a few creative young people like you around my firm." He put his hand lightly on Gerry's arm. He didn't pat or squeeze; he made only a gesture to familiarity for old time's sake. Kathleen's eyes followed that hand and she noticed how attractive it was. Well-shaped and beautifully manicured, it was uncluttered by rings. When she looked up again, he was still looking at her curiously before finally taking his leave. "It was great seeing you, Gerry."

"Nice to see you, too, Richard." Richard Jacobsen melted away, swallowed up in the crowd milling about the long hall. Gerry watched even after he was gone and spoke into the space Richard had left.

"Richard interned with me, Kathleen. Years ago. Such a bright young man. So focused. So intense. I always thought I taught him everything, but there were some things he did not learn from me." Gerry fell silent. Kathleen looked toward the milling people, but Richard Jacobsen did not reappear, so Gerry reanimated himself and touched her arm. "We soon parted company. He went the way of an ambitious young man. I had my suspicions that he was walking an unusual path."

"It couldn't have been that odd, considering his success."

Gerry looked at her, a wry upturn of the lips transforming him into the man Kathleen remembered.

"I think parts of Richard Jacobsen are like a rubber band. They bend and pull in odd directions. And another part is made of quicksand because of the way he absorbs information, making it disappear as if it never existed, then spitting back his own version. But mostly, he's made of steel. One never knows about Richard, and I've long since been truly curious. We went our separate ways. Perhaps I should have gone with him." Gerry chuckled, then thought again. "Perhaps not. And we must do business with all sorts, mustn't we? Funny thing is, I can't really say what sort Richard is."

Kathleen walked with Gerry. Louise was long gone, and a hush had fallen suddenly over the now deserted halls. Those who had business with the court were either doing it or had been sent away. Richard Jacobsen had simply evaporated. He left behind him a sense that Gerry and Kathleen were now less than they had been, that the triumph before Judge Kelley was minor.

Although she might be on a new ladder with Gerry, Kathleen knew she was still on the bottom rung. Richard Jacobsen was on the top and he wasn't looking down. She'd have to climb some to reach him, but that was where she wanted to go. Maybe she wouldn't go all the way to the top; she wouldn't be that arrogant. But up. She wanted to go up. After this morning's performance, she knew that she could. If she made it to the middle of that ladder, Kathleen knew she wouldn't ask for anything more.

"Shall we stop for breakfast, Kathleen?" Gerry asked as they stepped out of the courthouse. Gerry looked about, squinting into the sun, Richard Jacobsen forgotten. Kathleen had forgotten even Gerry for the moment.

"We have an appointment, Uncle Gerry. We need to start on the Brooker problem right away. The sooner we do, the sooner it will be over."

And I can start climbing.

Marlene Wong was late. They were early so they waited in the coroner's gift shop. Gerry sat on the straight-backed chair in the corner fanning himself with the three-page catalogue. Kathleen, her forehead dotted with perspiration, her hair slicked back behind her ears, held up a fluffy, white beach towel resplendent with a black body-outline. She refolded it, remembering this was Los Angeles. She wouldn't want to give anyone on the beach any ideas.

There was a mug.

A picture frame.

A call.

"Gerry?"

Kathleen turned toward the door that led elsewhere in time to see Gerry smile and greet the woman with a kiss on the cheek.

"Marlene, it's been a long time."

"You've been out of the loop lately," she drawled. "Like the last ten years. What've you been doing?" White coat and clipped words couldn't hide her obvious affection for Gerry O'Doul.

"Haven't I been working, Marlene! Sure, that's why you haven't seen me. How nice you missed me."

"I'll take a working stiff over a regular one any day, Gerry. Come on, I've got what you asked for." She cocked her head, her thick, short, black hair glinting in the fluorescent lights; the pink-beaded chain attached to her glasses swayed as she moved.

"Come, Kathleen," Gerry held out his hand. Marlene gave her a once-over as she joined them. "My niece and new associate. She's lead attorney on this; I'm only here to make myself feel useful."

Marlene Wong sighed at his blarney. "Then I guess you'd both better come. But watch out, we're full up and there's no place for tea."

Gerry held the door. Kathleen looked straight ahead as she followed Marlene Wong down the hall to a glass-enclosed office. There was nothing to see, but the mere idea that somewhere in this vast building was a room full up with dead bodies was enough to make her feel queasy. They entered a small, neat office.

"Here we are. Got the file. Looked it over. Have a seat, Kathleen." Marlene Wong was already sitting down. Kathleen did as she was told, slinging her purse strap over the back of the chair and putting her hands in her lap. Gerry sat after the women were settled. Marlene Wong looked at Kathleen. "What do you want to know?"

Kathleen looked quietly at Gerry, who didn't look back. She was on her own, and he waited patiently for her to state what she wanted.

"I want to prove that Lionel Brooker didn't intend to take his own life. So I guess what I'd like is any medical information that might help prove he was just hoping to get high. Is there any information you have that might help us prove that?"

"That's pretty broad."

Gerry stepped in, much to Kathleen's dismay. If he hadn't wanted her to handle this, then he shouldn't have set her up.

"Is there something in the toxicology reports, Marlene, that might lead you to believe the dosage was such that Mr. Brooker wanted simply to pleasure himself?" Gerry filled in, gently protective, Kathleen imagined, of her feelings. He needn't be. Kathleen was a quick and grateful study, all he needed to do was show her the way.

"That's a tall order. I've seen kids in here who look like they've got everything to live for. Cheerleaders who jump off cliffs 'cause their horse has fleas. How in the heck am I supposed to know what this guy intended? Heroin was in his system; he died of an overdose. He could have misjudged the dosage; but then again, he could have calculated it that way."

"Perhaps, then, you could give us a run-through on the report. Anything that doesn't ring true to your educated ear, we'll listen." Gerry nodded as if encouraging her to take center stage at a recital for which she was ill-prepared.

"Okay." She took a deep breath through her nose, tipped her head back and her glasses down. "It wasn't my case, remember. I didn't do the actual autopsy."

"Not to worry," Gerry murmured.

"Just wanted you to understand. The great man himself did this one." Marlene, practical and political to the last, gave them both a look to make sure they understood. "Guess that in and of itself is pretty bizarre. By the time they got Mr. Brooker in here, it was late—or early, depending on how you look at it. Dr. Greischmidt is usually out of here by five and doesn't come in until nine-thirty—which is his prerogative. He has so many administrative duties to attend to, it must be exhausting." Marlene ran her finger down the report in the folder.

"So, I'd say *that* was pretty out of the ordinary. Not extraordinary, you understand, but somebody would have had to have made a special request. He wouldn't have come in without it."

"What was so special about Mr. Brooker? I mean, why would Dr. Greischmidt take notice, especially at that time of the morning? He had to have been called from home. Could we ask him about that?" Kathleen asked.

Marlene gave Gerry a Cheshire grin that, until now, had been carefully guarded, but she talked to Kathleen.

"Sure, and we'll invite him to tea." Marlene and Gerry laughed. "Dr. Greischmidt isn't exactly a fan of mine or your uncle's. About fifteen years back, Gerry pushed hard during a trial and embarrassed him a lot. A young girl had allegedly been killed by her brother three hours after dinner. Dr. Greischmidt had thrown away the stomach contents which were pivotal to the prosecution. Gerry embarrassed the good doctor by making a big deal about that."

"Did you manage to get the brother acquitted?" Kathleen asked.

"He did." Marlene answered for him.

"What she's not telling you, Kathleen, is that the boy was guilty. That one made me think twice, I'll tell you," Gerry mused. "Ah, the days of maneuvering like that, eh, Marlene? Kept me young."

"Kept us all young. Guess that's why Greischmidt lets us underlings do everything now. He sticks to the paperwork. So, back to the work at hand. Let's see how good he was on the paper this time." Marlene was still smiling as she read. "Stomach contents were saved. Brooker hadn't eaten in a while. Pretty empty except for some grains. No alcohol. Heroin in the system along with an overabundance of vitamin C and E. Our man was a vitamin-taker. That's kind of weird if he's a drug-abuser."

"Would you say it was a massive overdose or miscalculation?" Kathleen asked.

Marlene raised a shoulder and cocked her head toward it nonchalantly. "I'd venture to say just about anything would be considered a massive overdose. This guy had to play it safe." Marlene looked over the top of her glasses. "Brooker had an enlarged heart. Not a terrible problem on its own, unless you're doing the kind of drugs he was doing. Then it would have definitely disturbed the balance in his body. He wouldn't have been able to take the same dose as someone who started with a strong and healthy heart. Heroin shoots straight to the brain; signals shoot back down to the heart, and—boom!"

"Then he might have committed suicide." Gerry's comment was matter-of-fact. It was too early in the game to throw in the towel, but Kathleen didn't want to consider it. She had not only convinced Judge Kelley of the rightness of her stand, she'd convinced herself.

"Or it could have meant he wasn't particularly smart," Kathleen offered. "I mean, is there some kind of manual that tells people how much they're supposed to use? I wouldn't know how much to use."

"I think, if you know where to buy it, you know how to use it." She went on to the next point of interest. "We also don't know what grade of heroin he was using. It could have been contaminated. Can't tell from this what he knew and what he didn't, but I'm willing to bet he hadn't been shooting long."

"Why?"

Marlene Wong opened the file and laid it flat on the desk. It was apparent she didn't want them to focus on the typed form on the left but on the autopsy photos so neatly tacked to the right side of the manila folder.

Kathleen looked at the corpse of Lionel Brooker for the first time. Fascinated and curious, Kathleen was astounded to find herself neither revolted nor sympathetic. Were these the emotions of a lawyer? But she was a woman with a history of compassion: empathy for her father's disillusionment, for her mother's disappointment, for her fiancé's limitations. Funny, she'd thought she'd left only Banning behind; now she realized she'd left part of herself there. She wondered if she should try to find it again.

"I'm sorry, Dr. Wong," Kathleen said quietly, her personal epiphany put away for her to consider later and alone—if ever. "I don't know what I'm looking for in these pictures."

Old eyes still sharp, Gerry had flipped from the full-body photos to close-ups of Lionel Brooker's head, torso, legs, and—finally—arms. He was the one who answered.

"Here, Kathleen. Look here." A long, thin finger indicated the midpoint of Lionel Brooker's arm. She followed the instruction and shook her head again. "Clear, my girl. His skin is unblemished. There are no tracks, Kathleen, no bruises. Indeed,

Mr. Brooker may not have known what he was doing. Lionel Brooker was not a junkie. If he had a drug of choice, it wasn't injected heroin.''

"Still sharp, Gerry. So, it could have been his first try." Marlene Wong added her two cents. "There are a few other things that bother me." She flipped back to the picture that showed the left quadrant of Lionel's unclothed body. "There is no note of a fresh needle-mark, but . . . see here? It looks like . . . something . . . on the neck." She made a little circular motion to draw attention to it. "This picture isn't great because the good doctor didn't turn the head fully, procedure I would call sloppy if it were anyone but Dr. G. But the really strange thing is, if you look with a glass, there seems to be a slight tear in the skin. There's also a contusion on the back of his right thigh and one on the back of his right arm near his elbow.

"Like he'd fallen," Kathleen muttered.

"No," Marlene said thoughtfully.

"Then what?"

"Like he'd struggled."

Chapter Six

Kathleen had pirated Gerry's slightly larger office to depose Sarah Brooker, but it was still uncomfortably crowded. The stenographer had settled in an upright chair in the corner, her machine at the ready on a portable stand. Tony Maglio was sitting in one of the bucket chairs purloined from the reception area. Kathleen was behind Gerry's desk and Sarah Brooker was across from her. There were approximately ten-square-feet of floor space that wasn't being tapped upon by a set of feet. And, in the free space, Becky flitted about refilling coffee cups or water glasses. She looked pale and terrified. The audience was too big, the activity more than she'd seen in all her years at O'Doul & Associates, and she wanted everything to be right. The air-conditioning was on full-force. Perhaps that was what kept everyone from getting hot under the collar.

"Sarah—" Kathleen crossed out number sixty-three on her list of questions. "—did your husband spend much time away from home?"

Sarah slid her eyes toward Tony. Kathleen followed suit. Tony, unfortunately, wasn't quite on top of things. His eyes were crossing. The expression *pulling teeth* took on a whole new meaning as Sarah looked down again and shook her head.

"Mr. Maglio?" Kathleen looked for a little help with a raised brow. She had long since overcome her awe of him. He cleared his throat and pushed back his coat, letting his hand rest on his hip.

"You'll have to speak for the record, Sarah." Tony fell short of giving her a nudge on the shoulder. He'd said the same thing sixty-three times.

This, Kathleen decided, must be legal hell. Sarah, sitting with her hands in her lap, her gray sweater hanging over her thin shoulders, her dishwater-blond hair falling from a middle part to hide her face ... the court reporter's fingers at the perpetual ready, only to be stretched for seconds by one-word answers ... Tony playing imaginary cat's cradle with his fingers, and ...

"No," Sarah finally said, her voice as flat as a pancake.

"I'm sorry, I've forgotten the question." Kathleen looked toward the reporter.

"Did Lionel stay away from the home for long periods of time?"

The woman's mouth hadn't moved. Kathleen glared at Louise. She'd forgotten Louise, who had been progressively banished farther from the table where counsel and client sat. The reporter looked at Louise just to make sure she wasn't going to say anything else. When it was clear that there wouldn't be a duet, she spoke.

"Did Lionel stay away ..."

Kathleen nodded politely. The woman stopped. Kathleen and everyone else in the room looked at Sarah, who looked back with deer-eyes—the kind that were wide and scared and caught in the headlights Kathleen was shining on her.

"Sarah?" Kathleen prodded.

"No. He was always home." This time her voice was almost defiant.

Louise snorted. She was ignored by everyone—except Sarah Brooker. Slowly, Sarah turned to look at Louise. The picture was stunning. Louise in her black-satin jumpsuit—breasts pushing out the top; high-heeled, sandaled feet pushing out the bottom—sat confidently at her end of the spectrum. Her nails were white. Louis Armstrong blew into a gold trumpet. Louise's own lips were outlined in pewter and colored in with plum. Tammy Faye didn't have a thing on her.

On the other end of the spectrum sat Sarah. The sweater she'd worn in court still hung over her shoulders despite the heat outside. Today it covered a denim dress, neatly pressed, too long, too big to bring to mind any prurient interest. Yet, on her unpainted face there was an expression of such courage she seemed as formidable as her counterpart.

"Lionel was home every night because that's where he wanted to be. That's where he felt safe." The reporter typed like crazy, happy to have something to do. Sarah looked back at Kathleen, her piece said.

"Was there something that made Lionel feel unsafe?"

The odd choice of words alerted Kathleen. The picture Sarah painted of her life with Lionel was crucial to Kathleen's argument and Sarah knew it. But whatever else was in Sarah's head was now tucked firmly away.

"Nothing. There's nothing. He just liked the feeling of being at home." She hesitated. "Lionel liked being away from everything loud—and vulgar."

They all thought about that for a moment. Louise inspected the tip of her nail. The guise of indifference was well-assumed, and, because it was Louise, believable.

"Did Mr. Brooker ever verbally or physically abuse you, Sarah?" Sixty-four was checked off.

Sarah rose to the occasion, defending her dead husband. "No. Not Lionel. Whoever said that is a liar. Every word out of Lionel's mouth was truthful and loving toward me."

"No one has accused him of anything, but everybody thinks there was something wrong at the end of Mr. Brooker's life."

Kathleen put her hand to her head, winding her fingers through her hair. She looked at Sarah Brooker and opened her mind. The belief that Sarah wanted to talk was a far cry from knowing how to tap into that desire. Obviously her desire was fleeting.

"I want to go home."

Sarah pleaded with her attorney. She refolded her hands.

Tony Maglio looked through her. Finally, she turned the full force of her frightened and anxious attention on Kathleen.

"I want to go home." This time she appealed to Kathleen. "I've told you everything there is to tell. Lionel was a good man. We were very happy. We loved each other. I know that you people can make things seem different. I know you're smart with words. If I could, I'd give you all the money just so you would go away and let Lionel rest. But I can't. It's not up to me." She hung her head and the curtain of hair fell again. She spoke from behind it.

"He never did drugs. He loved the world. He was a spiritual man and we were so happy together. Now he's dead and nobody is interested in how that happened. You don't care about Lionel, so just take what you want. You can ask me things a hundred different ways, but I can't tell you that Lionel was ugly or mean or selfish. He wasn't. *He wasn't.*" She raised her head, memories of Lionel giving her courage.

"I know he didn't kill himself. I know that for sure because . . ." Sarah's voice rang out like an evangelist. Suddenly realizing how curious they'd become, she backtracked. "I know that because I know him. I don't know how the drugs got in him, but you'll never convince me that he was so sad he didn't want to live. He finally had a good life." She slumped back in her chair. "Now it's gone and you are all picking at his corpse. That was my husband. I loved him. He loved me. There's nothing more. So, please, can I go home now? I want to leave."

The silence was a canvas with Sarah's last words painted on it in big letters for all to see. Tony Maglio craned his neck so he wouldn't have to look at Sarah. Kathleen looked at her notes. Never in her whole life had she felt so guilty. She had scored one today. A big one and she felt terrible because Sarah Brooker wasn't her opponent. Sarah was only a sad, little widow, afraid of her own shadow.

"Oh, Lord," Louise finally muttered from her exile. "Lionel wasn't a saint." The spell was broken. The court reporter typed, and Becky slipped into the room, staying only long enough to whisper in Kathleen's ear.

Though she listened, Kathleen watched Sarah Brooker

closely. The body language screamed martyr, but there was something else inside her. When she glanced over her shoulder toward Louise, Sarah Brooker began to shake and Kathleen understood. That something else inside Sarah was honest-to-goodness fear. The questions were *how deep did it go?* and *how real was it?* Sarah's eyes snapped back to her lap, and Kathleen turned a curious eye on Louise. There was, of course, one other question. Who was causing such fear?

"Mrs. Brooker," Kathleen said gently, jotting a note to herself regarding Becky's information before looking at Sarah. "Can you think of anything in Lionel's life, or yours, that would cause him to become despondent or to feel as if he would be doing anyone a favor if he took his own life? If there is one small thing, it would help so much to wrap this up."

Sarah shook her head. When she looked at Kathleen there was no fear, just an expression of extreme weariness. "No," she answered softly. There would be nothing else from Sarah Brooker, but Kathleen had to try one more tactic, a question she asked the women in Banning who came to her, bruised and battered, to find out what they could do to protect themselves from an *unnamed person* who wanted to hurt them—an unnamed person who usually turned out to be their husband. In this case, that wasn't a possibility. There was, however, another person whom Sarah Brooker might fear.

"Sarah, is there anyone you're afraid of?"

Sarah Brooker bolted upright, her narrow, fragile shoulders shaking under the heavy sweater. If it were possible, her face paled even more, the freckles across the bridge of her nose taking on a three-dimensional look. Her eyes lowered; they slid left toward Louise. Kathleen watched closely for any sign of accusation. Those eyes slid right toward Tony Maglio and, finally, they looked fearfully at Kathleen herself.

"I just want to be left alone."

Kathleen stood up. The court reporter packed up her things, left a card on the desk, and went away. The transcripts would be in Kathleen's hands the next day. It was hardly necessary. Kathleen would remember everything: the words the nuances, the inflections. Sarah hurried out the door and Becky said goodbye to everyone in turn. Tony Maglio stuck out the hand that didn't hold his briefcase.

"It's been a pleasure," he said.

Kathleen shook his hand.

"It's been interesting."

"Yeah." He hoisted the case and Kathleen wondered what could make it so heavy. "It was pretty painless."

"For you, maybe," Kathleen reminded him. It took him a minute to realize he was supposed to murmur an empathetic statement on Sarah's behalf. He tried, but it didn't come easily.

"Well." He had a proposition to discuss. "Look, Kathleen,this estate isn't worth the paper it's printed on. I'm only here as a favor to Brooker's brother, you know. He liked the wife. He didn't know her well, but he has a lot of respect for the way she felt about his brother." He glanced over his shoulder. They were alone. He laid it out. "Anyway, you've got a better shot at getting the bucks out of All Life. Everything in the estate is tied up with Sarah anyway. She was Lionel's beneficiary on the company-paid policies—retirement, house, everything. She thinks she can just give it away and that will be that, but I'm here to tell you it would be a mess." Now he put the briefcase in front of him and held it with both hands. He lowered his head close to Kathleen's. She leaned into him to hear what he had.

"There was some stock in Lionel's name and a separate savings account Sarah said he had opened to save for his farm. The guy worked twenty years and he left less than thirty in personal assets. Our fees are going to be substantial because of this suit. It comes out of the estate before there's a penny on the settlement. We've cooperated *pro bono* on this depo. What do you say you talk to your client? I'll expedite the probate. Sarah will have some bucks in the bank and still have her house. You put your efforts into All Life. That's where the money is." He glanced over his shoulder at Louise, knowing her ears were as big as her greed. "That's what your client wants anyway. It's pretty evident. Cut and dry. You're good enough to get All Life. Why not do it?"

"I'll think about it. I promise."

She took his arm and moved him out of the office, standing taller under the mantle of his compliment. If anything else was going to be said, she wanted it said out of earshot of Louise Brooker. She wrapped things up with him; but before she could go back to Louise, Becky stopped her.

"This came by messenger. One for you and one for Gerry."

Kathleen took the cream-colored envelope, noted there was no return address, and opened the seal. She was quiet while she read it once, twice, and then again.

"You okay?" Becky asked. "Bad news? I hope not. I have some soda. Want some?"

"No." Kathleen shook her head and tried not to grin when she looked up. She didn't do a very good job. "No, it's not bad news. In fact, it's very good news. Did Gerry get the same thing?"

"Yep."

"Then pencil me in on his calendar. We have a date at Shay, Sylvester & Harrington on the thirty-first. We've been invited to a fund-raiser for Carl Walsh. I guess Gerry's networking is paying off."

"Wow. That's cool. Can you imagine? A party at the biggest law firm in the city. You're sure going to meet some neat people."

"Yes," Kathleen muttered, "I think you're right."

She put the invitation back in the envelope and headed toward Gerry's office. She wouldn't get her hopes up. She wouldn't make any plans. She wouldn't even allow herself to imagine that Richard Jacobsen even remembered what she looked like. She wouldn't do anything until the day was over. Then she'd dream. Boy, would she dream. But now, Louise was waiting and she'd give a dollar to pop any balloon of good cheer Kathleen sent up. Composed, Kathleen walked back into Gerry's office, pocketing the invitation.

"So, do we have enough?" Louise asked.

Kathleen started cleaning up for lack of anything better to do that would keep her from looking at Louise. "We've got a lot."

"A lot isn't a win." Louise stood up and adjusted the top

of her outfit. Her breasts moved this way and that, only to fall into place the minute their owner stopped her fussing. Kathleen put all the coffee cups to one side, no longer impressed by Louise's antics. Louise wasn't the kind of client she wanted to represent. Shay, Sylvester & Harrington had those clients. Louise wasn't the kind of person she wanted to know. Richard Jacobsen was.

"There aren't any promises, Louise." Kathleen stopped. She could only rearrange the cups so often. She gave Louise the courtesy of her attention, limited though it was.

"I'm not asking for a promise. I just want to know if the judge will understand this. I mean it is kind of an iffy thing, this intention-stuff. It makes me nervous."

"This *intention stuff* is what's going to get you what you want, Louise. If I were you, I wouldn't open my mouth in the courtroom, try to explain anything, or add to it. I'm doing everything that needs to be done, and Gerry knows everything that's happening. I've talked to a psychologist and Lionel's doctor; we've deposed Sarah, and I've been to the coroner. I've got the police reports to go over. I'm going to Tysco to check out things there. There are still a few things to look into, the paperwork to do, and the appearance. Now you know everything I know. You know that I'm doing everything I can, and I hope that's good enough for you."

Kathleen looked straight into Louise's eyes. Today the contact lenses made them a bright green, the color of money, the color of jealousy. Kathleen looked deep, trying to sense something in the other woman that would make her fearful, but there was nothing. Louise might make her feel small and unworthy and almost stupid, but all that had changed with a cream-colored invitation from a man who worked only with the rich, the famous, and the powerful. The invitation had brought a little bit of that to Kathleen. So now, looking at Louise, Kathleen only wanted to know if there was an evil in Louise Brooker that Sarah understood but Kathleen couldn't fathom.

Louise looked back, thinking thoughts of her own. Instinctively, Kathleen knew those thoughts were about her. It was the first time the two women had faced one another without confrontation. A truce was too much to ask, but Kathleen would count herself lucky when Louise left with only a jab at the way she dressed instead of the way she comported herself as an attorney. But when Louise spoke, lucky wasn't how Kathleen felt. Thunderstruck was a more apt adjective.

"Okay. Thanks." Louise picked up her purse, a curious thing that couldn't decide whether it was a suitcase or a knitting bag.

In the silence that followed, Louise Brooker turned her back on Kathleen Cotter and quietly closed the door, remaining inside the office. The Louise who now regarded her was tired or worried—Kathleen wasn't sure which—but subdued, nonetheless.

"I know you don't care much for me. I know you think this mess is as low as the lowlifes that caused it. I can understand that. I'm not stupid, you know. I've got a handle on myself. I'm not sure you have one on yourself, but everybody has a little baggage. If you want to fool yourself that there's more than this out there, fine. But I'm straight, Kathleen. I'm not out to screw anyone, least of all that little dishwater-blonde. What I feel about her is pretty personal and wrapped up in a whole lot of stuff. I don't have time to worry about it. If I took the time, I'd never do anything else. But the insurance-thing, that's different. It's got a beginning and it's going to have an end."

"Louise, I'm your lawyer. I don't need to know any of this. I don't make judgments about my clients." Uncomfortable with confession, she let her eyes drift away.

"Yes, you do." Louise smiled sadly, a wiser woman than Kathleen. During the hours of the deposition, her lipstick had worn off and, for the first time since Kathleen had met her, Louise Brooker seemed less than a caricature. "Never kid a kidder, Kathleen. I didn't want Lionel to die. I sure as heck didn't want him to go the way he did. But it's over and done and now there are possibilities for me, you understand? Lionel's life is over, mine isn't. It's as simple as that. I mean, do you think we went through all that hassle getting an insurance policy because we thought Lionel was going to live forever? He was going to kick off sometime. So, I don't know why you're looking down on me for wanting what everybody planned on.''

"I'm not looking down on you . . .''

Louise stood tall, or so it seemed to Kathleen. Her eyes took on that steely look again. Kathleen Cotter might as well have stepped on her, so insulting was that lie.

"Yeah, whatever, Kathleen. Just do what you have to do, and then we'll call it quits, okay?'' And she was out the door for good.

"Yes,'' Kathleen muttered as the door slammed. "Then I'm gone. I'm gone.''

Minutes later, Kathleen was out of the office, too, catching up with Louise a half a block away.

"Louise.'' Kathleen slowed her pace as she approached the other woman. Wary still, she spoke from ten paces then closed the distance slowly. "I'm sorry about the way we've been. I'm not usually rude. If I have been to you, I'm sorry. You just kind of got all caught up in my expectations when I was way down.''

"Funny, that's exactly how I feel about you.''

"Fair enough.'' Kathleen looked toward the street. It was quiet. A car passed them. She looked past Louise toward Wilshire Boulevard. Even two, long blocks away, she could see that the street was packed with cars. Most were turning north, not south. That's where success was and yet Louise and Kathleen stood here, on South Beverly, below Olympic, far beneath the people who traveled Wilshire. None of it mattered right now. All that mattered now was the answer to one mystery. "If you didn't love Lionel anymore, why are you so hard on Sarah Brooker?''

Louise smirked and shook her head, amused to find that Kathleen was so naive.

"It's this way,'' she said, holding out her hands to help in the explanation. Louise Armstrong tooted away on the tips of her nails. "If Lionel loved Sarah—a mousy, weak kind of woman who hides from the world—and if he loved me, then it must mean she and I have something in common. I don't

want to look at her tortured little face and think that Lionel
saw the same thing when he looked at me. I don't want to
think I was ever that weak. I have my pride.''

Louise's head was up, her eyes ablaze. The memory of a
man who disappointed her in life, and disappointed her by
marrying someone who was everything she wasn't, made her
angry. Lionel had negated her. That was tough to take.

"I don't think Sarah Brooker is weak at all," Kathleen
countered cautiously. "I think she's scared. Do you know what
she might be scared of?"

"Life," she snorted. Vintage Louise was back.

"Is there someone she should be scared of?"

Louise put on her sunglasses and lingered a moment before
turning her back on Kathleen without giving an answer. She
walked away. Kathleen didn't follow.

Instead, she raised her face to the late-afternoon sun. She
never would have done that in the desert, but here a privileged
breeze cut the heat down to warmth.

When she opened her eyes again, Louise was two blocks
down, one hip thrust out, her hands on both as she stared at
something in a window. Kathleen wondered if Louise was
planning how to spend the fortune when, and if, it was won.
Perhaps she was looking at something she knew she would
never have because she had no faith in Kathleen's ability.
Perhaps Louise could buy whatever had caught her fancy. Who
knew what Louise Brooker was really about or what she already
had? There was money to pay O'Doul & Associates, to have
those nail masterpieces painted, to buy so many cheap clothes
that Kathleen hadn't seen the same outfit twice. Perhaps it was
all smoke and mirrors. Perhaps Louise was exactly what she
was, an unfathomable mystery. But solving *that* puzzle would
bring Kathleen nothing. Doing her job and finding out what,
if anything, Lionel Brooker intended before that needle went
through his skin was something else. Much as she hated to
admit it, Kathleen Cotter was hooked on the challenge Louise
had brought to her. One battle had resulted in an uneasy peace
between the two women as they faced the final strife. It was
time Kathleen put together her arsenal and her armor.

Sighing, she turned away from Louise, feeling lonely. She seemed to be the only one who cared what really had happened to Lionel Brooker. Judge Kelley only wanted enough to allow him to legally override All Life. Louise wanted the same. Sarah wanted to be left alone; she already knew as much as she wanted to know about Lionel. If Kathleen found evidence that Lionel had wanted to take his life, Sarah would never believe it. Gerry wanted Kathleen to succeed. So, there she was, alone with the enigma of Lionel Brooker, a clear calendar for midafternoon, and a feeling that today was the day she should spend anywhere but inside the office with only Becky for company . . . Becky, who would be crushed to know that Kathleen dreamed that the invitation from Richard Jacobsen might be her ticket to the other side of Wilshire.

Hurrying back to the office, Kathleen grabbed her purse and briefcase and was back out the door with a warning for Becky to take any messages—as if there would be a flood of them. Feeling free and in control and dedicated to her mission, Kathleen got into her car, turned the radio loud and the air-conditioning on high. She drove and pretended that she hadn't heard some of the words Louise had used that drew parallels between them. She even allowed herself to think that some good might come out of this. If she beat All Life and Tony Maglio, if she convinced Judge Kelley that her suit had merit, there would be talk. And the talk would be of an attorney who had come out of nowhere and made her mark. Richard Jacobsen might take notice. And, if she were so lucky as to actually have the man's ear for a moment, she would toot her own horn. Mom would turn over in her grave; but then again, Mom had lived and died in Banning. Now, *that* was something to consider.

Forty minutes later, chilled from the air-conditioning, her ears ringing with the decibel-level of the car radio, plans she wasn't sure she could carry out still pinging around in her head, Kathleen Cotter pulled into the parking lot of the sprawling Tysco complex and knew instantly this was a place where she could hide from the little demons and big hopes that chased her.

The compound was as big as a city.

To the left, long, low buildings sprawled over acres of land. Hangars yawned on the south end and, beyond that, scrub brush and, finally, barbwire-topped fences. Helicopters stood at the ready; jeeplike vehicles spotted the tarmacs. A private jet sat idle, painted white with the Tysco logo on the tail. A tall, chain-link fence surrounded a portion of that portion of the complex.

Kathleen's eyes slid right, then left again and finally noted the tunnel-like building to the north which connected the one-story buildings to the many-windowed high-rise. A grass strip ran the length of the windowless tunnel, merging with a flower bed that snaked S-like out from the last third of the low building. In front of the high-rise, the landscape became a full-blown celebration of horticultural ecstasy. Nestled in this floral jubilation was a sculpture of the world gone awry. Huge bars of brass and steel converged in an oddly shaped sphere. The artist had left mammoth gaps through which black metallic arrows were thrust. The design was so deftly done that a visitor with less interest in the place would have subliminally blocked out the dreary south end and focused only on the northern structure.

Kathleen crossed her arms over the steering wheel and lay against it, focusing on the high-rise where Lionel Brooker had come every day of his working life. Sarah had said it was a long drive from his home in the canyon. Kathleen couldn't fathom why he'd made it. Certainly there was no glamor in being one of a hundred auditors who labored anonymously in a place like this. Then she thought of Banning, Dorty & Breyer and her caseload. She had had a reason for being there; Lionel could have had a thousand reasons for toiling like an ant in a hill, not the least of which was safety. No one ever asked you to prove how worthy you were in a huge place like Tysco or a schlock office like Dorty. You simply had to be and do. At least here Lionel's salary had been good and the benefits solid. There was job security, and that was a good thing. There was predictability. That could be a good thing.

"Good things, Lionel," Kathleen said to whatever part of

his spirit had been left here. "You don't leave good things. You leave bad things, a world where people don't care. But Sarah cared. Your brother cared."

Lionel left Louise because she wasn't a good thing. Lionel stayed with Sarah because she was. Lionel saved for a farm. That was a good thing. Lionel worked and died at Tysco. Tysco seemed a good thing, but then again this might be where the good things had changed. God, she hoped not.

Reaching for her purse, Kathleen refreshed her memory. Lionel had been found in the bathroom on the second-floor south wing just where the tunnel intersected with the high-rise. There would be nothing to see in the bathroom. It would have been scoured clean the moment the investigating cops gave the word. But there would be a lot to see on the sixth floor where he'd worked. There would be people to talk to. That's where she would go.

She signed in at the huge desk and, sporting the plastic-encased badge that identified her as visitor, followed directions to the elevators. She stood posture-perfect, as always. She waited, as always, patiently. But when the doors opened, Kathleen's mouth fell open and she ducked right to avoid the stampede from all six elevators.

Men and women, short and tall, well dressed or not, spilled out at her. They pushed through the crowds silently, cursed under their breath, or talked frantically as they headed for the front door and freedom. One-by-one, the doors closed and the elevators zipped up their shafts to collect those desperate and left behind. Kathleen managed to slip behind door number three. It wouldn't have waited for God, and she breathed a sigh of relief when she made it. On the sixth floor, twenty people hovered, their faces a collective show of disappointment that they would have to wait one second longer to allow Kathleen out before they smashed inside.

Apologizing, she crab-stepped through the crowd as she went. The other elevators called and the twenty people disappeared, leaving Kathleen alone to ponder her own circumstance.

Perhaps O'Doul & Associates was not the most glamorous place on the face of the earth, but Tysco was akin to being buried alive, judging by the way people fled at the end of the day. Perhaps Lionel had simply snapped, unable to face another day with hundreds and thousands of people who arrived, worked, and ran.

"Oh, I hope you didn't, Lionel," Kathleen muttered even as she thanked her lucky stars that she'd never ended up in a place like this. Dorty, at least, had always been surprising. She moved on.

Like the lobby, the office floors were well-appointed though uninspired. The carpet was new, short, and easy to care for, wheat-colored. A small, wooden plaque on the wall pointed the way to auditing. Kathleen followed the directions. It was one of her specialties.

She went left and followed the next arrow right until she reached the end of the hall and her destination. While the doors on either side of her opened to single offices of no particular distinction, the double glass doors ahead of her led to a huge room filled with gray desks. Kathleen had the almost uncontrollable urge to press her nose against the glass. Instead, she stood quietly and looked.

Kathleen prided herself on her ability to sense the state of things. Her mother's house had been filled with disappointment. Even after her death, after the cleaning crew had taken everything away and just before the house was sold, Kathleen could tell that no matter who bought it, the house would always be filled with disappointment. Her home had been filled with loneliness. Gerry's offices were filled with hope. Though her first impression had been one of failure, she had come to realize it was only hope that had collected dust. And here, standing where Lionel Brooker had tread, Kathleen didn't sense discouragement. No black fingers of discontent reached out to give her a chill, no Oliver Twist cowered in a corner asking for more. This was just a place to work.

A bank of average-size windows and strips of fluorescent lighting ran the length of the cavernous room. There were framed prints on the wall that, from her vantage point, offered a corporate attitude . . . perhaps renderings of goods manufactured elsewhere in the sprawling complex. There was one tall plant in the corner, but no padded walls divided up the big room. There was a water fountain with a bulletin board over it. Kathleen wondered where the coffeepot was. She imagined there was a grindstone about that these people kept their noses to, yet Kathleen didn't find it terribly unpleasant. She pushed through the glass doors. If possible, the quiet behind the doors was even more profound than the silence of the recently deserted halls. She pulled her purse closer.

"Can I help you?"

Kathleen jumped. A woman materialized from a small room cut out of the beige wall. Kathleen glimpsed a Xerox machine, noted the sheaf of papers in the woman's hand, the impatient expression on her face, and the purse slung over her shoulder. It didn't take a rocket scientist to figure out that she was trying to catch up with the rest of the pack.

"I'm looking for the supervisor."

The woman jerked her head toward the back. "He usually doesn't leave until six. But there's always the exception. I saw him in the hall about fifteen minutes ago. He didn't look like he was leaving for the day, but you never know."

"Thanks."

Kathleen nodded. The woman went around her.

"No problem."

She put the papers on the desk nearest the door, pulled open the bottom drawer, retrieved something that fit in the palm of her hand, and went on her way without a backward glance. Kathleen went the opposite way.

Up close, the situation was no better. The desks were laid out five to a row, ten rows. It was a long room and the boss had an actual office in the back, though *office* might have been a generous description. Actually, all the poor guy got was an extra glass wall that cut him off from the unwashed masses. Kathleen wondered how long he had had to work for the privilege. The office was empty and, since anyone who came in could see that she was not stealing anything, Kathleen was bold. She went in.

Far from finding anything to steal, she was hard put to find anything to look at. The desk was neatly stacked with ledger sheets and memos. A hand calculator pulsed green with a number in the six figures in front of the decimal and three after. It had been left precisely in the middle of the desk, offset by a lamp, a standard-issue pen, and three perfectly sharpened pencils. There were no pictures, no children's drawings, no sport paraphernalia, no joke-gifts given to the beloved boss last Christmas. The office gave Kathleen the creeps. She imagined a robot-person coolly eyeing those he supervised from his silent, lonely, glass-enclosed office.

Kathleen's senses were on overload. The quiet of this deserted place made her uncomfortable; the starkness of the office seemed ominous. Deciding another time, a more active time, might be more conducive to a conversation with the person who inhabited this place, Kathleen turned on her heel. She clutched her purse tighter. She'd make an appointment. She'd send a letter. She was about to reach for the door when she saw him.

It was a Kodak moment. Music should have swelled. Her heart should have stopped instead of stuttered. The man standing in the huge room, halfway between the big glass double doors that led to the hall and the single glass door behind which Kathleen waited, looked neither surprised nor curious. He was gorgeous.

He was tall; his hair dark, straight, and thick enough that Kathleen hardly noticed it receded slightly at his brow. His face was narrow, his features refined. But there was an edge to his good looks: Thick dark lashes rimmed deceptively serene eyes; the authoritative set to his lips kept them from being full; his nose was a bit too hewn to be aristocratic.

There was no pocket-protector; no wing-tip shoes; no short-sleeved, easy-wash, no-wrinkle dress shirt tucked into sans-a-belt polyester pants. His tall body wasn't languid, but held at the casual ready. Lean, it was also defined. The long-sleeved shirt was rolled up past the wrist, open at the neck, and tucked into jeans that skimmed a pair of Dockers. He was a billboard come to life.

Kathleen, speechless and immobile, could only watch as he walked slowly, but surely, toward her. He paused, hand on the knob, then opened the door without a smile of welcome or a grimace of displeasure. He walked past to the desk and said, "Are you looking for me?"

"Are you the supervisor?" Her voice squeaked. He looked at her. She could swear the very tips of his lips moved up. Almost a smile.

"Am I sitting here?" She was wrong about the smile.

"Are you always rude?" She tried to set herself apart. Perhaps if she felt superior, she might be able to make it through the next few minutes without sounding like a love-struck schoolgirl. She had never been so excited by her own audacity. He didn't quite soften, but he did her the favor of sitting back in his chair and giving her his full attention.

"No, actually, I'm rather nice. And I don't think either of us meant to be rude. I just have a lot to do, and I'm assuming since you made it this far you knew whom you were coming to see." He crossed his legs, laced his hands behind his head. "What division are you from? Who's complaining?"

"No one that I know of. I was hoping you could tell me."

Kathleen looked around, as much to identify a chair as to cool her heels. A man like this knew exactly what effect he had on women like her, and Kathleen didn't fool herself that he couldn't read her like a book. Confidence radiated from him while Kathleen's was running for the door.

She breathed deeply through her nose, dug in her purse, managed to come up with a business card and a half a stick of gum. She handed him the card, noticed the gum, took the card back, and extricated her fingers from the offending mess. Redfaced, she handed him back the card.

He hadn't cracked a smile.

Thank God she didn't work for him.

"My name's Kathleen Cotter. I'm from the firm of O'Doul & Associates." He read faster than she could talk and put the card aside before she'd finished. She sat down without an invitation, knees together, her thoughts on his eyes and ways to fill the expectant silence. Uncomfortable, Kathleen realized the man was still looking her in the eye as he had since the moment he'd seen her. As if he read her mind, taking pity on the poor girl he had to know wasn't as sophisticated as she looked, the supervisor glanced once more at her card. Before she could breathe, he was looking her in the eye again.

"Michael Crawford. What can I do for you?"

"I'd like to ask you some questions about one of your employees." Kathleen cleared her throat. She sounded better. Not great, just better.

"Should I have a representative from our legal department here?" he asked. She was just another part of his day. She resisted the urge to tug at her skirt.

"I don't think you need to, but you're welcome to call someone if it will make you feel more comfortable. I don't mind waiting." Kathleen mentally whacked herself. She sounded as if she were asking if he wanted a pillow for his feet. She cleared her throat and added an addendum. "But it really isn't necessary, I assure you. From a legal standpoint, that is. But if you start feeling uncomfortable—"

"Okay." He picked up a pen and ran it through his fingers. Long fingers with a streak of red across the knuckles. An injury he couldn't have gotten pushing papers. "Shoot."

She licked her lips, which were dry—from the recycled air, more than likely.

"Yes. Fine. Sorry." She laughed once. She smiled. So did he, thank goodness. "Okay, I appreciate you giving me some time. I won't take up too much of it. I represent a woman named Louise Brooker. Her husband Lionel worked here and we are in litigation with the insurance company regarding Mr. Brooker's policy. I'd like to ask you a few questions and determine if, perhaps, a deposition might be in order or if, perhaps, an affidavit might provide me with the information I need."

Or if, perhaps, you have a clue as to what I'm talking about.

Kathleen paused for breath. That really wasn't bad. Off the cuff, just enough legalese and him looking at her all the while. He didn't say a word. What else could she say?

"We don't believe that Mr. Brooker intended to take his own life," she explained. Nothing. "I'd like to get some comments from you regarding his state of mind at work. I won't subpoena you unless it is absolutely necessary." He lowered his arms, no longer cradling his head, and tossed the pen on the desk. His scrutiny made her uneasy. "Even then, it's likely you won't have to appear in court. I'll make this as painless as possible for you."

"That's very kind of you."

"Not at all," Kathleen said quietly. He shifted in his seat, leaning over the desk. Everything he did looked comfortable and casual and made her feel uptight and prim. She bet his mind worked the same way, casual and sure. She would kill for a mind like that.

"Unfortunately, I don't think I'll be giving you anything, or going anywhere, much less to court. I haven't got a whole lot to tell you that a judge would be interested in."

"Mr. Crawford, I promise you the information you share with me will be used verbatim. I don't want to do anything to hurt Mr. Brooker's memory, but I also don't want to go into court with a losing proposition and waste my client's time and money. I just want to understand his state of mind so I can make a decision regarding this suit."

Michael laughed. "I don't care who you tell about our conversation. I'm one of those people who actually has nothing to hide. You can believe me when I tell you I doubt I know anything that's going to help you, really."

"He did work here, didn't he?" Verbally she tapped her toe. He wasn't phased.

"He did."

"You are the supervisor of this department aren't you?"

"I am. The problem is I've only been in this department about two months. Lionel Brooker died a few weeks after I came on board." Now his smile was big. His teeth were white and straight, and smaller than she imagined. The overall effect was charming, and there was no doubt he was having fun.

"Oh." Kathleen slumped. "Darn." She crossed her legs, and for the first time, he took his eyes off her face. She didn't notice. She stared stage left with her chin planted on her upturned fist, then she looked back at him. "You know, I thought I was being so smart. I came all this way without calling because I wanted to experience where Mr. Brooker worked. I wanted to see if I could get a feeling for him.''

"Would you like some coffee?'' Michael didn't move. A man of few wasted gestures, he waited for her answer.

"No, thanks.'' Kathleen shook her head.

"Just as well. It's not bad in the morning, but by this time of day, I wouldn't vouch for it.'' Michael picked up a pen, then discarded it once again. ''I don't know if I can give you a feel for the guy. The best I can do is tell you that Lionel seemed to march to the beat of a different drummer. He was right out of the sixties: hair, dress, kind of a spiritual quality about him. I'd bet my bottom dollar he didn't do drugs, though. He knew his job. He did it well. He went home on time.'' He shrugged; the smile disappeared, replaced with an expression of charming hope. ''Does that help?''

"You didn't notice anything before he died? Nothing suspicious in his behavior?'' Kathleen dropped her fist and folded her hands.

Michael leaned forward.

"This isn't the most personal place, Ms. Cotter.'' He didn't have to refer to her card. ''I suppose I should restate that. This isn't the most personal place unless the powers that be want to single you out and make it personal. Then it can get downright intimate. In fact, the company can live in your hip pocket. I didn't really know Lionel, but I'm pretty sure he wasn't the kind to draw an undue amount of attention to himself. When he died, I went through channels and asked some questions.''

"That's sort of odd since you hardly knew him.''

"He was in my division. It didn't seem that anyone else was going to bother. There were a few things that appeared odd enough to me that I thought someone should at least ask a question or two.''

"Like?''

"He was found dead four floors down in a transition area of this building, for one thing. Our work in auditing doesn't take us traveling. It's all paper.'' He considered his desk . . . the calculator that pulsed, the pen, the three pencils. He took inspiration from the simplicity or at least he ordered his thoughts with it. "There were other things. The man had never been late, never stayed late, was never disoriented. In the few weeks I had to observe him, he didn't do anything that could be considered clandestine and the only personal phone calls he ever made were to his wife. I know that because he asked permission." Michael Crawford raised only his eyes to her. "That's not the profile of a drug-user."

"I thought you couldn't tell me much," Kathleen said.

"I can tell you what I saw. Even in a few weeks, I would have seen some sign if he'd been a junkie. I'm a very observant person."

Her heart didn't stop, but the heat went up. He was looking her in the eye again.

"Did you point all this out to the authorities?" Kathleen's fingers went to her fringe and she combed through it briefly.

"The Tysco authorities, yes." He fiddled with the calculator. He flipped it off and shoved it aside, looking displeased. This was the second time he'd intimated Tysco wasn't the benevolent, if boring, Big Brother Kathleen had assumed. "I was never asked to talk to the police."

"You went to a lot of trouble."

"I don't think so. There are some things that are just right to do." Michael Crawford's head tilted to the side; he seemed boyish and animated.

"That's it? You did all this because it was the right thing to do?" It wasn't the answer she'd expected, but then this man wasn't whom she'd expected to find in this place.

"Yeah." He nodded and sat back again, bouncing a little in his junior-executive chair. "What're *you* trying to do?"

"I'm trying to prove that Lionel Brooker didn't intend to kill himself."

"That's admirable."

Kathleen blushed.

"It's my job." Kathleen stepped over his comment and went on. "I want to prove that Lionel didn't want to die. If he was an addict—which is getting hard to believe from the little I know about him—I want to prove that Lionel might have meant to get high but that he wanted to live.''

"Sounds like his ex-wife must really have loved the guy to have hired you to prove that. Too bad the marriage didn't work out.''

"She's the beneficiary on a life insurance policy. She can't collect if he actually committed suicide. I need to prove Lionel had a lot to live for,'' Kathleen said bluntly, still anxious to distance herself from Louise.

"You're a funny lawyer.''

"I don't mean to be,'' Kathleen said.

"I meant unusual-funny. You're very honest.''

"I try to be.'' Kathleen needed some fresh air and she needed it fast. "Look, I'd just like a little history on Lionel Brooker, even if it's recent history. Was he despondent? If so, over what? Was he given to emotional outbursts? That kind of thing. I honestly believe Lionel Brooker's death was an accident. That's it. It's nothing more unusual than that.''

"Think you can prove it?''

Kathleen's eyes widened. She blushed. "Yes, I think I can . . . if it's true. So, could you just help me out a little? Please?''

Michael Crawford actually grinned. "It's been a long time since someone said *please* to me.''

"That's too bad,'' Kathleen answered.

"Yes, it is. I appreciate the courtesy.'' His glanced up long enough to let her know he really meant it.

The blue-bound book he put on the desk looked official. The drawer shut with a metallic click. Michael Crawford flipped through the pages. They were blue, too, and made a restful, flapping sound, spreading themselves neatly under his strong fingers. The motion stopped as quickly as it had begun.

"Look, I'm sorry I can't make this easier on you, but at least I can try to point you in the right direction. You need to talk to Lionel's former supervisor. He worked with him for a good number of years. I was going to give you his extension, but why don't I try to set something up?'' He picked up a pencil, made a notation, and closed the book before he stood.

He looked at Kathleen's card, then at her. "I'll call you and let you know what I find out."

Kathleen stood, too. He was even taller than she'd realized. "Shall I call you?" she asked.

"No. I won't forget."

"Okay." She checked him out, looking for the lie. It wasn't there. "Okay, then, I'll wait. But I don't have forever."

"I understand."

"Well, I'd better let you get back to—" She waved a hand over his desk. But on the back swing, she felt him take her hand. He shook it. Nothing personal, yet her body reacted like it was. She let her fingers slip through his. "You don't seem like the kind of man who would be working in a place like this."

"You don't seem like a Beverly Hills lawyer," he countered.

"I'm not. Not really. Not yet," Kathleen admitted, knowing it would be hard to explain that to a man like Michael Crawford.

"I'm not really an auditor."

Kathleen smiled. She said all the right words of goodbye, sure that she didn't sound too reluctant to go. She didn't look back until she was on the other side of the glass double doors. He was working, not watching her, but Kathleen wasn't disappointed. She knew she would hear from him again.

Chapter Eight

The day was a good one.

Henrietta Poole had been wheeled into Kathleen's office by a male nurse. The woman, although in her eighties, was gorgeous, sharp, and knew exactly how the carpet company she was suing had been negligent. She'd brought photos of the establishment, of herself lying on the floor (though how she'd managed to convince the carpet store-owner to take that picture was beyond Kathleen), and X-rays of her hip. She'd brought doctor's records and a few stories of a very well-traveled and colorful life. Her case was valid, and she was a far cry from the proper, old woman Gerry had led her to expect.

Kathleen would have loved to have pointed this out, but Gerry was gone, as he always was these days, coming back late in the afternoon with reports of whom he'd talked to and what kind of business they might expect and always bright with the belief the hoped-for work would be forthcoming before the end of the millennium. Kathleen listened to the dreams. It was the best she could do since she didn't share them. Nor did she remind him that at the conclusion of Louise's suit, she planned to find more mainstream employment.

Life had fallen into an oddly comfortable routine with just

enough normalcy, just enough challenge, just enough work that Kathleen had almost forgotten what it was she had wanted from this leap out of Banning. So, Kathleen listened to Henrietta Poole, filed the proper paperwork, directed Becky to have the subpoenas served and to follow up with the clerk for a court date once the case was assigned.

Michael Crawford called while Kathleen was with Mrs. Poole, and Kathleen found herself holding the pink message slip close to her breast when she walked back to her office and closed the door. By the time Kathleen had composed herself, and put on the lawyer cap she needed to wear when she called him, he had left his desk. She wondered if he'd managed to set up an appointment with Lionel Brooker's previous supervisor. She wondered if he had found out anything that might have an impact on her case. Then she wondered if, by some stretch of the imagination, he might just want to talk to her.

Kathleen went to lunch an hour late, just in case he came back and called.

She found a dollar on the sidewalk when she went to lunch and returned to find she had a new client—Becky's boyfriend. He wanted her to handle the articles of incorporation for his new business. Kathleen charged him Dorty & Breyer rates. In her heart of hearts she still wasn't sure she was worth the $170 an hour Gerry charged for her time, and she knew Becky's boyfriend couldn't afford it if she were. Maybe when his business flourished, Gerry would thank her for the lapse and reap the rewards.

At three, she picked up her new dress from the tailor, a dress she'd insisted she didn't need and Gerry had insisted she did.

By five, her makeup was perfect: pale-as-porcelain skin, redder-than-red lips, and eyes just smoky enough to make a statement. She slicked back her short, blond hair and donned her new dress. She felt almost as beautiful as Gerry told her she was; she felt more vital than she ever had in her life. Kathleen Cotter knew it wasn't the clothes but the destination that made her feel this way.

"Don't forget, Kathleen, the people I told you about. Carl, of course, is one you wish to impress along with Richard.

There's also James Ellis, who is Carl's right-hand man. Gloria Pennin is a big supporter of Carl's, and she runs Power Records. Oh, what am I saying. Talk to everyone, hand out your card. Let the world know you're here and that here is O'Doul & Associates.''

"I know. I know. And if you talk about it any more, I'm going to start getting nervous." Kathleen turned Gerry toward her and straightened his bow tie. She stood back. He patted it.

"Don't let them see that you're on edge. Who would want to hire a nervous attorney?''

He laughed. Kathleen didn't. He was absolutely right. Who would want to hire her if she appeared less than capable? There wasn't another moment to even consider it. The elevator doors opened, and Kathleen Cotter saw what she had expected to see all those weeks ago—offices of stunning proportions that screamed success. They stepped out into the reception area of Shay, Sylvester & Harrington.

People were everywhere, drinks in hand, balancing plates of food, laughing without really sounding amused as they passed. A low hum of conversation was background music to the conga line. Most of the women were dressed in dark suits. The few women in dresses seemed to hug the walls. Spouses, Kathleen decided. Men followed the same pattern as their professional female counterparts. This was the A-team, no slouches about. Kathleen blessed every article in every fashion magazine she had ever read. On Gerry's arm, she moved into the heart of the firm.

Here the serious gathered. People smiled as they engaged in deep conversation while their eyes searched for someone they could engage in an even deeper, more lucrative dialogue. There was a subtle difference in the way these people were dressed, the jewelry they wore. Kathleen smelled money. Kathleen was finally north of Wilshire.

A waiter passed by with a tray full of small cakes, and Gerry moved into his wake. The first person who stopped to nibble was reeled in by Gerry O'Doul. Kathleen was thrilled to be cut loose so soon. The ball had just begun, and she was determined to make it to midnight with her shoes on.

* * *

"Carl? A refill before you face your supporters?"

Richard held up a decanter, its many facets catching the light and shooting prisms toward the corners of Richard Jacobsen's office.

The mayor looked over his shoulder, checked out his glass, and shook his head. He was tired and looked it. Facing a camera or a city council meeting, a group of well-wishers or a reporter, he bloomed. Alone, without the jarring light of public scrutiny and the fuel of public adoration, Carl Walsh was a shadow man, blending into his surroundings. Tall and stooped, he looked less a politician than a disenchanted college professor. But out there, he became animated and talkative, back-slapping and glad-handing. "No, I'm fine. I'm just worried."

"No need. Everything is going very well. Out there you'll find some of the most sycophantic folks in the entire legal system, all willing to reach deep into their firm's coffers—and their own pockets—to support you. They believe you will be their next senator. They want your good favor, Carl. They want your ear when you reach Washington." Richard poured himself two fingers, replaced the stopper, and held his glass. "And in here, you have your campaign committee. Me, myself, and I. Believe me, between everyone out there and me in here, you haven't a worry in the world."

Carl walked from one end of Richard's office to the other. It was one of the most beautiful he had ever seen. Richard, unattractive as he was, had a marvelous eye for beauty. Carl couldn't have begun to describe the place or figure out how he managed to pull it all together—antiques, modern furniture, artwork, and collectibles. He made a statement so elegant, visitors almost forgot who, and what, Richard Jacobsen was.

Carl put his glass on a small table nestled by a big chair and walked back to Richard, sinking into a carved chair that had a mate on the opposite end of the long table that served as Richard's desk. He propped his elbows up. He'd had a bit to drink, just enough to put him on the edge of depression.

"I'm not sure we should make the budget-thing our lead on

the campaign. I mean it's an incredible story, but I don't want to get caught up in anything—you know—that the press could make anything out of.''

"Carl, Carl, Carl, please.''

Richard laid his head back on his chair. He sounded weary. Unlike many small men, he hadn't opted for a power-chair. The one in which he sat was tasteful and perfectly proportioned to his short, almost-misshapen body. Everyone who realized this nod to practicality was impressed by it. Richard Jacobsen, they assumed, was a man with no ego. He put his fine mind to work brilliantly for the clients of Shay, Sylvester & Harrington and he put himself second. They assumed wrong.

"Don't use that voice, Richard,'' Carl begged, his head now falling into one upturned hand. "You sound like a school-marm.''

"And you sound like a man who doesn't really want what he says he wants. You sound like a child, and all this time I thought I was playing with a big boy.''

"Richard,'' Carl whined. Both hands were over his face now. "It's just that now we're going to start screaming about it. It's one thing to have it on paper where the press can pick it up, but I don't want to debate—''

"If you're tired of everything, go home. If all you want to do is practice instead of pitch, I'll find someone else to support for the Senate. I need a candidate who is willing to take some risks. I thought you were that man.''

"I am,'' Carl grumbled miserably. "I was only saying that I think the emphasis on issues should be spread out a bit more to protect us. All of us, Richard.'' He tried to give Richard a knowing and harsh look. He succeeded only in looking as if his bodily functions had suddenly gone awry. He tried again. "What we've been doing isn't going to be so easy when we're dealing with federal budgets. You know that and I know that. A city is one thing. I controlled the city, but Washington is different. With the way the press is these days, if I toot my horn too much on one topic they're going to come back at me hard. I don't want anyone snooping around. I just want to win this election, settle in, and leave it at that.''

"It will never be left at that, Carl. This is politics. Nice-looking as you are, I'm afraid you won't be able to swing votes on that alone."

Richard Jacobsen stood up in a surprisingly fluid motion. He was a legal vampire, appearing and disappearing with little fanfare, but always carting away the blood while everyone else was still arguing about how much there was to suck. He was a smart cookie, and Carl had done well listening to him. What Carl lacked was Richard's surety that everything he did was what should be done. Richard never attached words like *right* or *proper* or *moral;* he simply did what he had to do to reach an objective that seemed logical to him. There was little he was passionate about, and his passion was usually reserved for very special people. Carl was not one of them.

He wrapped his hand around Carl's upper arm and helped him up, though Carl wasn't sure he had wanted to go just then. Richard steered him toward the door.

"It's time to meet and greet. Put on the face, Carl. It's a wonderful one. Tomorrow, have your medication checked. I think your chemical imbalance has shifted again. Leave everything else to me. Everything. It will all be just fine. You will be hailed as a fiscal God; I will have what I want, and my good friends at Tysco will have what they want. That is even more important to me than your ultimate destination. No one will get in our way. I promise you. No one."

Richard opened the door to his private office. It was a stunning design. Though he could see many of the three hundred people milling about in the outer offices, they could not see him.

"Look at them, Carl. To them you're already in the Senate. To them you've already got the power. All you have to do is turn on the charm. Shake their hands. Tell them what they want to hear. We've talked about that. It's a different story for these people than it will be for those on the street. These people want to know their money is being spent right. The guy on the street wants to know that you're saving him a buck. Just do what you've been doing, and all will be well."

"You really think so, Richard?" Carl asked, looking into the short man's soft, brown eyes.

"I know so, Carl. I know so." Richard gave him a pat on the back. It felt good to both of them. Carl smiled, but the glow faded quickly.

"Oh, Lord. He's here. Gerry O'Doul. I don't want to talk to him."

"I think you should. I think it might be a very, very good thing," Richard mused.

"I think it would be dangerous as hell. That old man is sharp as a tack, Carl. I don't want him anywhere near city business." Carl moved back into the shadows. Richard remained at the door, eyeing Gerry O'Doul and the woman beside him.

"You might be right. I don't know," Richard said, more to himself than to his candidate. "Just give him some rein. Keep him on the line. With a name like his, it wouldn't hurt. There are still those around who remember. If we can get you elected and out of the mayor's office before he becomes a problem, then you're home free. Just keep smiling. Tell him you and I are working on something for him—for old time's sake." Richard watched Gerry without a sigh of admiration or compassion. It would be good for Gerry O'Doul to concentrate on something other than the Brooker business. "The old can be so tedious, but they do deserve some consideration. Some more than others."

With a slight push, Carl Walsh was out the door, Richard looking after him. It was a sight to see, Carl Walsh turning on. People were his batteries; he glowed the moment he plugged into them. He would do well in the coming months. Very well, indeed, and Richard Jacobsen would do even better because his hands were on the reins guiding this wagon train. As long as Carl remembered to head in the direction Richard pointed, all would be well.

The door was almost closed when Richard saw Gerry O'Doul moving in on Carl Walsh. Richard paused, watched, and was satisfied that Carl was giving Gerry just enough of his time and attention. Richard's eyes darted over the immediate crowd surrounding the two men. O'Doul's niece was nowhere to be seen. Richard closed the door. He wasn't surprised. She was probably out on her own. A handsome woman like that wouldn't be clinging to an old man when there were so many other, younger, more interesting men around. He knew so well how hard it was to keep the interest of a young and handsome companion. Kathleen Cotter, he wondered, what is it that would keep you around?

Closing the door, Richard went to the private bathroom, the door a hidden panel in the wainscoting of the wall. It was as well-appointed as the office. He washed his hands, combed his hair, and managed a glance at the woman in the picture he kept on the antique bureau in the small dressing room.

How he loved her. How little she understood him. He slipped out of the bathroom, out of the office, and into the flow of the human river that ran through the offices of Shay, Sylvester & Harrington.

"Do you like them?"

Richard Jacobsen was beside her and Kathleen hadn't even sensed his coming. It would have been understandable if she were still in the middle of the muddle near the main bar, but she wasn't. She was alone in a conference room, smaller than the impressive one in the main office. Meaning to stay for only a moment, Kathleen had been mesmerized by the amazing oasis she had stumbled on.

Hung on the sand-colored walls were paintings so surprising in their brightness and intensity, their fluidity of style, that Kathleen felt positively transported to an exotic place full of life and passion. They were happy paintings, feel-good paintings inspired by white, romantic beaches on exotic islands. Kathleen couldn't imagine what kind of legal work was ever accomplished under their influence.

Perhaps it was the comforting influence of the paintings that kept her from being startled by Richard Jacobsen's sudden appearance. After all, in exotic places, strange and wonderful things happened.

"Do you like my collection?" he asked as if they'd been together contemplating the big canvases for some time.

"Yes, I like them very much."

"I do, too," Richard said, moving over a few steps to stand in front of one that was long and bright. Tall houses huddled happily together like good friends leaning into one another with great camaraderie. The houses were painted in shades of peach, red, and yellow. She wanted to live in one. "This one is stunning, don't you think? The artist has caught the feeling of community. He seems to rejoice in that sense of belonging. It's as if the houses and buildings cannot exist without the next one to hold it up."

"I hadn't really thought about it like that. I'm not much of a connoisseur." Kathleen chuckled quietly, looked at the painting through Richard Jacobsen's eyes, and wondered what in the heck she was supposed to say next, given this surprising interpretation of the art.

"I don't think you have to be." He turned his face toward her and she was struck again at how sad a face it was. Now it seemed softer than it had in the corridors of the court building. Perhaps, in this room, he could relax and let down his guard; perhaps, in this room, he dreamed of the places that he considered better than the one he was in. Funny that bigger-than-life flowers, boats, and beaches were the subject matter of Richard Jacobsen's daydream. He looked back at the canvas, diverting her attention. "I think you have to feel certain things. This artist is from the South. Alabama, I believe. Mathis. Tom Mathis is his name. A wonderful find, don't you think?"

"Absolutely."

She waited for Richard to speak. She wanted to be led in the direction that would be most impressive to him. Her hand was warm around her cold drink, and she worried it would slip from her fingers. Then he would see that she was someone he shouldn't waste his time with. But Richard Jacobsen didn't seem to notice how tautly she held her body, how bright her eyes were with interest. He spoke to her as if she were a friend.

"Yes," he said again, "Mr. Mathis will be very popular soon. I've found him before the masses, and I enjoy him every time I use this room. My personal conference room." He said the last as though it were underlined and Kathleen came about.

"I'm sorry. I didn't know. I thought the entire office was open to the party. I apologize." She moved toward the door. Her purse still lay on the table; she retraced her steps to retrieve it. He stepped in front of the path of retreat.

"No, Miss Cotter, please. I didn't mean that at all." Richard almost smiled, his calm a wonderful contrast to her fluster. "It's very nice to find someone who appreciates the same things I do. It's unusual these days to have anyone linger over paintings in a law office. Usually their noses are buried in paperwork. They don't bother to look up."

"Maybe they can't look up. They don't have the time. Billing pressure in a firm like this must be incredible." Kathleen came right back at him.

"I never thought of it that way." Richard chuckled. "You only get to look up when you're my age and you're the one with the personal conference room. I suppose when you're trying to get there you keep your eye on the ball."

Richard Jacobsen was metamorphosing before her eyes. His uncouth features melded into the kindly visage of a man who has overcome much and who, recognizing a need in someone else, is generous with his time and experience.

"I suppose. I don't know." Kathleen moved about the room, unsure if they were having a conversation or if she were simply listening to his musings.

"You don't? That's very interesting." Richard Jacobsen turned to her full-face, the paintings forgotten. "Aren't you shooting for the stars along with all your contemporaries?"

"Yes, I am." Kathleen laughed, then sobered. "I am. I'm just a little late getting on the rocket that's going to take me there."

"I can't imagine you feel that way at your age."

"I only feel that way because of my age. My resume isn't very impressive. I don't know that a solid, good firm would feel comfortable letting me handle anything."

Kathleen tried to chuckle, but it was impossible. Standing here, in the midst of the trappings of such great success, she realized how little she could bring to the table.

"Most young people want to earn the big bucks. It's funny

you should mention clients and responsibility.'' Richard pulled out one of the chairs surrounding the simple table. Kathleen sat, looking up at him over her shoulder.

''That's because this profession isn't really about money, is it? It's about what we can accomplish, the truth we can reach when we're working with laws we didn't write. I've always been fascinated by that. But only the large firms get a chance to practice that kind of law. The rest of us just dance around it and talk ourselves blue in the face trying to take care of everyday problems.''

Richard's hands lingered on the back of her chair as he watched her, a moment short of making her uncomfortable. Easily, he perched on the table so that he looked down on her.

''That's an unusual take. But then, when your uncle is Gerry O'Doul, I can understand the calling. Gerry was never one to worry about money first. With him, it was style . . . challenge . . . justice. He built a career on such high ideals. You should be very fulfilled working with him.''

Kathleen stopped moving. She almost stopped breathing. This was a moment that could be used. Conscience pulled at her. She owed Gerry more than to talk behind his back, but Richard Jacobsen was here, now, waiting for her to say something. He'd given her the opening. She couldn't pass up the chance to do something for herself.

''No, Mr. Jacobsen, I don't think working with my uncle will be fulfilling. Interesting, yes, but not what I was hoping for. I didn't realize that his firm had fallen on hard times. The clients that come to him aren't the clients I had hoped for. They're unusual, to say the least.''

''Are you by any chance referring to the problems of the lady I saw you with the other day?'' Richard chuckled, a dry and papery sound.

''Louise Brooker?'' Kathleen gave him a wry look. They shared a collegial chuckle. ''She is different, and the case is unusual. Her husband was found dead in the bathroom at Tysco Industries at their manufacturing facility in Culver City.''

Kathleen was revving up, but hadn't quite hit her stride. She was still lucid enough to realize that her audience was not, perhaps, as interested as she'd thought. Richard Jacobsen was staring at her. He seemed to be listening, but his mind was a million miles away. She pulled up short.

"I'm sorry, I'm boring you. You've got so many guests, and I'm monopolizing your time." Kathleen started to stand. Her exit would be graceful. If nothing else, he would remember that.

"No, not at all," Richard insisted, suddenly shaken out of his reverie. He put out his hand, insisting she stay though he didn't touch her. "I'm sorry. I was just thinking that it seems a bit unusual that Gerry would be handling a murder case. I'd understood he was semi-retired and doing only civil work."

Kathleen laughed. So, that's where he'd been. In the past, trying to place the Gerry of long ago with the old man who milled about in the outer office.

"No, it isn't anything like that. He died of a self-inflicted drug overdose. Louise's alimony agreement included a life insurance policy on Lionel Brooker. Now All Life won't pay off because his death was ruled a suicide. I think we can prove that he never intended to take his own life. I think—"

"Richard, there you are!"

Carl Walsh bounded into the room, followed by two tall, strong men who were less than light on their feet. Kathleen's eyes flitted over them. They looked back at her. They weren't lawyers. Richard slid off the table and went to meet his guests. He ignored the big guys, shook Carl Walsh's hand, and turned him so he faced Kathleen squarely.

"Carl, I've been having a wonderful chat with Ms. Cotter here. She's Gerry O'Doul's niece, his associate now. A very, very bright young woman. Perhaps you can convince her to volunteer for you. You're always looking for intelligent, attractive young people."

Kathleen glowed under his compliments. She stood and proffered her hand.

"I've heard a lot about you."

He shook her hand.

"Gerry is a sweetheart," Carl answered heartily. "Don't believe a word he says. Richard either."

"Even if they say good things?" Kathleen flirted. From the corner of her eye, she saw Richard Jacobsen's benevolent smile. She was fitting in, on her own.

"Oh, if they're good things, I want to hear all about them," Carl laughed, and the two men behind him unwrapped packaged smiles. Carl's eyes followed Kathleen's. "My associates. Bob and David. Go-fers. You know, go for this, go for that."

Kathleen nodded their way, watching for any sign of embarrassment. There was none. Richard still sat quietly on the edge of the table. Carl laughed into the silence. Kathleen was suddenly uncomfortable. Somehow she had ruined the party and wasn't sure how.

"Well, I should leave you to your business." She turned to Richard. "Thank you for the gallery tour. It's wonderful."

"I hope you'll come back again." Richard took her hand in his. "I still want to know the end of your story, though." Richard put his hand on her arm. She looked at it, then up at him. He was smiling. Carl Walsh was not. "It's been a long while since I've heard something so intriguing. What is it you plan to do for Brooker's widow?"

Jacobsen's hand fell away, his touch had been so light she hardly remembered the feel of it.

"Oh, Louise isn't his widow. Sarah, his second wife, is. But Louise was due the death benefits. It's kind of crazy and complicated. I just hope to prove that her husband wasn't suicidal so that we can get past the suicide exclusion."

"A unique solution. Unprovable, I would think. I'm surprised Judge Kelley gave you the go-ahead."

"I convinced him that there are actions taken by reasonable men that wouldn't be taken by a man ready to take his own life. I'll dig until I find those reasons," Kathleen said humbly, praying this man would think her strategy as meritorious as Gerry did.

"Fascinating. Commendable," Richard breathed, then added quietly while he kept his eyes on Kathleen, "isn't it, Carl."

"Very," the other man answered, but it was obvious he hadn't been listening. Kathleen was so taken with the attention of Richard Jacobsen, she didn't notice that Carl Walsh was tired of her and anxious for her to leave.

"Perhaps you'll keep me up on the progress, Kathleen." Richard, sensing the change of mood in the room, guided her toward the door. "I'd enjoy being young again, pursuing such colorful matters."

"Just say the word." Kathleen would jump from the tallest building to keep Richard Jacobsen interested in her professionally. Both of her hands were in his as he wished her goodbye.

"I just might, Ms. Cotter. I just might. Thank you for such a lovely respite. Now, I'm afraid, there's business at hand. Good night and thank you for coming. You have no idea what it meant to me."

"Or to me," she said, and there could be no doubt she sincerely meant what she said.

Outside Richard Jacobsen's private conference room, Kathleen Cotter took a deep breath and pinched herself. She checked her watch. Fifteen minutes alone with a man who could make Carl Walsh a senator. What could he make her if he took the time to think about it?

Aglow, Kathleen floated through the throng. More than one head turned to watch her go, but when Gerry looked up from his conversation to give her his leprechaun smile, guilt tarnished that glow. If it hadn't been for Gerry, she never would have met Richard Jacobsen or roamed the halls of Shay, Sylvester & Harrington. If it hadn't been for Gerry, she'd still be in Banning. Then again, if it hadn't been for Gerry and her mother, Kathleen would already have the resume that would make a man like Richard Jacobsen take notice.

Pretending she hadn't seen him looking proudly and expectantly at her, Kathleen turned toward the bar. Her white wine was replaced by a scotch. She stood alone and listened to Carl Walsh's speech, his promises of the same fiscal responsibility on the federal level that he'd shown as mayor. When he was done, when she had written a check to his campaign that was small but, she was sure, noticeable, Kathleen found Gerry. She took his arm, knowing she had taken steps that evening to secure her future. Midnight was striking when they left the

party. The book was closed, the place marked, but the fairy
tale wasn't over.

She dropped Gerry at his house, kissed his cheek, and waited
for him to get inside before she drove away. Her message
machine was blinking when she got home. Michael Crawford
was asking her to meet him at two-thirty in Marina del Rey.

Undressed, she crawled beneath the covers and listened as
William called out love messages to Paul from the street below.

"You're not in Banning anymore, Kathleen," she murmured.
Just before she fell into an exhausted sleep, with images of
Gerry and Richard Jacobsen and Michael Crawford melding
together in her head, she muttered, "Thank God."

Chapter Nine

"You were wonderful, Henrietta."

Kathleen pushed the wheelchair that Henrietta sat on like a throne. They'd done their work well this morning. Henrietta had given her version of the accident in clear tones and precise language. Kathleen found nothing in her statement that would keep her from testifying in front of judge or jury.

"Thank you, my dear. I thought I did rather well." She fussed with her gloves, carefully pushing her fingers into them. Bo, her strapping nurse, took over for Kathleen as soon as they exited the building. The women were now side-by-side.

"They aren't going to settle, you know." Kathleen slipped on a pair of sunglasses, new ones that gave her a sort of Jackie O-gone-platinum look.

"Oh, I know that," she tsked, suddenly facing Kathleen as her chair was twirled wrong-side around and placed on a platform that would lift her into the van she'd rented precisely for this purpose. Bo was behind her, waiting patiently until they'd finished their conversation to turn on the lift motor.

"So, you ready for court?"

"I think it will be a great deal of fun." She leaned forward and gave Kathleen a pat. "We're such a fine team, how can they possibly turn us down? I didn't ask for this to happen, after all. There was no warning whatsoever. That bolt of carpeting came out of nowhere. There were no signs indicating a loading zone. I'd been led there by one of their own representatives and told to wait. No one called to alert me that I was about to be torpedoed. I think the judge, or whatever, will be very sympathetic.''

"You know what I think?" Kathleen leaned down and whispered, "I think you could argue this without me."

"Oh—" Henrietta giggled. "—you are ridiculous. Of course I need you to do that. It's perfect staging. You look as if you could be my granddaughter. Who could resist that? A granddaughter fighting for her poor, old grandmother. I think it will all work very well. And we're not asking for the moon, you know. That should go over well. Just asking for a proper and moral settlement for all my pain and suffering.''

"You think fifty thousand dollars is enough? You've been suffering a lot." Kathleen looked over the van, the handsome attendant, Henrietta's perfectly coifed hair and lovely clothes.

"I know, dear, and I'm bearing up as well as can be expected," she teased back. "I'm sure fifty thousand dollars will do something to ease my pain." A final tug on the gloves. "Can I drop you somewhere, Kathleen?"

"No, thank you. I've got some paperwork to do, then an appointment at two-thirty. Busy day.''

"I hope some of it will be fun. Go have a facial, dear. It does wonderful things for the psyche." She gave a barely-there wave to Bo, and he moved further back into the van.

"I'll remember that. But today's a little tight.''

"Well, whenever. I'll tell you what—" she called, her voice drowned out when the gears on the van-lift kicked in. Henrietta was raised above Kathleen. She looked perplexed when the mechanism jolted to a sudden stop. Composing herself, she spoke again. "I'll treat you to one with our settlement.''

"Gerry would have my head if I knocked a few dollars off your fee for a facial.''

"Don't be ridiculous. That man thinks you walk on water. Besides, this would be a tip for services rendered.''

Henrietta was pulled into the interior of the van. Bo secured her. She called goodbye, and the doors closed. Kathleen waved, though she doubted Henrietta saw her. Henrietta was a busy woman, too busy to linger over the niceties. Kathleen didn't have much time either.

She took care of her paperwork over a burger in a corner coffee shop. By the time she'd indulged in a piece of chocolate, banana cream pie, it was time to hit the road. Marina del Rey was a new part of the world to her, and the last thing she wanted was to be late for her meeting with Michael Crawford.

Marina del Rey wasn't a bit like Oz. It wasn't green. It wasn't just one color at all but a whole scheme—blue set off by white and defined by brown. Blue skies over blue water . . . white sails on the boats dotting the bay, white hulls on those moored to white docks . . . tanned bodies lounging on teak decks or speeding along the walk on roller blades. There were restaurants with names like Charlie Brown, Acupulco, Thank God It's Friday. It seemed like a playground for adults who preferred not to grow up, where the happy hour was perpetual and youth extended like a taut rubber band. Kathleen figured that out when she stopped for the third time to ask directions within the concentric circles of the area's layout and she dashed into a small shop she'd passed more than once. Surrounded by the smallest bikinis she had ever seen and assisted by a curly-haired girl in a backless dress, Kathleen was finally pointed in the right direction. Her destination wasn't a house, an apartment, or a business, but a slip where a boat was moored and a man was sitting. A man who was definitely not Michael Crawford.

"Excuse me." Kathleen stood beside the boat and called up to him. He sat on a deck chair and looked as out of sync with his surroundings as Kathleen felt.

His hair was cut short and slicked down as if to stretch it back to some fetching length. His glasses were big, black, and broken. Tape held the nosepiece together. His shirt was blue and short sleeved. His shorts were plaid and baggy. His socks were white, his shoes black, his skin as pure as the driven snow, and his voice as deep as a radio announcer's.

"Are you Kathleen Cotter?"

"Yes, I am. I'm looking for Michael Crawford."

The man nodded and put down his book, a hardbound anthology of MAD cartoons. He picked his way gingerly over the deck. Kathleen looked away when he disappeared below.

She took a few steps down the dock, stopped and just stood. The whole world moved up and down as if the ocean were sighing in its sleep. Toward the horizon she saw the curve of the breakwater that helped shelter the harbor. Sailboats floated out to sea. A perfect day for sailing. The slips were quiet; only intermittent sounds broke into the songs of the gulls that flew overhead. Under their wings, the water glistened and stretched large and Kathleen Cotter was overwhelmed. Life could be so beautiful.

"Hi."

Twirling, she squinted toward the sound of the greeting, but the sun was in her eyes, shining behind the man on the deck of this more than respectably sized boat. All she could see was his silhouette but there was no doubt it was Michael Crawford. Still tall. Still lean. Still well-turned-out. His hair ruffled as the breeze picked up strands and the sun shined through them. Smiling, Kathleen moved so that she could really see him. When she did, she saw that he was reaching for her. She took his hands without a second thought. They were warm and strong.

"You'll have to give a little jump now," he instructed, nodding toward the deck, then looking back at her. His eyes went up and down. He gave up. "Not going to work. Hold on. It'll be tough in that skirt. Would you rather sit on the grass?"

She glanced at the boat. Polished, well-kept, inviting. Painted black and gold and white, it told her more about Michael Crawford than the pristine office where she'd initially met him. She wanted to go on deck, poke about, and see what else she could find. Instead, she said, "I suppose it would be better on the grass."

"I could lift you. It's nice up here," he coaxed.

"I have no doubt," she answered and wondered if her voice had been too soft for him to hear or her blush too faint for him to take notice. He stayed where he was, giving her a chance to change her mind. He changed his first and jumped down onto the dock. It rocked gently; he stood his ground as if shaky was where he felt comfortable. Michael's guest came out of the galley. Kathleen reluctantly changed her focus.

"Michael, I have everything."

The MAD man was back.

"Thanks, pass it on down." Michael reached up and, with one hand, took a canvas bag the other man held with both hands. Interesting, if this were evidence he was about to turn over to her. "Come on down, Harold. Ms. Cotter isn't quite dressed to climb up on deck."

"Okay." The bespectacled man climbed over the side, but with an awkward jump, he ended up sitting at Kathleen's feet despite all his precautions. "Hi. Harold Douglas."

"Nice to meet you."

They shook hands. She helped him up and they both followed Michael to a grass strip. Today he wore shorts, frayed at the hem. His legs were long and strong. He wore a T-shirt that touted the virtues of a bar in the Baja. Another place she'd never been.

Folding himself onto the grass strip, he pushed his dark glasses up his nose, though they seemed well-settled without the effort. A neon-orange tube of fabric was attached to both ends of the glasses and looped around the back of his head. Here, he was a happy man.

"I don't know if you've eaten, but I figure everybody likes to munch while they're talking. I've got beer, soda, cold chicken, and pretzels. Oh, some Twinkies." He held up the plastic-wrapped, lemon-yellow cakes with the three distinctive, cream-filling tattoos on the bottom.

Kathleen laughed. "It's a feast." She sat beside him. Close but not too close, legs politely tucked beneath her. She wished the skirt on her dress were full. "I'll take a beer and the pretzels."

"No Twinkies?" He twirled one to entice her. He grinned when she shook her head. "That's what I like, a woman with self-control. Harold?"

Michael's eyes were on the skinny fellow who appeared to analyze the grass for signs of something distasteful before sinking to his knees and leaning back to rest upon the heels of his very hard shoes. His hands were on his knees.

"What is it you have again?"

"Chicken, soda, Twinkies, pretzels," Michael said patiently. Harold shook his head. He shuddered.

"No, thank you."

Michael took him at his word and served himself, taking a beer and a chicken leg before crossing his legs. The floor was open for discussion.

"I've been trying to get hold of Lionel's previous supervisor, but it's been tough tying him down." He shrugged. "Sorry about that."

"That's all right." Kathleen nibbled on a pretzel then took a sip of beer. It had never tasted quite so marvelous as it did on this August afternoon. Even her disappointment was easier to swallow.

"But I brought you the next best thing. Harold was a friend of Lionel's, and I thought he might be able to help you." Michael used the chicken leg like a baton. The floor belonged to Harold.

"Correction, Mr. Crawford. I wasn't a friend. I never would have presumed upon my relationship with Lionel by assuming anything as intimate as a friendship. I was his admirer. I was grateful to be his student. I was working on being worthy of his friendship, but fate did, indeed, step in and remove that particular prospect from my agenda. Much, I might add, to my distress."

Harold's fingers were incredibly long and bony. He tapped his knees with them. He bit his nails. A subdural twitch seemed to grip Harold Douglas, yet his body remained rigid, his voice remained calm. He never cracked a smile. Sincere and serious, approaching his topic as though presenting his credentials to the queen, Harold Douglas had no time for small talk. Yet he seemed in no hurry to leave.

"How long had you known Lionel, Mr. Douglas?" Kathleen asked.

"I'd worked alongside Lionel for four years, Miss Cotter. They were the best four years of my life." He glanced down, lifting his fingertips ever so slightly, as if to hold up history for her approval. "I have no delusions, Miss Cotter. I know that people like me are considered throwaways. Nerds. Society has little use for the less-than-stylish, the less-than-self-confident, the less-than-beautiful. We are a reviled subset of our culture when we are in our formative years and ignored when we have passed through them."

Harold took a breath, keeping his eyes on her. He almost began again but changed his mind. Quicker than lightning, he reached into his back pocket, withdrew a huge white handkerchief, and sneezed a sneeze of incredible proportions into it. Even Michael took notice—not that he hadn't noticed everything that had happened up until that point. Kathleen was not unaware of his intense interest in Harold and in her.

"Forgive me." Harold honked once more, put the handkerchief away, and resumed his speech. "I apologize. I've drifted from the subject. I only wanted to paint the background so you could see why I thought so highly of Lionel Brooker."

He stopped and blinked at Kathleen. Waited. Nothing.

"And why was that, Mr. Douglas?" she prodded.

"What?"

"Why did you think so highly of Mr. Brooker?" Kathleen repeated clearly. Beside her, Michael uncrossed his legs, reclining on one elbow to watch the proceedings. Kathleen looked at him, mentally tripped when she focused on his legs, then looked back at Harold, trying not to make any comparisons between the two men—or think to which she was more suited.

"Lionel Brooker managed to break the mold, of course," Harold answered with dignity. "He had crossed over. A man completely aware of his status as a second-class citizen, yet somehow he rose above the discrimination afforded men like us. Lionel had style. He had heart. He had confidence. Lionel Brooker knew exactly what life was about.''

"And what was that, Mr. Douglas? Can you tell me?''

Kathleen set aside her beer. It toppled in the lush grass. She reached for it at the same time Michael did. Their hands touched.

"Thanks.''

"Hate to waste a good brew,'' Michael said. Harold Douglas watched the exchange with not a small bit of awe. Kathleen resumed her questioning.

"Did you know a lot about Lionel's life outside the office, Mr. Douglas?''

"Lionel's life was perfect, Miss Cotter.'' Harold paused, sad for a moment. Removing his glasses, he breathed on them. Lacking an appropriate cloth with which to finish the job, he put his glasses back on, looking at the world through a slowly disappearing fog.

Uneasily, Kathleen watched, chancing a glance at Michael Crawford to see if he, too, was affected by Harold. Michael looked at the man from behind dark sunglasses, his feelings cloaked. When Kathleen finally saw Harold's eyes again, they were trained at some point beyond her and swam with tears.

"There was no reason for Lionel to take his own life. I don't know what happened in that bathroom. I don't know that there was anything in the world that would have caused him to harm himself. Lionel was a very spiritual man, you must understand.'' Harold shared this with both of them equally but finally settled on Kathleen. "He believed in nature in its purest form. That's why he held no animosity toward his first wife. He said their divorce was just part of the journey. We would have lunch and he would share his journey with me.''

"You mean he was sort of a born-again Christian?'' Michael asked. He reclined now, propped up on his elbow, one knee up and one leg extended.

Harold shook his head, "No, it was more than that. His journey was one of personal growth. He was the only man

I ever knew who thought so deeply about himself and his environment. He continued to try and carve a place for himself that was self-satisfying while honoring his responsibility to the world at large. He felt guilty about Louise. He felt he'd married her without giving thought to how they fit together in the universe and that was why they hadn't made it. Do you understand?''

Kathleen was all sympathy. ''I think so. Like when people marry too young and find out that there's no place for the captain of the football team and the head cheerleader in the real world.''

''Exactly.'' Harold pushed his glasses up, smiling quite a lovely smile. ''That's exactly how Lionel felt, and that's why he took responsibility for Louise. He believed he had done her a disservice.'' He was excited now, warming to his subject. ''You see, Lionel believed everything was tied to nature. It was Louise's nature to desire material things. It was natural for her to be upset when she realized that Lionel had never valued the things money could buy. Her nature was unchangeable. His was at least refinable, if that makes sense.''

Harold knelt up, tiring of leaning on the hard heels of his shoes.

''Lionel was gentle, spiritual, kind, respectful of all the living things that inhabited his world, even the people who sought to take advantage of him. He took pride in his job because he believed that he was using his God-given talents to the best of his ability. He was taking care of his first wife and his second by honoring the commitment he made to Tysco. In short, Lionel Brooker was a very proud man and I say he had every reason to be.''

''And no reason to kill himself?''

Harold glanced at Michael, surprised to hear him speak and looking almost peeved that his soliloquy had not been allowed a moment of respectful silence. When he'd spoken of Lionel, he had seemed to grow taller, his shoulders had become broad with pride that he'd known such a person. But Lionel was gone. Harold shrank back, sitting on his heels once more.

"No, there was no reason for him to kill himself. He was upset in the weeks before he died about something that had happened at work. I might even go so far as to describe his behavior as *distressed*. He didn't confide in me except to say that life is full of disappointments and sometimes you just have do what you can when you run into them."

"And you didn't take that to mean that he was resigned to solving his problem by taking his own life?" Kathleen questioned him now.

"No." Harold shook his head slowly, thinking hard about his answer because he knew it was important. "I didn't. In fact, I don't believe it was Lionel's problem. The way he spoke of it was more like he was angry at other people. I don't think Lionel made a mistake. I think someone else did and he was taking it upon himself. At least, that's the impression I had. He wasn't depressed. If anything, he was energized."

"Did he say how he was going to do this or who else might be involved?" Michael was sitting up again, offering Kathleen the chicken. She shook her head.

"I'm sorry." He looked Kathleen's way. "We weren't intimate in that way. I admired him. I don't think he knew how much. We ate lunch together, said good morning and good night, but I wasn't privy to Lionel's most private thoughts. Without Lionel's opening the door, I would never have burdened him with mine."

"He must have been a very special man." Kathleen's voice was another note in the summer sounds. She waited for a car to pass through the parking lot behind them, then leaned forward and put her hand on Harold's. "I hate to ask this, Mr. Douglas, but I have to. If you weren't the best of friends, how do you know that Lionel might not have turned to drugs?"

Harold turned a cold eye on Kathleen. "I know because Lionel wasn't that kind of man. I would testify to that in court, my hand on the Bible. If no one else will speak for Lionel Brooker, then I will. You see, Miss Cotter, people like Lionel and me, we realize very early that we are life's square pegs. That's why our senses are honed and our thought process is keen. From the time we are young, we know that we won't have many friends, so we treasure the ones we do have. Lionel was a lucky man. He had Sarah and he had me. I will speak out for Lionel Brooker. I will be his character witness.''

Kathleen sat silently, considering the grass. There were a few large blades that would have made marvelous whistles. Had she been a girl, she might have plucked one up and whistled a tune. But she was a grown woman with a purpose, and that purpose had suddenly taken a very personal turn. She wouldn't be swayed. Harold's feelings were not evidence.

"You're very astute, Mr. Douglas. I appreciate your honesty and your insights. But the information I need has to be more concrete. Did Lionel ever share with you any plans for the future in the last weeks of his life? That would be truly helpful if you could come up with some concrete evidence that Lionel felt he had a future.''

Her voice was hypnotic. The sea breeze took her words, spoken so gently, and spread them between the two men. Beside her, she could almost feel Michael Crawford's mind turning as he tried to help her.

"He talked about the farm he wanted to buy someday.''

"Did he talk about that in the last few weeks?''

Harold hung his head. There was nothing more he could add and his word alone wasn't enough to convince anyone that Lionel Brooker thought he had a reason to live.

Kathleen patted his hand. "I wish I had a friend like you, Mr. Douglas.''

"I'm surprised you don't, Miss Cotter,'' he answered with equal sincerity. Michael Crawford had no comment.

"Well, if you can think of anything else, I would appreciate hearing from you.'' She poked into her bag and pulled out a card. Harold took it reverently, tucking it safely away in a zippered change bag that hung from a clip around his belt loop.

"I promise I'll call. Right away.'' He stood up. His knees were pocked with the pattern of the grass; one white sock had worked its way down around his ankle. Michael stood up and shook Harold's hand. He said all the things a boss would say to an employee, but he said them with impressive warmth.

"I appreciate your coming all the way out here, Harold. I'll see you at work on Monday."

"Sure thing. I was glad to do it for Lionel." Harold tugged at his blue shirt, bent and picked up his book. Before he left, though, he had another thought. "Mr. Crawford? Has Lionel's desk been cleaned out?"

"It has. I thought the same thing, Harold."

"Too bad. It might have helped to look at his desk to see if there was anything he held back," Harold suggested. "Well, if there's anything else, let me know."

He gave a waist-high wave with his goodbye. Kathleen shaded her eyes to watch him go, only to call him back briefly.

"Was there anyone at all whom Lionel disliked, Harold? Or anyone at work who particularly disliked Lionel?"

Harold shook his head. "Lionel gave everyone a fair shake, even if they didn't reciprocate. No one ever really dislikes guys like us. They just don't pay us much mind."

"They don't know what they're missing, Harold."

"Thank you, Miss Cotter."

With that, he was gone. A mince and scurry and he was at his car. Kathleen watched him go. Michael Crawford watched her watch.

"I'm sorry that wasn't much help." Michael was already sitting down, leaning back on his elbow again. Kathleen's legs were cramped. She stood a few seconds longer before joining him on the grass.

"Not at all. It was very helpful to meet him. I think you can tell a lot about people from the company they keep." Kathleen finally picked up the beer and popped the top Michael had put back on. She took a sip, thinking while her tastebuds adjusted to the cold, bitter taste. "Lionel sounds very nice. Accommodating. Worried more about other people than himself. He was either one in a million or he was on drugs and that's why he was always on an even keel."

"Maybe, but I doubt it. It's hard to hide something like a habit. Especially heroin. It can be done, but it takes someone extremely controlled."

"You sound like you know something about it."

"Something." Michael crumpled the pretzel pack and cleaned up the chicken bones. Kathleen handed him the napkin she'd been using. "Have you talked to his wife?"

"Same story from her. Lionel was this perfect guy, content in his own little world. But even she confirmed he was upset about something. She didn't give me any indication that it was anything earth-shattering. Did you get that impression from Harold?"

"Nope. It just sounded like Lionel had something to take care of. He was playing it close to the vest and that all seems very mysterious, but it sure didn't affect his performance. If the problem drove him to suicide, I'd assume someone would have seen some majorly out-of-character behavior. I'd say whatever had his feathers ruffled was in the context of normal, everyday living. No big problem there."

"Shows what you know." Kathleen nibbled on her last pretzel. "Any good attorney can take a molehill and build a mountain faster than you can say 'I object.' And the insurance company's attorney is pretty good." Kathleen chuckled and waited for Michael to politely speculate that she could probably give as good as she got. He didn't. She stopped laughing and cleared her throat. "Look, I appreciate your going to all this trouble. I didn't expect you to get quite so involved. I know it's been an imposition."

Michael shook his head. "Not really."

"You don't say much, do you?" Her legs were going to sleep. She recrossed them, put the beer aside, laid the unfinished pretzel on top. Michael took it all and put it into the trash bag; that went into the backpack. They made a great housekeeping team.

"Sorry. It's a failing. I guess I like to watch and figure out what needs to be said, then I say it."

"Smart thing to do, as long as you don't lose your nerve when it comes time to say what you've been thinking."

"I've never lacked for nerve, but I must say I'm pretty darn careful about what I say and whom I say it to." Michael stood up, towering over her. He hoisted the backpack and looked ten feet tall from where she sat. "Do you have to be somewhere right now?"

"No."

"Feel like working anymore?"

"No."

"Good." He held out his hand. She took it. Michael pulled Kathleen up until she was not just upright but close. She still had the flutters, still the ridiculous awareness of the sheen of his hair, the feel of his hand in hers; but now she felt something more, and the more didn't have an adjective to go with it.

He hoisted his bag and held her hand tighter. "There's nothing like the open sea to clear the brain."

"You mean sailing?" Kathleen choked. "I've never seen the ocean before today. I don't know if I'm ready to bob around on it."

"Come on. What's it worth being alive if you do the same thing every day? Come on." He tugged at her hand and grinned. "We'll just go past the breakwater . . . unless you've got something better to do . . . someone waiting for you."

"No. No one waiting, nothing better to do." Kathleen looked at the beautiful boat. She would like to sit on the deck chair, her face turned up to the late-afternoon sun. She'd like to feel something other than the hard, unforgiving ground under her feet. She'd like to spend a minute more with Michael Crawford.

"Okay. Why not?"

"Good. Great." He gave her hand a squeeze, friendly and inviting. Kathleen thought no further than beyond the next minute. Lionel Brooker was forgotten. Louise could leave a zillion messages. Gerry could hold down the fort without her. The day belonged to her and Michael. But they hadn't cleared the grass before they were stopped.

"Mr. Crawford? Miss Cotter?" Harold was back. He was leaning half out the window of his car. Kathleen crossed to the white picket fence that ran the length of the marina and separated it from the parking lot. Michael waited where he was, still close enough to hear. Harold was flushed, perspiration dotting his forehead and the bridge of his nose. The little car lacked air-conditioning. "I remembered something else. I don't know if it's important, but Lionel was wearing a suit on the day he died. He never wore a suit. It was just something I thought was odd. Him wearing a suit. That's all. Just odd.''

His car stuttered. He revved the motor and drove away again without a wave or a second look.

Chapter Nine

It was more beautiful than Kathleen could ever have imagined. The horizon was endless, the sea stitched to the sky with the delicate, invisible thread of some brilliant cosmic seamstress. The blue of the water had changed from robin's egg to the deep navy that can seem black in the endless reaches. Here and there white sails dotted the grand expanse, canvases billowing.

Michael hadn't bothered with his sails. Instead, they cut through the water powered by an unseen and almost silent motor. Their wake was pleasing to the eye, the slight rock and rise of the boat soothing to the soul; and when Michael Crawford cut the engine and sat beside her on the deck, he redefined the meaning of the words *alone together*.

Michael had brought drinks with him. Water, this time, in clear, plastic bottles. He handed her one, the plastic fogged and perspiring with cold. Kathleen took it and held it, not wanting to disturb her perfect posture. She was reclining in the chair, hands crossed at waist level, face tilted toward the sky but at an angle where she could slide her eyes toward him. Her legs were stretched out, her stockings and shoes discarded—privately in the cabin below—to make maneuvering the slick deck easier.

"So, what do you think about the suit-thing?" Michael kept his eyes on the sea, his hands on the steering wheel that guided the craft he had named *Gentle Reminder*.

Kathleen didn't move. Contentment had paralyzed her. Never in her wildest dreams could she have imagined a day quite so perfect. She wouldn't spoil it for anything. "I'm not sure I should think anything about it. Sometimes people feel like dressing up. Or is that just a female-thing?"

"It's been known to happen in our ranks, too." Michael chuckled. Kathleen laughed lazily. He reached down and pulled a lever or pushed a button, the conversation never breaking stride. "It is unusual at a place like Tysco, though. Especially in a department like auditing. We don't do the big meetings. Lionel reported to me. I report to those above me. It's very cut and dry, and I've never required anyone to dress when they meet with me. What's really strange is that he died in another part of the complex. He really had no business being there. That's always bothered me. Who in the heck was he going to see? Now, add the suit and you've really got a mystery."

"Maybe he was dressing up for someone. You know, like a lover. Do you think Lionel Brooker could have been having an affair?"

"That would be a case of still waters running more than deep." Michael laughed, and she knew he was looking at her from behind his black glasses. His gaze lingered, his voice softened. "Besides, he was already dealing with two women. That's more than enough for any man."

"Could he have been interviewing for a position in another division? I mean, can't people move around within Tysco?"

"His wife would have said something. If they were such soul mates, he wouldn't keep plans like that from her."

"Maybe he was in another area so no one would recognize him and ask what he was doing because he truly was an addict." That didn't sound right even to Kathleen, but Michael played along.

"What about the suit, then?"

"True." She licked her lips. They tasted like salt. Her lipstick was long gone. That gave her pause, but Lionel Brooker was a more interesting subject to consider. "Okay, how about this? He dressed up to kill himself. People do that, right? They have some big statement they want to make. So, Lionel got dressed up because he wanted to be found in his Sunday best." Kathleen's fingers drummed on the back of the chair. "But what was his statement? This particular day was important to him. He was going to try to escape some dissatisfaction by taking to drugs and the suit signified the transition . . ."

Michael snorted, but it was an elegant expression of disbelief rather than off-putting. "Never happen. A man doesn't plan to become a junkie like he plans to go out to dinner. It just happens. Lionel had to have tried it once before, then he had to want to do it again. It's not like you can decide to take up drugs the same way you take up smoking. You can't buy heroin at a corner drugstore. He'd go back to whoever turned him on in the first place, buy the stuff, get the syringe, pick a time, worry about being caught."

"Unless he did want to kill himself, then he wouldn't worry about being caught."

"Then he'd be near his normal department. I mean, whose feelings would he be trying to spare by doing it a few floors down? Harold's? Naw, he wouldn't worry that he was dressed right to make a buy if he didn't worry about what he wore to work every day."

"Okay. Bear with me. I'm just throwing things out. If Harold thought the suit was so unusual, then there had to be an unusual reason for wearing it. Obviously nobody bothered to look into what Lionel was trying to say by dressing so out of character. His statement was lost because . . . because . . ." Kathleen searched for the logical conclusion to her argument. Michael stood up and looked out to sea, then back to her.

"You are really something." Michael abandoned his station. Going past her, he settled himself in the middle of a padded bench that did double duty as storage. "Do you always think the best of people?"

Kathleen raised a shoulder. "I suppose. Why not?"

"Because for the most part there is no universal best in people. Most people aren't concerned with what's right or wrong but with what's expedient, easy, and self-serving. You want to know why nobody wondered why Lionel Brooker was dressed to kill—excuse the expression? Nobody cared what kind of statement a man like Lionel Brooker wanted to make. They wanted to push it under the rug. If there had been a note, it probably would have made the six o'clock news. Since there wasn't a statement, his suicide meant nothing.''

"That's pretty cynical,'' Kathleen complained, vexed to find this handsome, rather personable, obviously intelligent man was so mean-spirited, so small-hearted.

"Not at all. That's just the way things are,'' he answered evenly.

"Didn't anyone ever teach you generalizations are dangerous? Don't you know that there's an exception to every rule?'' she shot back, surprised at her own intensity.

"Are you the exception? Would you have thought to wonder why Lionel Brooker was wearing a suit?''

"I might have.'' He rolled his eyes. She sat up straight and leaned forward. "I just might have.''

"And if you had and if you'd found out that Lionel Brooker was making a statement about being so unhappy with his life that he dressed up and purposefully took it, your whole case would be blown right out of the water.'' Michael sat back and the boat bobbed.

"You've forgotten one thing. I'd at least know the truth.'' Kathleen tapped the middle of her hand with one finger.

"But you'd have to find some way around that truth in order to do your job,'' Michael countered. Something had changed. The edge in his voice had sharpened; his words felt dangerous. Kathleen sat up and paid close attention.

"You're assuming I would continue with this case if I knew that to be true.''

"But that's what lawyers do if they find a truth that doesn't suit them. They rearrange it.'' His superior attitude was more infuriating because it was presented with such maddening confidence.

"Boy, you sure know how to ruin a perfectly nice day.'' Kathleen threw up her hands. "You're full of assumptions.

What makes you think that I don't care about the truth or that all lawyers do the most expedient thing? You are an incredibly negative person. Look at the life you live. You have a safe job that pays for this boat. You haven't got a worry in the world, and you don't have to prove yourself. You don't have to make life and death decisions every day. You live in a safe little cocoon between your office and this boat. You have nothing to be afraid of, but maybe Lionel Brooker did.''

A speedboat passed. The swell it created caused the boat to tip. Kathleen slid forward in her chair, and Michael Crawford moved quickly. He put his hands on her shoulders, holding her so she didn't end up sprawled at his feet. He looked into her eyes, and she could just see his through the smoky lenses of his glasses. When he spoke, his voice was low and flat.

''I'm not cynical, I'm realistic. I'm not afraid, I'm cautious. And there are other forums besides the public one in which you operate.'' He set her back on her chair, bent over, let his elbows rest on his knees, and took off his sunglasses.

His eyes were beautiful, but they had no depth. They were hard and honest, and Kathleen knew she had made a big mistake in challenging him. She waited for him to speak, but he had changed his mind. He put his glasses on and went back to the wheel. The engine came to life. Michael threw the wheel. The boat responded, kicking up a question mark of a wake as it headed to shore.

Kathleen was alone, looking back at the horizon toward which they had been headed. She didn't want to go back to shore, back to her apartment, or back to the office. She stood up and then found herself beside Michael Crawford.

''I'm sorry. That wasn't very nice of me. I shouldn't make assumptions.'' Silence. A sigh. She tried again. ''When I came here, I assumed that my uncle was still the handsome, successful attorney he'd been when I was a kid. I was angry when I found out he wasn't. I guess I made assumptions about you, too. I don't know which—if not all—are wrong, but I'd like you to set me straight. When I meet the real Michael Crawford, then I'll apologize to him.'' Kathleen waited a beat and added, ''If it would be appropriate." Another beat. "Is that fair?" A gull cried. Kathleen asked, "Michael?"

He started talking when they passed the breakwater. It took twenty minutes to maneuver the boat back to its slip. In that time she found out that Michael was an army brat. Ten schools by the time he was fifteen. High school in Germany. He loved Germany. He loved the chance to learn and do anything new. The world was just full of opportunities no one took advantage of. His father was a desk jockey, his mother a housewife. His parents had an extraordinary marriage, especially considering they were a military couple. There had been a brother, Michael's twin. His name was Charlie and he'd been killed in Vietnam.

Kathleen helped secure the boat while Michael analyzed the differences between his brother and himself. Charlie had been more outgoing and adventurous, Michael more intellectual. Michael was a thinker who sought out experiences, Charlie had taken them as they came. Charlie was a ladies' man; Michael liked a commitment. He had been engaged once but never married. He couldn't really explain why. Perhaps they hadn't been right for one another; perhaps he had waited too long and analyzed the situation too fully. Marriage was an important step, but maybe he should have tried it out instead of letting it die on the examining table. He wanted it to last forever. His caution, perhaps, made his intended feel like the courtship would last forever. He couldn't blame her. There was also the risk factor. His posting in Vietnam with the Special Forces wasn't idyllic. Even Kathleen understood the implication of that piece of news. Michael Crawford was the best of the best, the most courageous of men in America, a man of impeccable credentials. And she, a woman from the desert who had lived her whole mundane life on the cautious edge, had accused him of taking the easy way out.

Michael stopped long enough to let her get back into her shoes and stockings before he leaped onto the dock and held his arms out for her. She went into them without a second thought and, in a movie-moment, the sun seared red and gold as it sank behind the horizon before he put her down. They walked toward the marina and a small Mexican restaurant where they found cold margaritas, hot salsa, and a back booth.

"My parents are still living. They're retired in Palm Springs."

"I spent my life in Banning, not too far from there," Kathleen said.

"I know where it is." Michael nodded and had the decency not to comment further.

"Do you see them often?" Kathleen asked.

"I confess to being the perfect son. I see them as often as their schedule allows. They're pretty active. I think the happiest day of my dad's life was retiring from the service."

"What about you? I would have thought that the service for someone in the Special Forces would be an ideal life." Kathleen rested her arms on the open menu. The waitress had been over twice and had finally figured out they probably wouldn't be ordering any time soon.

"I really loved the military. I went in with my eyes open and I served well, but I was ready for something different. I wanted to live like the rest of the world. Heck, maybe I just wanted to see how I looked with longer hair." Michael shook his head back like a fashion model and Kathleen laughed.

"Fine."

"What?"

"You look fine with longer hair. More than fine." Kathleen took a chip and too much salsa. Thankfully the spice brought tears to her eyes. When she looked back, she couldn't see him clearly. It would have been awful to have found her compliment wasn't welcome.

"Thanks." There was a scarlet tinge to his skin that could have been a trick of the light or a blush of pleasure. "Anyway, Tysco was there waiting in the wings. I was snapped up and put in the computerized weaponry division, international contracts. My business card was pretty neat." He chuckled and she knew it was at himself for being so impressed by something like that. Kathleen looked at the table. They shared a failing. She hadn't thought he ever failed.

"I bet you wore a suit and everything."

"Very astute." Michael dipped into the salsa, but it dripped back, his chip forgotten, as he continued. "I was on that fast track, Kathleen. I was interfacing with the military, making huge bucks—"

"The boat?"

He put the chip aside and raised his salt-encrusted glass to toast the lady.

"You think an auditor could manage that?" Michael grinned, but there was a sadness in his hindsight. "Anyway, I found out I had been signing contracts that weren't viable. The products that were being delivered weren't up to contractual specs. Tysco was cutting corners and what they were shipping was dangerous. I went through channels. I protested. I did my homework and wrote extensive reports, then I was patted on the back and told not to make waves."

"So, what did you do?"

"I blew the whistle." The pride in his voice was shaded with regret. "I went to the military, explained the situation to men I thought would understand the danger. They didn't. Those men were bureaucrats. They said they would look into the problems. For all I know, they did. But that's where their interest stopped. The men on the line, those guys like me, weren't in a position to do anything about it. The equipment being shipped was substandard. They might be killed by it or because of it, but they couldn't do anything to stop the corner-cutting." Michael took a long drink, stabbed a new chip into the salsa, and ate the whole thing. "I went to the press, but Tysco had a great PR machine." He shook his head. "Poor Lionel if he went the same route. I wish he'd asked me before he did anything." There was no pain when he looked back at her. He'd dealt with that long ago. "Anyway, the stories were buried. Nothing ever happened except that I'd rammed my head into a brick wall. It was almost terminal."

"I can't believe they didn't fire you." Kathleen was all ears and disbelief.

"You're the lawyer. Think I would have had a great discrimination case? That would have gotten a heck of a lot more press than what Tysco is really doing.''

The waitress was back. This time she wasn't leaving without an order. Kathleen looked at the menu, ordered a burrito. Michael did the same. Anxiously, she leaned close.

''So they kept you on and—''

''And made life miserable for me ever since.'' Michael munched another chip, taking his time with a story that had obviously been long lived. ''That was three years ago. In that time they have transferred me four times. Finally, I ended up in auditing. In the very unglamorous world of defense work, heading up the auditing division is about as bad as you can get. They took their time, but finally they put me in my place.''

''Lord, Michael, what on earth are you still doing there? How can you exist in a situation like this? How can you work for people like that?''

''How can I not?'' he said evenly, without a hint of the martyr. ''Every day I walk the halls of Tysco, I am a reminder of their failings. They know what's in my head. They know they're the ones between a moral rock and a hard place. They've done the worst they can do. I still exist; so does the problem. Even if I never see the men who called themselves my peers, the ones who gave me not only the opportunity to do my work but the responsibility to do it well—they know I am still around. I'm a watchdog that no one bothers to feed.'' Michael laughed, pushed the chips away, and sat back. He eyed Kathleen casually. The outrage had flared then burned itself off like good cooking wine, leaving behind the essence of itself. Few knew of his situation. Fewer still agreed with it, thinking his life wasted in a vain attempt to take a stand that would never accomplish much. Now he'd laid the problem in front of Kathleen Cotter, a woman he barely knew. Now he would know a little more. ''So, what do you think?''

She didn't hesitate. ''I think you're a very unusual man.''

''A stupid man?'' he asked.

''A brave man,'' she said.

Michael smiled. It was enough. All he'd ever needed to hear. ''I appreciate that. Unfortunately, this brave man is in no position to really help you. I'm a nobody in a place that only reacts when you're somebody. I can't even get Lionel's old supervisor to call me back. The guy seems to spend more time out of the office than he does in."

"That's okay. I have a feeling that if you're determined to get in touch with him that's exactly what you're going to do."

"And when I do?" Michael asked, one finger trailing her hand lightly. "Do you think you might be available to discuss it over dinner?"

"Just let me know when," she answered, knowing she'd discuss physics sitting inside a cave at high tide with Michael Crawford.

Chapter Ten

"Ladies and gentlemen, the evidence put before you today may seem minimal, but I assure you it is not. It is powerful in its simplicity. There were no signs to warn my client she had wandered into a loading zone . . . my client who, I might add, is eighty-eight years old and unable to rush even if the devil himself were after her."

Kathleen looked over her shoulder at Henrietta Poole, who was appropriately turned out in a subdued, gray suit and white gloves. She sat primly in the very, very big wheelchair she had rented for the occasion. Henrietta believed it would make her look smaller and more vulnerable. *All the world is a stage,* she had intoned gleefully to Kathleen when she'd arrived in the monstrosity. Kathleen let her gaze linger just long enough. She was finally getting the hang of this jury-thing thanks to Gerry's tutelage and her own blossoming talent. She raised her arms wide.

"There were huge rolls of carpet all around her. To anyone, it would seem like an extension of the showroom. She was thinking about what color would look best in her home when, out of nowhere, a roll was flung in her direction by two men. As you heard from their own testimony, through the court's interpreter, they didn't look where they were throwing the bolt, they didn't call out in warning. The salesman on the showroom floor had stepped out for coffee because, as he testified, he assumed his client would soon realize she could not afford anything in the establishment.

"Well, of course that shouldn't even be a consideration when it comes to providing service, or simply being chivalrous to a woman of her years." Kathleen clucked as if they were all good friends who were chatting about the matter over tea. She dared to put her hand on the railing that separated her from the jury. The woman closest to her smiled. Kathleen smiled back. She bet the lady had a daughter just her age, unmarried no doubt. She'd seen enough of those smiles to know. "So, what I'd like to do today is to ask you to find in favor of my client, a woman who was doing nothing more than browsing in a public place when she was struck by six hundred pounds of nylon plush in pony beige. Think of your own mothers and grandmothers. Think of their welfare and send a clear message to those who serve the public that the public's safety should be first and foremost in their mind. I ask that you award my client not only her medical fees but also punitive damages for pain and suffering in the amount of $50,000. I ask that you make your decision today so that Henrietta—" Kathleen's beautiful eyes rested briefly but affectionately on her client. "—when she is lifted out of her wheelchair tonight, may rest easy knowing that, at least for now, her future is secure. Thank you."

Another touch. Another smile, this time to a man in the third row, who gave his shyly and then looked at the judge.

Kathleen returned to her seat and offered a pat on the hand to Henrietta, who, in turn, gave her a surreptitious wink. A satisfied client was a lovely thing. If only Louise Brooker could be equally amenable. Kathleen folded her hands and listened as the judge gave her instructions to the jury. The points of law were tedious and there was nothing in the instruction that would obstruct the verdict Kathleen hoped for. The fee would be wonderful; Henrietta would be satisfied, and Michael Crawford would be calling one day soon. Life couldn't get much better.

Instructions over, there was a bit of a flurry as those in the courtroom rose and left through different doors—the jury through the one on the side, preceded by the bailiff; the judge through one cut into the paneling, her chambers hidden behind; and Henrietta out the back with Kathleen following. Kathleen was past the third bench when her step slowed. She didn't stop, but it took all her self-control to walk through the door behind Henrietta and not turn to look behind.

"I'm going to the coffee shop, Kathleen. Would you like to come? I'll buy even though we don't know if I've won my case." Henrietta winked. It was a charming invitation, as always, but Kathleen declined.

"Thanks, no. I'll wait out here for a bit just in case I've been so smooth the jury comes back in five minutes."

"If they do, give me a holler. The way the elevators work around here, it will take that long for one to call up. Come along."

Henrietta tapped the mute Bo with her gloved fingers and they were off. Kathleen looked about. The hall was empty, which was not surprising since spectators had been few and it was close to three. Kathleen waited, counting the seconds as they ticked by. She'd give herself five more before she went back into the courtroom, but she only needed three to be sure she had seen whom she thought she'd seen. He came through the swinging door and looked directly at her as if he expected her to be there. The man never wasted a movement, or a thought, she was sure. What she couldn't fathom was what had brought Richard Jacobsen to the very courtroom where she was arguing a minor personal injury case. Whatever it was, she didn't care. Kathleen stepped into the opportunity, heart pounding, wishing she had had time to redo her lipstick.

"Mr. Jacobsen, I thought that was you." Kathleen smiled and held out her hand. Lord, it felt damp. He took it without comment and shook it without verve. His smile seemed faded under the fluorescent lights, but his eyes were sharp and on her.

"It's delightful to see you in action, Ms. Cotter. You have quite a way with the jury."

Richard Jacobsen had somehow managed to back her into a corner between the wall and a concrete bench. Kathleen felt too tall, too big for the space, and suddenly Richard Jacobsen looked properly proportioned, almost graceful.

"Thank you. I'm honored you stayed to watch."

Kathleen's fingers suddenly ached. She'd been clutching her briefcase tight. She loosened her fingers. The word relax flashed in her mind. Richard Jacobsen was only another lawyer, after all. A man. A rich man. A well-known and powerful man. Her fingers tightened again. He'd stayed to see her perform. She felt sick. She smiled anyway. Even her dead mother's ghost rising from the grave wouldn't distract her from what she was about.

"Actually, I'd expected to meet a colleague, but it seems I had the wrong information regarding his whereabouts." Richard held out his small hands, fingers pointed toward her as if she could put the right information in them. Would that she could. "But if you have to be somewhere else, Ms. Cotter, I shouldn't keep you."

"Not at all. I'm delight—" Kathleen paused and cleared her throat. Her voice had risen an excited octave. She lowered it, rotating her neck as if she could twist out the knot of nervousness that had made itself at home. "—delighted to run into you. I should have written you a note. I enjoyed our talk in your office very much. I wanted to thank you." She sounded like an advertisement. Her smile broadened and she tried desperately not to try too hard. Richard Jacobsen wouldn't stand for anything so crass as groveling. "You were very kind to spend so much time with me."

"Not at all. It was truly my pleasure." He moved and Kathleen followed. The sign of a true leader is that he moves the troops without a word or a look. He led her out of the corner and in front of the bench. "I've actually been thinking about you." Kathleen almost fell off her pumps. "That's why, when I realized it was you arguing, I thought I might stop and watch. It's always good to see both sides of someone who has left an impression. The professional and the personal. You liked my artwork, that was enough to give you an A on the personal front.''

"And professionally?" Kathleen asked.

"You did very well. But I must confess, I was hoping I would find you working on Mrs. Brooker's case. It sounded terribly interesting. Truly unique."

Kathleen laughed uneasily. He hadn't been impressed enough. He wanted to see her tackle something more intricate than Henrietta's hip.

"We're on Judge Kelley's calendar. I could call you."

"No, no. As delightful as that would be, I think I've seen what I need to see." He began to walk again, with short thoughtful steps. Kathleen kept pace, hoping he didn't hear the disappointing thump of her heart. There must be something she could do to keep his interest.

"When do you expect to wrap up your work with Mrs. Brooker?"

"Six weeks," Kathleen blurted out.

"Do you feel confident, Ms. Cotter? Do you believe you'll triumph over the insurance company, big as it is? I've known Bob Morton for years. Do you think you can best him?"

Kathleen stopped. This time he followed suit. "Yes, Mr. Jacobsen, I think I will. I believe I can prove that Lionel Brooker wasn't suicidal. I think, given time, I could probably prove that Mr. Brooker wasn't even a drug addict. The more I hear of him, the more convinced I become that there is some mystery to his death."

Richard Jacobsen's face changed. He was every skeptical teacher Kathleen had ever had.

"And now you'll become an investigator, not an attorney? That would be such a loss to our profession."

Kathleen laughed uneasily. She'd never been able to please her teachers. "No. That's not in my future. I'm just hoping to get All Life to consider a settlement."

Richard tried to laugh. Kathleen thought he needed more practice. "A challenge, to say the least. Attempting to prove more than his state of mind, to prove there was no intent to take his life at the moment of his death, is a unique and risky road.''

Kathleen couldn't believe he'd been listening so carefully during the few minutes they had had together in his office. She was flattered beyond words.

"Would you quit? Would you pursue this course?''

He looked at her hard, and his face changed again. Though unattractive, he suddenly seemed ugly; quiet, he suddenly seemed eerily silent. Finally, he spoke.

"I wouldn't presume, Ms. Cotter, to advise you on any matter while you work with O'Doul & Associates.''

"Of course not, forgive me. That was very forward of me. I apologize.''

Richard reached out and took Kathleen's free hand. He held it between his palms.

"Unless, of course, you don't feel that Gerry is on top of this. If that's the case, then, of course, I'd be willing to help in any way I could.''

In another moment Kathleen would have thought something was amiss with Richard Jacobsen; but the light changed as they were jostled by the group of wailing women who suddenly came out of Department 36 followed by two bewildered children, and Kathleen realized he had meant only to be helpful.

"I would like it very much if you would call on me to fill in the gaps of the fine education Gerry will give you.''

"Thank you.''

"Goodbye, then.''

"Goodbye. And thank you, Mr. Jacobsen.''

He turned in a fluid motion and Kathleen was forgotten. Or so she thought. He wasn't gone three steps when he came back to her and asked, "Are you happy where you are, Ms. Cotter? Happy with the rather odd problems you're handling at O'Doul & Associates.''

Kathleen didn't breathe when she answered. She did hesitate, though, but for just an instant. For a second, while Gerry's face flashed in front of her mind's eye. It was the face first of young Gerry, then of his old and wizened visage.

"No.''

"I thought not."

Richard Jacobsen left her. She wished she were walking away with him.

Michael had seen him before. They called him Jack. Nobody knew his real name or how long he'd been at Tysco. The best estimate was that he'd worked there for twenty-six years. The best guess on what he did was something in the quality-control section—not hands-on, just paperwork. No one Michael had ever talked to knew where Jack's office was; they had no idea where he lived, and most swore they'd never heard him speak. Jack had fallen through the cracks of the mega-corporate Tysco system. He pulled his pay; he showed up and—if the twenty-six year guestimate of employment was correct—he would be eligible to retire in four years fully vested. Until then, he wandered the halls like a specter, dressed in his corporate camouflage: brown shoes, brown pants, brown tie with a gold-tone 25-years tie clasp and white, short-sleeved shirt. He carted a sheaf of papers with him so that if anyone had the inclination to stop and ask him where he was going or what he was doing he could hold them up as proof he was a necessary cog in the wheel. Michael had thought long and hard about Jack. He shared, after all, a rather sad affinity with the man. But there was one big difference. Michael had no intention of disappearing. He refused to be relegated to the land of the living dead, and Lionel Brooker was the catalyst who propelled him through the halls of Tysco, past Jack, up to the tenth floor of the main building, and into a suite of offices that shared a common reception area and secretary.

"Morning."

Michael smiled at the woman behind the desk. Cute. Late twenties. Sedately dressed. She still had the idea that this was her ticket to a career. Little did she know.

"Good morning." She swiveled on her chair. Michael was reminded of android technology, so smooth was her chair, her delivery, movement, and smile.

"I'm looking for Jules Porter."

"Do you have an appointment?"

"Nope. I've been trying to get one." Michael turned on the charm. A warm smile, a casual leaning toward the desk, a helpless opening of his palms. It didn't work.

"Mr. Porter is scheduled today." Her movements were silk. Porter's calendar was open. "He isn't available until at least three this afternoon. I can pencil you in, but of course, that would be subject to change if Mr. Porter finds himself running over."

Michael had the most marvelous images of Porter as a bathtub, Porter as beer. No doubt he would run over. No one in this place ever did anything with urgency, and efficiency was questionable. Suddenly, Michael had an image of Porter that was three-dimensional when the man himself walked purposefully through the door and into the office that bore his name etched into a brass-toned plate. Michael gave the very efficient lady behind the desk a thumbs up and walked right after the man. The lady at the desk protested briefly but was apparently terribly attached to her chair. She didn't try to follow.

"Jules Porter," Michael said heartily, hand out. The other man took it. A natural reflex from olden days when knights protected themselves by extending their lances. Today it was their hands. Keep the opponent at arm's length until you can figure out who he is and what he wants. "Michael Crawford. I inherited your old desk over in 42B. You've come up in the world."

"Yes. Yes." Porter extricated himself; the half smile faded. Michael was under him in the pecking order. "What can I do for you?"

"I was hoping you'd have a minute." Michael slid into a chair. It was nicer than any they had in auditing, and his people sat all day. He'd have to do something to rectify that situation. "I've been trying to get you for a couple of days now, and I understand how busy you guys can be, running the company and all."

Michael smiled amiably. Porter appeared perplexed or tired. He was definitely cranky and off his game.

"I'm afraid I'm still very busy. You should make an appointment with Miss Hutchinson, though, I must say, I don't have time to help you with anything at the moment. I would suggest you go through channels. If you're having difficulty with the department, there are procedures outlined in the handbook. If it is something that I initialed, you can send it interoffice. I'll get back to you when I can.''

Jules Porter dismissed Michael easily. Michael ignored him graciously.

"Well, look, this problem really doesn't have a solution in the handbook and it sure as heck doesn't have anyone's initials on it. It's sort of a personnel problem.''

Jules Porter removed his Italian jacket, took a black-and-gold Mont Blanc pen from his pocket, and sat down in his standard-issue, Tysco executive chair. Instead of giving Michael his attention, he opened the dark-brown portfolio he had carried into the office and concentrated on his papers. His dark head was down so that Michael could see the meticulous part. Moments later, Jules Porter was looking at Michael Crawford's large hand as it covered the multiple-columned financial report. Porter looked up. Crawford was ready for him. He smiled. Porter did not.

"Look. I know who you are. You're a troublemaker and I don't want any trouble.''

"Then give me a few minutes of your time, Mr. Porter, and I promise not to make waves.''

Porter considered this, then made an executive decision. He sat back. Michael closed the portfolio and put it aside, patting it into place like a father putting away a slow child's toys.

"Jules. I may call you Jules?''

Silence in the war of types. Porter despised men like Michael Crawford—those who hadn't the courtesy to dress right, speak when spoken to, offer only the kind of creative ideas that would please those on the next rung. But he also feared men like Michael Crawford because you just never knew what quirk of fate would put them on that rung above you.

"Well, Jules, I have a question about a man who used to work for you—and me, for a few weeks. I assume you'll remember him. He had a long history with the company. A history as long as yours. But he's not in a nice office like this. He died in the john, on the second floor, quite a ways away from auditing. Apparently he killed himself. A suicide in our hallowed halls.''

Porter turned his head away. He looked pale. Some people lost all blood pressure when they were angry. Some when they were guilty. Some because they were simply the sensitive type.

"Can we get on with this?"

"You're right. This has got to be tough for you. It must be difficult to speak about someone you must have been close to.'' The sarcasm wasn't lost on Jules Porter. He moved in his chair, trying to rearrange the coals in his belly that fed some emotion at Michael's impertinence.

"Who told you we were close?" Jules demanded, his head whipping back Michael's way. "I want to know who told you. It's a lie.''

"It was just an assumption," Michael said, curious about such an emphatic reaction but not willing to let Jules Porter know that. "I figured since you'd worked with the guy for almost ten years you probably took some kind of personal interest.''

"I knew him. Lionel Brooker. He was a troublemaker, too," Porter grumbled.

"I didn't find that to be the case. He seemed quiet and efficient. But then, I imagine we would have differing views on things.'' Michael settled into his chair. He crossed his long legs. "I'm just interested in the facts of his employment during the time you were his supervisor. I've talked to others who worked with Lionel, and their impression was that he cared a great deal about his work and his job here.''

"The man didn't know when to quit. That's all I can tell you. He was not efficient. He was a nitpicker. He thought he knew how the whole place worked. He took everything very personally. This is a business, Mr. Crawford, a big business.'' Porter found at least one of his balls and leaned forward in his junior-executive mode. "People like you and Lionel Brooker think a conglomerate like Tysco can be run like a corner grocery where you give credit to the widow who needs some bread.

But we don't deal in bread. We deal in products that make the world work. There's pressure here. No one expects the world to be perfect or the structure in which our goods are manufactured to be impeccable. We all simply try to manage the beast; and if you try to micromanage it or give it a name and a personality, then you sacrifice efficiency.''

"What about someone's life? Someone who might have been so upset about what happened inside these walls that he took his own life or tried to forget his worries with drugs.''

Jules Porter stiffened. He looked sick.

"That is only one person and he was obviously unbalanced. There are over twelve thousand who work here. You don't see all of them committing suicide, now, do you?''

"I'm not sure that Lionel Brooker did. I think he might just have been looking for a little peace. With your kind of attitude, I might have tried a little junk myself.''

"Don't get personal, Mr. Crawford. Bad things happen to people who get too personal.''

"That sounds oddly threatening,'' Michael drawled. "But don't worry. I have no intention of trying to, Mr. Porter. I believe it would be next to impossible to get personal with you.'' Michael stood up. He was itchy. Only something physical would relieve his discomfort and he didn't want to do anything he'd regret. Not that he'd regret popping Jules Porter all that much. "What was Lionel Brooker up to just before he died? Anything you were aware of? Think carefully before you answer, because I have to answer to a lawyer who is looking into Lionel Brooker's death. If she doesn't like what I tell her, you might just end up on the other end of her subpoena. And you know how much time that would take out of your busy day.''

"Have you checked with legal on this?'' Jules Porter demanded, still under the false impression that anything he said would make an impression on Michael.

Michael spread his hands on Porter's pristine desk and got up close and personal.

"Fuck legal,'' he whispered.

Porter thought about that, then began to talk.

Michael thanked him when he left, but it was Jules Porter who had the last word.

"You know, nobody really cares about you anymore. You and your stupid stand. You know that, don't you?"

Michael kept walking. One of these days, he would return the knife Jules Porter had just put in his back.

"Hello, hello! Becky, the next burrito is on me. What a day! The jury came back in an hour and a half and gave Henrietta five thousand more than we asked for. She was ecstatic."

Kathleen closed the door behind her and tossed her briefcase onto one of the reception chairs. She was just about ready to sink into another one. Becky stopped her without ever looking up from her typing. The in-box was always full now, and Becky was on five days a week.

"Don't even think about it. Gerry's waiting. He's got company."

"New client?" Kathleen righted herself.

Becky shrugged.

"Haven't a clue." She stopped typing long enough to open her top drawer. "I hope he's got terrible problems. I wouldn't mind seeing him every day or more. Cookie?" She held up something white with dark chocolate and a green-icing dome. Kathleen made a face and picked up her briefcase.

"Then I better give my hair a brush and get to it." She was in and out of her office in record time. She rounded Becky's desk, knocking on wood. "Remind me to tell you what else happened." Her hand was on the doorknob. "What's this guy's name?"

"Michael Crawford." Becky sighed. The cookie disappeared at the same time Kathleen did.

"Kathleen," Gerry admonished, "You didn't tell me Michael was such a delightful young man. I think she wanted to keep you all to herself." He winked to show his pleasure, then stage-whispered. "Worried that I'll become too stimulated with all the changes around here, but this ticker is just fine. Sure, though, I don't know what I'd do without my Kathleen around here.''

Kathleen refrained from rolling her eyes. She'd caught on. Gerry was about as much an invalid as she was. He had her number and dialed it often, but Kathleen knew she was just about on the verge of making it unlisted. She grinned at him, nonetheless, and then improved on it when she took Michael's hand. She talked to Gerry; she looked at Michael.

''It was hard to describe Mr. Crawford. I wouldn't have wanted to do him an injustice.'' Kathleen settled herself. Michael half stood, put his hand on the back of her chair, and said hello.

''Isn't that just like you?'' Gerry chuckled. ''Mr. Crawford, indeed. After all the wonderful things he had to say about you, I would have thought you were on a first-name basis.''

Kathleen shifted. The twinkle in his eye was downright embarrassing, the interest in Michael's completely welcome.

''We've spent some time together. But it was purely professional.'' Kathleen was flirting, and it felt great.

''Yes, yes, yes.'' Gerry nodded, with a wink at Michael. ''A sail on the sea is always a good way to depose someone. Did I ever tell you I tried my hand at boating, Kathleen? Michael, perhaps I could impose one day . . .''

''It would be a pleasure, Gerry.''

''All right,'' Kathleen interjected. ''I give up. You two have obviously been at this for a while. I can't imagine you came all this way to tell my uncle what a great guest I was on your boat.''

''You're right, of course.'' Gerry still smiled, but Kathleen, now used to the signs, understood they had done more than talk about the boat. ''Niceties aside, I'm afraid Michael does have some news that's very interesting, Kathleen. In fact, it might create a bit of a problem when you argue for Louise.''

Kathleen's butterflies that had batted about in honor of Michael Crawford's pheromones now took a different, more ominous turn. She unfocused on his eyes, his hair, his lips and focused on what was coming out of them. She sat down, noting he checked out the lay of her legs as she crossed them. His interest lasted a second more, then he looked up at her.

"I finally spoke with Lionel's previous supervisor. Jules Porter, by name. He toes the company line like ninety-nine percent of Tysco employees, but this guy believes the chapter and verse. He was wired tight. I'm beginning to think Lionel was either crazy or a saint to work in a department headed by that guy. Ten years, no less." Michael shook his head as if Lionel's feat were more heroic than his own.

"What did he say?"

"Lionel was upset specifically with Porter. Seems that Lionel had received an interdepartmental envelope that had been misdirected. Instead of repackaging it and sending it on, Lionel took a really good look." Michael spoke to Gerry. "Lionel was one of those very smart guys. Almost a photographic memory. He took one look and the numbers were analyzed instantly." His head swiveled again. Kathleen was all ears and motion. She'd taken a pad of paper from Gerry's desk to jot notes. "So, he didn't send it on because he had instantly determined that the information didn't add up. He took a closer look, then brought it to Porter. Porter took one look at the departmental designation and told Lionel to get back to work and not waste his time. It wasn't any of their business."

"Wouldn't that kind of support make you want to do your best for the company?" Gerry mumbled.

"Incredible incentive," Kathleen agreed wryly.

"The whole thing seemed incredibly urgent to Lionel, but Porter didn't want to be bothered. He had his agenda; Lionel was asking him to deviate. And it wasn't just the time that concerned Porter. Believe me, I talked to him long enough today to figure him out. He's a guy who chalks up ten percent of product to loss. If there were a discrepancy in the billing, he'd rather see it go through the system than rectify it."

"Just gives you a lot of faith in the people who are making our bombs, doesn't it?" Kathleen muttered.

"They make toilet paper, too." Michael chuckled. "I suppose, in a way, Porter has a point. I mean, what do we care about the paperwork as long as the damn things don't explode before they get where they're going?''

"So." Gerry pushed them along. "Lionel was very unhappy with what he'd found and received no satisfaction from his supervisor when he tried to rectify the matter. How long was it before Mr. Porter left the department and you came in?"

"About three weeks, maybe a month. Lionel had discovered the problem at least a month earlier. Porter says he lost track of the whole mess. He couldn't even remember the specifics. A guy like him wouldn't have remembered what Lionel looked like the day after they talked."

"And Lionel never brought it up to you?"

Michael raised a hand and rested his chin on it. "Nope. He never approached me about anything. Not that I can blame him. If one guy tells you it doesn't matter, why would you think the next one to take the chair would think any differently? Even if he went over Porter's head, he probably got the same reaction. Remember, Lionel had been there ten years. He knew what was what."

"But whatever he saw made him—angry enough to try to buck the system? Do you think he was angry?"

"I don't know. Porter wasn't great with adjectives. Basically, he said Lionel was a pain in the ass."

"I'm sorry to hear that." Kathleen tapped her pen on the pad of paper. Her notes consisted of circles in which she'd written *Porter* and *Brooker*. "Well, what do you think we've got with this bit of information?"

"I think you have a problem with your theory, Kathleen. If Michael's Mr. Porter is called to testify and gives the same impression to a jury that he has given to Michael, that jury might see justification for Lionel's taking his own life."

"Because he was dissuaded from bringing up a billing discrepancy?" Kathleen scoffed. "I don't think so."

"Because his job might have been jeopardized," Michael filled in and Gerry nodded in agreement, beaming at the younger man.

"I see. What you're saying is, with a supervisor like Porter, Lionel might have felt threatened."

"Exactly," Gerry agreed, opening his hands in a papal and inclusive gesture to show his delight. "That's a powerful motive for suicide. Look at what you know about Lionel."

Kathleen ticked off the list. "He was conscientious."

"Not a good thing in a corporate structure like Tysco unless it is to work only within designated guidelines," Michael offered.

"He was spiritual, gentle."

"Could be interpreted as high strung, delusional." Gerry added his two cents.

"He was honorable."

Both men thought for a moment, and it was Michael who commented.

"Might be viewed as a man with a conservative complex. Sort of a born-again type. His version of right was the only one."

"And therefore, Lionel would be highly distressed if he felt the entire twelve thousand employees of Tysco thought nothing of the problems he'd found," Gerry added.

"He had a goal. To own a farm and live a quiet life with his wife," Kathleen offered.

Michael countered. "He believed his dream wouldn't be attainable if he lost his job."

"He was consistent, a ten-year work-record," Kathleen shot back, hoping to salvage some positive shred of evidence.

"He was unemployable elsewhere," Gerry pointed out. "Paranoid and afraid to leave, but feeling himself above the rabble at Tysco. He was between a rock and a hard place. Many would become homicidal in that instance. Look at the postal workers. Gentle, mystical Lionel possibly became suicidal."

Gerry ended with a flourish, the old skill still intact. If Kathleen had been on a jury, she would have bought into the argument that rather than a gentle, caring soul, Lionel Brooker was a paranoid rascal with a personal agenda that was designed to set himself above and apart from a system that was well-respected throughout the world.

"Oh, Lord." Kathleen sighed. Defeat made itself comfortable in her lap. It was a heavy child.

"Kathleen," Gerry tsked. He let his head hang as he stood

up and came round his desk. Leaning against it, he raised his hand. For a moment Kathleen thought he was going to pat her head the way he used to when she was small. But he let his hand fall, along with the tenor of his voice. "Are you going to give up so easily, my girl?"

"I don't know what else to do."

"Why not ask yourself the question you'd ask the jury?"

Kathleen raised her eyes, but not her head. Michael was sitting quietly, watching Gerry intently. There was a deeply thoughtful look on his face—almost too personal.

"What question?"

Gerry let his eyes linger on Kathleen an instant longer before looking over his shoulder at Michael.

"Why would they believe that about Lionel?" He looked back to Kathleen. "Aren't they good people themselves? People who understand that honor and truth and empathy are the most valuable qualities in the world. Aren't they people who have been mistreated by employers, companies, and associations, too? Aren't they folks who have been misunderstood because of their very pure motives? How many times have words been put in their mouths and their efforts to do the right thing been foiled?" Gerry pushed himself off the desk and stepped around Kathleen so that his hands were on the back of her chair. With him came an energy that pulled Kathleen up straight as if he were tugging at her puppet strings. He leaned close but spoke in a voice that commanded attention. "Make it personal, Kathleen. Point to the lovely widow Sarah—if she'll come to the proceedings as proof that Lionel was a good and loving man. Find out how he lived. Did he pay his bills on time? He was saving for a farm, for goodness sake! The great American dream. Put Mr. Douglas on the stand. Paint them a picture of *your* Lionel, Kathleen. The Lionel you believe existed and Sarah believes existed and even Louise believes existed."

"Yes, that's exactly what I need to do. That will work, won't it?" Kathleen sat forward in her chair and asked the question first of Michael, then of Gerry.

"Who knows?" Gerry laughed, and Kathleen's face fell. Reaching out, he touched her chin, lifted it up, and spoke only to her. "But if you believe, then you'll be able to convince them. Everything is in that heart of yours, Kathleen. When you translate that and speak it loud and clear, there's every chance you'll win."

Kathleen covered his hand with hers, sure he was right. Then he dropped his hand and Kathleen looked at Michael, and the hole in her heartfelt confidence opened a bit. There was always a chance that she'd speak her heart and mind and lose. It happened to good people like him. She just didn't want it to happen to her. Not now, not when someone like Richard Jacobsen was watching and someone like Lionel Brooker was waiting for vindication.

"If it helps—" Michael leaned over and touched her shoulder. Kathleen came out of her reverie, putting away her ridiculous thoughts. She could be in worse company if she lost.

"What?"

"If it helps, I went through Lionel's records. He was a whiz when it came to his records. There wasn't anything out of the ordinary. If he'd been upset, I imagine he got over it and sent the docket back where it belonged. I'm no lawyer, but I'd imagine without the documents it's your word against Jules Porter's about how upset Lionel was."

"Guess I'll have to have a talk with Mr. Porter, huh?"

"It'll be tough. I don't think he's at his desk longer than fifteen minutes at a time."

"Then I'll go where he is. Think you could arrange that?"

"No, I don't think I was Mr. Porter's favorite visitor, but I could sneak you up to his office and let you see how far you can get on your own. It will have to wait until tomorrow." Michael stood up and put his hand out to Gerry. When the old man took it, Michael covered it with his other hand and moved closer. "Gerry. It's been a pleasure. If I come back for Kathleen at five-thirty, do you think the day's work will be done? She promised me if I delivered I could take her to dinner."

"You don't need my permission." Gerry beamed. "But if you can't convince her, then I'll step in. I'll order her to go as my associate."

"You'd better watch what you promise, Gerry," Kathleen

said, standing shoulder to shoulder with Michael. "It seems I have another professional admirer, and if you don't treat me right, I'll just have to pay a little more attention to him."

"Oh, ho." Gerry grinned from ear to ear, still holding onto Michael's hand. "There's competition. I knew it wouldn't be long before the word got out that she was an enterprising young woman." He dropped Michael's hand.

"I hope I don't have the same problem when it comes to her social life."

Michael held out a hand. Kathleen walked into the gesture and they both went to the door.

"I'll see you about five-thirty."

Kathleen followed him out the door.

"Kathleen," Gerry called. She stopped. She turned and held onto the open door. "Just so I know what I'm up against, who is it that's nipping at your heels?"

"Richard Jacobsen. Shay, Sylvester & Harrington, Gerry. He came to watch me in court today. How's that for hitting the big time?"

Kathleen looked at the old man, knowing the minute the words left her mouth that she had meant to wound her uncle. In that instant, she thought she paid him back for the years of silence and the disappointment of finding out life wouldn't be what she'd imagined. She hated herself for it, especially since there was the element of a lie in her story. Richard Jacobsen had made no offer; he had done nothing more than inquire about her status.

"Impressive, Kathleen. Very impressive, indeed." Gerry smiled, but the light in his eyes dimmed. The words were hard for him to get out.

She closed the door gently. Behind her, Gerry whispered to himself.

"Oh, Lord."

"What's your pleasure. Chinese? Japanese? A burger? Johnny Rocket's?" Michael ticked off the list. Kathleen sat beside him, her head leaning against the upturned window, the air-conditioning blowing her hair back from her face. "Are you not hungry or just not listening?"

"Michael, I'm sorry. I am hungry. In fact, I'm really, really hungry." Kathleen scooted around so that she was cradled between the door and the seat. "But I can't eat until I have some answers. Would you be up for a little drive?"

"Mountains, beach, downtown, desert? You name it; I'll head that way."

"You're scary, you know that? You're far too obliging. Don't you have any faults?"

"Stubbornness. If I didn't have that fault, I'd be somewhere else making a ton of money, have a great car and fabulous babes falling all over me instead of sitting in a ten-year-old BMW, sticking my tongue out at Tysco managers who've all but forgotten why they hate me, with a . . ."

". . . thirty-year-old lawyer who doesn't quite know what she's doing and talks like she's been breathing helium?"

"With one fabulous babe," he whispered, laying his arm across the back of the seat, making sure his fingers touched her bare neck. She believed him.

"Thanks for that."

"Thanks for giving me something to care about again. I was digging that rut pretty deep at Tysco. I'm glad you fell into it." Michael touched her hair. He touched her arm. "You're cold. Sorry."

He flipped the switch and the air went from hurricane force to a mechanical version of a breeze. Kathleen crossed her arms and rubbed. Goose bumps marched under her short sleeves, under her bodice, and across her chest. Air-conditioning had nothing to do with her goose bumps.

"Wow," she whispered.

"Yeah. Twelve years on the road and still going strong. I don't know many marriages you can say that about, much less cars." Michael readjusted some of the vents then sat back, satisfied. Kathleen watched him, taking in every nuance of his body, every inflection in his voice, and packaging them away just in case he got tired of chasing around with her. She'd want something to dream about.

"You're a really nice man, Michael."

"And you are a really nice lady. So I think we'll just assume that we will keep exploring how really nice we can be together." He gunned the engine and threw it into gear. The car purred. "But right now, what is it you want to do?"

"I want to see Sarah Brooker. I want to ask her about this problem at work and get her perspective on it. I want to find out how mad Lionel was at Jules Porter. I've got her address. Is it far?" She showed it to him, noticing the gold streaks that shot through his hair when he leaned over to look.

"No problem. I have a general idea where it is. It's the mountains just above Malibu. We'll find it." He sat up. "So. Eat first or drive first?"

"Drive," Kathleen said, and he did. He was already in traffic when Kathleen confided, "I can't do what Gerry wants me to do. I'm not good enough to defend Lionel if I'm not telling the truth. I'm not as good as Gerry thinks I am."

Michael opened his mouth, but changed his mind about what he was going to say. Instead, he covered Kathleen's hand with his own and said, "Let's just talk to Sarah."

Chapter Eleven

By the time Michael turned the car around and headed back through the canyon for the third time to begin at the beginning, Kathleen had come to two conclusions. Southern California was an amazing land of contrasts. She'd been impressed by the difference between Banning and Beverly Hills. Marina del Rey and the ocean were fabulous, West Hollywood was more than colorful, and now this. Up the coast from Santa Monica and inland from the ultra-rich Malibu colony, there were mountains full of brush and canyons that looked like fairy-tale forests.

It was also amazing that, in a state with more than a million people, Sarah Brooker seemed to have lost herself.

"There it is."

Kathleen peered through the Hansel-and-Gretel dark. The sun had set an hour ago. Signs that were difficult to read in the light of day were almost impossible in pitch-black. There were no lights on the road and the few homes that could be seen at all were hidden by trees and bushes, accessible off small tangential roads. Michael turned the car onto a narrow paved road and Kathleen relaxed. Asphalt, the bread crumbs of the modern age.

"There are people in the desert who live like this. Way out, away from everyone. Most of them are crazy.'' The sound of her own voice added another dimension to the comfort of the asphalt.

"You spent time with Sarah Brooker,'' Michael reminded her. "Do you think she's crazy?''

"I wasn't thinking about Sarah. I was worried about breaking down before we find her. I don't want to ask to use the phone at one of these places.'' Kathleen lifted her chin to indicate a house nestled behind a stand of eucalyptus. Three pickups defined the perimeter, two were on blocks. A Confederate flag covered the front window, and an ax leaned leisurely near the front door. They were past it before Michael could look, even if he had had the inclination.

"Keep the map handy, but I think we're just about there. If this is the access road, the Brooker house should be up at the top. Boy,'' he mumbled, focusing on his task, "Lionel must have had to start at five in the morning to get to work on time.''

"Not my idea of fun,'' Kathleen said back before they both fell silent.

The map was open on Kathleen's lap, but she didn't bother to look at it. Her eyes roamed the forest as if it were an alien landscape. It all seemed blacker than black, yet the moon was full and there was enough light to see that there was nothing to see but shadows and shapes and imagined spooks. This was the kind of place where people disappeared. This was the kind of place where hikers happened upon bodies in shallow graves.

"Here we go.''

He slowed, pointing the headlights at a free-standing, bright-blue mailbox. A gray whale had been lovingly painted on the side, its huge mouth opening to gobble up whatever the postman brought.

"This is the place.'' Kathleen laughed quietly. "Lionel drove Louise crazy with his interest in whales.'' The map crackled as she shifted her weight. Sitting straighter, she strained to get a better look at where they were going.

"Doesn't she sound special? I don't think I've ever met anyone who hates whales.'' Michael took his foot off the brake and maneuvered up the long drive, which was really nothing more than a wide clearing through the forest. Michael stretched his right arm. His shoulder popped. "You did tell her we were coming, didn't you?"

Kathleen shook her head. "I was afraid we'd scare her off if I called."

She leaned forward, suddenly anxious. Images of Sarah Brooker came at her fast and furious, all jumbled up with Louise's pronouncements and her own observations. It was Louise's assessment of the lady that won out. Sarah Brooker was a mouse, small enough to scutter through an opening where Kathleen certainly couldn't follow. A phone call would have been wrong, Kathleen was sure.

"What if she's not home?"

Michael pulled to a stop, stretched his arm across the seat, and put his hands against Kathleen's neck as they sat in the dark. She trembled when he did. She wanted to throw herself into his arms. Lust was the last thing on her mind, the need to hide from ... something ... was the first. A specter in the night had skittered over the hood of the car and poked its pallid puss through the windshield.

Mom? Dad?

Kathleen took hold of herself. The other life had been banished. She was surprised it didn't know its place. "Believe me, she'll be home."

These were only trees. She was used to the desert. This was a canyon, and down was not her favorite direction. She was anxious because she'd made a decision on her own, without anyone's permission, to intrude upon this person. She still wasn't used to that—making decisions or intruding. Nor did she like the claustrophobic feeling of the night here. But those same trees, this same dark, probably made Sarah feel safe.

"She's there," Kathleen muttered, more to herself than Michael. Without Lionel, where else was there to go?

"I wouldn't bet on that." Michael no longer touched her. He draped his arm over the steering wheel. He was studying the well-kept cottage in the partial illumination of the head-lights. Every window was dark.

"Maybe she goes to bed early. The car is here." Kathleen

pointed. Michael looked. The nose of a Volkswagen peeked out of the shed to their right.

"You want to wake her up?" Michael's eyes were on her, blacker than the night and, to her credit, Kathleen was able to look right into them without any thought but to do what they'd come for. The sooner they did that, the sooner they'd be out of here and looking at each other over a glass of wine. Then she would have very different thoughts.

Kathleen's hand wrapped around the door handle. "After everything it took to get here, I'll camp out before we drive back again."

"You'd be sleeping on the ground alone." Michael chuckled. Simultaneously they got out of the car and closed the doors behind them, leaving the headlights on. Standing side by side, they considered the house.

"This is a neat place, isn't it?" Kathleen whispered, her little-girl voice sounding almost wistful. Gone were the creepy crawlies of a few minutes ago. "It looks just like I thought it would. Sarah and Lionel were probably very happy here." Relaxing, Kathleen put her hands on her hips and breathed in the clean, still air. "I'm glad I came. Seeing this makes me realize that there is no way Lionel Brooker killed himself. He wouldn't have wanted to leave this."

Kathleen took a step toward the house. Night dust danced in the twin beams that burned two holes through the darkness.

"And the drugs?"

"There's got to be some explanation for that. It just doesn't add up. Oh, look, a raised garden . . ."

Kathleen's heels crunched on the gravel that transitioned the drive to the area around the cottage. Michael reached for her arm, his mouth open to warn her about the uneven lay of the ground. Kathleen turned her head. She was smiling. His fingers brushed her arm. That's when it happened.

The wooded silence erupted with a deafening explosion. A bright light flashed to their left. Then it flared again and disappeared like ball lightning. Kathleen wasn't sure if another explosion came the second time since her ears were still ringing from the first horrendous noise. The ground around them seemed to implode, but it was only the kick of buckshot slamming into it that made it shudder and sputtered beneath their feet.

Kathleen screamed at the same moment Michael hurled her to the ground. Her head hit hard, her shoulder was on fire with pain. Before she knew what was happening, Michael had rolled atop her, driving the air out of her from the bottom up like a toothpaste tube.

Another shot. She bucked and screamed again.

Michael barked an order Kathleen couldn't hear, but she knew enough to understand that he wanted her to be quietly hysterical. She whimpered and took flash-card comfort from the fact that she wasn't alone. She didn't have long to linger over the thought. They were moving. Turtlelike Michael raised up and flipped her over, ordering her to hightail it to the raised garden, the only bit of protection within twenty yards. Breathing hard, they threw themselves toward it, rolling on their backs behind the wooden forms no more than a foot high. There was at least enough cover to afford them a moment to think.

"Okay. Okay."

Michael whispered as he squeezed Kathleen's hand tight. Hers shook so hard her bones seemed to rattle. His was steady, dry, and strong. His breathing was even; hers came in ragged bursts. Michael's heart beat tight and fast in his chest—the proper, controlled, combat reaction. He could only imagine what Kathleen's heart felt like if his was thundering in his body. He rolled his head her way. The ground was hard packed and well-kept. No loose dirt to blind them, only a few stones to cut them. These were good things, he would tell her that when she calmed down. She wasn't about to listen now with her cheek pressed down hard as if she could squash herself into the earth. Her eyes were covered by her hair. With his free hand, Michael brushed it away.

"We're fine. We're fine. Kathleen, I need you to open your eyes." He laid his fingers on the side of her throat, leaving them there until he could feel her breath coming in deeper gulps. The panic left her reluctantly. "Okay, honey. Okay. That's it."

He was careful to keep his voice lower than low. The enemy was about; and every sense he had was reaching out to the world around him, trying to figure out where that enemy was. When he was sure Kathleen was breathing almost normally, Michael lifted his head slowly. In another moment his eyes would just clear the wooden forms. In another second . . .

"Sarah! Sarah! Call the police!"

Michael, cool under fire, jumped out of his skin and flattened himself again. Rolling over Kathleen, he clapped his hand over her mouth and slapped his cheek against hers so hard their jawbones ground painfully against one another.

"Shut up. Kathleen, shut up, for God's sake," he hissed, but either she wasn't listening or couldn't respond. Kathleen's mouth worked against his fingers. "Quiet." His hand tightened until he could press no harder. Her eyes flew open, big and bright, blue and horrified. "Quiet. Okay?" He pushed once more for emphasis. This was no game and she'd hurt a lot more if she couldn't figure out how to play it now. Whoever was out there with the gun wanted them dead. Those had been shots that missed their mark, not a warning to stay away.

"I'm going to take my hand away, okay?" Kathleen nodded. He loosened his hold. She remained quiet. He released her, letting his hand hover near just in case. Her mouth motored, lips flapping silently until she finally found a shard of a voice.

"Michael, Michael . . . we've got to let Sarah know . . . we're out here, Michael. She's the only one who can help. She's the only one for miles. Michael. Michael. I'm so scared. We have to tell her. . . . We have to . . ."

He shook his head vehemently, their brows as close together as they could be, their lips kissing-distance. Kathleen watched those lips carefully, knowing she'd go mad without focus. "No. No. We have to figure out what's going on first. If you call to Sarah, you'll let whoever's out there know exactly where we are." Michael cupped her head with both his big hands and pulled it even further toward his. He smelled like dirt and sweat. He smelled almost safe. Brow-to-brow with her now, he closed his eyes and talked. "They may already have Sarah. We don't know. But to save ourselves, and help her, be quiet. Please,

please, Kathleen. You're with me, right? You can be brave, right? You can. We've got to figure out what the situation is . . ."

Michael stopped talking, primed to pounce again if he had to. Kathleen had gone rigid beneath him. Opening his eyes, Michael raised his head slightly. Kathleen Cotter wasn't looking at, or listening to, him any longer. The tip of a gun barrel pressed into her temple seemed to have distracted her. Black, double-barreled, and in good condition, it was the most frightening thing he'd ever seen. Sliding his eyes down, he saw legs, but before he could look higher, Kathleen managed one more strangled word.

"Sarah?"

The gun barrel pushed deeper into Kathleen's temple. Cautiously, Michael turned his head a millimeter. Sarah Brooker stood above them, holding a gun almost bigger than she was. Alice in Wonderland turned Rambo. She had the butt firm against her shoulder. If she pulled the trigger, the kick might send her flying, but Michael and Kathleen wouldn't be around to see where she landed.

"Sit up." The barrel of her gun still leveled at Kathleen's head, Sarah stepped back slowly. That step was sure; her voice was not. "I said sit up, both of you." Michael moved, but he was too fast. The barrel swung his way. "Slow."

He eased off Kathleen as carefully as if she were a sleeping lover. But Kathleen didn't sleep, nor was she aware of Michael. She remained frozen in position, her mouth open, her eyes on Sarah Brooker. Michael sat on his heels, his hands in plain view. Sarah's knuckles were white she gripped the gun so hard. There was fear in her face and, sadly, determination.

"Her, too." Sarah was more comfortable with the situation now. Her voice didn't quaver. Neither did the gun. "Get her up."

Michael pulled at Kathleen, but it was like trying to move a corpse. Rigor mortis couldn't have made her stiffer. Still, he did what he had to do.

"Come on, babe. Do what she says. Come on," Michael murmured. Finally, Kathleen was sitting beside him, her legs sidesaddle. It was an unfortunate position if she needed to move quickly, but it would have to do. He looked directly at their captor. Sarah Booker was satisfied. She stepped forward once more.

"Who sent you?" She pushed the barrel closer to Kathleen, who went cross-eyed as it neared her nose. "I want to know who sent you."

Mutely, Kathleen's lips formed the words *no one*. She shook her head frantically, her eyes still focused on the barrel of the gun as if begging for another chance to do better. She found her voice. "Nobody. Nobody. Nobody, Sarah."

Kathleen swallowed hard, then took a deep, deep breath that actually reached her lungs. She shuddered, yet instead of collapsing, she came together. Afraid still, her voice was stronger this time around and she managed to force herself to look at the other woman instead of the shotgun.

"Sarah, I'm sorry we didn't warn you we were coming. Don't you recognize me?" Kathleen's voice started shaking. She took another deep breath. "I'm Kathleen Cotter, attorney for Louise Brooker. You were in my office. This is . . .''

"I don't care who that is!" Sarah's scream was punctuated by a hiccup or a sob, and this time the gun shook. Not a good sign. Kathleen closed her mouth, clamping her lips shut until they hurt. When moments had passed without anyone doing anything, Kathleen slid her eyes toward Michael. Through the dark she could barely see him, but she knew that he was looking right at her. It was hard to focus on him or know what he wanted her to do. Taking a stab in the dark, Kathleen kept talking since Sarah refused to acknowledge Michael's existence.

"Sarah," Kathleen began cautiously, "I just want to ask you some questions about Lionel's work—"

A ratcheting sound stopped Kathleen cold. Even she knew Sarah had racked a round. She was going to die in the middle of a nowhere that was worse than the nowhere she'd come from. At least Banning had been her home. Now she was staring down the barrel of a shotgun held by a crazy woman in a forest in a canyon. Kathleen hadn't soared skyward, she'd sunk to new lows. And for what? If Sarah Brooker were crazy, then Lionel probably was, too. Heck, Lionel probably did himself in to get away from Sarah and Louise. Two crazy women in one lifetime was enough for any man. Kathleen didn't want to die for a man she didn't know or because of a ridiculous lawsuit, and she didn't want to die before she had a chance to really live. There were so many things she hadn't done.

Kathleen wasn't going to have a chance to make a list. She was knocked aside, her head hitting the raised, wood garden-frame as Michael flew past her. He was nothing more than a denim blur, and he hit Sarah Brooker like a torpedo while Kathleen fought to stay conscious. Sarah cried out in surprise. Michael grunted and the gun went off so close to Kathleen she was thrown backward again just as she was struggling to sit up. It was only the searing pain that screamed through her body that kept her awake enough to pray.

"Hail Mary . . ."

A great calm washed over her. Either her soul was leaving her body or her wits were fleeing.

"Full of grace . . ."

She felt almost light-headed.

"Kathleen!"

Michael was shouting at her soul, disrupting her prayers.

"Kathleen! Wake up!"

No, Michael was hollering at her. She opened her eyes. She wasn't dead at all. She pressed her hands against her head, her chest. She was alive! Sore, but alive. Ecstatic, she looked at Michael and saw the blood.

"Oh, Michael," she wailed. But it was only his hand that was cut; it wasn't his heart that was blown out.

And Sarah's head. A bloody bruise was beginning to swell beside her eye. Relieved that they were all alive, Kathleen bolted up, only to collapse again as the world spun.

"Kathleen?" Michael was breathing hard. It had taken more effort than he ever would have imagined to subdue Sarah Brooker. He had her in a headlock, but was afraid to move. She was stronger than she looked and more defiant than he'd first imagined. It was a deadly combination. "Kathleen? Please? Can you stand up?"

"Yes. Yes."

She got to her feet, scraping her knee and forcing herself to focus. Her legs gave way once, but she recovered nicely while Michael maneuvered his captive. He managed to get Sarah's hands behind her, holding them painfully high and tight against her back. Sarah, disoriented, seemed to lean into Michael for support. One look in her one good eye, though, convinced Kathleen her submissiveness would last only as long as her daze.

"The gun, Kathleen. Please?"

She moved like a child eager to please and picked it up. It was heavy. She held it against her chest, hoping to God there weren't any more bullets in it. Michael struggled to stand, bringing Sarah with him. They were a tumble of legs and groans and, finally, they were on their feet. He was huge and heroic. Sarah was small and scary. He cocked his head.

"We're going in."

Kathleen stepped in front of them.

"No." He barked and pushed Sarah forward without letting go of her. "Her first." His voice softened to a mild command as they passed Kathleen. "Just in case."

"In case what?" Kathleen danced around, catching herself just as she stepped in front of them again, only to fall back, talking fast from behind them.

"In case she's not alone," Michael growled.

"Do you think there're more? Sarah? Are there any more people who want to hurt us?" Kathleen scurried forward. She hopped and skipped beside the other woman, dipping her head to look into her eyes. She held the shotgun away even though Sarah couldn't have scratched her nose if she'd wanted.

"Get back," Michael ordered, and Kathleen fell into line, still talking.

"Sarah. Sarah, is there anyone in the house?" No response. The tiny woman stumbled. Kathleen reached for her instinctively, only to pull back hard. She was learning the fine art of caution. Sarah righted herself with Michael's help and glared silently at Kathleen as she stumbled on. "Sarah, what on earth were you thinking? Why would you want to do this? If there's someone in that house, tell us now. Don't let this go any further." Kathleen half hip-hopped alongside as they made their way to the house. Sarah was unmoved, so she appealed to Michael as they went. "Michael, tell her. Did you notice no one came? Did you notice that? Nobody came to see what the shots were about. We should call the police."

They were at the porch now. Michael helped the taciturn Sarah up. Her head moved from side to side. Michael tightened his hold, knowing flight was on her mind. The last place he wanted her was in the woods. With Kathleen's chatter providing background music, Michael kicked at the door. It opened easily and he cleared the threshold, pushing Sarah ahead of him as far as he dared. Relieved when nothing happened, he pulled Sarah Brooker up tight against his chest. Her head barely reached his shoulders. Using his heel he shoved the door shut as soon as Kathleen was in, putting his lips close to Sarah's ear. They stood in the dark, an unlikely, intimate group.

"Is there anyone in here? Anyone!" He pulled up tight until he thought he might break her shoulder. He heard a sharp intake of breath, but no cry of pain. She was a tough cookie. Sarah shook her head and closed the eye that wasn't already swollen shut. Michael gave her a beat more to change her mind then raised his head. "Turn on the lights, Kathleen. Stow the shotgun."

"Okay. Okay. Lights. Lights." Rushing forward, she slammed her shin into something hard. "Ouch." She hopped about, caught sight of Michael's rigid silhouette, and remembered her charge. "Forget it. I'm okay. Okay. Lights." Off she went again.

Using her free hand as a blind woman would, she searched the space in front of her. Silence. Then a triumphant, hysterical giggle came along with a click. All three blinked though the bulb-wattage on the table lamp was low. Kathleen stood back, beaming at her success. One look at Michael and her pride faded. She wasn't finished. Hugging the shotgun, Kathleen cut a wide berth around Michael and Sarah and opened the first closet she found. Brooms, brushes, detergent. Gun. She put the gun neatly alongside the dust mop and closed the door.

"Here you go, Mrs. Brooker." Michael tossed Sarah onto a small overstuffed chair that had seen better days. He pulled up a straight-backed one for himself, straddled it, shook his head, and glanced at his bleeding hand before looking at her. "That was quite a welcome you gave us. Let's talk, Sarah. What about it? You do that to everyone who drives up after five?"

Quietly, Kathleen moved beside him, though she still stood apart. This wasn't a movie. Michael didn't exactly have the time to sweep her into his arms for comfort, so she wrapped her own around herself and did her best to help.

"Sarah, we didn't come here to hurt you. We only wanted to ask you some questions. We heard something about Lionel that we'd like to clarify. Sarah?" Kathleen's voice lowered an octave. "It's not about money, Sarah. We're not going to take your house. It's about the kind of man Lionel was. We know he probably didn't do drugs." Kathleen winced as Sarah tried to open both eyes to cast a look of anger at the mention of her husband's name. She failed miserably. Kathleen moved forward a step. "A great number of people admired Lionel, but one of those people said that he'd been upset at work just before he died. We want to know what upset him. That's all. That's really all we came for."

Sarah Brooker's long hair fell in curtains over her as she lowered her head. One angry eye could still be seen burning with hatred and suspicion. The blood around the other was drying. Kathleen reached out to push Sarah's hair back, but the woman jerked away and nailed Michael with her Cyclops vision.

"Who is he?"

Kathleen stepped back and put her hand on Michael's shoulder. "This is Michael Crawford, Sarah. Lionel's supervisor."

That was it. Before the last syllable was out of Kathleen's mouth, Sarah Brooker went nuts. She bolted, fast as a newt. She zipped past them, swerving like a quarterback. Michael was on her heels. Her hands were on the closet doorknob where the gun was stashed, but Michael was taller and stronger. He reached out above her head and slammed the door shut before she could get inside. Thwarted, Sarah spun away from his grasp. The front door was her next target. A standing lamp bit the dust, thrown behind her in a defensive move. Michael fell over it. He wasn't happy.

"Sarah, wait!"

Kathleen sprinted around the end table after Sarah but not fast enough to keep the front door closed. Sarah flung it open, her hair flying as she looked over her shoulder at her pursuers, but freedom just wasn't in the cards. Sarah Brooker was flung back into the room, pushed hard by someone reacting to the surprise of a body hurtling out the door just as they were reaching for the bell.

Stunned, everyone stopped. Sarah lay on the floor, her arms, legs, and hair splayed out around her; Kathleen froze midstride, and Michael stopped as he opened his mouth to howl in outrage. They all stared at the open door as Louise Brooker stepped into the living room, grinned and gave a Miss America-wave. Her nails were lapis. Rod Stewart was the guest rocker.

Sarah Brooker had beautiful china. It was old and hand painted with lilacs. Another time, Kathleen would have asked its history. Another time, Kathleen would have actually enjoyed fixing tea and sitting in this little house in the canyon, surrounded by trees, settled in for a long chat over a warm cup. As it was, she was cranky and dirty and not a little unhappy that Louise was standing in Sarah Brooker's kitchen, too.

"Gerry told me where she lived. What's the big deal? My horoscope said, 'Make peace and financial gain will be yours.' It was a sign, Kathleen. Besides, I thought I could just talk to her a little, you know, convince her woman-to-woman to tell me anything that might help this case. If she had, I was going to drop the whole nonsense against the estate and then she wouldn't have had to worry about her future." Louise scratched her head, nail-tips only. Kathleen's eyes narrowed. The Pinocchio move. "Whatever future she had, that is . . ." Kathleen huffed.

"I was doing just fine, thank you. I was doing what a responsible attorney would do. I was methodically gathering information and following up leads." She yanked open the pine-wood cabinets, found the tea, and put the tin on the counter before turning to look at Louise. "You weren't coming to talk to her at all. You were going to browbeat her and she could have sued the pants off you, Louise. Where are your brains? Not only that, that woman could have killed you."

"Oh, right," Louise scoffed. Those nails were now more interesting than Kathleen. Louise buffed old Rod for good measure.

"Okay, don't take my word for it. Grab a flashlight. Take a look outside. Those aren't woodpecker holes out there in that wooden garden. Take a look at us! Take a look in the front closet. She shot at us." Kathleen fumed and ripped off the top of the tea tin, wishing it were Louise's head. "With a shotgun. If Michael hadn't been here, I would have been dead."

Kathleen ran the water into the kettle. Behind her Louise breathed a sound that seemed like a horrified *no,* but when Kathleen turned triumphantly to receive the other woman's apology, Louise had abandoned her. She was mincing back to the living room on Lucite wedgies, her arms held out toward the one-eyed Sarah.

"You didn't. Did you really take a gun to these two?" Louise cooed in a voice one might use to compliment the hostess's lemon cake.

Louise settled herself beside Sarah, who sat stiff with terror. A more unlikely pair one could never hope to see. Sarah swathed in another gray sweater (this one with a shawl collar), a nondescript blouse tucked into her jeans; Louise in a gold-lamé blouse and black, skin-tight jeans that sported open latticework. The peek-a-boo ran down the outer side of the legs. The less-than-demure cutouts let the world see that cellulite was not a problem for Louise Brooker. Louise crossed her skinny legs and took Sarah's hand.

"You are one gutsy little broad," she said solemnly. Louise

picked up the ice pack Sarah held against her head and checked out the bruise. It was ugly. "Wow, I didn't realize how bad that was. How're you feeling?" Louise clucked, touching the miserable knot on the side of Sarah's forehead. "I didn't think you had it in you. That's really amazing, you standing your ground like that. I didn't think the estate meant that much to you."

"It doesn't," Sarah groused, coming to life as she eyed Louise warily. Rudely, she pulled the ice pack back. Louise crossed her arms, taking no offense. On she talked, addressing Sarah, the watchful Michael, and Kathleen, who brought out two cups of tea and put them on the coffee table before going back for two more. Louise raised her voice so Kathleen wouldn't be left out.

"This is something, isn't it? To find out that Sarah and I have something in common, after all. I suppose we had to have had something in common. Lionel wasn't a dummy, was he, Sarah?" Louise batted her lashes at her new friend. They were blue-tipped with little balls of iridescent mascara. "That's what I loved about him. He was smart. His priorities were just a little screwed. But the thing that bothered me was, he wasn't consistent. First, he marries someone like me." She actually raised a hand to her coifed hair as if they needed reminding of exactly who—or what—she was. "Then he goes and does the same thing with someone like you." The look she gave Sarah was pitying. "It didn't make sense till now. But now I get it." Louise raised her arms as if inviting them to join in a refrain. "Strong women. That's what Lionel needed. Really, really strong women. You had me fooled, Sarah. You really did."

"Excuse me, but can we cut the bull?" Michael retaped the gauze on his hand and looked at Louise, nonplussed.

Louise lowered her flashy lashes and her voice as she leaned toward Michael. "You're not much of a woman's man, are you? If you're thinking of bullying this little lady—" She jerked a thumb toward Sarah. "—you just watch it, 'cause I'm here now."

"And so am I." Kathleen rejoined the group of misfits.

"And I'm not going to let anyone do anything that isn't legal or appropriate."

"Don't look at me; it's him. He's the one that wants to be so heavy-handed, or haven't you taken a look at Sarah's eye? What's your name again?" Louise pushed her chest out just a tad more. Sarah, while now a sister, wasn't half as interesting as a good-looking man.

"Crawford. Michael."

"Oh, I love a man who talks like that." Louise pulled back and turned a cold shoulder his way to show she wasn't as impressed as she really was. "And what's your business here?"

"I came with Kathleen," he said evenly. Any other time, he would have found Louise Brooker interesting; at present, she was a pain in the butt. "I was Lionel's supervisor."

"Oh, God," wailed Sarah, burying her face in her hands. The ice pack fell to the floor with the muffled thump of half-melted ice against rubber.

"What, honey, what?" Louise crowded her on the small chair. Sarah would have ended up on the floor if Louise hadn't grabbed her around the shoulders. She gave Michael a scowl that didn't make a dent in his peevishness.

"Kill me," Sarah wailed, lowering her hands, raising her face. Joan of Arc about to be tied to the stake couldn't have looked more pathetically heroic.

"This is ridiculous." Michael stood up. Sarah tried to. He turned on her. Kathleen didn't bother to move. "I'll tie you to that chair if you move again. Now, start talking some sense. Kill you! Ridiculous. No, you don't." He whipped a look at Louise, who was about to leap to Sarah's defense. "I swear I'll tie you to her and I'll gag you. Now, both of you listen up. I'm an auditing supervisor at Tysco Industries. That's it. Nothing more. I came here because Kathleen wanted me to drive her to see Sarah. All I wanted to do was take her to dinner. But now, I'm here. My hand is killing me. I've been shot at and I've groveled in the dirt. I'm a mess and I'm surrounded by crazy women. Excuse me—" The latter he directed toward Kathleen, who nodded back curtly, acknowledging herself as the exception. "Now, if you don't mind, I'd like to get what

we came for, and what we came for is information. That's all.
We don't want to pillage. We don't want to kill you. We just
want to know what had Lionel riled before he died!'' Michael
did a three-sixty, his hands in his hair. He gave a frustrated
tug to the hair at the sides of his head and looked back at Sarah
Brooker. The silence grew fat and heavy and almost unbearable.
''Are you going to say anything?''

Another strained moment and Sarah nodded.

''When?'' he asked.

''Now?''

It was going to be a long night.

''He wasn't mad in the way you think. Lionel never got
upset that way—like with himself. Did he, Louise?''

Michael and Kathleen leaned forward, straining to hear
Sarah's voice. Louise plucked at her cuff, trying to snag a tiny
thread that eluded her talons. She shook her head.

''Sarah's right there. You could walk all over Lionel, and
he wouldn't even get mad at you, would he, Sarah?''

''No, not at all, but I never tried to take advantage,'' she
reminded Louise shyly, pointing out that there were some differences between them, after all. ''Lionel really hated unfairness.
That made him crazy. Cheating, that was another thing that
made him crazy. Meanness, too. That's why Lionel never felt
badly toward you, Louise.'' Sarah's narrow, pale brow puck-
ered, but it hurt her eye, so she let her face relax. ''You never
tried to cheat him, Louise. He respected that.''

''And I appreciate your telling me. I want you to know I
never hated Lionel, Sarah. I just hated the time I wasted with
him. You understand?'' Louise gave up the thread hunt, her
attention riveted once more on Sarah.

''I do. I do,'' Sarah said sincerely. ''Time is so important.
I never realized that until Lionel was gone. You had too much
time with him, Louise, and I didn't have enough.''

Kathleen slid her eyes Michael's way. Sarah's kind of love
for Lionel was rare indeed, but neither could take too much more
of the budding affection between Louise and Sarah Brooker.

Michael cleared his throat. Sarah blinked. She was back from the past and still wary of the only man about.

"Yes, I'm sorry. Well, I don't really know much about it, you understand. This thing that was bothering him, I mean." She was back to picking at her sweater. "Lionel liked working at Tysco. Everything was in its place. He knew what his job was; they paid well, and the benefits were very good. It was a perfect situation. That job left his mind free to pursue the more spiritual aspects of life. You know, to just sort of enjoy all of this."

"You're kiddin . . ." Louise started to laugh. Kathleen was close enough to give her ankle a kick. Louise closed her mouth, and collectively they contemplated the small, well-kept house, the grounds, the pretty china. Kathleen thought there was something to be said for Lionel's priorities. Sarah sighed. She looked pitiful with her swollen eye and worn sweater.

"One day something came across his desk. Some bill or some kind of accounting document that was meant for someone else. I don't know a lot about this," she said again, apologetic and distressed by her ignorance. Her audience nodded their encouragement. "Well, okay then." She took a deep breath. "Lionel said that, no matter what department they were from, they didn't look right. In fact, he was really, really angry. He said the system was like an idiot-child that did whatever a smart person told it to do, even if it were an unscrupulous smart person who was telling it to do things. Lionel believed that the actual cash flow in the part of the company those bills came from, and maybe some others, was being manipulated."

"That would be pretty tough to do," Michael commented, one hand over his eyes, a barrier to deflect whatever nonsense was to come. The other arm, the injured one, dangled over the side of the chair.

Sarah gazed at him mournfully. "I don't know anything other than that. I'm not very good with this kind of thing. I work at the potter's down the way. We don't bill anybody. They just buy their pot and leave."

"It's okay," Kathleen assured her, but even she was weary.

This was one of those times when Dorty & Breyer looked like a step up. "Just go ahead."

"Well, Lionel said he went to his supervisor with the problem and was told not to worry about it. But Lionel couldn't just ignore the whole thing. So, he went a few times more, but his supervisor got angry. Lionel found out who his supervisor's boss was and he was going to go to him." Sarah rubbed her temple gingerly. Kathleen winced. Sarah did not. "He said he'd go to the top if he had to. When he put on his suit, I knew that it had probably come to that. He didn't say it had, but why else would he put on a suit? He looked very handsome." This she directed to Louise, who was kind enough to simply nod as if she, too, admired the image of that reed-thin body turned out in his Sunday best. "I didn't want him to do anything crazy. If he lost his job at Tysco, I didn't know what we'd do."

Kathleen couldn't resist a glance at Michael. He smiled. He was gorgeous, even after their tussle on the ground. She put her hand to her hair and pushed back her bangs, then gave up on hoping that she might make herself look at least presentable. It would be great to have a brush and her lipstick. Not that it would have mattered to Michael; he was getting into his conversation with Sarah.

"Lionel didn't ever mention a name? Jules Porter, who was his supervisor before me. He didn't say whether or not Jules Porter had threatened him with a personnel action for pushing the matter?"

"No." Sarah thought hard. She only knew what she had been told; there would be no extrapolation that might enlighten them. "He just went off. He kissed me goodbye. I've always been grateful for that. The next thing I knew, Lionel was dead. I was devastated. He was my best friend. I really didn't have anyone else."

"You do now, kiddo." Louise lifted the sofa cushion to look underneath, only to sit down when she didn't find whatever she was looking for. Kathleen thought a codicil—*whether you like it or not*—should be added to that statement, but she remained silent.

"Anyway, I was home lying down all day after I'd gone to identify his body. I couldn't believe he was dead and I never believed that he took drugs. Just to be sure, I searched this house top to bottom looking for something that might prove that he did."

"And you didn't find anything?" Michael again.

"No drugs, no." Sarah wound a length of hair around her finger. She didn't look at anyone. "I just fell apart. I went out to feed the rabbits. I just sat there with them, feeling how warm they were. I cried a lot. The hutch is back in the real woodsy area. I thought they'd like it there. You can see it from the house, but just barely. So, I just sat there, trying to figure out how drugs had gotten into Lionel. Then, the day I went to court, the first day I saw all of you?" She waited while they nodded. "When I came home, I realized someone must have put drugs in Lionel. I knew then that someone had killed my husband."

"Sarah," Kathleen breathed. "Why on earth would you think that?"

"Because someone's trying to kill me, too." Sarah looked from one to another. She wasn't asking for their belief or their sympathy. She was simply stating a fact. "Whoever they were broke into the house when I was back with the rabbits the day Lionel died. They moved things. They stayed in my house. I watched, but it was dark when they came and I was scared. I didn't see exactly who it was. I'd never been so afraid."

Sarah stood up. She was still afraid.

"I convinced myself it was a burglary, even though they didn't take anything. But they were odd burglars, because they had suits on and they were very, very big." Sarah clasped her hands in front of her and continued with her recital. "Then, after I went into court and said what I had to say, I was really upset. I went to see my rabbits the first thing when I got back here. This time I knew something really bad was happening because of Lionel. All my rabbits were dead. All of those sweet little rabbits with their necks broken. I went to get a shovel. Those men had been inside again. This time, the house was ransacked. They would have killed me if I'd been here. I know it.''

Sarah wound her fingers together tightly and held her hands chest high. There were tears in her good eye.

''I picked everything up; I buried my rabbits out back. I got the gun, and I waited. I almost gave up because nothing's happened for so long. Then you came and I shot at you. I'm glad I didn't hurt you, but you've got to understand how it's been around here ever since Lionel died. I don't know any of you people. I don't know if you want to hurt me or help me. I loved Lionel, but I don't want to die because of him.''

That was the end. She was done talking. Sarah walked out of their circle and went to the closet where Kathleen had put the gun. Michael tensed and half stood, but Kathleen held him back. Calmly, Sarah set up a step stool and pushed open a slot in the closet ceiling and rummaged about. When she returned, she was holding a manila envelope, not the shotgun.

''I'm sure this is what they wanted. This is what got Lionel killed. I found it when I was looking for drugs. He'd hidden it up there.'' She held it out to Michael. It lay gingerly on the open palms of her hands as if she feared spontaneous combustion.

''Then if he were killed—'' Kathleen mused with awe.

''—We're talking murder,'' Michael muttered.

''—We're talking settlement,'' Louise scoffed.

Chapter Twelve

"Good morning."

Kathleen sat on the edge of the chair nearest the couch. She'd been watching Michael for at least ten minutes, a juice glass in her hand, before she realized what she was doing. When he opened his eyes and smiled, she thought she'd die of desire—and embarrassment.

"Good morning," she said, horrified to find herself whispering. A bedroom voice is what her mother had called it. Kathleen had been forbidden to use it in her mother's house. But this wasn't her mother's house and this wasn't her bedroom. How liberating. She grinned and held up the small glass as if to prove she had no intention of seducing him. "I brought you juice. I don't drink coffee, but I could run down to the corner and pick some up if you want."

Michael put his hands by his sides to push himself up. He didn't get very far. Wincing, he examined his bandaged hand.

"It wasn't a dream?"

Kathleen shook her head and tried out a hangdog expression, " 'Fraid not."

He shook out the pain and scooted into position. The sheet fell away from his bare chest. It was a very fine chest, sprinkled with dark, curling hair shot here and there with silver. The hours on the boat kept him more than fit. The hours under the sun had turned his skin golden brown. Kathleen stood up and handed him the glass. He took it. She didn't let go.

"You have a very fine couch." He talked as if he woke there often. "I hope Sarah slept as well."

Kathleen laughed gently, happy to play the game. But she knew that he knew that she was feeling less-than-comfortable. "Sarah probably isn't sure what hit her. Can you imagine being carted away by Louise Brooker?"

"I don't know, those ladies seemed to be well-suited to each other in an odd sort of way." Michael wriggled to settle himself. Kathleen kept talking.

"It was nice that Louise offered Sarah a place to go. That poor lady has to be scared out of her wits by all this. No wonder she wanted Louise to take everything. She probably thought Louise had sent some hit men out to get her."

"I can see why she might have thought that," Michael murmured. He looked at the juice, then he looked up at her. "My arm's getting tired."

"Oh." Kathleen let go of the glass. He took it, but before Kathleen could turn away, he caught her hand with his good one.

"No you don't. Come here." Gently, he pulled her toward him, tugging until she figured out that he wanted her to sit. He wanted her near. She complied.

Carefully, Michael put the glass on the coffee table and his hands around her waist. Then, with the most marvelous subtle moves, he pulled her down until her hands lay flat against his chest and her lips touched his lips. He kissed her lightly once, twice, three times, and then he wasn't kissing her anymore. Michael Crawford was looking at her, smiling a smile that would have banned him from her mother's neighborhood for life. If only Mom—and Cherie—could see her now. "How are you feeling?"

"Nervous," she answered, not completely in her right mind.

"I mean, how are you?" He laughed.

"Sore."

"Where?"

"My head." Kathleen dipped her head and smelled the sleep on him. He kissed her head.

"Anywhere else?"

"My shoulder."

Michael touched the neck of her T-shirt and pulled it away to bare her shoulder. His lips missed their mark and hit that fabulous spot just to the side of her neck.

"Other shoulder," Kathleen managed to say, and he obliged.

"Better?"

"Much."

"Your knee?" Before she could stop him, he leaned sideways and planted a kiss on the bandage on her knee and Kathleen felt a stab of painful pleasure just north of his lips. It made her think the world had opened up and was ready to swallow her. She had the most awful urge to start praying that it would.

"All right?" he asked. All she could do was nod. "Good." He sat her halfway up and scooted so that he was nestled back against the pillows. His hands held her wrists.

"I like the new you."

She lowered her eyes. It was the same old Kathleen, the one she worked so hard to improve, and she couldn't imagine how he could like her this way. Her *face* had always seemed so important to her, her carefully made-up face. Magazines told her that no one paid attention to a woman without it. Every successful woman on the television and billboards and the streets of Beverly Hills had it. Now, Michael Crawford was telling her he could care less.

"The T-shirt's nice, too."

She turned her head. "We used to give them out at Dorty & Breyer. To new clients. It was silly. It was a law office not an ice-cream parlor."

"Why are you so ashamed of it?" A finger under the chin brought her back to him.

"I'm not. I'm not," she insisted and looked at him. He knew she was lying. "Okay, I'm kind of ashamed. It was an office in a strip mall. I handled divorces where there were no assets. Anybody could have filled out the paperwork. I used to pretend

I was the receptionist when I answered my phone, then put on my attorney voice just to make it seem like we were an honest-to-God law firm with a staff and everything. I wanted to look like I knew what I was doing.''

"Last night I figured you knew what you were doing."

"No, not like that. I wanted to feel that I controlled what I was doing and that what I was doing was important. I've been living in a bubble for so many years that I wasn't sure I could make decisions anymore. The only thing I did on my own was go to law school when my father didn't want me to. After that, I was just kind of pulled back into doing what everyone else wanted. My dad died just before I was going to head out to seek my fortune. My mother made me feel guilty for wanting to leave a widow. Then, when she got sick, I couldn't leave an invalid. My friend at Dorty made me feel guilty for wanting to better myself. When I finally left, I walked right into Gerry's life. I was looking for some high-powered action; instead, I found an old man with dreams of grandeur and a way of letting me know he doesn't expect anything except blood.''

"You don't call what happened last night *action?*" Michael laughed.

"This wasn't exactly what I had in mind. I don't think most attorneys in Beverly Hills get shot at while trying to do their job." Kathleen stood up, afraid she was going to start saying things she didn't want to say. He held onto one hand. She clucked her tongue. "I sound ungrateful and whiny. I don't mean to. It's just that my life has been very strange since I've come here." She laughed and handed him his juice, extricating herself. "My life was very strange before I came here, too. It's not like I had a purpose, like you. I had been drifting while I stayed in the same place. Then, when I finally made my move, I was disappointed when I found I couldn't leap right to the top and play with the big boys. That's selfish and unrealistic, I know. It's a really childish attitude. You might as well know that now before we get any more involved. If you want to just kind of bow out now, I'll understand."

Michael sat up straighter, the smile disappearing from his face. "Thanks. I'm glad you told me. That's kind of you. I was awake all night wondering how I was going to just get back to my life and forget all about you.''

"Really?" She sat heavily on the coffee table, her eyes wide with hurt.

"No." He laughed. "For your information, I was exhausted last night. I couldn't have stayed awake if you'd walked naked through this room." His thick lashes lowered, his eyes lingering on the D and Y in Dorty that were kept afloat by her fine breasts. He looked at her knees, bared and just a bit bony and so damned sexy. Then, he looked at her. "Well, I might have been able to stay awake for that, but not much else. Besides, I figure if I hang around you, I might just jump-start my life."

"I wouldn't imagine that would be a problem."

Michael threw off the covers she had put over him the night before, his killer grin going the same way. He'd slept in his jeans, but barefoot and bare-chested he was a sexy package.

"I didn't think it was. I thought I was actually doing something till I started hanging around you." He pulled his jeans up at the waist, a ploy so that he wouldn't have to look at her while he confessed. "Jules Porter told me no one knew who I was anymore. I think he was right." He touched her hair then cupped her chin with his hand. "I think I've been fooling myself, Kathleen. One moment does not a lifetime define. Maybe if I help you unravel the mess around Lionel, I'll have finished something. Remember that rut I told you about? I think it was deeper than even I knew. Comfortable, deceptive, and deep." He took a breath. Self-flagellation was tough. But it was over, he was hardly bleeding, and Kathleen didn't seem to think less of him. He smiled. "Bathroom?"

Mesmerized, she pointed the way. Her apartment was small. It wasn't hard to find. When he came back, she was still where he'd left her. He walked right up to her and took her in his arms. He kissed her, letting his hand wander down to gently cup her rear. Kathleen melted as sure as if she'd been ice cream set out in the sun. Michael had just the opposite reaction.

"Thanks," he said when her head fell back and her eyes didn't open.

"For what?"

"Looking like that," he whispered. "Bringing the outside in. I'd kind of forgotten all this good stuff existed. I thought I was standing alone in a fight, but I was just standing alone. So, thanks."

"Anytime," Kathleen breathed, her eyes still closed, her lips still ready. He kissed them again and asked, "Where'd you put that folder?"

"It's in the bedroom."

"Shall I get it?" Michael asked. "Or do you want to get it together?"

Kathleen opened her eyes. She smiled without teeth, that mischievous glint back in her eyes. It was a great offer. She thought about it a minute too long.

"I'll get it," she said.

"You sure?"

"Yeah. But I'll put it back there sometime. Then we'll see what happens when we go looking for it together."

"Meanwhile, let's kick some butt. Whaddaya say? Think the two of us from the wrong side of the tracks can tackle whatever it is that did Lionel in?"

"I haven't got a clue." She wriggled out of his arms, almost sorry she hadn't taken him up on his offer. But when she did, it was going to be so fine. Kathleen held onto that thought and got the folder, checked herself in the mirror, and reached for her red, red lipstick. Thinking twice, she chucked it back on the dresser. He didn't think she looked so bad without her *face*.

His shirt was on and tucked in by the time she got back. She laid the folder on the coffee table and watched Michael slip into his shoes. He ran his hands through his hair, picked up the folder, and started to work.

This was the instant, the moment, the millisecond that marked a turning point in her life. Time could be marked like that, and all the other marked minutes of her life were forgotten. When Michael looked up at her, Kathleen listened intently because these first words she heard, in this new part of her life, would be terribly, terribly important. She leaned forward, anxious to drink in every sound, every nuance, every tone of his voice.

He touched her hand and looked into her eyes. He asked, "Do you have Louise's number?"

"Come in, Kathleen."

Gerry waved at her from behind his desk, coming toward her a second later. Kathleen stood with the door held against her chest as she smiled at Carl Walsh and tried to figure a way to duck out.

"No, you're busy. I'll come back. I didn't realize you had appointments today."

Gerry was too quick. He had the door in his hand and was pulling it open. "Nonsense. Come in here and say hello to Carl. He's been asking about you."

Carl Walsh stood up politely and nodded to her. He had a lovely, vote-winning smile. She'd give him her vote if he would just sit down. She motioned him down; but when he remained standing, Kathleen walked slowly, and reluctantly, into the room. She was stiff from her roll in the dirt and both men took notice, but Carl covered up his surprise smoothly.

"I was just telling your uncle that I hope you're finding the Los Angeles area to your liking." She grinned gamely as she limped in. He kept going. "It's always nice to get a new citizen's point of view."

"I like it very much, thank you," Kathleen said, eager to be done with the amenities and get on with the business of the day. Gerry had no idea what was waiting for him. She wasn't about to fill him in in front of Carl Walsh. She stopped and hoped she wouldn't have to walk any farther. Of course, Gerry insisted.

"Kathleen, what on earth has happened to you?" Taking her by the arm, he stared at her knee where the huge bandage bulged under her stocking. Carl Walsh held out a chair. "Sit down."

"Hope that didn't happen on city property." Kathleen grimaced. There was nothing like sincere concern, and Carl Walsh didn't have it. "If it did, I'd have to give O'Doul & Associates the case so you'd have a conflict of interest and couldn't sue us.''

"No, it's not really as bad as it looks and it happened on private property. It's a long story.''

"One I'd like to hear.'' Gerry clucked, deftly covering his anger. "I thought you were off to see Sarah Brooker last night and then to dinner with Michael. Neither seems an agenda that would lead you to bodily injury. Michael didn't have anything to do with this, did he? If he did, I'll sue Tysco for all their worth. Employing a dangerous man like that.''

"Gerry, please.'' Kathleen tried to hush him. "Michael helped me. I'll tell you about it later. Mr. Walsh, I'm sorry. Sometimes my uncle forgets that I'm his associate and not his daughter.'' She stood up stiffly and smiled as best she could. "It was great to see you, but I have some people in my office.'' To her uncle and associate, she added, "I'd appreciate it if you'd come over when you can, Gerry.''

Kathleen offered her hand. Carl Walsh shook it. Kathleen gritted her teeth, anticipating that her next move was going to send a shooting pain up her back. Funny that she hadn't noticed all that this morning when Michael was offering kisses to make it better.

"I've really got to be going,'' Carl said, suddenly anxious to be out of the office. Not that she could blame him. Between her and Gerry, this place must seem like a nursing home. "Gerry, you go ahead with Kathleen. I'll see myself out. It sounds like she's got her hands full on some front.'' He shook Gerry's hand, too, holding it longer than was necessary. Kathleen limped away and disappeared behind the closed door of her office. Carl watched until she was safely away then walked toward the door with the old man. "Tysco business, Gerry? Business must be better than I thought.''

"Sure, don't I wish that were the case. Tysco is only a small part of a problem we're handling for Mrs. Brooker. Though even I must admit it gets more interesting by the moment.''

Carl Walsh nodded and the two men parted. Gerry gave Becky's desk a knock as he passed and stole a chocolate kiss from the pile in front of her before opening the door to Kathleen's office. He stood right there and cocked his head.

"Well, 'tis a party, I see." He smiled grimly. Stone-faced Louise, Sarah, Michael, and Kathleen looked at him. "I can't wait to hear what the occasion is."

Carl Walsh hadn't intended to go back downtown. In fact, he had intended to pick up a game of racquetball at his gym, sweat a little, and check out the action. If there wasn't any, he was going to give one of the stand-bys in his little black book a call for dinner. There was always a photographer hanging around the gym and a photo of him looking fit as a fiddle with a lovely woman on his arm wouldn't hurt. Huey and Dewy, the bodyguards, were off for the day, not that he needed them when there wasn't a crush around or special business to take care of. Now his plans had changed, and the change threw him off the roll he'd been on.

Instead of enjoying his one afternoon off, away from a planned event, fund-raiser, or campaign speech, he was driving back toward Shay, Sylvester & Harrington, chewing on his lip and cursing the streetlights. More than once he picked up the mobile phone to make a call, only to change his mind and put it down again. Mobile technology just didn't provide the privacy he was going to need.

Sweating lightly by the time he pulled into the underground garage, Carl parked in a handicapped space and walked quickly toward the elevator banks. He ignored the curious looks of people who thought they'd seen him someplace before. The last thing he wanted was to stop for a little talk with a voter. He could feel a blue mood coming on fast, but he kept it at bay till the elevator deposited him at the offices of Shay, Sylvester & Harrington.

"Richard."

He bypassed the receptionist with one word. She was on the phone fast to warn the man in the big corner office. Richard took the news well. He was smiling when Carl walked through the door. Carl was not. There would be no small talk.

"I paid a courtesy call on Gerry O'Doul. He'd been calling my office. I thought it would get the old man off my back. Damn. Damn, I'm glad I stopped by. Damn." Carl was pacing like a caged dog. He pointed at Richard with a long finger. "You won't believe it."

Richard handed him a drink. Carl grabbed it, but it took him a minute to notice Richard was standing behind a chair waiting for him to sit. He shook his head and his free hand.

"Not this time, Richard. I'm not going to let you calm me down with one of your talks about your taking care of everything. You've been taking care of everything, and I will admit you've done a hell of a job till now; but, Richard, it's going to fall apart. I'm not kidding you."

"All right, Carl. Fine. Let's talk. I'll sit. You walk if it makes you feel any better."

"That niece of his, she comes in to the office and what does she talk about? Some supervisor at Tysco and Brooker. Sarah Brooker. I can't believe it. I'll never forget that name as long as I live. That idiot's wife. That blonde was talking about the one guy I thought we didn't have to worry about anymore. That tall—" Carl spun toward Richard. "What's her damn name? Jesus!"

"Kathleen Cotter." Richard filled in the blank softly.

"Who cares?" Carl took a swig of his drink. "I swear, I can't believe it. This isn't good, Richard. This isn't good at all. What in the hell do you think they're doing? Christ. This is incredible. First, the boys can't find the billing, and now, this. Thank God I went over there." He stopped. He drained his glass. His hands were shaking. "What in the heck do you think they're up to? That damn old man. I should have known something was up. Bumping into me that way. Calling the office. Damn old man's trying to make a name for himself on my back."

"He's not up to anything, Carl. I suggest you relax." Richard soothed him patiently. His cool expression infuriated Carl almost as much as his condescending words.

"Right. That's what you told me when we found out Brooker was asking questions."

"And everything was fine, wasn't it?"

"If you call suicide a solution." Carl snorted.

"We were lucky. The man was unbalanced," Richard answered evenly. He picked up a brass cube from his desk . . . an award, but he didn't remember where he'd gotten it or from whom, but still, it felt good and heavy in his hand. He would have liked to have used it to knock some sense into Carl Walsh.

"Well, I don't think we can count on Gerry O'Doul doing the same thing. The guy is relentless. He'll have his niece on our tail until they find out everything. Would you figure that someone who looked like her would even have the brains to ask the right questions?"

"As a matter of fact, Ms. Cotter is quite competent. As to Gerry, let him be." Richard put the brass cube down. If he hadn't he might have been tempted to throw it at Carl. If he killed him, they'd only have to find another candidate. "There's nothing to worry about. This is a small problem. Kathleen Cotter is representing Brooker's ex-wife against the estate and the insurance company. It's no more sinister than that. It's a civil matter. It will run its course."

Carl stopped cold and stared indignantly at Richard Jacobsen.

"You know about this? You know that those two fools have been sniffing around Tysco? You invited them to the party knowing that?"

"It's wise to keep your enemies close, Carl. These two barely qualify, but . . ." He raised his hands as if to ask what could they do.

"Then I must be a hell of a smart guy, Richard, because I practically live with you." Carl started pacing again.

"Thank goodness you don't," Richard drawled. "I prefer my world to be a little more ordered than yours."

"Come on, come on cut the crap. This is not the end of the world. It's an annoyance. That's what you're telling me?" Carl put his glass on the desk. It hit too hard and Richard gave him a look. It was enough. Carl crumpled into a chair.

Richard leaned forward. Carl had never seen Richard nervous. He was like a human calendar, ticking off projects, adding new ones to replace those he'd successfully completed. The indirect lighting caught his glasses and reflected the light so that it appeared there were no eyes behind the lenses.

"Carl," Richard said patiently, "the business arrangements you and I have with one another and the arrangements we both have with Tysco among others are simply that—business arrangements. I want you to remember that. Because if you don't remember that now, you will have a difficult time dealing with the future. I can't imagine these histrionics when we must accomplish as much in Washington." Richard moved less than an inch, but Carl could now see one myopic eye watching him. Carl shifted, too, trying to find the spot where Richard's eyes were hidden behind the reflection. He was unsuccessful, and Richard went on, unaware that he was giving Carl the heebie-jeebies.

"What is happening here is just a dry run. There is nothing to worry about. I have covered all our bases. Worst-case scenario, we end up in court. If we do, a defense is at the ready. Our arrangement is nothing that hasn't been done before. The only thing that sets us apart is the scope of our project. Remember that. We have almost four years invested in this. Now, pull yourself together. Let me monitor the situation with Gerry O'Doul and his lovely niece. You make the speeches. I'll manage the rest. If it makes you feel any better, I know a simple way to diffuse the whole thing."

"You'd better, Richard, or I'm out of here." Carl shot up. "I mean it. I'll just go it on my own—win or lose. If I hear one more word from Gerry O'Doul, if that niece of his shows up on my doorstep asking questions, if whoever they're dealing with at Tysco starts sending me memos, then I'm cutting myself out of this picture."

"I wouldn't advise that, Carl. I have a great deal invested. We all do," Richard reminded him quietly.

"Yeah, well, I've got a whole life wrapped up in this—a reputation, not just money. Money means nothing."

"Oh, yes, money means something," Richard said, but he was talking to the mayor's back. That in itself was surprising. Carl Walsh had never turned his back on Richard before. If Richard had his way, he never would again.

Alone, he sat back and thought. He thought about the person in his life to whom money meant everything and the woman in his life to whom appearances were everything. He thought about himself and what meant everything to him. Few people would guess it, but love and acceptance meant everything to Richard Jacobsen. Only one person really knew that. Pity it wasn't the right one.

An hour later, he put a simple plan into action. While he waited for his call to be put through, Richard thought about the world and knew that he understood it far better than Carl Walsh or Kathleen Cotter or even Gerry O'Doul.

"Did you have that looked at, Sarah?"

Gerry touched her hair, careful not to rub against the ugly bruise beneath it. She shook her head. Kathleen's leg was propped up on an open drawer. She had stopped tapping her pen and was waiting for an answer.

"No, Louise took care of it last night. It's much better, thank you. I can open my eye now." She tried, and the effect was horribly unattractive. Gerry patted her shoulder.

"I still think you should have had a doctor look at it. I think all of you should have had a doctor take a look at you."

He tsked at them all and their antics while he let his gaze roam around the room. They had moved to his office to be more comfortable. The place looked like a triage ward— Michael with his hand bandaged; Kathleen with her scraped knee, sore muscles, and bruised head; Sarah with her terrible knot. Only Louise had emerged without a scratch. That didn't surprise him.

"Gerry, we're fine. We're more concerned with the matter at hand. What do you think?"

"I don't think you have a leg to stand on," Gerry said, stifling a laugh, "if you'll forgive the pun."

"I don't know how you can say that," Kathleen huffed. "We've got overwhelming evidence that Lionel was on to something not-quite-kosher at Tysco. Someone didn't want him to know about whatever it was. Why else were those two men snooping around Sarah's house? I don't know many burglars who go to work in suits. Her rabbits are dead. Lionel felt strongly enough about what he had found at Tysco to bring home paperwork and hide it. He was going over his supervisor's head to try and get some satisfaction, and he didn't do drugs.'' Kathleen looked to her cohorts for help, knowing she'd missed something.

"And the police report," Michael reminded her.

"Yeah, what about that? And the coroner's pictures.'' Louise snapped her fingers triumphantly.

"Yes. Look, Gerry.'' Kathleen shuffled through her own papers and held one out to him. "See, here? The police report says that there was blood on the collar of the deceased's shirt. On the collar!'' Gerry raised a brow, unmoved. "Gerry! Remember the coroner's photo? There were no track marks, which meant Lionel wasn't an addict; but there was that jagged mark at his neck. He was injected in the neck. Sarah checked the clothes that he wore. There was a smudge of blood on the collar right where the neck wound was.''

"Ah, yes, that reminds me. Marlene sent me a copy of the coroner's report on Lionel with a note. Kind of her. She spoke to our good friend Dr. Greischmidt. Unfortunately, he can't remember where the lethal injection was introduced. This doesn't surprise me. The man can't remember what he did with an entire stomach, why should a syringe prick be any different?'' Gerry said.

"See, that must be the injection point. I checked with the free clinic over on Pico. Heroin injected there is for seasoned junkies looking for a final high. For someone who's clean, it's certain death," Kathleen crowed.

"The only thing I will grant you is that it seems Mr. Brooker—'' He nodded to Sarah in deference to his memory. "—was not an experienced drug-user. I would even grant you that he never, ever used drugs before that fateful day. Sarah, did Lionel ever mention that he had an enlarged heart?'' Again she shook her head. "There, that is no help. If he were aware of a medical problem, then he probably wouldn't have attempted to inject himself with heroin, a drug that immediately affects the heart. But more interesting still, there is no damage to the veins in Lionel's arms. There wasn't one collapsed from overuse, no tracks, nothing to indicate that this man had ever injected heroin before that day. His nasal passages were clear. There was no breakdown in tissue to indicate he was snorting. His lungs were clear. In short, Lionel seemed to be what everyone you've spoken to say he was—a man who believed his body was, indeed, a temple.''

"There, see?" Kathleen was delighted he saw it their way.

"I knew he'd understand." Louise put her arm around Sarah, who still looked bewildered by her attention.

Only Michael was quiet. He watched the old man, who watched him right back.

"The problem is, it's not enough, is it?" he asked Gerry.

"No, Michael, it's nothing. There's nothing you've told me that would convince me to go to the authorities. They would laugh in our face if we asked them to reopen the case on Lionel. No threats of violence against him. No enemies. You don't even have a handle on the work difficulty. I'm afraid you all have been overwhelmed by what happened last night.''

"There *is* something wrong, Gerry," Michael reminded him. "I haven't had a chance to go over those invoices, but I can see why Lionel didn't like the looks of at least two of them. They seemed inflated in certain areas. It will take awhile for me to give you something definitive, though.''

"Michael, it won't matter, even if you do. What can you really tell the police? Can Sarah identify the men who were in her home?" Gerry pinned her with his gaze. She hung her head. "No, I thought not. Can either of the Mrs. Brookers provide us any insight into Lionel's dealings at Tysco?" Louise checked out her nails. "No. He didn't confide in them. He kept his professional and private lives separate. And, Michael? You haven't any evidence to bring to the table. No threatening notes, no people popping in unexpectedly to whisper in Lionel's ear while he worked. You told Kathleen that Lionel was a good worker, steady, and hardly eccentric. The only person who thought something was bothering Lionel was his friend Harold.

You checked that out and Mr. . . . Mr. . . .'' Gerry snapped his fingers. ''Forgive me, I've forgotten his name.''

At that moment the door opened and Becky motioned to Kathleen, whispering *telephone*. Kathleen slipped out to take the call in Gerry's office. The last thing she wanted to do was interrupt the proceedings. Going behind Michael, unable to resist, she let her fingers trail across his shoulders just as he answered Gerry.

''Jules Porter?''

''Yes, Mr. Porter, Lionel's former supervisor. They'd had many years together and, while he may not have been polite, the man answered your questions, did he not, Michael? Did he appear to be stunned or nervous about your questions? Did he attempt to hide anything? Have you thrown out of his office?''

''No, he didn't.''

Michael turned his head away, bringing his fist to his chin. They sat in silence, the two men and two women. Emotions toured the room, lighting on all their heads more than once. Frustration, the feeling that the answers were just around the corner, sadness, anxiety, the need for a challenge, the desire to know the truth about Lionel were all borne in thoughtful silence.

''We can settle this entire matter quickly in two ways,'' Gerry said finally.

They all looked at him as Kathleen slipped quietly back into the room, her phone call completed. She stood apart, lingering by the door, her hand on the knob as if she were anxious to be off somewhere else instead of in this room with the people who had come to mean so many things to her. Her eyes remained fixed on Gerry, her expression was one of profound sadness and even more intense determination. No one noticed. Their attention was on the old man.

''If Lionel was murdered, then he was murdered. We will keep that belief to ourselves, and we will take what we know about his state of mind and physical condition to the court. Kathleen will lay it at Judge Kelley's feet. I believe that we will prevail and Louise will be granted her benefits by All Life.

Of course, I would also suggest that we withdraw our suit against the estate.''

Louise nodded. "That's okay with me." Her whiter-than-white nails with Michael Jackson painted on them never once headed for her hair. Sarah smiled at her sweetly.

"We can also call Bob Morton and suggest that we meet and attempt to settle this matter with All Life before we get to court. Since he can expect full disclosure anyway, we might as well do it sooner than later, wrap this up, and get on with other business.''

"Then there's the second long and arduous road that will, more than likely, lead nowhere." Gerry paused. He looked at them each in turn.

"We can continue with what we're doing." Michael picked up the ball. "Perhaps someone owes it to Lionel to find out the truth about his death.''

"And who will take on that job, Michael?" Gerry became devil's advocate. "The police won't want anything to do with this. This is Los Angeles. The authorities are so overwhelmed they often can't pursue investigations on those who are gunned down in cold blood on our streets with twenty eyewitnesses. They aren't waiting for a mysterious challenge. And who will take it upon themselves to exhume Lionel's body, assign and pay investigators, criminalist, and goodness-knows-who-else? You? Do you intend to quit your job for Lionel? Kathleen? Me? Is that what the practice of law is about or would we be overstepping our bounds? Sarah? Dear Sarah, who wants to tend her garden? Louise? Would you like the job? Would you like for us to secure your insurance settlement only to see it frittered away on an investigation that may not have a conclusion? Which of us will do that? Which of us will take on Lionel's cause if, indeed, there ever was foul play?''

Sarah lifted her head and pushed her hair out of her face. Dressed in purple and white, she looked like an odd Harlequin. But no one was laughing. They couldn't meet her eyes, for each of them knew their answer was *no,* they would not take on such a responsibility.

"How about all of us?" Sarah asked, her voice small, her question profound.

She looked about, and there was no expectation in her expression. She and Lionel had lived a reclusive life; there had been no need for anyone to share it when it was good and she didn't really figure anyone would want to share her sorrow or her fear. But she asked the question anyway.

"I'd go for that." Louise's voice.

"I'd figure out the Tysco stuff," Michael added.

"I could help with the legal work needed for the exhumation and investigators," Gerry said. "Kathleen will speak with All Life. We'll try to wrap that up as soon as possible. After that, we'll look into the matter of the strange death of Lionel Brooker. Is that it, then?"

Yes, they all agreed, and then Gerry O'Doul smiled at his niece, waiting for her sweet voice to be added to the chorus.

"No," she said solemnly. "That isn't it."

Chapter Thirteen

They sat facing each other, neither moving though there didn't seem that much more that could be said between them. Still, Gerry wasn't ready to let go. He wasn't ready to end the afternoon, at least not on this note.

"Sure, Kathleen, aren't I excited to death for you? Really. Richard Jacobsen is quite the man. To be offered a position at Shay, Sylvester & Harrington is flattering indeed, considering he has only run into you once or twice."

"Three times. I've seen him three times."

"Ah, yes, once he came to watch you in court. When you were arguing for Henrietta, I believe." Kathleen nodded. "Then 'tis really something that he offered you a position. On an environmental case, no less. One that's even made the news as I recall."

Kathleen made some noises of agreement. She crossed her legs, focusing on a scuff mark on the side of her beige slingbacks. She hated scuff marks. She hated doing this to Gerry O'Doul. Didn't she?

"It should be very exciting for you. Yes, yes, indeed," he mused. "After only three meetings. And not a formal interview between you. Fancy that."

"Uncle Gerry, I know this can't make you happy." Kathleen squirmed. Her guilt and his graciousness were making her angry.

"But of course it makes me happy. Sure, I couldn't possibly offer you the career advantages you'll have with Richard. It's only that I want you to be very sure, very careful of the decision you're making."

Kathleen unclasped her hands where they lay in her lap and put them on the arms of her chair. It had been too much to hope that this could be taken care of with a simple look of surprise, a hug of encouragement, and a send-off with a smile.

"I can't explain this, Gerry. I realize it's unusual. It's as unusual as your letter asking me to come work with you. Maybe my stars are in the right place or the moon is full or I was meant to be working for you so that I could meet Mr. Jacobsen. Whichever it is, I appreciate the opportunity you've given me, but I can't turn my back on the one he's offering me. I can't. It's the dream of every lawyer to work for a firm like Shay, Sylvester & Harrington. For someone like me, it's closer to a miracle."

Gerry let his hand waggle. "Now, now, don't sell yourself short."

Why not. she wanted to ask, everyone else in her life had. Even he had, for a while.

"I won't," she said quietly. Her fingers went to her silvery bangs. "But I've got to see if I can do this."

"Oh, Kathleen, I don't think there's any doubt that you can. None at all." Gerry's faded, blue eyes didn't twinkle anymore. He was serious. Relieved, Kathleen allowed herself a smile.

"Thank you. I appreciate the blessing. I really do. And we'll see each other often. I'll need your advice, I'm sure."

She was out of the chair, her fingertips still in contact with nubby brown upholstery, when Gerry revved his engines and came at her full-force.

"Of course, I'll be here when you need me, and naturally I wouldn't want anything to keep you from what you need to do; but, Kathleen—" He held up a finger. She knew that tone of voice. It was too kind, too selfless. She stiffened. "Do you think you might possibly ask Richard to postpone your employment just a wee bit? Given what you've been through with Louise, given Sarah's precarious position and Michael—of course, Michael—you might want to stay with us a little longer. You know, with your friends. For Lionel. Not that I'm asking for myself, you understand . . .''

At that, Kathleen began to shake. It was just a little shivering inside, a small twitch in her hands. She clamped her lips shut and looked to the left of Gerry and then took an interest in the door. She wished she had a magazine to flip open, an article to read on anger or making your eyes look bigger with the right shadow. She wished she had a place to hide where she could nod and agree and make life smooth. But there was no magazine and this was not her mother. She had to hold that thought. If she didn't, she would continue to paint on a face instead of turn a real one to the world.

''It *is* for you, Uncle Gerry,'' she said quietly, and he responded with his own dead silence. ''It's for you, not Michael or anyone else. You want me here because you're lonely. But I've been there, done that. My mother wasn't really sick for years. She was lonely and she was scared. I knew that somewhere inside me, but I stayed anyway because I was lonely and scared, too. We were each other's excuse. I did it because I figured I wasn't worth much to anyone except her, and it was you who made me feel that way. When you left, you took all the hope and stardust with you. Mom and Dad never talked about you after that. You didn't call. There was just this big, awful silence like it was my fault you were gone. So I made up for it by staying. But I'm not going to stay behind again. Mr. Jacobsen says he needs me immediately. It's a big case and they've lost a key player. I'm not going to stay because someone asks. Not again.''

Kathleen stuck her hands into her pockets. She'd said too much, but she couldn't stop the rest that was coming. She didn't look at Gerry for fear the hurt on his face would weaken her resolve. At the very least, it would make her shut up, and she didn't want to do that ever again in her whole life.

''You wouldn't stay even for me and I thought—'' Her voice

shook. "—I thought you cared." There was a rent in time where everything stood still. All clocks, all motion, as if the world were waiting for the truth. "I thought you loved me. You didn't care enough to stay in my life, so why should I stay for you?"

"Kathleen, I did love you. More than you'll ever know."

"So much that you walked out?" She tilted her head to let the tears trickle back the way they came. "At least I'm giving you the courtesy of a little notice. I'm giving you a reason. You didn't give me either."

"Then, sure, Kathleen, I'll give them to you now."

Gerry came toward her. She moved away. If she'd been smart, she would have run. But she wasn't that smart.

"I had no wife, no children, and you were the apple of my eye. I wanted you to have everything. Not so much you'd forget how to work, but enough to make the road easier."

"Oh, I never forgot how to work," Kathleen said. "I had to work for every little thing I had. My father thought education would be wasted on me; my mother thought clothes and makeup were a waste on someone so tall and big and ugly. What was it you wasted on me, Gerry? Your time?"

Gerry hung his head; the top of it was smooth and reflective. The little bits of hair that were combed across it looked pitiful. He raised his head to speak to her.

"Time, Kathleen. Time is what I wasted. But I only wasted the time I spent away from you. And it was only because of the money."

"There never was any money," she shot back.

"Yes, there was," he said quietly. "There was quite a bit." Kathleen sat down, unable now to take her eyes off him. "There was a trust fund for you, Kathleen. Your mother and I arranged it with the provision that your father would never know. Your mother was the trustee."

Gerry walked past her, lost in his memories, choosing the proper words for his story, seeing her, she was sure, still as a young girl eager for the stories of his glamorous life.

"Your father chased every scheme that came his way. And every one he pinned his hopes on failed him. That's why I didn't want him to know about the money. In those years I represented some pretty shady characters. I worried I might not always be around to take care of you. That's why I made your mother the trustee.''

Gerry landed by the window and looked out. She knew what he saw. An alley. Nothing more or less. There was no glamor there, but he seemed to draw inspiration from it.

''Your mother managed the fund for many years. She sent me the statements that were sent to her. You should have had enough not only for school but to set yourself up in a tidy practice if you liked. Unfortunately, your mother was a weak woman. She told your father about the trust fund. When he asked her to withdraw the money, she did.''

He looked over his shoulder at her. The collar of his shirt still bobbed about his thin neck; the years wore on him. She saw hurt and regret on his face. Mostly regret.

''I could have forgiven her that, Kathleen. What I couldn't forgive was her righteousness. When I confronted the two of them, she sided with your father. She said it was their right. She looked me in the eye and told me that the money I'd worked hard for was, by rights, theirs because they had so little. It was about them. Not you or me, but them. I imagine your mother knew in her heart she was wrong, but her pride kept her from apologizing. I was so hurt I cut myself off from my sister and her husband. In the process, I lost you, too.

''And it went on that way until there were years between us.'' Gerry found his chair again. He seemed tired. ''Everyone was at fault except you, and you suffered the most. 'Twasn't what I wanted at all.'' Gerry cradled his cheek in his palm. ''Sure, didn't I think your mother had told you the sorry tale, Kathleen? I thought that's why you came. Now that you know, it will be why you leave.''

Numb, Kathleen stood up. She slipped on her high heels, then righted herself. For the first time in her life, Kathleen spoke the honest-to-God truth, out loud, without qualification or concern for anyone's feelings but her own.

''That's not why I'm leaving. I'm leaving for myself, Uncle

Gerry. I want what Richard Jacobsen has to offer, and Richard Jacobsen wants me."

"I need you."

"It isn't enough now. I don't want to be needed anymore. Not in that way. I'll take care of All Life. I'll call Bob Morton in the morning."

"You'll be leaving Sarah just when she needs you the most."

"Gerry, she's not my friend. We all aren't bound to each other. You treat Louise like she's your daughter. You've taken Sarah under your wing. You've seen Michael twice, and you're ready to have him up for cards."

"And you, Kathleen, how have I treated you?"

"Like my mother did," Kathleen said and regretted it the moment the words were out of her mouth.

"I'm sorry, then. I can only wish you well." Gerry stood and gave her a formal bow, stopping her as she reached for the doorknob. "I'm sure Richard will want you to start as soon as possible. I'll take care of Louise."

Kathleen hesitated.

That hurt.

As she left for the day, the sun was setting.

Her heart was, too.

"I thought you'd still be here."

Michael stood in the doorway of Gerry O'Doul's office. The front door was open; Becky was long gone, so he had walked right in. His long legs were parted, his thumbs hooked in the pockets of his jeans. He was a shadow-man because Gerry hadn't moved from this chair since Kathleen had left, not even to turn on the lights. Gallant as always, he did so now, though it was obviously a great effort to pull the little gold chain on the banker's lamp he'd had since he'd passed the bar. That grand occasion seemed a hundred years ago. The lamp still worked; Gerry was beginning to wonder if he still did. He blinked and held his glass up toward his guest.

"Come and raise one with me, Michael. We've been deserted by the woman we love and there's nothing left but the bottle."

Gerry's sad chuckles were like wilting rose petals strewn in Michael's path as he sauntered in. He smiled at the old man who had shed his jacket and turned up his cuffs. The watch on his wrist was silver with an elasticized band, the substantial timepiece of a substantial man. Gerry poured two fingers and put it in front of Michael.

"You do love my Kathleen, don't you?" he asked as he sat back in his chair.

"I don't know, Gerry." Michael took the glass and sat down. "How about I just confess to liking her a heck of a lot so far?"

"That's fine for the time being, Michael. But don't wait too long to decide on the other. Kathleen is moving, Michael, moving so fast. She'll leave us all behind if we're not careful, and she may not be happy when she does. When she wants to come back, we may not be here to welcome her home."

"Is that what she's doing? Leaving us behind? I thought she was just taking advantage of an opportunity."

"No, no, my boy." Gerry poured himself another drink and toasted Michael. He sipped and put his head back on his chair. "Ah, I say, getting older has its good points. I don't even feel this brew as it goes down." Gerry licked his lips and let his eyes roam over the ceiling. "She's run away is what she's done, poor thing. The problem is she's run the wrong way, into the jaws of the wily beast."

"Jacobsen?"

"No other." Gerry slid his head along the back of his chair and his eyes came to rest on Michael. "You're a good man, Michael. I could tell that the moment I met you. I'm proud to know you. But Richard Jacobsen is a man I've never trusted. He worked with me, don't you know, so I'm not talking through my hat. He was a brilliant young man, but there's something odd that drives him. Something dark, it is, and I've never quite cared for it. I can't condemn him. We've all played the game, each of us just has a different way of staying on the board. I used Richard when I could. He used me. How could I, in good conscience, tell Kathleen anything other than good luck? She's on the board now, Michael. If I were still one of the big boys, she'd be safe here with me instead of going to him."

"You think she's in some kind of danger?"

Gerry shook his head, "Not in the way you mean. It's just that I don't want her to be disappointed, Michael. I don't think she has the cold heart she'll need for a place like Shay, Sylvester & Harrington. I think this was a bad decision, truly I do."

"And you didn't tell her?"

"After confessing to her that all the adults in her life had done her wrong? Me the worst offender?" Gerry snorted. "Sure aren't you the optimist? I'm assuming she told you when you drove her home."

"She did." Michael still held his drink. This wasn't the social hour, just some time he could give an old man he admired. He wished he could do more.

"And you think she would have trusted my advice?"

"I don't." He reached for the bottle and checked it out. Fine scotch. When he put it back on the desk, he finally had a taste. It went down smooth. "She's got her pride."

"Don't we all?" Gerry laughed. It was good to sit with a man, talking like a man. No flowers, no hearts, no worry about who would be hurt. Gerry confided in his new friend. "My pride kept me from changing with the times. In my colossal arrogance, I assumed quality would win out, and the one thing I always had to offer was quality. People got what they paid for." Gerry chuckled at his own nonsense.

"But fashions changed. No one wanted ethics and reason; so few people wanted the truth. And there was the press. I always spoke so truthfully to the press, but the time came when they turned the words around so blatantly I sounded like a fool. People forgot Gerry O'Doul and the way he understood the law. I didn't see that people wanted to be entertained and shocked. They wanted gossip, not thoughtfulness. No one cared about the truth or the deftness of a battle waged by the spirit and letter of the law. My pride kept me from running with the pack, so I was left behind. I was not the darling any longer. People like Richard Jacobsen were. Money talked. Designer-name law firms got the business. Those who could sell rather than argue their case were the champions."

The two men considered, Gerry's opportunity lost. There were pros and cons to standing still. They had both done it. There was something to be said for compromise, too, but they wouldn't argue the fine points now.

"And you, Michael, how has pride changed your life?"

"Pride fooled me. Pride lulled me into thinking I had accomplished something when in fact I'd simply been hollering into a vacuum while the bad guys kept doing what they wanted to do."

"Very bad guys?" Gerry asked.

"Semi-bad. Immoral, unethical. That kind of bad." Michael shrugged.

"Then we'll toast the bad guys, for sure their time is just about up, don't you think?"

"I guess that depends on you. You've got an unusual group here who aren't quite sure what in the heck they want to do. We'd fall apart without someone to lead us through the Lionel thing. Are you still in, even without Kathleen?"

Gerry opened the top drawer of his desk and took out two cigars. He handed one to Michael. They snipped the tips and lit them. The office filled with the aroma of a fine tobacco. They sat comfortably together.

"I'll make some inquiries, Michael, but I think I'll reserve committing myself just about now, if you don't mind."

"I don't mind. It will take me awhile to figure out the paperwork. We'll just sort of agree to look into things."

"I think that's wise." Gerry puffed again and watched the cloud above his head take shape. At first he thought it looked like a woman in the gray smoke, then he realized the apparition looked like Richard Jacobsen. A little misshapen, so difficult to define, impossible to pin down. "Yes, I think I'll be keeping my eye peeled. I'd appreciate it if you'd do the same. Keep your eye on everything, Michael. Especially my Kathleen."

Chapter Fourteen

"So, Bob Morton's thinking it over?"

Kathleen stabbed at her Chinese Chicken Salad and came up with everything but chicken, so she started all over again. Her appetite wasn't what it should have been, so she let her fork rest and looked at her companions. Sarah, in a floral dress, looked pretty now that her bruise had faded and her eye was back to normal, Louise in lace and leather with Marilyn Monroe on her chartreuse nails was true to form. Gerry was spruced up in a new suit of beige linen. Only Michael was missing. Somebody had to work, she supposed. She sure as heck wasn't working. At least not the kind of work she'd thought she'd be doing.

"Well, he doesn't have much time to make up his mind, does he?" She put on a brave smile, hoping they wouldn't see how much she wanted to know everything that they were doing. "We're supposed to . . . I mean, you're supposed to be back in court next week, right?"

"Hardly seems possible." Gerry was jovial. His good humor did nothing to relieve the pall that had settled over their luncheon table and his own private ire. They had come with such good intentions to celebrate her new job and show there were no hard feelings. Instead, they had found Kathleen, beautiful as always, looking forlorn and trying to hide her frustration. He kept smiling and trying. "So, then, that means that you've been gone from us for almost three weeks. How are you finding life at Shay, Sylvester & Harrington? Is Richard treating you well?"

"Yes. Definitely. Yes, he stops in to see me every so often. In fact, he even had a painting I admired transferred into my office from his personal conference room." Kathleen smiled, too. She looked sick. "You'll have to come up and see it. It's really beautiful. Really."

Kathleen's enthusiasm was less than convincing, but all the heads around the table nodded politely, Louise most heartily since she was the one who understood about keeping up appearances.

"So, then, what are you doing in this new office of yours? Bet it's nothing as exciting as us, huh, Sarah?" Louise gave her new friend a wink only to be rewarded with a true, but shy, smile. Kathleen thought she would cry except for the fact that Louise was looking at her expectantly.

"I'm working on an environmental case. It's very important. If we successfully defend our client, there might actually be sweeping legislation that will change the water pollution laws across the country. It's very, very exciting."

"Wow," Sarah breathed. "Are you going to go to Washington when you win and make the laws?"

"Well, no. I don't think they'd have me."

"Are we going to see you on TV? I watch that court TV show all the time," Louise chimed in. "That would be great to see you on TV, but you've got to wear something more colorful. I swear, you've got dowdier since you flew the coop."

"Well, no, I'm not actually going to be doing the trial work." Kathleen colored and picked up her napkin. She couldn't look at Gerry. She didn't really want to look at any of them. "It's kind of dry, actually. We're all specializing, you know."

Feeling Gerry's eyes on her, she chanced a glance at her uncle. She didn't hold his gaze long. He knew. She knew he knew. She was nothing at Shay, Sylvester & Harrington. Fourth seat is what she was on a huge, convoluted case that might never see the inside of a courtroom. She spent most of her time pouring over emissions records. The thought of years of this made Kathleen more than miserable. Gerry knew, all right, that she was nothing on this case. Worse than that, he pitied her when he should have been proud of her. She changed the subject. She'd get through this lunch if it were the last thing she did.

"So, what are you all up to besides getting ready to get Louise her money from All Life?"

"Michael hasn't told you?"

Kathleen shook her head. "It's been hard to see him. I have to bill so many hours a week, I hardly have time to breathe. He's been busy, too, I hear."

"He's narrowed down those billing records. Gerry's been making phone calls all over the place." Louise leaned over, her substantial cleavage on the table like a forbidden desert. In his younger days Gerry might have enjoyed such an eyeful. Now he just wanted to watch Kathleen and make sure the misery he saw on her face wasn't a trick of the light. He would never rejoice in her suffering, for certainly that's what it was, but he was curious about it and took exception to it and blamed Richard Jacobsen for it.

"Louise, we shouldn't be talking about our investigation," Gerry warned her.

"Gerry," Sarah breathed, "it's only Kathleen. She wouldn't tell anyone."

"Darn right she wouldn't," Louise intoned.

"I don't have anyone to tell anyway. Besides, no one would believe what you guys are doing. So tell me something exciting." Kathleen regrouped like a girl at a slumber party. "I want every detail."

"There isn't much, Kathleen," Gerry interrupted. "I've managed to find out a few interesting details about the coroner, that's all. Minor things that aren't worth talking about."

The one that was most interesting he would never share with her: An attorney had requested the coroner himself be dispatched to autopsy Lionel Brooker. It had been a lovely piece of work, Marlene talking with a friend who talked with a friend who tracked down someone else who remembered an offhanded comment made by the big man himself when he arrived for the dirty work. Lovely piece of work, indeed. Kathleen would have enjoyed it. Thankfully, she didn't press for information he wasn't ready to share. Louise had her ear and was directing Kathleen to look under the table. Their heads were together like two inept spies.

"Look, we got this great camera. Sarah and I are going to go out to Tysco and snap some photos. We're going to see who comes and goes and then try to see if Sarah can figure out if any of them kind of look like the guys who went out to her house."

"Louise, there are thousands of people who work out there. That's ridiculous." Louise lowered the tablecloth and stashed her bag. Kathleen sat back. Sarah hung her head, fidgeting with her napkin.

"Well, we don't have much choice. It's not like we've got a whole lot of help," she sniffed. "Not like the backup you've probably got. Computers and things. Besides, we're not going to take pictures of the women, so that cuts it down by half. And we're not going to bother with the people coming out of the manufacturing facilities."

"The men who came to my house wore suits, I know that," Sarah offered.

"Yeah, so that means we've gotta concentrate on the suits. And we know they're big guys," Louise offered.

"And we're especially going to watch out for Jules Porter. If Lionel was giving him a bad time, then we should find out if he's doing anything weird outside the office that might have affected what was going on inside." That was Sarah talking, and they all had to lean close to listen.

"And does Michael know what you're doing?" Kathleen missed all this. She laughed, grateful that they hadn't forgotten her. At O'Doul & Associates, there were people to talk to and problems to solve, listening to these two made Kathleen wish for the good old days. At Shay, Sylvester & Harrington, there were emissions reports to sift through. Forms to fill out. Associates so concerned with their own status on the partnership track they were afraid to talk to Kathleen, much less befriend her.

"Not to worry, Kathleen. If these ladies get in trouble, I'll defend them with my last breath." Gerry grinned at all of them with a smile that didn't reach his eyes. Kathleen saw it and answered his sympathy with a simulated smile of her own. "But I'm afraid we all have things we must do. Kathleen, we wouldn't want to keep you from your work. So important, those billing hours. I'm glad I'm old and infirm," he said with a commiserating wink. "Sure, I couldn't keep track of such mathematics anymore. Shall we, ladies?"

Chairs went back, napkins were put on tables, skirts were smoothed, and little things said all around as they trooped out of Maple Drive, onto the street, and across it to Shay, Sylvester & Harrington. Louise and Sarah left them in the lobby of the building.

"We're going to take off, Gerry." Louise leaned into him for a kiss on her cheek. He kissed the air instead and patted her shoulder—if, indeed there were a shoulder under the incredible pads in her jacket. She looked a bit like a packing box. Satisfied, she did the same to Kathleen. "We want to get down to Tysco and stake out before the four o'clock shift leaves. We'll pop in and see Michael, too. Anybody have a message for him?"

Sarah and Louise looked at Kathleen. Gerry answered.

"Ask him if he'd mind postponing dinner this evening. Tell him I'll call him tomorrow."

"Okay, Mr. O'Doul." Sarah stuck out her hand. He shook it gently, bowing slightly.

"You were going to have dinner with Michael?" Kathleen asked, trying to sound casual as they headed to her office.

"He says he asked you, but you pleaded work. I was second choice, don't you know?"

The elevator called for them. Kathleen went in. It was late. She'd have to make up the extra hour that evening. She was all alone. Then Gerry joined her.

"You don't have to come up, Uncle Gerry."

"Nonsense. I've been so patient waiting for an invitation to see your new place of business, but I've not had one. So now

I'm taking matters into my own hands. I'll just pop in and say hello to Richard while I'm here.''

Kathleen punched the number sixteen. The elevator shot up. Her stomach fell to the floor.

"He's awfully busy, Gerry. I don't know that you should just walk in on him. There's a definite protocol in this place."

"Yes, yes, I know." Gerry patted her arm. It was a touch filled with a lifetime of experience that told her there weren't many places you couldn't go if you acted like you belonged there. "But it's really not as daunting as it seems, Kathleen. I promise you it isn't." Gerry O'Doul stopped the elevator. He pressed a button that had a warning to press only in the case of emergency. Kathleen's mouth dropped. He had pushed it as if he were ringing a doorbell. This wasn't a three-story building on South Beverly. This was a towering high-rise in the heart of Beverly Hills. This wasn't the place for a heart-to-heart, but Gerry didn't seem to think the rules applied to him. She supposed he never did.

"Kathleen, these are just people. They are a little scared like you, a little daunted by the fact they are working on problems that affect the country, not just a widow who lives in a canyon with her rabbits. It's all right to be nervous as long as you're doing your best. But, Kathleen, if you're unhappy here, that's another matter. Don't be afraid to stay and work like the dickens, but don't be afraid to leave either. It wouldn't be a failure; it would be a choice. Choose the kind of life you want; and if it's not the kind Richard leads, then my door is open or I will help you find the right door."

Kathleen met his gaze head on and was proud of that. She was touched by what he said; but more than that she was embarrassed by her own idiocy, and *that* she would never admit. Besides, he didn't need her. Nor did Louise or Sarah. They had everything under control.

"Thank you, Gerry, but I think it's all going to work out fine here. I've just got to remember things take longer in a place like this. Mr. Jacobsen wouldn't have offered me the job if he didn't think I have what it takes."

"No," Gerry answered. "No, he wouldn't."

He pushed the button and they were off again. A moment later, they were walking through the lobby where they had partied not so long ago. They went down the long halls, past secretaries and paralegals and big offices with windows that didn't open for a breath of fresh air. They passed an enormous library, a production office where reams of paper were printed and copied and stapled for court appearances, internal distribution, and storage. They passed the offices of junior partners and, finally, came to Kathleen's where Gerry made noises of appreciation over her Mathis oil and tried to ignore the closetlike dimensions of the place she called her own. Stacks of reports waited for her attention and a grid pulsated on her computer screen. When Gerry was finished with his admiring sounds, he kissed her cheek.

"I'll leave you to your work, Kathleen. Why don't you and Michael come for a drink Saturday?"

"I'll think about it. We're supposed to go to a movie; but the way I feel now, all I want to do is sleep."

"Life in the fast lane." Gerry chuckled. "But I'm afraid that's no excuse to leave an old man on his own all weekend." Gerry stepped back, the smiling fading. "I'm sorry. I didn't mean to pressure you. I'm sorry, Kathleen."

"No offense taken," she said. "I'd love to come. I'll try. I promise. I'll tell Michael to kidnap me if he has to."

Kathleen waved him out the door and sat back at her desk, forgetting lunch, Michael, Sarah, and Louise as she opened the first of many tomes on environmental testing. Only Gerry O'Doul stayed on her mind. It was nice to know her uncle's door was still open. Not that she'd ever do anything about it, but it was nice to know.

Gerry was almost buried by the cushions of the low, deep chair in which he sat. He was so small that he seemed almost inconsequential. If Richard Jacobsen had his way, he would have *been* inconsequential. Instead, Gerry O'Doul was making himself all-too-important.

"Richard, I don't want to create a problem for Kathleen. I

know you won't hold it against her because her old uncle has come to check up. But there are things that just seem a bit unusual here and I thought, being her only living relative, that it is my responsibility to keep an eye on her.''

"Of course, I completely understand your concern for your niece; what I don't understand is why her employment here would be the cause of that concern.''

Richard bounced ever so slightly in his perfectly proportioned chair while his eyes remained fixed on the old man. Beneath the desk, out of Gerry's sight, he played with a pen. He wanted Gerry O'Doul gone. Shay, Sylvester & Harrington did not function as O'Doul & Associates did. A slap on the back, a handshake. Absurdities in an era when business was the law and the law was business.

Gerry leaned forward, escaping the suction of the overstuffed cushion with a great effort. He straightened his tie when he was finally in a position that allowed him to speak to Richard man to man.

"We'll be blunt, Richard. Kathleen is a smart girl. In the right circumstances, she could even be brilliant. The jury returned more than the asking when she handled Mrs. Poole, and look at what she did for my client in the Brooker case. I believe All Life is going to settle with us because of her innovative arguments. In fact, we're going to be doing more than that. Sure she even managed to put us on the track to prove that there had been some sort of foul play. Unfortunately, you took her away before we could have the benefit of her thinking.''

Richard's lips tipped up. Had Gerry been looking closely, he would have seen a glimmer of joy.

"Obviously, I chose well. Shay, Sylvester & Harrington likes their associates to be innovative. Perhaps I overstepped the bounds of propriety by not asking for her professional hand first and that's what makes you uneasy.'' The sarcasm was evident. Gerry ignored it.

"No, Richard. It's not about the way you did this. It's about why.'' He dug in his heels, not about to leave, and that didn't make Richard happy. He glanced toward the door, then back at his guest.

"I have a full calendar today, Gerry. Perhaps we could get to the point."

"I've known you many years, and never have I known you to do anything that was not calculated for a return on your investment. I never believed those rumors about the incident in Mexico. Scandals of a sexual nature were never what I would have expected from you. That is why I don't imagine your interest in my niece is personal. But I must ask the question anyway, Richard. Did you hire her because you fancy Kathleen?"

Gerry had never heard Richard Jacobsen laugh before. He imagined, given the volume and intensity of Richard's amusement, that there were quite a few people in the halls listening to the odd sound coming from this usually silent office.

"Oh my. Oh my, my, my."

Richard reached into his pocket for a handkerchief and dabbed at his eyes. In a twinkle, Richard Jacobsen was back to his old, smooth self, his tiny hands clasped together, pink and soft-looking. He held them out to Gerry as if to show he wasn't hiding a thing. Gerry couldn't look at them and think Kathleen's name at the same time. He found nothing amusing about any of this. The more Richard danced around his questions, the more uneasy Gerry O'Doul became.

"Your niece is a very attractive young woman, but believe me, that's not what I found so intriguing about her, Gerry. Quite simply, we needed a bright, quick-thinking associate and we needed her quickly."

"Analyzing mathematical data truly takes a bright mind. A lesser one would be put to sleep," Gerry snapped. "Although, in my day, any paralegal could have created the charts Kathleen is toiling so diligently to complete."

Richard ignored him. "She is a hard worker and a quick study. We didn't want a paralegal. We wanted an attorney who might offer insight into courtroom arguments after the data has been analyzed. Money isn't your niece's motivation, thank goodness. Even you must see how unusual and desirable that is in a young attorney. We are top-heavy with fiscally driven young people and a volatile team of egotists on the case to which she was assigned. I'm counting on her for many things, not the least of which is her attitude.''

"But why the urgency, Richard?" Gerry pressed, wanting to lift his feet to allow for the flow of bull.

"We had an opening. Those don't happen too often," Richard answered narrowly.

"She's working on a minute portion of a case that will never see the inside of a courtroom." Gerry sat comfortably in the big chair, his fingers tented and his eyes just as bright as always. He forced himself to mildness but didn't fool Richard at all. "I smell a rat, Richard, one I think I should ferret out."

"It would be a waste of your time," Richard answered with equal discretion. "I admire you greatly, Gerry, and I would hate to see you waste precious time on something that is no mystery."

"I've already wasted time where Kathleen was concerned. What little I have left, I want to devote to making sure she is happy and content."

"She's a woman who has made a career-decision, and I would suggest you respect that. If you don't, you might find yourself lonelier than you are now and Kathleen might find herself on the street. I can't imagine she would look kindly on your meddling if it caused this firm to think twice about her employment."

They both thought about that great, big horrible possibility. It was a bald-faced threat, but before he had time to explore all the angles to see what was hidden behind them, the phone rang. Richard answered it, rudely dismissing Gerry with that gesture.

With dignity, Gerry nodded to Richard Jacobsen, a man of dubious integrity whose back was now turned to him. Standing tall, Gerry turned on his heel and walked, shoulders back, to the vestibule just outside Richard's office.

When he cleared the door, he stepped aside and leaned against the wall, knowing he couldn't face even a secretary until he'd composed himself. His heart hurt. He had failed Kathleen, and this was her reward. This ridiculous situation where she would be used for God-knew-what-reason, only to realize it too late.

Five years from now when there was no partnership offering, when her resume read Shay, Sylvester & Harrington, Associate, Kathleen would be turned loose only fit to work for another Dorty & Breyer. It was his fault. Richard was paying him back for something, and he was using Kathleen to do it. But what had been so awful in their history that Richard would ruin a young woman's career to prove the point?

Richard's voice droned on behind him, clear and sure as always, as Gerry's thoughts swung back and forth like a pendulum that had sliced his good intentions in half. In this state, he planned a strategy. He was weakened by this encounter but certainly not down for the count. It was through these thoughts that Richard's conversation floated, and suddenly Gerry knew what he had to do and where he would find the answers.

"You heard?"

Richard replaced the receiver and looked at the man who had come from his private bathroom and still held a towel in his hands.

"Every word." He pulled the towel through his hands and made it taut. "I can't believe it. Richard, this is getting ridiculous. I don't know how you can sit there like it's nothing. I don't think he's going to give up. We've got to do something. These stopgaps aren't working. These people are nuts."

"I'll get on the phone to Bob Morton and talk to him about settling. He owes me a favor. It will be over once that Brooker woman has her money. When that happens, the others will lose interest."

"That's what you said when you brought Cotter over here."

Richard stood up. He felt antsy. It was a feeling he seldom had, and it never occurred because of nerves. There were other, more personal, situations that caused Richard Jacobsen to feel as if he might jump out of his skin. When one got older, that's how things were. Business could always be taken care of. Yet, standing here, now, he felt that tingling in his groin, that sense that he better put a lid on the jar before all the fireflies were gone. Intellectually, he knew this was ridiculous. These were truly minor matters played out by bit players. All he had to do was tweak the script. He turned back to his companion and smiled.

"You do whatever you can on your end; I'll take care of it over here. We'll stop this nonsense once and for all. Together, the way we did before."

"It's not nonsense, Richard, and it sure as hell isn't your butt if this comes down. It's mine." The man tossed the soiled towel on the couch. That made Richard wince. He didn't feel antsy any longer. "I've got to get back to work."

Richard watched him walk across the plush carpet.

"Will I see you later?" The man stopped, his back still turned to Richard, who was more specific, just in case he hadn't been heard. "This evening, perhaps?"

The man waited a beat, then left without answering. They were all guessing. Richard was no different. It was time he sweated, too.

"Gerry! What are you doing?"

Carl Walsh was halfway across the room, wondering what was happening in his outer office, when Gerry O'Doul flew in. Carl's secretary was hot on his heels.

"I can do what I damn well please because I pay my taxes, Carl Walsh. You're the mayor and I want answers. You're up to something, and I want to know what it has to do with my niece."

"I don't know what you're talking about."

Carl scooted back a few steps. Gerry could read his face like a jury. Carl Walsh did know. If he didn't, why would he turn away? Why would he wave off his secretary? Why would he color with surprise and discomfort? Gerry pressed his advantage. Small and wiry, it was hard to believe he could move so quickly at his age. But move he did, right around the tall man so that Carl had no choice but to run, and that would certainly have proved Gerry's point. Carl seemed to know that, too. He stayed where he was.

"Sure, don't you know, Carl? You know what game Richard

is playing. I heard him on the phone to you. 'Twas a mistake I heard since I didn't eavesdrop. I have more pride than that. I'm more of a man than both of you because I went directly to him and asked right out about Kathleen to his face. He wouldn't give me an answer and I was tired. I'd only lingered for a moment outside his office, but I heard him tell you everything was all right. That Kathleen was settled in, that he would be talking to Bob Morton. He said you weren't to worry. He said you wouldn't have to worry about Gerry or any of them anymore.''

"It wasn't me he was talking to." Carl turned left. "An interoffice call." He danced right and made it around his desk.

"It didn't sound that way to me. Though I certainly could ask to see the employee records and find out how many Carls are employed at that esteemed firm. I want to know what you're up to. Who are the folks you needn't worry about, Carl? What is it that Kathleen . . ."

"You're demented. I can't believe you'd do that. What a nut case." Carl cut him off. His face was blazing red, but Gerry was certain it wasn't with anger. It was shame and embarrassment and guilt that caused him to boil. But the man was good in front of a hostile crowd. He stared Gerry down and tried to turn the tables. "Let me be straight with you, Gerry. You've been acting like a nut since that niece of yours came to town. You think you can use her to revive what little is left of your career, but you can't. A pretty face and a passable talent just won't do it. You can't flaunt her and expect all of us to be so impressed that we'll send business your way."

"So that's why Richard hired her? Because she is a passable talent?" Gerry would have spit if he weren't such a gentleman. "I don't think so. Nor do I think he hired her because he has lust in his heart. Not our Richard. You make no sense, Carl. You and he are thick as thieves on something. I don't really care what it is, but I don't want Kathleen involved in it."

"And what gives you the right to make any decisions about anyone? Your niece is way past the age of consent if you haven't noticed. You are not involved in city business, my business, or Richard's. You have a few piddling lawsuits and a fantasy that you still can figure out what's what. We've all tried to be kind to you, Gerry, for old time's sake, but we've had it. You're a crazy, useless, old man; and if you don't get out of my office right now, I'm going to have you thrown out. I don't care what you were to my father. All you are now is a pain in the ass with dreams of grandeur for that mediocre niece of yours.''

''I repeat, if she's so mediocre, then why does Richard want her?'' Gerry pleaded. Carl had worked himself into a fit and lost his guilt along the way. ''Just tell me, why would Richard be discussing her with you? Carl, for the love of Mike, something is afoot. I'm worried . . .''

They weren't alone. The big men that Gerry had seen at the hotel all those weeks ago were now here, protecting hiz honor from the likes of Gerry O'Doul, but Gerry didn't know it until one of them spoke.

''Mr. O'Doul, the mayor is busy now.'' The taller one's voice was so low he seemed to pull it up from his toes. Gerry didn't move, nor did he acknowledge the beasts behind him.

''Carl, I'm sorry.'' Gerry composed himself and put up his hands in a sign of peace. He lowered his voice. He'd not intended to raise it in the first place, but everywhere he turned now there were questions. Kathleen's name was whispered and spoken and her attention taken by men who shouldn't have given her the time of day. He'd known something wasn't right from the first and tried to bury his concerns, but he couldn't ignore them any longer. ''I've no desire to disrupt your working day. I would like to have a talk with you. I'm sure there is a plausible explanation for this interest in Kathleen; I'd simply like to put my mind at rest. Please, Carl. I would like ten minutes of your time.''

Carl Walsh was backed up against the window. He glanced over his shoulder as if to make sure his city was still there, behind him. He nodded to the large men who converged on Gerry.

''Please, Carl,'' Gerry begged. He sounded old. Even he heard it in his voice. The men each put one hand on his shoulder. Their fingers felt like weights. Gerry's resolve was quashed beneath those hands. "Whatever the game, Kathleen will do you no good. She's not meant for the back rooms and the wheeling and dealing. Carl, you are Richard's good and dear friend. Tell him that for me. Just tell him that she won't live up to whatever expectations he has for her."

A hand tightened on his shoulder, and this time Gerry didn't fight it. How could he? This was City Hall.

Chapter Fifteen

Kathleen swerved, but the front tire of her car popped over the curb anyway. At an angle, she sat with one hand tight on the wheel; the other pressed the phone tight against the side of her head. She counted to ten.

"Are you there? Michael? I'm sorry." Now she held the car phone to her ear with her shoulder, threw the car into reverse, almost lost the phone when the car clunked back onto the street. Finally she pulled parallel to the curb and turned the damn thing off. "I'm sorry. I'm sorry. I can't get used to talking on this thing and this car is so much bigger than my old one. I don't even know why they gave it to me. A company car! Where am I going to go? And a phone? Who's going to call me? What clients am I going to take to lunch?"

She lay her head back on the seat, feeling completely ridiculous with all the trappings of Shay, Sylvester & Harrington's best and brightest and none of the responsibility. She listened as Michael made pitying noises. She didn't miss the underlying chuckle. He'd been there, done that, but at least he'd actually been the top dog. She sighed. "Yeah. Yes. I think I'll hang up. I'll call you after I talk to Gerry. I hope he hasn't gone to bed. I'm so late."

She listened. Michael absolved her from any social obligation to him with a few sweet words. *Take care of Gerry. Spend some time with him.*

Understand what you've given up.

She hung up, trying to ignore his subliminal and kindly finger-wag. It was hard though. She'd been wagging that same finger at herself. The job wasn't what she'd imagined. There. She'd admitted it. Fourth seat on an environmental case. Fourth! She was the homemaker of the team, putting everything in order so that the big guns could eventually get up and argue the case. She'd been an idiot. She would have admitted that to Michael if he hadn't already hung up. She was just tired enough, just disheartened enough to admit it to Gerry, too, if she had the chance.

Sighing, she got out of the car and pushed the nifty new key chain that beeped before locking down the incredible hunk of gray metal. Two good men in her life and she'd disappointed both. Two good men who never said a word against her—either in disappointment or anger—and Richard Jacobsen was on the other side of the scale. The man never said much to her anymore. Although he was pleasant when she did see him, there weren't any more chats about Tom Mathis and his fine paintings, no more philosophical discussions in Jacobsen's private conference room about the challenge of law versus the bottom line. Wouldn't Cherie be laughing up her sleeve now?

Hoping Gerry wouldn't laugh at her, too, Kathleen started up the flagstone path only to stop and look over her shoulder when she heard a bleep that sounded quite like the one her car made when the locks were being opened. Her car was dark, safe and sound. She looked up the street. A young, dark-haired, besuited man looked back at her briefly before ducking into his green sedan. She was glad she couldn't see him clearly. She felt a wreck. He drove away moments later. Gerry's street was as silent as a tomb once again, so she headed up the path. The sooner she talked to Gerry, who had been surprisingly insistent that he see her that night, the sooner she would be in bed with the covers pulled up over her head.

She took the three low-rise steps to the oval porch, rang the bell, and admired the house Gerry had lived in for over fifty years. Modest by comparison to its neighbors, it was worth a fortune. On the right side of Sunset, Gerry had bought the place for what most people now spent on a car.

Lost in her thoughts, Kathleen didn't know how long it had been since she'd rung the bell, so she tried it again. This time she added a knock for punctuation. She peeked through the long, leaded windows that ran floor to ceiling on each side of the wide front door.

She could see a snippet of the living room on the left and the dining room on the right. Both were straightened and clean. The foyer was empty; the flowers on the side table were fresh. She scanned the street. Nothing. Not even a sound. No dog barking in the distance, no maid carting out the trash. Lights burned behind elegant windows on homes set back from the street. Some were ringed by wrought-iron fences, others set apart by meticulously cut hedges.

Kathleen's eyes flicked left to the trees and bushes surrounding that side of Gerry's house. Her eyes darted right to the driveway. She went that way. Stepping off the porch, she walked across the manicured lawn, leaving her self-pity on the porch, replacing it with curiosity and just a dash of concern. Lifting the latch on the gate, she slipped through and headed for the back. It was a warm evening and Gerry had a soft spot for the night-blooming jasmine. He could often be found in his garden, alone with his thoughts, surrounded by the jasmine's heavy perfume.

"Uncle Gerry?" she called, walking more slowly.

Knowing how easily her heels would sink into the sponge of the grass, she picked her way across the stepping stones that led to the patio. Deflecting the unease, she took note of all the normal things around her: the neat coil of hose, the garage door that was latched on the outside, the patio furniture that Gerry washed down every Saturday whether it needed cleaning or not and, yes, the night-blooming jasmine, whose heady summer perfume lay heavy on her senses. She hesitated on the fifth paver and looked about, breathing deeply. Closing her eyes, Kathleen found she was smiling. Though children had never played here, though she had never set foot on this ground until she moved to Beverly Hills, Kathleen knew a truth beyond reproach. She was home. Nothing that had been done couldn't be reversed. No decision that had been made couldn't be rethought. She'd share that with her uncle. He'd been waiting to hear that for a long time.

"Gerry! Uncle Gerry!"

She hurried up the back steps. His shoes were by the back door, the polish sitting out. She knocked on the back door and her heart stopped. Instead of hearing the hollow sound of a fist on the door, she heard the door swish as it opened onto a meticulously kept kitchen. Dread skittered out like a cat shut in too long.

Kathleen made excuses. The door was open because he'd rushed back in, in search of a rag to polish those wing-tips or new laces to replace the ones that were frayed. She would help him. They'd talk. It would all be okay between them. Or maybe the phone had rung. He'd gone back in and hadn't closed the door all the way. She'd wait, curled up in a chair in his office while he finished his call—unless it were personal. If that were the case, she'd make herself some tea and wait under the jasmine tree.

"Uncle Gerry?" There were a million reasons why the door wasn't closed and locked, not the least of which was Gerry O'Doul's belief that in his home he was safe. Kathleen stepped into the kitchen. A coffee cup and plate had been placed neatly in the drainer. There were no cooking smells but Kathleen expected that. Gerry preferred to eat out or microwave soup. At his age, he was fond of saying, he didn't need much to fill him up.

Kathleen poked her head into the TV room. An old picture of her and her mother sat framed atop the television. A book was open on the table by the recliner. She caught the name of the author, Donald Tivens, and the visage of Uncle Sam in mourning on the cover. It felt like an omen. The television was off. She left the lights on.

A short hall connected a guest room and the master bedroom. Kathleen could see the edge of the guest bed, made up and

waiting for friends who never came. Gerry was the last of his
breed. She turned the opposite way, opened her mouth to give
him a heads-up and then remembered the shotgun a surprised
Sarah Brooker had greeted her with in the mountains. Not that
this was the same situation. Still, once burned, twice remembered. She walked cautiously down the hall, glancing into a
small room Gerry used as an office. Memorabilia, a desk, a
chair, nothing more.

"Uncle Gerry?" she whispered, and the words sounded like
a child's quiet cry in the night. She hadn't meant to say anything
until she knocked on the door but there it was, done now. No
voice came back to greet her, but she knew beyond a shadow
of a doubt, that he was there in his room. Only him. No one
else. Heart sinking, Kathleen quickened her step, checked out
the clothes laid on the bed, heard the sound of the shower, and
for one minute allowed herself to be relieved. But when she
walked to the door of the bathroom, her knees shook. When
she raised her hand to knock her arm felt too heavy. She forced
herself to rap on the door.

"Gerry?"

His name came out in three syllables. She knocked three
times and laid her cheek against the door, straining to hear his
answer. She called again. Louder now. Then once more. That's
when it sounded as if she were going to cry.

"I'm coming in, Gerry." Kathleen sniffled. "You'd better
be decent. I'm telling you, I'm not used to being in a man's
bathroom." She tried to laugh, but her breath caught and she
put her hand to her mouth to keep the sob inside.

Swallowing hard, Kathleen lay her left hand on the hard,
solid wood of the door; her right she used to turn the knob and
push open the bathroom door. She knew there was no need to
call anymore and no need to hurry.

Kathleen Cotter stood her ground and felt her shoulders
slump. While she surveyed the scene, she reminded herself to
be attentive. There would be questions. After that, there would
be tears and self-recrimination and sadness. But now, she
needed to pay attention.

Gerry O'Doul's hand was slung over the side of the bathtub,

white and lifeless. A fine spray of water shot through the partially open shower curtain, making the tile slick where the rug didn't quite cover it. A white, fluffy robe was laid neatly over the toilet, a towel on top of that. A glass had left a ring on the sink top, but now it was shattered on the floor near the tub.

It took three steps to reach the tub and one quick movement to pull the shower curtain back then close it again. It took a second or two to do that, yet it seemed like an eternity. Kathleen concentrated on his face in those few seconds, looking for any sign of life. She had reached through the curtain and put her fingers to his neck, praying for a pulse and knowing her prayers wouldn't be answered. At the other end of the tub, she reached for the faucet and held back. The police might want to see everything as it was. She backed off, turned, and crunched glass underfoot. Scotch. He'd been drinking Scotch, but he'd hardly had a sip. The smell was slight and the entire contents of the glass seemed to be on the floor.

Perhaps he had felt it coming—the fall, the heart attack, the slip—whatever had caused him to hit his head and die. Perhaps he had reached for the side of the sink to right himself and that's when the glass had fallen. It was the only thing in his whole, lovely home that was disturbed. Even Gerry didn't look disturbed. Only perplexed and that, she supposed, wasn't a bad way to go. Better than her father, dying with a scowl on his face. Her mother had turned her face to the wall, refusing to look at Kathleen, much less the world around her. Yes, perplexed was probably okay, Kathleen thought, as she stepped over the glass, walked to the bedside table, picked up the receiver, and dialed 9-1-1 and asked for help.

Then Kathleen Cotter crumpled to the floor and tried very, very hard to breathe so that when she cried she would do it very, very well.

"He just lost his footing and hit his head. It happens all the time with the old folks. Their equilibrium isn't what it used to be. There isn't a thing you could have done about it."

"I could have been here sooner. He was expecting me sooner.

I don't know. I could have . . .'' Kathleen sniffled and tried to swallow, but the lump in her throat was huge and wouldn't go down easily. The officer didn't have time to wait.

"Yes ma'am," he mumbled and jotted her name and contact information in his little notebook alongside Gerry's name and vital information. Kathleen was prepared to tell him everything she knew about Gerry, that he was kind and considerate and she hadn't given him his due. Instead, the policeman walked away. She didn't believe him when he said she couldn't have done anything for her uncle even if she'd arrived a week-ago-Thursday and waited for the accident to happen.

Kathleen pushed herself away from the doorjamb where she'd been looking at the kitchen. It was so clean except for the dust around the back door where they had taken fingerprints. Only a precaution, she'd been assured. The door had been open after all; there was no sign of force. He had either left it open or forgotten to close it after a neighbor stopped by, but it seemed evident he had opened it himself.

Kathleen turned to the living room and wandered through it looking for the last bit of Gerry left behind. She sat on the sofa, in each chair, but couldn't find his spirit anywhere. She glanced out the window. The coroner's van was there. She was sorry she had not asked them to send Marlene Wong. She had only thought to call Michael, but she hadn't been able to reach him. The answering machine was on at the boat.

Trying to drown out the noise of police business-as-usual, she took refuge in Gerry's office, the smallest room in the house, the most like him. Kathleen sat in his chair. She laid her arm over his desk and her head on her arm then closed her eyes and tried not to feel so responsible. She wanted to wail that it was all her fault. She hadn't felt this way when her mother died. Then she had felt freed. Now she felt loss.

When she opened her eyes, it was just in time to see the gurney with Gerry's body being wheeled past the hallway door. Kathleen bolted upright, gasping for air. She would have turned away; but they were gone before she could move, and Gerry was gone with them.

Picking up a pen, she stabbed at a piece of paper, threw it

away, then began to rearrange his desk. She would clean it up. *For whom?* Put it in order. *For what?* Because he might be looking down from heaven and see what she was doing. *Niceties that she should have done while he lived.* This would be the only nice thing that she had done for him that was without a tinge of bitterness and disappointment. Grief was all she'd given him. He never let on that she'd disappointed him. Her tears started again but not before she'd noticed that the piece of paper she was holding was very interesting indeed.

Wiping her eyes on the back of her sleeve since the Kleenex in her hand was in shreds, Kathleen took the paper and nestled herself in the cracked leather chair that had been Gerry's favorite.

When she woke, she saw Michael.

"Are they all gone?"

"Yes," he said quietly. "I got here just in time. They were going to wake you."

"They should have," Kathleen murmured. She was stiff and her head felt like it was stuffed with cotton. She touched her cheek. It was cold and that reminded her of Gerry and that made her feel like crying again.

"I'm so sorry, Kathleen. I am so very sorry."

Michael was at Gerry's desk, but by the time he'd finished with those few words, he had moved and gathered her up in his arms. She sat in his lap, cradled like a child. For the life of her, she couldn't remember when she had ever been cared for in this way. They sat like that, her head on his shoulder, his arms wrapped loosely around her, for a very long time. He smelled so nice. Like Michael. Like a friend. His fingers combed through her hair now and again and when she sighed, he sighed with her.

"Do you want to stay here tonight? I'll stay with you," he offered.

"I don't know." She shook her head against his chest.

She couldn't find the strength to make a decision. She clutched her hands tighter, realizing that she was still holding the paper she'd found on Gerry's desk. She opened her fist. Michael took it.

"What's this?"

"A list. I found it on his desk. It's got everyone's name on it."

Michael looked. "Tysco. Lionel. Richard. Carl. Money. Money. Money." Michael chuckled. "Gerry had a one-track mind." He crumpled the paper and held her tighter. She reached halfheartedly for it. "It's nothing tonight. Now come with me." He kissed her forehead. She shook her head. "Yes. Come with me."

"I don't want to leave him."

"He isn't here anymore, Kathleen."

"Yes, he is," she whispered. Tears streamed down her face, falling onto the hands that were once again balled and fisted against Michael's chest. Michael dropped the paper to the floor and set her beside it. She didn't move while he closed the windows and locked the doors. When he came back he had her purse and that same purposeful look he'd had when she'd first encountered him at Tysco. Kathleen didn't think that odd, nor was she upset that there were no tears and no wailing. It was Michael's way, and she knew that his heart had broken in just as many pieces as hers.

Wrapping his arm around her shoulders, he walked her out of the study where Gerry had planned Louise's lawsuit and worried about Kathleen. It didn't escape her notice that Michael had closed the door to Gerry's bedroom. She nuzzled into him, all the thanks she was capable of giving at the moment.

Looking up as he led her to the front door, Kathleen realized he was right. Gerry was gone. He handed her out the door and turned to lock it behind them. That was when he allowed himself a private moment. That was when his eyes filled with tears. In his heart he raised a glass to his friend Gerry O'Doul, then took Kathleen Cotter to his boat where he let her know that she was as precious to him as she had ever been to Gerry O'Doul.

* * *

Richard Jacobsen sat in a carved chair that he had rescued from the vestibule of a soon-to-be-demolished church in Wales. It was old, made when men were not so large. It suited him well. He sat in the dark, his hands folded in his lap like a bishop. He considered the new twist to the story that had gone from a footnote in the script of life to an intriguing drama in its own right. He tried to pinpoint the moment when people had stopped doing his bidding and acted independently with such disastrous results. It wasn't hard to figure it out. What he couldn't understand was why he'd been unable to stop the snowball once it had started to roll. That had never happened to him before. But then, love had never blinded him before. He often looked at that picture in his private dressing room at the office and thought of the ways he would tell her how love had blinded him, what love meant to him. It meant so little to her, and so much to him. But he kept those thoughts to himself.

Sighing, he stood up and looked across the bedroom, letting his gaze linger on his sleeping, exhausted companion. It had been a long road, an unusual experience, and rather exciting. But now it was over. The fires had been put out—not the way he would have done it—but put out, nonetheless. There were, of course, loose ends to tie up. He wished there were someone else to do it. Since there wasn't, he left the room, closing the door quietly behind him.

In the hall, the early-morning light was pouring through the huge, round window above the grand staircase. He barely noticed the shadow patterns he usually found so artistically pleasing. Downstairs, the housekeeper was beginning his breakfast. He wasn't very hungry, but he was a creature of habit. She was the one who'd taught him the value of that. At the end of the hall he settled himself in his library—a huge, exquisitely decorated room—and dialed a number from memory.

"Carl," he said, "I have some news. Gerry O'Doul died last night."

The conversation was exactly as he'd expected. Carl didn't

seem the least bit surprised. He, at least, had been surprised. When their talk was done, Richard Jacobsen looked up the next number. He dialed it. The phone rang. No one answered. A machine clicked on.

"Kathleen, this is Richard Jacobsen. I just wanted you to know that we will expect you to take some time off given what happened last night. I want you to know how sorry—" Richard's voice cracked. That amazed him. He put two fingers to his eyes and finished up. "—how sorry I am to hear about the passing of Gerry O'Doul."

His lips on her lips woke her. His body, naked, against her body brought her to consciousness. Long, luxurious minutes ticked slowly by. With each languid trail of his lips, each hungry nip of his teeth, there was an explosion of sensation that ran the length of her body and embedded its memory so deep in her mind that Kathleen knew it could never be discarded. It filled up her head so there was no space for the sadness and pain she had felt the night before. He made remembering impossible—for a moment.

Kathleen reached for Michael and held him. They rolled together across the small bed and back again, instinctively knowing when the only place left to go was the floor. Floating was out of the question, they were both heavy with desire. The ocean rocked them, and the curve of the small cabin kept the sounds of their lovemaking private, as private as the conversation that followed when they lay in one another's arms.

In the end, Kathleen's head was cradled on Michael's arm, his free hand was cupped around her bare shoulder. She wished they could stay that way forever, forgetting everything—*everything*—else in the world. She would not put a name to that everything and she wouldn't let him either. Thankfully, he said, "You slept well."

"That happens when you're worn out." Kathleen kissed his chest. He smelled like sex. Better yet, he smelled like love. "I guess you're a morning *and* night guy."

"Kathleen, I can't tell you—"

"Shhh, not yet." She pushed herself up and put her lips over his, pushing hard and harder still until Michael had no choice but to kiss her back. He parted her lips. There was no question he had wanted her for a very long time. But he wouldn't let her run away from what she had to face. It wasn't his style. It never had been. He held her back. Kathleen's eyes were closed; her lips were parted, begging him to make love to her again so that they could just skip over the next days and months until she could open her eyes and look past her loss.

Gently, Michael lowered her and kissed her lips and both cheeks. Then he pushed her away and sat up. She had no choice but to do the same in the narrow bed. Tired, she made no effort to cover herself. Michael threw his legs over the side of the bed, gave her arm a squeeze, and got his shirt. Carefully he put it on her rolling up the sleeves, buttoning the front, and then he sat down beside her on the bunk.

"I missed." He pointed between her breasts. The shirt was askew. Kathleen looked down and fingered the small, white button he had overlooked.

"It's all right." She pushed on it but couldn't manage to get it through the hole. She pushed harder, fumbling with the fabric until she grunted in frustration and pain and her hands beat on the mattress that only moments before had cushioned their lovemaking. "Damn. Damn, Michael."

Kathleen threw herself against the wall, just to the right of a porthole. Her face was as pale as a foggy morning, the sea outside was as blue as Gerry O'Doul's eyes. Michael concentrated on her. He pulled the sheet around him and sat parallel to her, his back against the wall, the porthole between them. He looked through the window on the other side of the cabin while he spoke.

"It's going to be a rough day. A rough couple of weeks actually."

"I don't know if I can face it." Kathleen was quiet, still picking at the offending button but no longer trying to rectify the problem. "I didn't have this trouble with my parents. I just took care of things. I thought I could always just take care of things. Why do you think it's so different now?"

"Because you loved Gerry like a father. He treated you like a daughter."

"No, he didn't. My father stayed."

"Gerry let you grow. Staying doesn't really mean a damn thing, Kathleen. I think I realized that last night when I was driving over to get you." Michael picked at the blanket and put that across his lap, too. "Gerry never stagnated, you know? He stuck to his guns, sure. He never stopped working or looking for ways to move forward. It was a lesson I wish I'd learned years ago."

"What do you mean?"

"I guess he showed me that I wasn't being as heroic as I thought I was by staying at Tysco. It's harder to move and look for a way to do what you were meant to do. That old man had it all over me. He had it all over you, too." Kathleen hung her head. Michael waited, then coaxed her on. "Admitting it would help, Kathleen." He reached for her hand. She let him take it, then she squeezed to make sure his wasn't going to disappear. "I'm not going anywhere, babe."

"I think I would fall apart if you did, Michael. And I do admit it. I thought I wanted to hurt him, and now he's dead. I didn't really want to hurt him. Not really." She raised his hand to her lips and confessed the rest with that hand tight against her cheek. "It was stupid, stupid, stupid. I just wanted him to see that I'd waited and he was the one who had failed me. He hadn't. He hadn't. Michael, he gave me everything that really mattered. He gave me love and advice and hope. He gave me a chance. He wasn't wrong. My parents were and I was. When I became an adult, I could have picked up that phone, couldn't I?"

Michael nodded. "And when I stopped being effective at Tysco, I could have walked out, but I didn't. I was going to, though, when you guys didn't need me anymore. I wanted to sit and have a cigar with Gerry and tell him all the new things I was going to do."

"So, now?"

"Now, we stick together. We finish what we started with

Louise. Then we find out what it is we're supposed to do together. Think you're up for it?''

Kathleen sniffed and raised her eyes. They would never drain of all their tears. They weren't close to gone when she looked at Michael.

''Yeah. I can do that. I can, Michael.''

''Good.'' They came together in one of those moments— no longer Kodak or Hallmark—but their very own. They kissed like lovers who'd known each other forever and still loved. They clasped hands. Michael let them sit in silence for a moment and then said, ''I think I found out what was upsetting Lionel.''

Kathleen nodded. She stood up, shed his shirt, and went to shower. It was time to work.

Chapter Sixteen

Gerry O'Doul would have loved his funeral. The press was there. Not in force, not the way it had been after the Road Warrior case, but two reporters and a photographer stood on the edge of the crowd that had gathered to pay their respects. The reporters were jotting notes, collecting the names that would mean something to their readers. Most of the mourners were Gerry's contemporaries. There was the comic who'd become famous insulting people in the fifties. Now, kindergarten kids were crueler. There was the song-and-dance man who'd made a transition to television with a family sitcom. There was the host of a syndicated radio talk show, and a sprinkling of lesser personalities that might make the Where-Are-They-Now? page of *People*. They were all at Gerry O'Doul's funeral along with some the general public wouldn't know from Adam. Kathleen Cotter and Michael Crawford thought those were the people more than worthy of note.

Richard Jacobsen had murmured the proper condolences but Kathleen felt a distance from him, as if he no longer found her interesting. She put such a dramatic change of heart down to the daze of her own grief. There were five or six others from Shay, Sylvester & Harrington including Craig Nelson, lead counsel on the environmental case on which Kathleen toiled. She appreciated the show of force from her employer; she just wasn't sure why it was necessary. She hadn't had a personal bonding with her colleagues, Kathleen had not burst upon their scene like a bright professional light. Most of them were too young to have known Gerry in his prime. They had, no doubt, come out of respect for Richard. If he felt it was important to see Gerry O'Doul off, then it must be important.

There were businessmen, most of whom Kathleen didn't recognize. But Michael knew at least one. Mr. Grossman. From Tysco.

There were women who introduced themselves and shook Kathleen's hand. She smiled and murmured pleasantries as they each claimed to be Gerry O'Doul's one true love at some point in his life. Through their tears, each lamented that it hadn't worked out. Henrietta came, walking with a cane, Bo still by her side.

There were no children standing on the green grass, afraid to step on headstones in case the long dead reached for them out of the ground. Kathleen thought that was sad. No nieces, nephews, grandchildren. Just her. She would have to do. She hoped he'd look down from heaven when he got his angel-wings and see just how much she grieved for him.

"Kathleen?" Marlene Wong touched her arm. Kathleen smiled. The assistant coroner gave her a tight-lipped grimace that was close to a smile. Marlene was sad, too. "Nice service."

"Gerry would have liked Father Fallon's speech. I can see why they were great friends. Both of them knew how to lay it on thick."

Marlene chuckled and slipped on a pair of sunglasses. They were big and pink and made her look like a bright-eyed bug. She glanced around. People still stood about talking, slowly breaking up and heading to their cars. Kathleen followed her gaze. There wouldn't be many at the reception. The movers and shakers would be anxious to get back to business. Those who had none would be the ones at the buffet table.

"I heard you went over to Shay," Marlene noted, somehow managing to get Kathleen moving. The two women walked slowly away from the grave site. "Gerry told me when he called last week."

"Yeah. It's different."

"More lucrative?"

"Much," Kathleen assured her.

"Good. If you're going to be in a morgue, you might as well make some good bucks." Kathleen kept walking, staring at the black toes of her shoes as they came into view with each slow step. She remained silent, waiting for Marlene to lead the conversation. She didn't have to wait long. "Look, I don't know if it means anything anymore, but Gerry was after me to find out exactly who called for Dr. G on that Brooker thing."

"Did you find out?"

Marlene shook her head. "Nope, and that's what I wanted to talk to Gerry about. I had gotten pretty far. I knew it was an attorney, but the more I looked into it, the more the grapevine closed down. The fact that it seems to be a big, dark secret is something that's totally weird on its own and that's what I wanted to tell him about. I did check our logs. We got the call from the LAPD dispatching us at four-thirty-three in the A.M. The van rolled and everything was normal. Dr. Wipling was on duty; he signed the body, tagged and logged it. No big thing. Brooker took his place in line. I finally got to talk to Wipling about it—he'd been on vacation—and he had his nose out of joint. Dr. G showed up at eight that morning and actually pirated the examining room where Wipling was just starting on another subject. He had Brooker rolled in, ticked off to high heaven about having to dirty his hands, did a slapdash job on the body then instructed for it to be released. It was over in a couple of hours. Normally, Brooker's body would have laid there for days before anyone even looked at him."

"Dr. Greischmidt never said why it was so important to him?"

Marlene shook her head, "Last time he was out was for that model's murder. He likes the limelight. But if Gerry's to be believed, Brooker was a nobody."

"Believe it. There was no reason for special treatment."

"Well, it sure is suspicious behavior. The closest Wipling

got to an explanation was that someone Dr. G thinks is pretty nifty in the private sector pulled in a favor. Maybe whoever is handling the estate wanted the body to disappear so they could probate fast?''

Kathleen shook her head, ''I can't imagine Tony Maglio showing that kind of interest. I'm not sure he'd have that kind of connection even if he did.''

''I suppose you might be able to ask the good Dr. G directly. What've you got to lose? Who knows what the connection is? I'm sorry, wish it were more.''

''I'll think about it, Marlene. Thank you very much.'' Kathleen took her hand, knowing Greischmidt wouldn't give her the time of day. Marlene nodded and offered a few more words of condolence.

''You know, Kathleen, I did the autopsy on Gerry. He didn't suffer. I thought you'd want to know. It was quick.''

''Thanks.''

Marlene shook Kathleen's hand. ''If you're going to stick around this area, keep my number. Don't know what I'll ever be able to do while you're at Shay, but at least you can say you've got someone inside the coroner.''

Kathleen nodded and Marlene left. Richard was waiting.

''Kathleen, it was a lovely service.'' He called out the compliment before he actually took her hand. He was smiling now. Funny that a funeral service should make him seem almost lighthearted. Maybe it was just being outdoors. Maybe it was Father Fallon. Maybe it was the fact she wasn't going to be in for a few days. ''I want you to know I meant what I said about time off. A leave of absence isn't unheard of in situations like this. Close up Gerry's office. I can suggest a few private practitioners who might be able to take up a few of his clients. Or, perhaps, you'd like to sell the practice. Just let me know, Kathleen. Whatever you need, take as long as you like.''

You don't want me anymore.

''I appreciate that, but I won't be away long.''

I see it in your eyes.

''I just don't want you to be pressured.'' He reached for

her arm, as if he might give her an affectionate squeeze. Realizing what he was doing, he stepped back. "Nice service. Very nice."

Kathleen watched him go, keeping her eyes on him even when Michael came and took her hand. He was at his car and she was almost ready to turn away when she realized there was someone inside, waiting for Richard. There was a leg, an arm, part of a shoulder. A man in a gray suit whose dark head was shadowed, making him unidentifiable. He was dressed in a sharkskin suit, that kind of fabric that shimmered. Gerry had had a sharkskin suit years ago. She'd seen it in a picture. Now it had made a comeback. *Vogue* had shown it in the fall preview issue. Whoever was in that car was nothing if not fashion-forward. She looked back to the knot of people by the grave, to those who were heading to their own cars, and then back to Richard's. Had he been there? Wouldn't she have noticed a man dressed like that?

But looking back now, there was nothing to see. The passenger door was closed. Richard was already in the driver's seat. There was a ring on the stranger's finger. Oval and dark. Onyx, more than likely. But more importantly, it was a young hand. Not one of Gerry's peers, too dandy for an associate or partner. She would have remembered a man like that.

"You ready?" Michael asked, his hand lying protectively on the small of her back.

"Yes, I think so." She wrapped her arm around his waist. "Look, Michael. Someone was waiting in the car for Richard. Who do you think would sit through an entire service just waiting like that?"

"I don't know. Maybe whoever it was didn't feel well."

"Maybe he didn't want anyone to see him, like he was afraid to show his face?" Kathleen speculated as they turned toward the limousine.

"Like who?"

"I don't know. Who wasn't here that we should have expected? Who wasn't at the service that Richard knew and

Gerry knew?'' Michael shrugged and let his arm wind round her shoulder. "I know,'' she said quietly. "Mayor Walsh. He wasn't here.''

"They had words the day Gerry died,'' Michael said. There was no need to muddy the waters by pointing out they were about her.

"I didn't know that. Still, do you think that would be enough to keep him from coming to Gerry's funeral? There was such a history there.''

"I don't know, Kathleen. I'm having a hard time trying to figure out what the little we do know means. We've got enough mysteries to deal with. Why don't you call Walsh and ask him where he was? You could do one of those girl-things that make men think you're really worried about us.''

Kathleen laughed gently, "One of those girl-things, huh?''

"Yeah. I like it when you do those girl-things,'' Michael murmured and kissed the top of her blond head. "So, we'll put the mystery of who was in Richard's car on the back burner, and you can tell me who that lady was you had your head together with.''

"Marlene Wong. Assistant Coroner. She had a little twist to add to our story of Lionel Brooker. Dr. Greischmidt actually threw another body off the table to get Lionel's autopsy done fast. A regular van brought Brooker in; everything was going by the book, then Dr. G shows up, angry, muttering about favors and lawyers and misery.''

"Lionel didn't know anyone in high places,'' Michael reminded her.

"That's the point. Curiouser and curiouser, Michael. But maybe it was one of the Tysco attorneys who wanted to keep all this quiet. Do you think you could check that out?''

"Are you going to ask me to walk on water next?'' He kissed her lightly on the lips. "I'll get you the names, then you can call in an official capacity.''

He handed her into the back of the limousine. Inside, Louise sat with her arm around Sarah, who continued to cry quietly into a Kleenex that had seen better days.

"Thanks," Kathleen said.

"You two doing okay?" Michael folded himself onto the back seat. Kathleen gave Sarah a pat and Louise a sympathetic look. Louise had outdone herself. It was probably better she had taken Sarah back to the car after the church service. Someone might have tried to push her into the grave after Gerry if they'd gotten a good look at her in the sunlight.

Louise was as pale as a ghost, still shaken by Gerry's passing. Her eyes were red-rimmed, though no one had seen her cry. Her stiff upper lip was firmly in place only because she'd drawn it on with her lipstick. Her dress was black and, for the first time, her formidable chest was covered. Nonetheless it seemed as if the material was hard pressed to contain the mounds of flesh beneath it. She'd run her dark stocking and her nails were painted pearl with flesh-colored praying hands tastefully airbrushed on each tip. Gerry would have appreciated the gesture. So did Kathleen.

"Darn right, kiddo." Louise's voice was full of pebbles and Kathleen allowed her the little lie. "We're fine. We got pictures of everybody through the window. We know who was here. There's someone out there who had it in for Gerry. You're not going to convince me otherwise."

"No, Louise, no," Kathleen assured her. "Gerry fell in the tub. That's all."

Louise pulled Sarah closer and glared at Michael. "Do you believe that? After all you know, you believe that? This is all about money, and Lionel was killed because of money."

"It's looking that way," Michael agreed. "But I don't think there was any foul play with Gerry."

"Have you found anything else? I mean anything other than what Lionel left at the house?"

Michael shook his head. "I haven't been in the office since Gerry."

"I still don't understand it, Michael," Sarah said. "I'm so scared. I still don't know why someone would want to kill Lionel, and now Mr. O'Doul is dead."

Michael knocked on the dividing window of the limo and the car pulled away from the curb. He opened the bar and handed Sarah a canned iced tea. Louise shook her head, as did Kathleen.

"Okay, we'll go over it again. The papers you gave me were invoices from a Tysco's Office Supplies division, which sells to local government agencies, hospitals, schools, institutional kinds of places. Everything from pens to desks. That's big, big bucks for Tysco and big, big expenditures for those businesses and services. Lionel's invoices had the correct client code for shipping, but the billing code was incorrect. Over half the Tysco invoices for the city of Los Angeles sent during the last quarter carried a billing code for St. Peter's Hospital. So, the city gets the goods, but the hospital is paying for them and Tysco still gets the money."

"It could be an honest clerical error," Kathleen suggested.

"I don't think so. It showed up on every single invoice in increments that wouldn't be immediately identifiable to an untrained eye. I think this is exactly what upset Lionel," Michael said with certainty. "But I'm willing to give Tysco or the city or whoever's behind this the benefit of the doubt. The only way I'll be able to know for certain if this was a fluke or an ongoing problem—and I use the word *problem* lightly—is to search back through those division invoices. It's going to take some time."

"Why would anyone want to do that purposefully?" Louise had folded her hands and was listening intently.

"I don't know what benefit it would be to Tysco. I haven't figured that out yet, and they're the ones who have to be manipulating the billing. The city's bottom line would look great, though." Michael sat back and laced his fingers through Kathleen's. They sat quietly, looking out the window, knowing no one could look in. The car turned and turned again. They were getting close to Gerry's house.

"It could be a mistake," Kathleen reiterated quietly, wanting everything to be simple; wanting really nothing more than to give up.

"Yeah, it could," Michael answered.

Then they all listened to Sarah's sniffles. Kathleen wished she had the words to tell them it was over.

* * *

"Here's the last of the files. I think we've taken care of everything else."

Becky put the folders beside Kathleen and sank into a chair beside the desk that used to be Gerry's. She propped her chin on both hands and looked at Kathleen through her Coke-bottle lenses. A Tootsie Roll hung listlessly from her fingers, only the end nibbled and that, clearly, without much gusto.

"Have you finished the billing to date?"

Becky nodded.

"Did you notify all of Gerry's credit cards, the utilities, and everything?" Kathleen flipped through the first three folders, withdrew the second and set it aside.

"Yes." Becky sighed. "I just needed a break for a minute, you know. It gets so depressing sending the same letter out over and over again." She looked toward the ceiling. *"This is to inform you that Gerry O'Doul is deceased."*

"Becky, please." Kathleen closed her eyes and started to count. She got as far as three, then managed a smile. "I'm sorry. I guess I'm on edge. It's funny; I didn't think there was this much going on when I worked here. I had no idea he was on retainer with so many people."

"Yeah, I always thought that was really neat how he and his buddies stuck together. I mean all those old guys never got into any trouble, but they paid him like clockwork. Guess they all figured he'd be doing their estates and working out the fights between the kids once they kicked off. Now, look. He's gone before all of them."

Kathleen handed Becky the tissue box. Off and on through the last two days they'd both needed it. But now there was business to attend to. Gerry wouldn't have wanted her to sit around weeping when there was so much to do. In fact, she could almost hear him whispering in her ear to get on with the important things. There was no doubt in her mind what those important things were.

"Becky, look, I'm almost done for the day. Why don't you

take off? Get yourself into a hot bath. You'll feel better tomorrow and we'll start on the paperwork again.''

"Are you sure? It's only four o'clock.''

"Of course I'm sure. We only have two hearings pending—and Louise Brooker's trial of course. Luckily, we have another week or so on that. I managed to change the court date.''

"You didn't need to do that. Mr. Morton's office called. He wants to meet with you at the end of the week if you're not back to work at Shay, Sylvester & Harrington. Are you really going back there, Ms. Cotter?'' Big tears plopped into Becky's lap faster than she could wipe them away.

"Oh, Becky.'' Kathleen put down her pen. She stood up and patted the girl's shoulders, at a loss to know what to do. She'd never ever cried in front of her parents. Actually, she'd never cried in front of anyone but Michael. So, thinking of Michael, she did what she assumed would help. Bending down, Kathleen put her arm around Becky and whispered, "He would have really been proud of you, Becky. Gerry would have been so happy that you wanted to keep the office open.''

"He would have been happier to know that you did,'' she sniffled and then patted Kathleen's hand. The two women stayed locked together a minute longer and then Becky left, dragging herself out the door and home to the hot bath and whatever comfort her refrigerator had to offer.

Alone, Kathleen sat back down at Gerry's desk and pulled the file back to her. *Brooker, Louise* was neatly typed at the top. Bob Morton wanted to talk to her. It was settlement time, but happiness wasn't sitting there right along with that surety. Once this was settled, she'd have to make everyone see that she couldn't help them any longer. She wanted to forget about Lionel Brooker. There really wasn't any mystery; and if there were, she didn't have the heart to deal with it.

Who were they now that Gerry was gone? She opened the file to reacquaint herself with the issues, the arguments, and anything new Gerry had put there thinking he would be in front of Judge Kelley arguing the matter.

Quickly she perused the information only to find there wasn't much that was new. He had left her argument intact, making note of every piece of information regarding Lionel that she had managed to collect before leaving for her new position. There were notes and doodles on the manila folder and Kathleen smiled. She had never thought of Gerry as a doodler. She checked out the hearts and knives and books the artistic Gerry had penned, and then she saw something else on the top of the inside cover. She spread it out flat this time and took note. This was more than a doodle. Here were things that were on Gerry's mind: SS & H, Lionel, Tysco, money, money, money???? Bills!!! Billings!!! CW, RJ, Los Angeles, City of! Kathleen. Here was an extension of Gerry's doodling at his home desk.

It could have been anything. A laundry list of the things that worried Gerry O'Doul: his niece, his client, his competition, his worries. That would be a plausible explanation except for the boldly drawn arrow, the redundant circle etched around a woman's name and phone number. Kathleen had never heard of Mrs. Able and she was sure Louise never had either. Louise, who had an opinion on everything, would certainly have shared any opinion she had on Mrs. Able if she'd known the woman existed.

She tapped her finger on the number. Kathleen bit her lip. She picked up the phone and, before she lost her nerve or came to her senses, dialed the number.

"City Hall."

Kathleen was silent.

"City Hall."

"Mrs. Able, please?" Kathleen swiveled so she was exactly parallel to the desk. Slowly she picked up the pen she had earlier discarded and let it hover over the file folder where Gerry had made his cryptic notes.

"One moment, I'll transfer you." No problem.

"Thank you."

Kathleen's voice was small, no more than a whisper. Moving faster now, Kathleen rummaged through the drawers, finally finding a half used pad of paper. A file folder just wouldn't do. She flipped open to a clean sheet when a cheery voice floated over the line.

"Monica Able, how may I help you?"

"Well, I don't really know," Kathleen began. "I found your name and number on a file and I wanted to follow up."

"Oh, I see. Not to worry, I get calls like this all the time. One person leaves, another comes. Files are passed around. How about we start with your company name and the billing number on the file in question?"

"Actually, that's kind of the problem. I'm with a law firm, O'Doul & Associates. I believe Mr. O'Doul contacted you—"

"Oh, yes. I just heard about Gerry. My goodness, I thought my heart would break." Kathleen could almost hear the woman putting her hand to her breast as if to prove that her heart had been in peril.

"You're not alone, Mrs. Able. And I'm going to do my best to make sure his business is taken care of the way he'd want. I'm his associate and his niece."

"His niece." *Yes, good move, Kathleen.* "Oh, I know all about you—well, when you were little anyway. But imagine, old enough to be a lawyer! How wonderful. You know, I used to date your uncle. Many years ago, of course. He was sixteen years older than I. How wicked it seemed back then. Wish I hadn't let him get away." The woman sighed and Kathleen could swear she felt the phone line wilt. "Oh, but you don't want to reminisce. I'm sorry, what was it you're looking for?"

"I think Gerry called you recently. He jotted some notes on a file, and I'm afraid I can't read his writing."

There was silence, only this time it wasn't the quiet of good memories. Mrs. Able was being cautious.

"What did you say your name was again?"

"Kathleen Cotter. My mother was Gerry's only sister. We lived in Banning." Kathleen gave her credentials and tried to still her beating heart while she waited for Mrs. Able to decide if she were to be trusted.

"Okay. I just wanted to know because, really, what I did for Gerry was something I shouldn't have done, and I sure don't want to lose my job when I'm so close to getting my pension."

"No, I wouldn't want that either," Kathleen assured her

quickly and sincerely. "I promise to treat the information with the same discretion as Gerry would have."

"Okay. Okay." Her voice lowered almost to a whisper. Kathleen could hear the rustle of paper. She clutched her pen, ready to take notes. "Gerry asked me if there were any *special* procedures in the city billing department. I gave him the general numbers that we call when there are questions about bills that are sent to us from our major suppliers. Are you ready? Here they are."

Mrs. Able read the list and at the top were Tysco and Shay, Sylvester & Harrington, followed by a transportation firm, a cleaning service, and others.

"Thank you. That's great."

"Oh, but that's not all," Mrs. Able said quickly. Kathleen wondered if she talked fast because she was losing her nerve. Not that it mattered, really, as long as Kathleen got the same information Gerry had. Mrs. Able was chattering but her voice was so quiet it was hard to hear. "I did something I shouldn't have done. I accessed the mayor's personal phone records. It's not hard to do since the telephone bills come through this department. Gerry wanted to know if he had personally called the billing departments. Well, I found out that he had called a few numbers that showed up over and over again. They aren't the numbers for general accounting, but they are numbers for Tysco, the lawyers, and other suppliers. They seem to be special numbers. The mayor is the only one who calls those numbers."

Quickly, Mrs. Able gave her the numbers. Kathleen wrote them, big and bold, on her paper and then on the cover of the folder. She thanked the woman, assuring her that no one would ever know that she had done Gerry such a favor.

Taking a deep breath, she clutched the receiver tight, counted to ten, mouthed *go for it* and dialed quickly. The phone rang once, twice. It was halfway through the third ring when it was answered.

"Grossman."

"Hello. This is Mrs. Able from the mayor's office. Mr.

Walsh asked me to check in with you, Mr. Grossman. He wanted me to check about the special invoices." Kathleen took a deep breath and prayed that would be enough. It was.

"Oh, for God's sake," the man muttered. "Tell him we've got everything straightened out. They've all gone through the system without a hitch. You tell him, if he has any more questions to call me directly. I don't talk want to talk to clerks about this. Maybe I'll tell him myself. Put him on."

"Mr. Walsh called from his car," Kathleen ad-libbed. "He's not in the office right now. I'll tell him—" The connection was broken rudely, but Kathleen had what she wanted. Lionel had stumbled upon invoices from Grossman's division that assigned city costs to other Tysco clients. If this were happening at other suppliers, it meant the mayor's incredibly frugal budget, the foundation of his campaign platform, was a sham.

"Let's see who's next on the list."

Galvanized she dialed and got an answering machine attached to a private number. Kathleen compared it to her master list. From the prefix it seemed to be a private number within Corpraclean, janitorial services.

She began to dial again, but the other line rang before she could finish.

"O'Doul & Associates."

"Hi, sweetheart."

"Michael. I just talked to that man who was at Gerry's funeral. Grossman. The guy from Tysco."

"Funny you should mention him." He was excited and Kathleen was all ears. "Grossman heads up the food service division. They supply the city. I got the billing code for the city and cross-referenced automatic purchases for the city and other clients. Guess what?"

"The city bills have been assigned to other large clients where the charges would go unnoticed."

"Exactly. They've been buried in billing that goes out to other mega corporations and institutions. We supply a ton of them. Airlines, schools, hospitals, How many middle managers or clerks do you know that check the billing with a fine-tooth comb? I bet they're all eating big chunks of city costs, and Walsh is looking like a god because the city budget's balanced.''

''And there would be a lot to lose if a lowly auditor with a big mouth and an overblown sense of morality decided to make waves. This is the kind of thing that actually would get press. Lionel must have scared the hell out of Carl Walsh and Grossman and whoever else is involved in this scam. You don't think Carl killed Lionel though, do you?''

''No.'' Michael scoffed. ''He wouldn't have the guts. Besides, we already know they sent some goons to Sarah. They've got people on the payroll we'll never know about. You can bet their salaries don't show up on any billing records. What I still can't figure out is why the drugs? There had to be an easier way.''

''Listen, it's almost five. I want to make one more call.'' Kathleen held the phone against her shoulder, bouncing in the desk chair. ''Meet me at my place tonight. I want to start mapping this out so we can see where we need to fill in the blanks. I want to make sure when we go to the authorities we've got enough for them to open an investigation of Lionel's case.''

''Okay. I'll see you around seven. I want to run as many records as possible before the end of the day.''

As Michael signed off, Kathleen asked, ''Jules Porter was probably involved, don't you think?''

''Yeah, I do,'' Michael said definitively. ''I think Jules had been signing off on those invoices for years. Now that he's moved up, he's got to have someone else initialing this stuff, 'cause I sure haven't been doing it.''

''Be careful when you try to figure out who it is.'' Kathleen knew she should hang up, but there was another question she had to ask. ''Michael?''

''Yeah?''

''Do you think Gerry just fell in that tub?''

Silence. She could hear his thoughts; she just couldn't make them out.

"I do. I really do think so." Michael didn't hang up. He said, "You know, I thought you were going to give up."

"I thought so, too," she answered.

"See you tonight."

It was showtime. She dialed and listened and waited to go into her spiel once more. But when the connection was made, Kathleen Cotter was speechless.

"Richard."

She knew that voice as well as she knew her own. She'd listened to it. She'd believed it. She'd let Richard Jacobsen lead her away from Gerry O'Doul like the Pied Piper.

Kathleen slammed down the phone and began to sweat.

Michael kissed her goodbye at seven-thirty the next morning. Both of them were exhausted, not from their lovemaking, but from the long hours tossing and turning as they considered what needed to be done. None of their options were without risk, yet neither considered quitting. There was too much at stake: Michael's honor, Kathleen's proof of worth, justice for Lionel, Sarah's peace of mind, and, of course, Louise's money. Yet Kathleen knew that, even for Louise, this had become a quest for the truth. Now Kathleen was moving forward to bring them all what they needed. So, Kathleen dressed carefully and headed out on her own while Michael went the opposite way.

She nodded to the guard at the front desk and waited patiently for the elevator, trying hard not to wear her nerves on the outside of her skin. Kathleen did all the things she usually did once she got to the office. She put her briefcase in the back corner. She looked at the painting of the houses Richard had seen fit to put in this otherwise bare room. How easily she'd been bought. At least the purchase price made her feel better. She went for coffee and she waited for Richard to make his rounds, praying her resolve would see her through. She could be wrong about him, after all. It could be that Carl often called Richard's private number just to chat. It could be that.

Kathleen timed her departure from the coffee room to coincide with Richard Jacobsen's regular morning patrol of his domain. she ran into him near Doreen Cusler's office.

"Richard, good morning." She smiled brightly, her face painted on beautifully, her red lips smiling as they had never smiled before. She was taller than he, but her knees quaked when he drew near because he was more powerful than she. He might even have the power of life and death.

"Kathleen. I'm surprised to see you back. I thought you were going to take an extended leave to take care of Gerry's affairs."

Wouldn't you have loved that?

"There wasn't much to take care of. I still have to meet with Bob Morton. I think he wants to settle the Brooker matter. I don't know if you remember—"

"Yes, I do remember. That's fine. Excellent. I'm sure you'll settle with Bob equitably. He's a good man. Very fair. It's in everyone's best interest to wrap things up."

"He's a friend of yours, then?" Kathleen asked, stepping into his path. Richard eyed her curiously.

"Yes, as a matter of fact. I've known Bob for some time."

"That's nice. I'll have to call you if I need a good word put in."

Richard smiled and the temperature went down ten degrees. "I already have, Kathleen."

Slam. What a put-down. He might as well have asked her straight out if she thought she was smart enough to reel in All Life by herself.

"Thank you. That was very kind," Kathleen murmured. Richard took another step. His schedule was off and he was getting peevish. But Kathleen needed more. "I was wondering if you could spare a minute on another matter. Gerry's business is almost wrapped up, and I really want to settle down here. You know, really be a part of this firm. I wondered about the billing records for my client. I noticed them on Jake's desk and I was confused by some of the paperwork. I didn't want to do anything untoward, so I was wondering . . ."

"Don't wonder, Kathleen." Ice. His voice chilled her. Rich-

ard took a step toward her instead of around. "Just *do*. I want
you to perform for us as an attorney, not an accountant. Jake
will get the billing. I will okay the reports, and accounting will
do the paperwork."

Kathleen persisted. "I just didn't want to do anything detri-
mental. Everything was so easy at Gerry's office."

"I'm sure it was, and that's why Gerry had the kind of
business he did. Perhaps I made a mistake bringing you on
board, Kathleen. Perhaps you were cut out for something—
simpler."

He left her standing in the hall. She looked after him, pleased
as punch by his reaction to her questions. She wiped the smirk
off her face when she realized someone was looking right at
her. Kathleen looked over her shoulder. Doreen Cusler had
been watching and listening. Kathleen looked right back at her.

"It was a mistake, him bringing me on board, you know,"
she said to the astonished associate.

Kathleen sipped her coffee as she headed down the hall.
Richard Jacobsen would soon be finding out just how big a
mistake it was. Kathleen walked right past her own office and
stopped at the end of the hall, where she turned into the big
office. It took her three seconds to spot her prey. The lady was
at the first desk. Accounting was a busy place, so she smiled
at the girl, who looked like she could use a break.

"Hi, I'm Kathleen Cotter. Do you have a minute?"

"You know, this is really nice." The young woman's name
was Jenny and her morning drink of choice was cola. It had
taken her about five minutes to become Kathleen's best friend.
"Most of the associates don't even know our names, and the
only reason the partners do is because they worry about what
they'll have to divvy up at the end of the year. They think
we'll give them a heads-up if the balances look grim."

"See, that's exactly the kind of thing I'm not real sure
about. It's so weird, the expectations around here. I mean, I'm
supposed to know all the ins and outs, but I came from a really

small firm. It was nothing like this. It makes me feel like such a hick.''

"Yeah, I heard. Everybody thought it was pretty strange." Her eyes fluttered closed while she apologized. "I'm sorry, but around here we need any kind of gossip we can get. Most of the attorneys are so darn boring. I have to tell you, we figured they hired you because you looked so great. We never even saw a curriculum vitae from you. Everyone in personnel wanted to know where you'd come from."

"It's nice to know everyone found me so interesting." Kathleen giggled. She did the girl-thing when all she really wanted was the hard information she'd come for. "But I'll tell you, I really, really want them to admire me for my mind. The law doesn't worry me, it's the business part of the whole thing that makes me crazy. I want to make sure I look good on paper to this firm."

"Hey, that's not a problem. Just bill what they expect, and what they expect isn't forty hours a week. If you can hang in there at sixty plus, you'll do fine."

"So, I just fill out that time sheet with my hours. But I thought there must be something more to it because I heard Mr. Jacobsen gets the billing records. I sure don't want to do anything that's going to make him mad."

"Of course he does. He has to go over every single attorney's billing and make changes," she said, clicking her tongue as if this were the most ridiculous question in the world. Kathleen played along.

"Wait, now I'm confused. How can you change how many hours someone worked? I mean, what I put down is what I put down."

"Oh, it's not that you don't get credit for all your hours," the woman said, concerned that she'd given Kathleen the wrong impression.

Hurry. Hurry.

"Boy, that's good to know."

"Naw, it's just that sometimes adjustments have to be made to keep the clients happy. Business people do it all the time. Anyway, Mr. Jacobsen makes sure that no one inadvertently marks too much time to one client. Or if the firm needs to give a client a break, you know they want to look good to the client, Mr. Jacobsen transfers the hours between different dockets so that the bottom line looks the way he wants it to."

"Wow, that must be tough to keep everything straight. Do you each meet with Mr. Jacobsen to go over the changes."

She laughed. "You've got to be kidding. I'd quit if I had to go to all that trouble. We just tally the bottom line and input it into the computer. Then I initial it and send out the accounts assigned to me and make sure the receivables are up-to-date."

"Wow, I don't know how you keep it all straight." Kathleen shook her head admiringly. "Do you think I could see some of the final billing, just so I'm familiar with it if I ever have to justify anything to my client?"

"Sure. If you're that dedicated, you deserve all the help you can get." Taking a last drink of her cola, Jenny stood up and slid open a file drawer that was almost as long as the wall. "Here, this is the refinery docket. You can see exactly what you look like to the client on paper."

"Thanks. I really didn't mean to put you to all this trouble."

Kathleen forced herself to be casual. She flipped open the file folder and let her eyes run down the latest invoice. There she was, laid out in black and white, all her glorious hours, billed at a lowly associate's rate. But there was Craig Nelson, too, exclusive senior partner to city business. He billed triple her hourly rate and the refinery was picking up the tab for his services. If anyone noticed, they were probably pretty impressed that one of the senior partners was actually doing the daily dirty work on their business.

"Boy, I really admire you. I'd go crazy if I had to keep track of all these bits and pieces of hours."

"You get used to it." She preened, pleased to impress an attorney.

Kathleen's hands were sweating as she handed back the billing docket. "I didn't realize how much of your time I'd taken up. I better get going. Thanks for all your help. I hope I don't screw up."

"You won't. I'll bet you'll do just fine." The woman's smile faded as she turned away from the file drawer. Kathleen turned, right into Richard Jacobsen who stood in the doorway.

"I've brought this month's time sheets, Jenny."

He walked past Kathleen and deposited the paperwork. When he retraced his steps, he paused beside her, his expression quizzical. Kathleen began to perspire.

"I was just leaving," she whispered, standing and offering the only explanation she could think of. "I needed to change the beneficiary on my insurance policy. I mean, now that Gerry's dead. Tax information. You know. Thanks again, Jenny."

Kathleen glanced at her new friend, who looked a little sick. Kathleen hoped the woman wouldn't catch it for talking to her. When she looked behind her, she saw that Richard Jacobsen had already left accounting. He had no interest in Jenny. He was standing in the hall, looking thoughtfully after her.

Kathleen clutched her coffee mug with two hands, letting go of it only when she reached her office. Taking a deep breath, she picked up her purse and her briefcase and walked out the door, down the hall, and through the lobby. Eyes forward, afraid to look around in case Richard were there watching her, Kathleen waited for the elevator. She stepped in, let the doors close, and then collapsed into the corner sure that, at any moment, the emergency trap would open and Richard Jacobsen would be staring down at her, quietly informing her that she was about to die.

Richard would never go to such lengths to terrorize Kathleen Cotter. When Richard Jacobsen encountered a problem, he took care of it simply and swiftly. Picking up the phone, he called the one person who understood this predicament.

"It's me. I think there's a problem with Kathleen Cotter. I know, I know. I thought it would be all right now that the old man is gone. It won't be."

Richard listened. He objected. He listened again and, finally, was convinced.

They would meet that evening. They might never make it to bed. Once this was over, though, everything would be as it had been and they would take to bed for a week with no worries.

That was really all he wanted. He hung up the receiver just as Kathleen Cotter was picking one up outside at a pay phone. She told Michael the news.

Michael redialed. He called Sarah and Louise. They were all waiting when Kathleen got home.

Chapter Seventeen

Michael was on the couch, his head propped up on one arm and his heels on the other. Kathleen sat under his legs. She used his flat midriff as a deck and dinner table.

"More pizza?"

Sarah stood up and offered to refill their paper plate. All they had to do was tell her whether they wanted vegetable or pepperoni. They both shook their heads.

"I'll have pepperoni." Louise held out her plate. "Hey, look at these. Oh, Sarah, these came out great. I really should have been a photographer. I bet I would have been a fashion photographer if I hadn't gotten married so young."

Sarah handed Louise the pizza and Louise gave her a stack of photos—double prints, glossy finish. Sarah settled herself, then tried to settle herself again. Louise had taken it upon herself to make over Sarah Brooker.

The little widow's hair was now pulled to one side in a ponytail, her eyes were shadowed in a blue that made them look muddy. Half her mascara was on her lashes, the other half smudged under her eyes. Red wasn't her color and her chest couldn't hold a candle to Louise's, yet she had gamely donned one of Louise's halters. Over it all she'd thrown her gray sweater and pulled it around her for comfort while she looked at Louise's pictures.

"This one is really good." Louise leaned over, beaming at Sarah's compliment. The nail that delightedly tapped the photo was lavender; The Artist Formerly Known as Prince was illustrated in all his pouty-lipped glory.

"Yeah, doesn't that just look like something you'd see in the *Enquirer?* It has that look, you know, like he's done something really bad and he doesn't want anyone to know about it. What a slime. Him and that Richard guy. Show Kathleen and Michael. They haven't seen this batch."

Sarah did as she was told, offering Kathleen the stack with a shy smile. "They really are good, you know. Louise has a real talent."

Kathleen took them and almost put them aside, but she looked closer and shuffled the three-inch glossies like a deck of cards.

"Kathleen, here, look." Michael handed her a sheet of paper. "This one matches the file Lionel gave Sarah. It's from the office supply division at Tysco. So far I've found two divisions and one subdivision in on all this. No wonder Carl Walsh looks like a god to the voters. If you add up everything that's been misdirected in billing and put it back where it belongs, the city budget would skyrocket."

"Can I see?" Sarah put her hand out. Kathleen passed them over. She'd look at them later. Now it was the photos that had her intrigued.

"Poor Lionel," Sarah mused.

"Yeah." Louise pulled her knees to her chest. Her chest pushed up almost to her chin, but she managed to rest her chin on her knees. Her palazzo pants were purple, her peasant blouse white eyelet. She looked fetching. "I feel bad that I've been after money when that's what did him in. I feel just like one of those slime-balls."

Michael turned his head and looked at Louise. As often as he saw her, he never quite got enough of her. Louise was a piece of art, a work in progress. He looked back at his paperwork.

"I know where I've seen him. I know now." Kathleen had

paled. Michael watched her carefully. She handed him the photo.

"Jules Porter. I have to laugh when I think about his telling me that things fall through the cracks like it was just business-as-usual. He was the one making the cracks. I can't wait to find out who's been forging my signature to approve these." Michael held up recent invoices that had been initialed with an *MC* that looked close to his actual signature. I hope they made a heck of a lot of money, 'cause the gravy train is coming to a halt."

"No, I didn't see him at Tysco. I saw him at Gerry's."

"Gerry's. You mean the office?" Louise rocked back, raising her eyebrows.

"No, his house. The night he had his accident. This man was across the street, getting into a car."

They fell silent. Everyone knew what that meant. Gerry had been helped along with the slip in the tub.

"Oh, Lord," Sarah breathed. "Oh, Kathleen, I'm sorry."

The lump in Kathleen's throat came up fast, but she fought with that thought. She wasn't going to think the worst now. If she did, she would fall apart. Instead, she lifted Michael's legs off her and poked through the hundreds of pictures Louise and Sarah had taken during their surveillance. She picked out two, three, and—finally—five pictures of Jules Porter.

"He was at the funeral, too." She laid her fingers across the top half of one picture. "I recognize the suit. It was hard to miss. And that ring. He was in Richard's car at the funeral."

"Hah!" Louise scampered up as best she could with the yards of fabric that swathed her legs. She went through the photos like a whirlwind until she found what she wanted. "Wait till you see this!"

When Kathleen saw the photo in Louise's hands, everything went out of her head. Nothing but a flash of hot-white light remained. That and the full, complete, and painful realization that she had been stupid and ignorant and unworthy of Gerry when she'd put Richard Jacobsen above him. When she focused again, she was able to look at the photo with clear eyes and she saw Richard and Jules Porter. Richard's arm around the man's shoulder, like a father telling life's secret to a son. Two men with a great deal between them. At the very least, they were guilty of misusing her, Gerry, and Michael and abusing their positions as powerful men; at the worst, their sins included fraud, duplicity, and possibly murder. And for what? To elect a man senator.

"What, Michael? What did they want from all this?"

"I don't know, Kathleen. I don't think like them. I can't conceive of what drives them." He moved closer and took the photo from her hand, then wove his fingers into hers. She laid her head on his shoulder. Sarah watched silently. Even Louise didn't disturb the moment. It hadn't been just Lionel who had lost his life because of these men, but Gerry, too. A part of Kathleen died as well, now that she knew.

"What do we do now?" she asked them all, raising her head.

"What do you want to do?" Michael asked.

"Get them," she answered without hesitation. Sarah nodded. Louise, too. Those two women moved closer together. "What do we need?"

"Billing records from any of the suppliers. We need to talk to Marlene and ask her to reassess the autopsy with the idea that Gerry didn't fall. We need to go to the police and get the investigator's report the night Gerry died," Michael said.

"I'll call Marlene tomorrow afternoon. I'll subpoena Richard's phone records to see if he called Greischmidt at home. It will take time, so what else until then? Sarah?" The young woman sat up straighter. "Will you sign a request to have Lionel's body exhumed?"

"Yes."

"Michael. Will you come with me to the police?"

"You didn't even have to ask."

"Okay. Then there's only one thing left that I need to do." The three people around the coffee table strewn with pictures and pizza looked at the tall blonde with the very, very serious expression. She looked at each in turn. They were a funny collection, yet they were closer than any family could be, tied together by a man Kathleen had never met. She took a deep breath, her nostrils flaring. "Since we have to prove that the

Tysco billings aren't just clerical errors and we need to prove that there was a conspiracy and we need to make a case that these fine, upstanding citizens feared exposure enough to kill a Tysco auditor who was asking too many question—" Kathleen paused, a tiny, cold shiver gripping her. It didn't last long. There was no other decision she could make. "Since we need to do all that, I'm going to have to get the Tysco billing from Shay, Sylvester & Harrington; and I'd better do it soon, 'cause I don't think I'm long for that place."

They all had their assignments. Michael was going to take on Jules Porter. Sarah and Louise were off to City Hall to ask the mayor a few questions during the afternoon city council meeting, and Kathleen was headed into the Shay, Sylvester & Harrington office to see her new best friend in accounting. God knew how she was going to wangle the Tysco billing, but have it she would by the end of the day, even if she had to steal it.

"Morning, Kathleen."

She stepped into the elevator and smiled at Doreen. Rude though it was, she turned her back and watched the numbers slide by as the elevator took them to the office. Kathleen didn't have an ounce of small talk left in her. When the doors opened, she stepped out, thought twice about her silence, and realized later it could be construed as odd behavior. She waved at Doreen.

"Have a good one." Kathleen managed a smile that she hoped looked somewhat normal, nothing felt right. She had dressed as usual and put on her face as usual and it all seemed like a poor disguise. Kathleen wished she could throw it off and run to the marina. She'd make Michael take the boat out. She'd throw her head back and let the sun bake her. She would be renewed, reborn, and she would choose every step she took after that with such great care that she would build the life she wanted, not live the one she had once thought she wanted.

But that would be later. Now, she had chosen a plan of action. It was right and just and Gerry would have done it himself had he been there. So, she smiled at the receptionist as she went by. The woman smiled back, then did a double take.

"Oh, wait, Ms. Cotter. Come back."

Kathleen hesitated. She didn't want to be out in the open or noticed. She just wanted to be in her office, biding her time until she could make her move. But two other associates were headed her way and she was blocking the door that led to the offices. She had no choice but to retrace her steps.

"What is it?" she asked, resisting the urge to bolt for the elevators and run.

"Here. Mr. Blanco left this for you. He said you weren't even to have a cup of coffee, but to meet him as soon as possible. I really thought you'd be in earlier, so make sure you tell him that I gave you this as soon as I saw you."

"Sure, no problem."

Kathleen ambled away, hitching her briefcase, and opening the note with one hand. Harry Blanco was second seat on the suit the government had brought against her client. Harry Blanco was a good guy, but he sure had lousy timing. The request for on-site investigation had finally come through, and she was on call to follow up.

Kathleen looked toward the door, knowing she had no choice. To refuse would be career suicide. There would be questions, perhaps asked before she had time to get the backup she needed. Checking her watch, she saw that it was already inching toward nine-thirty. San Pedro was forty-five minutes away. Two hours with the guy max and she'd be back by midafternoon. Maybe it was better. Everyone was focused in the afternoon; there wouldn't be many roaming around looking for coffee or poking their noses into her business. Kathleen went to the phone in the reception area and dialed Michael.

"I won't be able to finish that business until this afternoon," she said, hoping she sounded as if she were just filling in a client.

"No problem. I got stonewalled when I called Jules this morning. I'm going to do some housekeeping around here and head in a little late."

"At least we're on the same timetable. I'll see you as soon

as I'm done. I love you," she said without giving a second thought to the fact she'd never said it before.

"I love you, too," he answered without one whit of hesitation.

That she noticed. It made everything all right.

The minute Kathleen was in the elevator, the receptionist picked up the phone.

"She's gone, Mr. Jacobsen."

"Excellent," he answered, and then made another call. "Meet me" was all he said.

The pictures in the file didn't do justice to the Ardol refinery and manufacturing plant. On film, the place looked imposing enough, but in reality it seemed to be some alien village transported intact to this scruffy place just off the Harbor Freeway in one of the less attractive parts of San Pedro. From afar she could see low-slung buildings that no one had bothered to prettify like Tysco. Huge tanks ballooned here and there, like Sumo wrestlers resting on their haunches on acres of untended land. Some were connected by arteries of bulbous pipes and veins of spidery ladders and catwalks, some stood stoically alone. The place appeared deserted.

Kathleen looked at her notes and turned left when she hit Anaheim Road, almost passing the small east gate where she was supposed to turn in. She flipped the wheel; the tires screeched, and she drove a quarter mile to a security gate only to find there was no security. But there were two cars in the parking lot. The place wasn't quite deserted. Slowly, she accelerated and parked next to the green sedan, squinting toward a small building off to the south that seemed to be a place where she'd check in.

She left her briefcase, but took her tape recorder and camera. Just as she was locking her fantastic new Shay, Sylvester & Harrington company car, she caught sight of someone out of the corner of her eye. A man in a hard hat left the small building and disappeared around the corner. Kathleen thought of calling after him, but the day was already warm and she didn't have the energy or the inclination to hurry. Her mind was elsewhere, which, when she thought about it, didn't come as much of a surprise.

She fiddled with the tape recorder, then put it back into her purse along with the camera as she took the three steps up to the office. Opening the screen door, she walked into a big, very empty room. Kathleen spent all of two minutes checking it out, then went back outside to stand on the porch. For a second she shaded her eyes, looking for the man in the hard hat. Unable to see him, she followed in his footsteps and walked into the bowels of the refinery.

"Damn. Damn." Michael kicked the back wheel of the BMW; then he kicked the front wheel. "Damn!"

Traffic slowed to look at him, hateful rubber-neckers on the North 405. Above him a traffic helicopter was no doubt issuing a Sigalert, and thousands of early lunch commuters would be cursing him for pulling over to the side and causing a distraction. God knew what was wrong with this heap, and only God knew why he was the last man in California without a car phone. With one final kick to the tire, Michael started to walk. The next freeway emergency phone was a half mile away. That would give him time to cool off. He didn't want to be crazed when he saw Jules Porter—he wanted to be fully in control when he ripped out that idiot's eyes.

Louise popped a breath mint and offered Sarah one. Sarah shook her head. Her hair was back to normal, parted in the middle, hanging over her eyes.

"You okay?" Louise asked.

"Sure. Yeah."

"Hey, don't you worry about anything anymore. We're going to have you home in no time. Tell you what, after all this is over, when they finally figure out about Lionel and Kathleen gets me that money from All Life, I'll buy you a present to cheer you up. New rabbits. How's that sound?"

Sarah swiveled her head, that shy little smile on her lips.

"That's a nice thought," she said quietly, but Louise wasn't listening.

"Oh my God, look who's coming. Can you believe it? The man himself. Guess we won't be going to City Hall today. That jerk. That idiot. Come on, Sarah," Louise said, reeling the seat belt over her substantial breasts, "let's go on a little road trip. Whaddaya say?"

Louise didn't need to ask twice. Rambo was back. Sarah turned the key and bided her time. When he drove out of the parking lot, she was on his tail like a pro.

"Hello! Mr. Nola? It's Kathleen Cotter. Mr. Nola?"

Kathleen stopped walking and did a half turn. She had no idea where she was or where she would even begin to look for the man she was supposed to meet. Three more minutes and she was out of there. She'd just have to tell Harry Blanco that she'd never connected with engineer Nola. She'd make another appointment. Of course, once she had the Tysco files, she wouldn't be keeping any more appointments. She'd probably never work in this town again, and that thought alone was enough to give her a giggle. Cherie was right, working in this town wasn't all it was cracked up to be.

"Mr. Nola!" She tried once more, finishing her turn just in time to see some movement. Her heart leapt to her throat, then settled down. The man was coming from between two cylindrical storage tanks. The odd shadows made his approach seem slow and sinister. Kathleen started forward. "Hi, I was worried we were going to miss each other."

She stopped the minute she heard his voice.

"Don't worry your attractive little head, Kathleen. I wouldn't miss this for the world."

Richard Jacobsen emerged from the shadows. Impeccably dressed, he looked as oddly out of place here as she did in her high heels and fine makeup.

"I didn't know this was such an important meeting that the general partner would show up," Kathleen said cautiously.

"Oh, this is a very important meeting. In fact, Kathleen, you have become one of the most important people in my life." Kathleen blanched, her eyes darted right, then left, only to snap back toward Richard as another man materialized. A young, good-looking man who discarded a hard hat as he came forward. Richard smiled at him and made the introduction. "I believe you know Jules Porter, if not formally, by reputation."

Kathleen nodded. Jules did not. Instead, he came close behind Richard, touched his shoulder, and let his hand run across his back as he positioned himself to the side and slightly in front of the older man. He was so close to Kathleen that she could smell his after-shave and see that his eyes were glassy. His hands shook ever so slightly, and the intimate pose of the two men made her more than uncomfortable—it made her afraid.

"I wouldn't suggest you try anything," she said and was disheartened to see that her warning fell on deaf ears. "There are others who know exactly what you've been up to. They know why Lionel Brooker was killed. Even if you hurt me, they'll still go to the police and tell them everything."

"And what exactly is it you know, Kathleen Cotter from Banning, California? Why did Lionel Brooker have to die?"

Kathleen was momentarily speechless. Richard hadn't denied any wrongdoing. Good Lord, she felt sick. Thinking of Sarah, knowing how afraid she had been and how courageous, Kathleen willed herself to the same bravado. If she didn't act, she would die of fright.

"I know that you've been manipulating city billing." She spoke slowly, looking for any sign that she was off base with her theories. There was none. Richard was so very, very confident. She couldn't look at Jules Porter; he was too frightening. Kathleen licked her lips and went on. "So has Tysco. I don't know why, but I know it's happening. I've seen the paperwork at Tysco."

"Crawford," Jules muttered.

"Just so," Richard answered back. Neither took their eyes off her. She had to keep talking.

"What I don't understand, Richard, is why? Why on earth would you do such a thing? You have everything."

Kathleen took a step, the first effort in a still-unformed plan to escape. Her heart sank when neither man looked concerned.

"No one has everything. The world isn't as limited as you would imagine, Kathleen. The reason you will always remain a little girl from a little place is because you have no imagination."

"I was willing to learn."

"You were. But you were too much your uncle's niece. You would never have been willing to play."

Reaching for straws, Kathleen bluffed. "Try me."

Richard looked at Jules. He looked concerned, even worried about the younger man, but Kathleen was asking him to prove his superiority. He couldn't resist.

"It was simply a beautiful plan. We have a marvelous network of men in positions of varying degrees of power, all of whom would like to be more powerful or be held in greater esteem. We siphoned off city costs to other clients where we knew the additional charges would be buried in piles of paperwork. The Pentagon does it all the time."

"To what end?"

"To get Carl Walsh elected to the Senate."

"Is he really that special? Will he be such a fabulous leader if he is elected fraudulently?" Kathleen felt light-headed. He was right. She wasn't cut out for this. None of it made sense.

"Carl won't be anything in and of himself," Richard answered. "And that's why I say your vision is limited. All we want is a friendly body where it counts. We've done well by the city; the business is prestigious and lucrative. We helped Carl's bottom line look good; he made us look good to our shareholders and board of directors by giving us city business. If Carl were in a position to funnel federal money to Shay, Sylvester & Harrington, Tysco and a few others, our billings would be incredible, our status in the business world beyond compare. Our influence would be worldwide. It was just business. Bottom-line stuff. We wanted Carl Walsh in Washington; he needed a track record no one could take exception to. Money always talks."

"And Lionel Brooker got in the way. He knew exactly what was happening at Tysco and that's why he died."

Jules laughed. Richard shook his head. Two little boys with club secrets they didn't really want to share with a girl. But, in the end, they were boys. They had to boast.

"No. That was not why Lionel Brooker died, and that's what makes this all so funny. Lionel Brooker." Richard took a few steps, clasping his hands behind him. Jules swayed, his hand remaining levitated now that his support was gone. Kathleen forced herself to look at Richard. He was such an ugly little man. Why hadn't she noticed that before? He didn't seem quite so formidable here among these giant structures, yet that didn't make him any the less dangerous.

"Lionel Brooker wouldn't have been even a footnote in Tysco history if it hadn't been for you and that client of yours. Lionel would never have gotten to first base with his allegations. Jules and Grossman had already seen to that. He had prepared the way for Lionel to fail no matter how he persisted. Things like this are buried all the time. It's nothing new, just as crusaders like Lionel Brooker are nothing new."

"Then why kill him?" Kathleen wailed. Richard raised a brow. Light glinted off his glasses. He looked blind, but his aim was good. He hit a deadly mark next.

"And Gerry, too; you might as well know that."

Kathleen's eyes flicked to Jules Porter. He looked neither shamed nor remorseful. She thought she might faint.

"Why Gerry?"

"Because Jules got nervous when he was pushing issues he didn't want to deal with. Because you both were keeping Lionel Brooker alive with your ridiculous arguments for that creature he used to be married to. A disgusting woman. You were digging too deep to prove that Lionel wasn't a suicide. If the authorities had listened, if anyone had put two and two together, you might have raised questions we didn't want raised."

"You and Carl?"

"No, Kathleen," Richard said quietly, turning his head toward her. "Jules and I."

Kathleen shook her head, confused beyond reason. "Because of the billing?"

"Because I love him."

Kathleen's head exploded. "What? What am I missing?"

"You're missing the whole point. You've been running around trying to prove that Lionel Brooker's character was beyond reproach. A noble thing to do, Kathleen. For a man's character is the crux of all things in this world. His character determines what he will be, how far he will rise. My mother taught me that." Richard turned and came back to Jules. He laced his arm through the younger man's. He lay his head upon his shoulder. "People will not respect those who are perceived to lack character. Corporations will not trust those who are perceived to lack character." Richard's head shot up; he edged away from Jules Porter, who stood zombie still beside him. "And my reputation—my character—if you will, was in jeopardy. If you had determined that Lionel Brooker was of sound enough character not to kill himself, then the authorities might have found out exactly how he died and I would have been ruined. My character would have been besmirched beyond repair."

Richard paced, short steps that led him nowhere. He spoke quickly, like a general informing the troops they had lost their comrades to a suicide mission.

"Yes, we were there when Lionel Brooker died. It was late. Everyone had gone home. I was leaving with Jules, but we had to make a stop in the men's room. We decided on one far from his office. There was no way to know that Lionel Brooker had been over that way, trekking around with his sheafs of paper, trying to drum up interest in his manipulation theory. Lionel Brooker had stopped to relieve himself after his last, humiliating interview with one of the people on our side." Richard shook his head, not so much amused as incredulous at the turn of fate.

"Then why kill him?"

He glanced up, surprised to see Kathleen there. He blinked. He smiled. "He died only because he was in the wrong place at the wrong time. Jules?" Richard looked at his companion.

The younger man unbuttoned the cuff on his shirt and rolled it up.

"I want you to know that, in many ways, I continue to be a man of impeccable character. Were I not, I wouldn't want you to know the truth. I owe Gerry's last living relative that much. I owe you the truth because you're a woman who actually exceeded my expectations." Richard took Jules's arm. "Look at the scars on his arms, Kathleen. Jules is a junkie. Dear, dear Jules, the man I love, loves something more than me. I would do anything to help him get what he loves."

He looked as if he would cry over Jules's battered arm. Instead, he turned his head her way, unmoved by the disgust he saw in her eyes.

"I couldn't let anyone know about Jules because there's someone I love even more than him. My mother, who stood by me when the world taunted me for my looks, my dour demeanor, my intelligence, my lack of humor. That woman is everything to me, and I would no more hurt her by having my dirty laundry aired in public than I would abandon Jules in his time of need."

"Richard, please." Jules's voice was hoarse. He loosened his tie, no longer quite the fashion plate he had first appeared. It was time for a fix.

"In a moment." Richard reached up and patted the younger man's head affectionately. "A moment," Richard leaned forward and kissed the back of Jules's neck. "I need you wound tight right now. I need you to act on instinct. Remember Lionel?" Richard's eyes were still on Kathleen, and for the first time she saw them come to life.

"Lionel walked out of that stall, Kathleen. He saw us, and that righteous little nothing told us he was going to call security. That little nobody was going to call security on me." Richard was energized by the memories of Lionel's impertinence. Lionel had been nothing to him, and Richard never thought about what Lionel Brooker might have meant to the rest of the world. "Jules came to my defense. Jules hit him like a football player and Lionel Brooker went down. They both went through the stall door. Brooker's leg hit the toilet. He reached back to break his fall. One does look over one's shoulder when thrown off balance that way. It was instinct that did Lionel in. I think Jules actually forgot he had that syringe in his hand. Jules doesn't think clearly when he's like this. As they scrappled, the syringe went in. It was surprisingly quick with Mr. Brooker. Over before we knew it. It actually took us a few moments to realize what had happened.''

"Did you call Dr. Greischmidt?" Kathleen's voice was barely a whisper.

He nodded. ''I was long gone by the time the police arrived. It was a simple matter to call the man at home once Jules was comfortable and settled. The doctor took care of the matter quickly. The police report was filed, and once Greischmidt made his ruling, no one bothered to look at it again. It was actually quite funny since the one thing they didn't have was a syringe. When Jules and I figured that out, we had a sleepless night. But no one really cared; the case was closed, the man buried. Some things are so simple. Other things that are simple can become large problems. And you, Kathleen, are one of those.''

Richard gave Jules a push so small Kathleen would have missed it if she had closed her eyes the way she wanted to. But they were wide open with fear and she saw him do it. Jules's reactions weren't as swift as hers. Fear will do that. Kathleen sprinted, thanking God for her long legs, cursing Evan Picone for the height of her heels.

A cry of outrage—or was it pain?—followed her, and she pulled her purse tighter. That was the last thing she wanted to lose and the first thing that Jules Porter grabbed. He pulled on the strap and Kathleen yanked back, managing another few steps before he pulled again and the strap broke. Kathleen went spinning out of control and slammed into one of the storage tanks. She saw stars for a second, then she saw a pair of hands reaching for her and she ducked. On her knees, she crawled, then scrambled up, only to be pulled down again. She screamed when Jules Porter clambered on top of her, then she stopped when his hands went around her throat. But his grip was unsure, his fingers shaking, and Kathleen was big and strong and, for the first time, that was to her advantage.

"No, you don't," she muttered and gritted her teeth. With a great yowl, Kathleen brought her knee up. Though it missed the bull's-eye, it made enough of an impact to send Jules Porter rolling away from her. Kathleen scrambled up and pivoted left. The maze of refinery equipment might hide her, but it also might hide the two men who wanted her dead. She'd take her chances in the wide-open spaces.

With that thought, Kathleen stumbled toward the parking lot. Just before she cleared the last tank, she tripped, the heel of her shoe wedging in a metal grate. She hit the ground again, hard on her hip. Whimpering, breathing hard and tight, Kathleen pushed one foot against the other, trying to get her shoe off; but her foot was twisted and Evan Picone had her trapped with tiny little straps that had once seemed so attractive, she had said she would die if she didn't have them.

Her eyes darted up, her head twisted, and still she saw no hope. She sat in the shadows of one of the storage tanks, scrabbling with the tiny buckles. Short of ripping her foot off, there was no way to unstrap the shoe before Jules, who was stumbling toward her with murder in his eyes, had his hand around her neck once more.

"Michael," she whimpered, moving back, scooting along the asphalt in a half circle since she couldn't move backward.

If there were a time she needed Michael Crawford, it was now. Michael of the Special Forces. Michael, cool under fire. Now, she thought frantically. Now is the time he should be riding in on his white horse. Jules was almost there. Jules was so close and looked so horrible that Kathleen couldn't tear her eyes away from him. She was positive, sure in her heart, that Michael's marvelous hands would soon be on Jules Porter. He would pull the murderer away from her. He would. . . .

Do nothing.

She hadn't even told him where she was going. It was over, and she cried out in anticipation of the pain that would soon come. From the corner of her eye, she glimpsed someone. Richard was coming to watch. Richard was coming to make sure that she would never tell anyone about his secret. Richard, damn, sick Richard Jacobsen was coming like the angel of death.

Kathleen stopped moving and, when she did, Jules Porter hesitated. Slowly, so slowly, she lay back on the concrete, aware of everything around her—the liquid rushing through the pipes overhead, the heat of the ground, the heavy breathing of the man who would kill her. Soon, she would think of nothing because she'd be dead.

Kathleen Cotter began to pray and that was when she heard an all-too-familiar sound. An explosion. The sound of buckshot hitting solid objects, pinging off tanks that could be filled with unstable gases, flammable liquids—but who cared? Death had been put on hold. Then she heard something she'd never heard before . . . the sound of buckshot hitting its mark.

She bolted upright just in time to see Jules Porter fall to his knees, looking quite surprised that his suit was being soiled by his very own blood. Stunned, Kathleen watched until he was face down on the concrete, so close that she could reach her good foot and touch his head. Instead, she looked toward her right in time to see Sarah and Louise coming straight at her, grim-faced given what had just happened.

They knelt beside her—Louise unbuckling Kathleen's shoe and freeing her foot; Sarah cradling the shotgun, just in case. Jules Porter died beside the women who finally wrapped their arms around each other and cried.

"Four, five, six."

Louise shook the box, and the last of the little white rabbits tumbled out onto the grass. Sarah scooped them up and put them in the hutch as fast as they came.

"Louise, you should pick them out like this," Sarah held the last one by the scruff of the neck and showed her. Louise made a face.

"It was enough that I drove them all the way here in the car and now you want me to touch them?"

"No, I don't want you to touch them," Sarah said, putting the last little guy away before closing the door.

"Thank goodness, kiddo. I like you, but I don't like you that much." Louise turned toward Michael and took his arm. "So, how does it feel to be a free man?"

Michael cocked a grin and looked over his shoulder. Kathleen and Sarah fell in step behind them. The last place he wanted to be was alone with Louise Brooker. "I don't know yet. I only gave my notice yesterday. How's it feel to be a rich woman?"

"Great. I don't even have to think about that one. Hey, Kathleen, did I ever say thanks?" Louise hollered over her one bared shoulder.

"Nope," Kathleen answered.

"Okay." Louise let go of Michael and stepped up onto the porch to get her purse. "Listen, I've gotta go. I have a nail appointment." She held up her right hand. Whoever had been immortalized on those talons of hers had been sufficiently mutilated as to make him or her unrecognizable. Kathleen felt as if she'd lost a friend, though she imagined it wouldn't be long until she saw another celebrity on the tip of those nails. They waved goodbye to Louise, and then it was time for Michael and Kathleen to leave as well.

"We're going to head out, too. Thanks, Sarah, lunch was wonderful." Michael wrapped his arm around Kathleen, who wrapped one right back.

"I think Lionel would have loved it. He would have been so proud of you," Kathleen added. "Are you going to be okay here alone?"

Sarah nodded and pulled her new sweater closer around her. It had been a present from Kathleen. It was gray, but the buttons were white.

"I'll be fine. I have my rabbits to take care of and I feel safe again. I can't thank you all enough for that."

"Don't include me in that. Kathleen was the one who really put herself on the line." Michael shook his head.

"And you're the one who explained to the police what Lionel

had found. You're the one who cleared his name. Harold was so pleased."

Kathleen smiled. Sarah could do worse than Harold, but she doubted she could do better. Kathleen touched Sarah's shoulder. Kissing her cheek had never quite seemed right.

"We're pretty happy, too. It looks like everything turned out for the best. Jules isn't dead—"

"I don't know that that's best," Michael mumbled.

"Richard is in jail. His head is probably still hurting from where you hit him. Carl is under investigation—" Kathleen talked over him.

"And O'Doul & Associates isn't closing its doors," Sarah added.

"I have to work somewhere," Kathleen said with a shrug. "Just do me a favor: Put the shotgun away. Much as I appreciate what you did, I don't want to be defending you anytime soon."

"I promise," Sarah said softly. Michael kissed her goodbye. When they got into the car, Kathleen lay back in the seat and watched the trees of the canyon turn to highway, the highway turn to freeway, and before she knew it they were walking along the dock toward the *Gentle Reminder*.

"Can you make it?"

Kathleen looked at her straight skirt. The day was over. No more meetings with Bob Morton. No more court. The office was closed for a long, long weekend. She didn't think twice. Kicking off her shoes, she handed them to him along with her bag. She hitched her skirt and was on deck in the blink of an eye. Michael kissed her; she kissed him back, and they smiled at one another.

"I'm going to change," Kathleen whispered.

"I'm going to cast off."

She went below; he went aft, and ten minutes later, they had both done what they needed to do. Kathleen half lay in the deck chair, dressed in jeans and a T-shirt, her head thrown back, her short, blond hair ruffled by the breeze as they headed out to sea. She didn't hear him coming, but she felt his hands on the arms of the chair; then she felt him tip up her sunglasses. She opened her eyes and looked at him.

"I love your face," she whispered.

He touched her cheek; there was no powder, no blush. He kissed her lips. They were tinged pink, but the Cover Girl had been left behind.

"I love yours, too, Kathleen Cotter. It has—character."

THE MYSTERIES OF MARY ROBERTS RINEHART

THE AFTER HOUSE   (0-8217-4246-6, $3.99/$4.99)

THE CIRCULAR STAIRCASE   (0-8217-3528-4, $3.95/$4.95)

THE DOOR   (0-8217-3526-8, $3.95/$4.95)

THE FRIGHTENED WIFE   (0-8217-3494-6, $3.95/$4.95)

A LIGHT IN THE WINDOW   (0-8217-4021-0, $3.99/$4.99)

THE STATE VS.   (0-8217-2412-6, $3.50/$4.50)
ELINOR NORTON

THE SWIMMING POOL   (0-8217-3679-5, $3.95/$4.95)

THE WALL   (0-8217-4017-2, $3.99/$4.99)

THE WINDOW AT THE WHITE CAT
                          (0-8217-4246-9, $3.99/$4.99)

THREE COMPLETE NOVELS: THE BAT, THE HAUNTED
LADY, THE YELLOW ROOM
                          (0-8217-114-4, $13.00/$16.00)

Available wherever paperbacks are sold, or order direct from the Publisher. Send cover price plus 50¢ per copy for mailing and handling to Penguin USA, P.O. Box 999, c/o Dept. 17109, Bergenfield, NJ 07621. Residents of New York and Tennessee must include sales tax. DO NOT SEND CASH.

HORROR FROM HAUTALA

SHADES OF NIGHT   (0-8217-5097-6, $4.99)
Stalked by a madman, Lara DeSalvo is unaware that she is most in danger in the one place she thinks she is safe—home.

TWILIGHT TIME   (0-8217-4713-4, $4.99)
Jeff Wagner comes home for his sister's funeral and uncovers long-buried memories of childhood sexual abuse and murder.

DARK SILENCE   (0-8217-3923-9, $5.99)
Dianne Fraser fights for her family—and her sanity—against the evil forces that haunt an abandoned mill.

COLD WHISPER   (0-8217-3464-4, $5.95)
Tully can make Sarah's wishes come true, but Sarah lives in terror because Tully doesn't understand that some wishes aren't meant to come true.

LITTLE BROTHERS   (0-8217-4020-2, $4.50)
Kip saw the "little brothers" kill his mother five years ago. Now they have returned, and this time there will be no escape.

MOONBOG   (0-8217-3356-7, $4.95)
Someone—or some*thing*—is killing the children in the little town of Holland, Maine.

REAL HORROR STORIES!
PINNACLE TRUE CRIME

SAVAGE VENGEANCE (0-7860-0251-4, $5.99)
By Gary C. King and Don Lasseter
On a sunny day in December, 1974, Charles Campbell attacked
Renae Ahlers Wicklund, brutally raping her in her own home in
front of her 16-month-old daughter. After Campbell was released
from prison after only 8 years, he sought revenge. When Campbell
was through, he left behind the most gruesome crime scene local
investigators had ever encountered.

NO REMORSE (0-7860-0231-X, $5.99)
By Bob Stewart
Kenneth Allen McDuff was a career criminal by the time he was
a teenager. Then, in Fort Worth, Texas in 1966, he upped the ante.
Arrested for three brutal murders, McDuff was sentenced to death.
In 1972, his sentence was commuted to life imprisonment. He
was paroled after only 23 years behind bars. In 1991 McDuff
struck again, carving a bloody rampage of torture and murder
across Texas.

BROKEN SILENCE (0-7860-0343-X, $5.99)
The Truth About Lee Harvey Oswald, LBJ,
and the Assassination of JFK
By Ray "Tex" Brown with Don Lasseter
In 1963, two men approached Texas bounty hunter Ray "Tex"
Brown. They needed someone to teach them how to shoot at a
moving target—and they needed it fast. One of the men was Jack
Ruby. The other was Lee Harvey Oswald. . . . Weeks later, after
the assassination of JFK, Ray Brown was offered $5,000 to leave
Ft. Worth and keep silent the rest of his life. The deal was ar-
ranged by none other than America's new president: Lyndon
Baines Johnson.

*Available wherever paperbacks are sold, or order direct from the
Publisher. Send cover price plus 50¢ per copy for mailing and
handling to Penguin USA, P.O. Box 999, c/o Dept. 17109,
Bergenfield, NJ 07621. Residents of New York and Tennessee
must include sales tax. DO NOT SEND CASH.*